AVARICE

A HOLLYWOOD MYSTERY

BRITT LIND

Editing, design, and distribution by Bublish

ISBN: 979-8-899890-10-9 (paperback)
ISBN: 979-8-899890-08-6 (hardcover)
ISBN: 979-8-899890-07-9 (eBook)
ISBN: 979-8-899890-09-3 (audiobook)

PRAISE FOR BRITT LIND'S BOOKS

Avarice: A Hollywood Mystery

Avarice - A Hollywood Mystery is a murder mystery crime story packed with intensity and action. Britt Lind's skill lies in creating a deep affection for Rosemaria and Josh in readers. The reader is drawn into a whirlwind ride full of twists and suspense, eager to learn who the assassin is, all while facing Hollywood's dark side. Curiosity about what happens next will keep readers turning the pages. Readers who enjoy inventive detective-style crime thrillers will enjoy Avarice, a story filled with love, money, conspiracy, and high-stakes situations. An awesome read that should be made into a film!
—Readers' Favorite / 5 Star Review Award

Avarice is an engaging and fast-moving page-turner that weaves a tale of mystery and murder in the upper echelons of Beverly Hills society. Through its vivid and engaging characters, this memorable novel illuminates the power of love and courage to bring both healing and justice. Written by the celebrated author, actress, and animal rights activist Britt Lind, this intriguing book engages the reader through its tapestry of suspense, humor, conflict, and eventual resolution. Highly recommended.
—Dr. Will Tuttle - Author of *The World Peace Diet*

If you're drawn to mysteries that explore the human psyche as much as the crime, Lind's Hollywood Mystery series will take you on a journey through the alluring world of the elite, and down into the dark underbelly of the City of Angels in this classic noir-style series.
—Chanticleer Reviews

In *Avarice - A Hollywood Mystery* Britt Lind's insight into the smoke and mirrors of the high end 90210 society paints a compelling picture of relationships, and dangerous secrets of the lives of the rich and famous. The story drives to a surprising conclusion as ex-cop now prosecutor Rosemaria Baker works with her buddies at Beverly Hills PD to track down a psychopath who is determined to kill her. Definitely a fast page-turning novel you won't want to put down.
—Rod Grier - Award-winning producer, director, actor

Malevolence: A Hollywood Mystery

"Rosemaria is an endearing and incorruptible protagonist who demonstrates tact and compassion while investigating the teenager's murderers and finding witnesses for her court cases…Her tender relationship with Josh and their banter are high points of the novel, and the dialogue ably reveals nuances of characterizations…As the murder reveals a political conspiracy with international implications Rosemaria finds herself pulled in different directions, and she must face the possibility that she may not be able to save everyone she loves…"
—Kirkus Reviews

"Britt Lind has created two excellent lead characters in Rosemaria and Josh, and their loving and supportive dynamic provides a unique backdrop to the grim and dark world of murder and international conspiracy. The mystery at the heart of *Malevolence* is highly engaging with enough twists and turns in the tale to keep audiences on their toes and excited to read what happens next. The dark nature of the subject matter is excellently counterbalanced by Josh's light sub-plot about getting his big break. As with the previous story, Rosemaria proves herself to be a capable investigator and an excellent pair of eyes for the audience to engage with the core mystery. The additional obstacles provided by her professional life contribute to the unpredictable directions that the plot takes as it moves forward."
—Readers Favorite, Five Star Review

"*Malevolence: A Hollywood Mystery* is the second book in the highly-rated series by Britt Lind. Like the first book, Malevolence weaves the themes of commitment and love, along with animal rights into the narrative. And in the end, those who should get their comeuppance do. For readers who like their police novels with a good heart, strong female leads, and a well- integrated animal rights theme, *Malevolence - A Hollywood Mystery* will excite and satisfy."
—Chanticleer Reviews

A Fate Worse Than Death: A Hollywood Mystery Prequel

"With a big talent for writing, Britt Lind again captivates the reader with a new mystery."
—Jonas Nordstrom, marketing head, *Adventure Box*

"Hollywood and mystery are a part of Britt Lind's history - from big screen to little screen and roles ranging from Clint Eastwood's *Play Misty for Me* to the iconic *Columbo*, so it's no mystery why she is a shining star of the written word in her Hollywood Mystery series including this prequel which gives us a glimpse into the childhood of her protagonist Rosemaria Baker."
—Bob Linden, radio talk show host, producer, and vegan activist

Deception: A Hollywood Mystery

"A thrilling page-turner about a group of flawed yet compelling characters caught in a cesspool of greed and ruthless ambition behind the scenes in Hollywood. I couldn't wait to find out the ending while simultaneously wishing the book wouldn't end."
—Lara Wickman, writer, producer, actress

"The story takes some refreshingly unexpected turns, picking a path through genre clichés and keeping readers guessing. The author has an easy writing style and a cinematic grasp of pace. Fans of silver screen crime should approve, as, in many respects, this reads like the novelization of a movie."
—Kirkus Reviews

"If you want to read a book that offers romance, suspense, detective work, intrigue, and feels like you're watching a movie, then this is your book. I highly recommend it."
—Tony Eldridge, executive producer, *The Equalizer I & II & III*

"*Deception* is a gritty rendering of the classic battle between good and evil played out in the milieu of Hollywood. As an actor herself, Britt is ably qualified to explore and articulate the disappointment and heartache of fame- obsessed performers as they struggle to make it in an unforgiving industry where fame is illusive and disappointment can lead to murder."
—Andreas Michaelides, writer, reviewer, blogger and natural health educator

Learning How to Fly
(Beverly Hills Book Award Winner)

"*Learning How to Fly* is the story of unstoppable passion. Britt Lind's acting career was filled with a seeming endless series of wins and setbacks, but she persevered. Readers with an interest in the tough and quixotic world of Hollywood movie-making will find much in Lind's story to hold their interest. I was surprised that even successful actors can find it a continuous and difficult challenge.

But the book is much more than a behind the scenes look at movie making. Lind's passion for acting is matched by her compassion for animals. Whether writing about rescuing cats, speaking up for fur seals and whales, or taking on the animal experimentation industry, her get-back-up-again

spirit is clear throughout the pages. Readers with an interest in the road to her animal advocacy will not be disappointed."
—**Rick Bogle, animal activist and author of**
We All Operate in the Same Way

"Britt Lind's journey to find her ultimate calling (a voice for the animals) is filled with highs and lows on her road to Hollywood, and you will want to keep turning the page."
—**Sylva Kelegian, actress, writer and award-winning author of**
God Spelled Backwards **and** ***The Dolphin Princess***

"Learning How to Fly is the inspiring story of a fellow activist who has hung in there through thick and thin for all of the 32 years I've known her. Fighting vivisection is a hard road and it takes both courage and incredible patience to stay in the battle. But Britt found a way to stay on course and still fulfill her passion for acting. Readers will find this book entertaining and humorous, but it's also her journey that provides guidance on how one can find their own way to a meaningful life."
— **Chris DeRose, founder and president of Last Chance for Animals and author of** ***In Your Face***

"As a young starlet, Britt Lind was a beauty who was cast in a Clint Eastwood movie and found happiness being married to a television producer and acting and raising a baby girl. But in a flash, her marriage ended, riches vanished, the house was foreclosed on and her career crumbled. Britt's story of disappearing success is poignant and unforgettable, and by the time she is beaten down in Hollywood and heads for New York with visions of Broadway, you cannot help but cheer for her and the animals she has dedicated her life to saving. This is a heartfelt, timeless story of shining on to create a life filled with love, beauty and triumph."
—**Janette Turner, writer, director and author of the forthcoming memoir** ***Magazine Crush: My Life as a Cosmo Addict.***

"These are the adventures of an innocent young girl from Norway, thrust into American culture, driven by a passionate ambition to be an actress in a ruthlessly unpredictable and sexist industry. Britt navigated through a life of obstacles, betrayals and disappointments with courageous resolve, a resolve deeply rooted in a firm moral foundation and strengthened by a deep compassion and a fiery desire to end the suffering of animals."
—Captain Paul Watson, founder of The Sea Shepherd Conservation Society and author of several books including,
Sea Shepherd: My Fight for Whales* and *Seals, Seal Wars,
Twenty: Five Years on the Front Lines with the Harp Seals,
Ocean Warrior: My Battle to End the Illegal Slaughter on the High Seas,
and *Hit Man for the Kindness Club*

*To my BFF Georgia Flambures, my beautiful stepdaughter
Lisa Howard, and my ever faithful friend Diane Dolphin-Torres
who surround everyone they know with love.*

"…true evil needs no reason to exist,
it simply is and feeds upon itself."
E.A. Bucchianeri

"For greed, all nature is too little."
Seneca

CHAPTER ONE

It was a perfect, eighty-five-degree summer day in Pacific Beach, and the town was crowded with tourists who decided California was everything they had expected when excitedly planning their trip back in Milburn, Ohio, or in some other land-locked state far away from the Pacific Ocean. Locals, who took their paradise for granted, were happy to share their bliss with the foreign hordes who boosted the economy and enabled them to afford their homes near the beach. Situated just south of La Jolla, where top rated golfers were playing in a celebrity tournament at Torrey Pines that very day, Pacific Beach offered visitors a plethora of shopping venues and the challenging decision of where to enjoy lunch in one of the many restaurants on the boulevard. Others were catching rays on the white, sandy beach or swimming or surfing in the cold waters of the Pacific. Joggers and cyclists crowded the bike path that ran in front of taco and souvenir stands and, farther south, where it passed pricey homes, situated side by side facing the ocean.

Anyone lying in a beach chair or playing catch with frisbees who happened to glance up at the good-looking man and his female companion who were slowly cycling south on the bike path, apparently in no hurry to reach their destination, would have been immediately arrested by the young couple's striking physical attributes. She was a beauty with a Dodger cap pulled down tight over auburn hair, her white T-shirt hanging loose over a toned body, and her tan shorts showing off legs that were shapely and well-muscled. He was unusually handsome, dressed in jeans and a blue T-shirt, muscular and tall with unruly blond hair. Both were grinning, enjoying the early June summer weather and the warm breeze that floated in off the water. The immediate thought that might have come into anyone's mind when they caught sight of the attractive couple was these two must be among the rich and famous people who lived just up the coast in La Jolla or owned one of the expensive vacation houses on the beach. Their curiosity would have lasted a few seconds before their attention would have returned to their own activities as the couple continued slowly cycling down the path.

The aforementioned blond man, Josh Sibley, reached out his hand toward his fiancée, Rosemaria Baker, and they briefly touched fingers as they meandered down the path on their bicycles. "I think we're holding people up," he said. "Everybody's passing us."

"I'm too busy enjoying my vacation to notice," Rosemaria responded and inhaled deeply of the salty ocean air.

"I think my meeting will be over by three or four. We can walk on the beach and then have dinner at the Mexican restaurant you spotted on the way here."

"Sounds like heaven to me."

She turned off the bike path onto a small walkway between two upscale houses, and Josh followed her onto a tiled patio that wrapped around the front and side of a magnificent three-story house of glass and steel. They stepped off their bikes and rested them on kickstands near the front door. The home they were about to enter glittered like a jewel in the noonday sun.

"I know envy is the ugliest emotion after self-pity, but right now, I feel sorry for myself that we don't own this house instead of Joell," Rosemaria admitted. "Does that make me a bad person?"

Josh shook his head as he pressed keys on the alarm pad. "I never cease to be shocked at the breadth of your shortcomings, my darling."

She followed him into the black-and-white-tiled entryway, light pouring down from a glass canopy three floors up. "And I try so hard to live up to your expectations."

Josh grabbed her and pulled her close. "I'm a very patient man. I will give you several years to improve."

Rosemaria whispered in his ear, "Actually, you think I'm perfect, don't you?"

"You wouldn't deserve me otherwise."

"Wise guy!" She pushed past him on her way to the kitchen, but he caught her from behind and held her by the waist.

"Don't get any ideas," she said. "Joell's driver is picking me up in an hour to take me to the gym. I worked hard to get rid of my spare tire, and I won't have you standing in my way."

He turned her around and kissed her. She melted.

"I was a strong, independent woman when I met you. And now look at me."

"Yes, I'd like to do that."

She sighed and let him lead her toward the stairs.

An hour later, wearing sweatpants and a clean T-shirt, she was seated in one of four tall chairs next to the marble-covered island in the perfectly appointed kitchen that had a view of the ocean through the family room. The cabinets were glossy white with platinum steel pulls and etched see-through glass. The appliances were stainless steel, and the floor was covered in beige travertine tiles. Rosemaria was enjoying the ocean view while sipping her lemonade from a glass. She became aware of Josh standing in the doorway, ready to head out, having showered and changed into a white shirt tucked into khaki slacks.

She turned to him. "I'm going to enjoy this swanky gym of Joell's. They don't let just anybody join, you know. Celebrities and rich people don't like having the common folk staring at them when they sweat."

"Joell's not like that, and besides, famous people don't sweat."

She stood up, rinsed her glass in the sink, and placed it in the dishwasher. She picked up her gym bag from the glass kitchen table and threw the strap over her shoulder. "Well, I do. Plenty. It takes a lot of work to keep the flab off these thighs." She looked up at him. "So why did she change the meeting to San Diego? I thought because she was playing in the pro-am, having the meeting in La Jolla would be convenient."

"She and her partner finished early, and apparently, she had some business downtown. I don't ask questions. Just follow orders. We'll be discussing everything about the European tour, all the logistics, checking into the hotels, tech rehearsals, local lineups, everything, so it could be at least four o'clock before I get back."

"I still get to see La Jolla, don't I?"

"We'll go there tomorrow, okay?"

"In Joell's shiny black Mercedes?"

"You sure focus a lot on the good life for somebody who's engaged to a starving musician."

She stood up, walked over to where he was leaning against the doorway, and wrapped her arms around him. "This will be your first tour as an honest-to-God famous singer. I will miss you terribly, but I'm so proud of you."

"Semi-famous—make that almost unknown. And songwriter, not singer. If it weren't for Joell being the biggest recording artist in the world and her having faith in me, I wouldn't even be going on this tour."

"By the time you get home, you'll be more famous than any of them."

He smiled and shook his head. "What am I going to do with you? You had the same kind of impossibly high expectations of me even when I was living in a rundown apartment in Hollywood."

"It's your talent, my dear. The first time you sang for me, I knew all this was inevitable."

"Even though I was a murder suspect, and all your cop friends were sure I did it?"

She took his arm, and he opened the door to the carport. "I may not be able to carry a tune, but I knew within minutes of meeting you that you weren't guilty, and after I heard you sing, your fate was sealed. I was going to hook my wagon to a star, baby."

They walked into the garage, where a black Mercedes and classic Jaguar were parked side by side. Josh pressed a button on a pad by the kitchen door, and the garage door slid open. He gave her a peck on the cheek and used his clicker to unlock the Mercedes.

As she watched him, Rosemaria felt a sudden shortness of breath and a premonition of impending disaster. It happened to her sometimes when everything seemed too good to be true. She shook it off. Nothing to worry about.

Josh was about to get into the Mercedes when he looked up at her and saw the stricken expression on her face. "Are you all right? What's wrong?"

She shook her head. "Nothing. Just a cramp. Female stuff."

"Okay, it looked like more than that, but I'll take your word for it. You waiting in the alley for Joell's driver?"

"Yes, you go ahead and pull out. He'll be here any minute." She walked outside, watched as he backed out of the garage, and waved before he disappeared around the corner. She set the alarm after the garage door slid shut and saw Raul approaching from the other end of the alley in Joell's Lincoln. She was tickled at the thought of the pampering she was receiving over this long three-day weekend. Yes, it was way too good to be true, and this kind of lifestyle was far above anything she had ever experienced in her life. But that didn't mean something had to go wrong.

* * * * *

Ten minutes later, she was relaxing in the front passenger seat as Raul drove. She had convinced herself to accept Joell's magnanimous offer to live in her rarified world for the weekend, but sitting in the back of a limo like some pampered celeb seemed a bit too imperious for a newbie prosecutor who was still on the low end of the salary scale. Joell's Rolls was back in Bel Air, so she had rented the Lincoln for the weekend, but today, she was being driven to her meetings by her manager and didn't need the town car. Joell had insisted that Raul, Joell's driver and bodyguard, a six-feet-four African American with astonishing green eyes that made his handsome face even more so, drive Rosemaria wherever she needed to go.

Raul glanced briefly at his passenger. He had accepted Rosemaria's desire to sit up front with him. Other friends of Joell's sometimes did the same when she occasionally asked him to drive them to the airport or home after having too many drinks. Even though Rosemaria was undeniably beautiful, she struck him as a woman who was indifferent to her looks and didn't have a narcissistic, self-centered bone in her body. "How do you like Pacific Beach so far?" he asked.

"I keep thinking I need to be somewhere, doing something useful, like time is going by, and I've jumped off the train and am losing ground." She shifted in her seat uneasily.

Raul laughed. "Sounds like you need to stay off the train and let it move down the tracks without you for a while. You're in serious need of some downtime."

"So, who is guarding Joell while you're driving a nobody around town?"

"She'll be surrounded by friends all day, and you're not nobody. Walk into the gym like you own the place, and everybody will believe you're somebody famous they can't quite place."

"Will you come in for a workout too?"

"Not today. I'll be waiting for you outside or in the lobby."

"I won't be too long."

"Don't worry about it. Take your time."

As she glanced out the window and up at the sky, she noticed some clouds moving in from the ocean. She hoped they weren't headed in their direction. She was looking forward to a walk on the beach and up the boulevard to the Mexican restaurant and maybe doing a bit of shopping. Raul was right; the train would move along just fine without her for a few days. She could do with some mindless relaxation. Rosemaria had thought that resigning from her job as a homicide detective in the Beverly Hills Police Department and becoming a prosecutor at the Airport Courthouse would have calmed her life down somewhat. But her first year as prosecutor had been almost as fraught with danger as when she worked vice in Hollywood. She didn't want to risk her life anymore. She was happy with Josh and lived in anticipation of his music dreams coming true. And it was all about to happen.

* * * * *

Standing in the shower after an hour's workout, Rosemaria was already thinking about what she was going to order for dinner. She mentally slapped herself. Darn! She wished she didn't love eating so much. Then she wouldn't have to work so hard to keep the pounds off. But her body was really shaping up, and she finally liked what she saw in the mirror every morning, even if Josh proclaimed her body was just as desirable with more flesh here and there. Yeah, right. All men said that until you got too fat, and then their eyes started wandering.

She dressed in her sweatpants and T-shirt and dried her hair with one of the dryers provided by the gym. A bean burrito, maybe, lots of chips and salsa. Hey, she could afford a few carbs. She smiled at the attractive young blonde girl at the front desk on her way out and saw several people waiting at the entrance. She was surprised to look out the window and see that one of those California rarities had occurred. A rainstorm had blown in off the sea and was drenching everyone caught unaware. Those clouds had decided to come their way after all. She looked around the lobby for Raul and saw that he was sitting in the driver's seat of the Lincoln. She walked out the entrance and waited for him under the awning.

As soon as Raul spotted her, he jumped out of the car and came running toward the front entrance carrying a large black umbrella. He huddled with her under the awning where five other people were waiting to see if the deluge would let up. "You want to make a run for it, or should I pull up in front?"

"Let's see if it stops first. I don't want you driving in this pouring rain." Rosemaria preferred to wait because the ride back to Joell's house was mostly on the 163, and the road from the gym down to the main street was steep and lined with trees and brush. It wouldn't do to get in an accident the first time Joell loaned Rosemaria her car and driver.

They walked back inside and stood in the lobby, looking out the window at people either still waiting under the awning or laughing and running for their cars. Rosemaria, a born-and-bred Californian from Simi

Valley, knew that heavy summer rain was unexpected and fun for people in southern California. They could hear cars whizzing by on the street on the hill just above the gym, the drivers ignoring the possibilities of an accident on the slippery, oily pavement. They waited five minutes, and the torrential downpour turned into a steady rain, but the black clouds remained. Rosemaria watched a man walking a small dog of dubious origin at the far end of the parking lot. The poor wet mutt was pulling at the leash, but the man was ignoring him. She saw he was wearing an earbud and intent on listening to something or someone. Even walking his dog in the rain, he couldn't stay off the phone.

"You ready to go?" Raul asked.

"Yes, let's do it."

They ventured back outside and stopped under the awning. Only two other people, a man and a woman were still waiting. Rosemaria again noticed the man walking his dog who looked in their direction and immediately began talking to his dog or to someone. Raul pulled open the umbrella, and the rain beat down on it in a steady rhythm as they walked, hunched over, toward the Lincoln a few yards away. She stopped and turned when someone tapped her on the shoulder. It was the blonde receptionist, who now leaned close under their umbrella. "You forgot your jacket." The words were barely spoken before she heard the sound of a rifle, the receptionist's head exploded, and blood splatter covered Rosemaria's face.

Raul grabbed Rosemaria's arm and ran. "Keep down! It's coming from up on the hill!" He pulled his Glock out of its holster and fired up the hill where he could see the sniper. A woman who had just stepped out of her car screamed and ran for the gym entrance. Rosemaria glanced back and saw the receptionist lying on the ground in a pool of blood, her face obliterated by the bullet.

The man with the dog dropped the leash and began firing at them with an automatic. Raul could see that the high-powered rifle on the hill was still aimed at Rosemaria, who had ducked down behind a car several yards away from the Lincoln. Raul fumbled the car key out of his pocket, and it slipped from his grasp and fell underneath the car. He fired back at the man in the parking lot then dropped down by the driver's side and slid under the car as bullets tore into the side of the Lincoln.

Rosemaria was close to the edge of the hill above the road that wound down from the gym to the freeway and decided her best bet for escape was to run down the hill through the thick brush and trees and make her way to the road below. She had left her own Beretta at Joell's house, not having anticipated that she would need it for a trip to a pricey health club. Maybe Raul could hold off the man in the parking lot long enough for her to get away, then somehow get in the car and meet her at the bottom. She cursed at herself for not being able to protect him.

From underneath the Lincoln, Raul saw the gunman minus his dog, making his way toward the edge of the parking lot where Rosemaria had disappeared. Raul fired three shots from underneath the car at the man's legs and saw him stumble and fall. The dropped keys were about a foot away, and he managed to crawl two feet forward without exposing himself to the sniper, grab them, click open the door, and pull himself inside. He didn't have to worry about the man on the hill once he was inside the car. Joell always ordered bulletproof glass on even her rented limos. A bullet slammed into the windshield as Raul started the car. He backed out of the parking spot and saw a man carrying a gun come tearing down the hill. By this time, no one was in the parking lot. Everyone had run inside and was huddled down behind locked doors. The wounded gunman had made his way to a black Ford, and Raul figured he had less than a minute to pick up Rosemaria at the bottom of the hill before they caught up with him. He raced out of the parking lot.

Rosemaria heard more gunshots. She ran and stumbled down the hill, now deeply covered in mud from the rain that was falling steadily. The root of a tree tripped her up, and she went down, hitting her head on something hard. She forced herself up and kept slipping and sliding down the hill, desperate to get to the road where Raul, if he had escaped the gunmen, would be waiting. She saw the Lincoln pull up, limped her way toward the partially open passenger door, and managed to pull it open enough for her to fit. She felt a pain in her shoulder and saw a black Ford bearing down on them.

"Get in!" Raul shouted. He took off before she was all the way inside, but he grabbed one of her arms and pulled her in. The pain in her shoulder was excruciating, and they were racing down the road fifty miles an hour before she finally was able to shut the door and fasten her seatbelt. By now, bullets were exploding on the back windshield. She whispered a thank-you to Joell when she saw they weren't penetrating the glass.

Raul drove like he was competing in the Indianapolis 500. Only once before, when he'd worked as a bodyguard for a much-reviled politician, had he had to drive like this to outrun a would-be assassin. But he had never experienced anyone as fierce and determined as the two who were behind him right now. He shot through the intersection at the bottom of the hill and hit the freeway entrance going eighty miles an hour. The Ford was right behind him. But he knew these streets and freeways like the back of his hand. San Diego was where he had grown up, and it was about to pay off. He knew all the dead ends and one-way alleys and had a friend who worked as a guard in a ritzy condo building. That's where he would head. But first, he had to try to get these dirtbags off his tail.

He was prepared to get off at the next exit but didn't move right until the last second. He whipped over two lanes and barely made it off and onto a side street. He glanced back and saw the other car was still behind him. Only professionals could drive like that. Someone had hired them to kill Rosemaria. He glanced quickly to his right and saw that she had passed out, and her head was leaning against the passenger door.

The Lincoln fishtailed as he rounded the corner of the next street, making the turn at the last possible second, but the Ford managed to skid and keep up. He headed for a freeway on-ramp but, at the last minute, turned in another direction to throw off the gunmen in the Ford and because he didn't want to be the cause of a massive pileup on the freeway. The driver in the Ford stayed behind him and was gaining ground.

He drove into an industrial area near an abandoned warehouse on the waterfront where there was a lot of construction going on. He remembered a complex of warehouses a few blocks away where he could drive through mazelike streets and hopefully confuse the other driver.

He clicked the phone on the dashboard, called his friend at the upscale building five minutes from where they were, and told him to open the gate and call the cops and an ambulance. The attendant's booth where his friend worked was protected by bulletproof glass, and they could bring down the steel door at the car entrance if they were far enough in front of the gunman.

Raul swerved the big Lincoln around one corner and then the next, not able to see how close the Ford was. Grateful the rain had let up, he raced to the far side of the warehouse block and headed for his friend's building. He didn't see the Ford following and looked down at Rosemaria, who was unconscious and covered in blood that seemed to be oozing out of the back of her head.

He was only two blocks away from the condo building when he again spotted the Ford. He floored the Lincoln and sped into the driveway of the parking garage and through the open gate. He shouted out the window as he drove past the attendant's booth: "Don't let those guys in!" The gate was already sliding down behind him. He came to a stop in a parking space near the entrance and stumbled out of the car.

Raul couldn't see what was happening outside the garage. Bullets were exploding into the steel door. But the door was impenetrable, and the cement walls that surrounded the garage only had a half a foot opening around the top. There was no way the shooters could get in. After the sound of a few more fruitless rounds, Raul heard sirens screaming in the distance and the Ford screeching out of the driveway, laying rubber as the assassins fled. His friend was inside the booth on his cell phone, making emphatic gestures and looking at Raul like, *What the hell, man?*

Raul felt a sharp pain stab his right thigh as he limped back to the Lincoln and saw that Rosemaria was still passed out in the front seat. He didn't touch her for fear he would cause damage before the EMTs came. His friend walked toward him, but all Raul could see was the vague outline of a person and sounds coming from that direction that might have been words. Soon, he was surrounded by a white fog that enveloped him in a welcome haze. The floor met him on the way down.

CHAPTER TWO

The emergency area around Hillcrest Hospital in La Jolla was jammed with sheriff's cars as Josh turned the Mercedes into the driveway. His heart was beating so hard it felt like a jackhammer pounding into pavement. He saw an ambulance at the front entrance, and, desperate to get to Rosemaria, he pulled to a stop next to a No Parking sign. He hopped out of the car, hit the ground running, and reached the back of the ambulance as two EMTs were placing someone on a gurney. An oxygen mask covered a woman's face, and one of the EMTs was holding an IV bag with a tube running into one arm. He recognized Rosemaria by her unmistakable auburn hair, even though much of it was now stringy and covered with blood. His heart stopped beating for a second. He couldn't speak. He was terrified.

The EMTs rolled Rosemaria through the glass doors and Josh had to run to keep up with them. "Will she be okay?" He tried to yell but choked on his words, and they came out as a whisper.

The EMTs didn't answer, just kept rolling the gurney toward the ER, and before Josh could catch up with them or ask more questions, two uniformed sheriffs grabbed him by the arms. "What's your business here, sir?" one of them demanded, his voice gruff and no nonsense.

Josh struggled to free his arms, but the sheriffs, one of them built like a middleweight and the other one thin and wiry but with a grip as firm as a jailhouse manacle, hustled him into a corner of the lobby. The middleweight put his face close to Josh's. "Why are you here? What is your interest in this person?"

Josh was desperate to free himself, and it took every bit of self-control he had to answer. "She's my fiancée!"

"You'll have to wait in the squad car until we check you out," the thin one said.

"Nuh, no, no!" He almost stuttered. "Please, I have to see her." The phlegm in his throat was so thick he felt like he was drowning in it.

The cops ignored his pleas and began walking Josh toward the exit door. With a strength born out of desperation, Josh broke free and ran down the hall toward the ER. No damned cops were going to stop him from seeing Rosemaria. He slammed through the ER doors with the sheriffs on his tail. Medical personnel looked shocked to see a disheveled man staring down at the woman on the gurney. One man, his face covered in a white mask, who looked like he was about to poke a needle into Rosemaria's arm, spoke in an angry whisper. "You need to get out of here if you care about her."

Josh glanced down at Rosemaria lying helpless on the gurney, her gym T-shirt soaked in blood. The man with the needle turned his back on Josh and began issuing orders to the other medical personnel in the room. Josh's legs almost gave way, and he felt the same mind-numbing fear he had felt years ago when he saw his father aiming a shotgun at his baby brother. Josh's instinct was to reach out his hand and touch her arm, but he was caught as if in a vice by the two sheriffs, then dragged backward into the hallway and cuffed behind his back. He knew it would be pointless to fight. Tears blinded him, and he sagged to the floor, unaware of the chaos all around him. The two sheriffs looked at each other in frustration. The guy on the floor was big. They'd need help to get him the hell out of there. One of them spoke into his shoulder mike. In less than a minute, another sheriff came running, and the three of them half dragged, half lifted Josh away from the surgical entrance.

They had finally managed to pull Josh to his feet when they saw a tall, blonde, very beautiful woman staring daggers into them from a few feet away. She planted both feet on the floor with an attitude only a famous diva can exude. "Uncuff this man immediately." Her voice implied she expected to be obeyed.

Middleweight glowered at her, "You need to step away, miss, or we'll have to arrest you as well."

The wiry one had recognized Joell. "Uh, you know this guy?" he asked as Middleweight looked at him in astonishment.

Josh, leaning against the wall, was slowly regaining his composure. Rescue in the form of Joell had arrived, and Rosemaria would be horrified at the scene he was making.

Joell spoke. "This man works for me, and that is his fiancée whose life is hanging in the balance while you harass and threaten him." Her voice was cold.

Wiry asked hesitantly, "You're sure he's her fiancé?"

Joell's imperious look had its intended affect.

"Fine, we'll let him go, but you need to control him."

"Take the cuffs off."

Reluctantly, they did as ordered, and Josh stumbled past them and sank down in a chair in the waiting area. He slumped over, cradling his head in his hands.

Joell put her hand on his shoulder. "Come on, Josh. Keep it together, for God's sake."

He barely nodded his head.

"You ran out of there so fast after the phone call I didn't get a chance to find out what happened. You didn't have to take off by yourself. I would have driven you."

He barely heard what she was saying. "I'm sorry."

"Oh, for heaven's sake, never mind. I'll see what I can find out." She stood up and walked toward the ER surgical entrance while Josh sat and waited. He watched Joell talking to a nurse outside the ER and then walk to the reception desk. He felt like his insides were about to explode, and old, unwanted memories of his little brother being shot flashed like lightning bolts in his brain.

Joell came back and sat beside him. "No news yet." They sat in silence for what seemed like an eternity. Finally, Joell said, "Somebody must know something by now."

When she stood up, she saw two gray-haired, middle-aged men, one of them Asian, both wearing nondescript off-the-rack brown suits standing directly in front of her. The Caucasian, who had a rapidly disappearing hairline, spoke to her. "Is this man the fiancé of the injured woman?"

Joell nodded, recognizing them immediately as the detectives they were. "Can't you wait until she's out of danger before you question him?"

The Asian man ignored her, took his detective shield out of his inside coat pocket, and showed the ID to Josh. "I'm Detective Loshi, and this is my partner, Detective Mack, of the San Diego Sheriff's Department. We need to find a room nearby and ask you some questions."

"I don't know the answers to any of your questions." Josh made an effort not to raise his voice as he felt anger threatening to overcome his good sense. "I'm the one who needs answers." He glared at Loshi. "Maybe you could have the decency to tell me what the hell happened to my fiancée."

Joell said to the cops, "Your timing stinks." To Josh, she said, "I need to find out about Raul as well." She got up and walked away toward the nurse's station.

Loshi and Mack looked at each other and sat down on either side of him.

Mack spoke first. "Your name, please."

"Josh Sibley."

Loshi nodded and looked down at his notebook. "Ms. Baker has a cut on her head and a concussion from a fall, a broken arm, sprained ankle, and bruising all over her body, and a bullet grazed her shoulder. She lost a lot of blood but is getting transfusions now before they wrap her leg and put her arm in a cast. After that, they'll do an MRI to check out what they think is a minor concussion."

His words gave Josh no sense of relief. "How soon can I see her?"

"That's not up to us. You'll have to ask the doctor when he comes out to see you. Meanwhile, we need information."

"You know more than I do, and I'm not moving."

Loshi sighed. "We thought you might have some idea of who would want your fiancée dead."

"She's been a cop for a lot of years and a prosecutor for a couple of years. If you're looking to find somebody with a grudge, there's a long list."

"Anybody stand out?" Mack asked.

Josh mumbled something and shook his head. The detectives looked at each other and stood up. Loshi handed him his card. "We'll get back to you. Let us know if you think of anything."

Josh accepted the card and put it in his jeans pocket. As the detectives walked toward the entrance, Joell came back and sat next to him. "She's going to be okay, Josh."

His hopeful expression as he lifted his head and searched her face broke her heart. "Yeah? The cops said that. They're sure?"

She nodded. "Raul is already in a room upstairs. I'll come back here as soon as I talk to him. A bullet grazed his leg, but it's not serious."

"What about your golf tournament?"

"Rory will have to find another partner." She smiled. "This is way more important, okay?"

She took his hand, but he barely noticed. He kept his eyes glued to the doors of the ER.

* * * * *

Rosemaria felt unspeakably tired, and, with extreme effort, forced her eyes to open into narrow slits. She could see blurred images of several people standing around her bed staring down at her. One of the figures, a gray-haired, middle-aged lady who was dressed in white, took her hand and held it while looking at a machine above her that was emitting regular beeps.

"Am I dead? Is this heaven?" Her voice was a hoarse whisper.

"No, honey, you're still on earth, just as alive as you can be," the lady in white said. "But you've been unconscious for two days. Nothing to worry about. You'll be fine." The woman released her hand and stepped back, and Rosemaria saw that one of the other figures by her bed was Josh.

Worry had carved new lines into his face, and he looked tired enough to drop into bed with her and pass out.

"You promised me you wouldn't get into more trouble." He leaned down and spoke quietly, his face close to hers.

"I'm sorry. I'm trying to do better."

"Try harder." He touched his mouth to her bruised forehead.

Her words came out in a rushed whisper. "I'm sorry I talked so much about money. You know all I need is you, Noor, Gilbert, and Suzi. I don't care if we live in our little apartment forever as long as I have the four of you."

Noor, a black panther, and Gilbert, a mountain lion, had been raised by Josh while he worked as a caretaker at the at the LA Zoo and now lived in a sanctuary. Suzi the cockatoo lived with them.

"And your dad and Larry and Vanessa."

"Them too."

She noticed then that her father had been standing on the other side of the bed, his craggy but still handsome face looking at her with a troubled expression. Then his eyes crinkled at the corners and his mouth curved in a slight grin. He took her hand and bent down and kissed it. "Always showing off how tough you are."

"Can't help it, Dad."

Her vision cleared somewhat, and she noticed Joell was standing behind Josh. Larry, her former partner, and his wife and Rosemaria's best friend, Vanessa, were standing at the foot of the bed, smiling down at her.

"I don't seem to be dressed for a party," she managed, her voice so soft she wasn't sure if she had even spoken.

Vanessa had tears in her eyes. "You look beautiful."

The nurse stepped forward and patted her hand. "No exertion. I'm shooing your visitors out of here in a few minutes."

As Rosemaria watched the nurse disappear out the door, her eyes closed, and she felt herself drifting back into a sweet, comforting inertia, but a sharp dagger of fear forced her out of her seductive somnolence. "Raul?" She gasped as the effort to speak choked off his name. "How is—?"

"He's fine," Joell assured her. "He was shot in the leg and, like you, lost a lot of blood, but he'll be fine."

"He-he saved my—"

Rosemaria couldn't keep her eyes open anymore, and she heard the nurse come in and order everyone out. Her last thought before drifting away was *Why? Why?*

The nurse ushered everyone out of the room. "She'll be asleep for a few hours. Why don't you all go get something to eat?"

Out in the corridor, Josh and the others passed two cops sitting on either side of Rosemaria's room door. "Don't let anybody in without making sure they are who they say they are," Josh said to them.

"Don't worry," one of the cops assured him. "And there's more of us here that you don't see."

Josh smiled and nodded as he walked with his friends toward the waiting area and they found places to sit close to each other.

They sat silently for a few minutes. "What a relief." Vanessa sighed. "I was terrified all the way down here yesterday. Now she's awake and totally safe from whoever—" She broke off, fighting back tears. "I'm so angry!"

Larry put an arm around his wife's shoulders as she vented. "She didn't deserve this. After all the hell she went through a few months ago."

Josh chuckled, and the other four looked at him, surprised. "You know what's going to happen, don't you?"

Steven Baker, who knew his daughter better than anyone, answered, "Yeah, she'll be wanting to track down whoever did this to her."

"Probably starting tomorrow," Larry said. And the others couldn't help laughing.

"She's the kindest, bravest person I know." Vanessa was tearing up again. "The thought of losing her is just too awful."

Larry pulled a handkerchief out of the pocket of his sport coat and handed it to her.

Vanessa blew her nose. "Thank God for an old-fashioned husband who carries handkerchiefs."

Josh, feeling like an ice-cold weight had lifted off his shoulders said, "I'm taking everybody to lunch. Joell, what's a good restaurant near here, anyway?"

Joell shook her head. "Sorry, I have a meeting to go to. The premiere of our movie is Friday, and then we fly out Monday morning."

"Oh yeah," Vanessa said. "I forgot all about the premiere. That's so exciting, Josh. Having your song in the opening credits of a movie then the tour to promote it. Too bad Rosemaria can't be at the premiere with you. Although she does hate all that red carpet glamour stuff."

Josh hesitated. He knew that, since Rosemaria was going to be fine, Joell would expect him to fly to Prague with the rest of her entourage next week. He didn't want that argument to occur here and now in the hospital. He wasn't leaving Rosemaria for the premiere, the tour, or anything else. Rosemaria came first. End of story.

Joell saw the determined look on Josh's face and feigned a bright cheerfulness she did not feel. "We can discuss that later, okay?" She and Josh stood up, and she kissed his cheek. "We'll talk." And she was gone.

He felt the questioning eyes of his friends on him. "Come on, let's go eat."

"Where are we going?" Larry asked.

"The Gaslamp District has a lot of restaurants." Vanessa said. "We'll go there."

They stood up and headed toward the elevators where the doors had already closed on Joell.

Steven Baker pressed the down button and said, "You know what Rosemaria would say about you not going."

"Yeah, I know what she'd say, but two maniacs are trying to kill her. You expect me to leave her alone?" He stepped into the arriving elevator, and the others followed.

*   *   *   *   *

The blinding hot fury that ravaged her consciousness was unwelcome and unfamiliar. The target had escaped and complicated her plans. She'd always thought of herself as the mistress of her own fate. Even when anyone else in her situation would have settled for crumbs, she knew she would end up possessing everything she ever dreamed of. She had always taken advantage of the slightest opportunity that came her way and worked it in her favor. *Ruthless* was a word she cherished, but subtlety was her middle name. It was that subtlety that had concealed her true intentions, that had brought her—almost—to the peak of her powers. Now she was standing in front of one of the floor-to-ceiling windows of her condo on the twenty-fifth floor of the most exclusive residential building on Wilshire Boulevard in Westwood, arms crossed, directing a fierce stare at the Century City skyline in the distance and fighting the urge to scream.

She and that idiot she was now joined at the hip with had probably jumped the gun. Uncharacteristically, she had panicked when she found out David Marchand had talked to the ex-cop. After careful digging and discovering Baker's formidable investigative reputation, she had decided to have the ex-cop killed to ensure no roads could lead back to her. She seethed as she recalled making her directions clear to the imbecile—she was willing to pay a lot of money for a clean hit and plane tickets for the assassins to get them out of the country as fast as possible. All the brainless moron needed to do was hire the right people online and keep her far removed from the deal. But he screwed up royally. She would have to get rid of him when all this was over.

Up until now, her life had been proceeding along the path she had envisioned years ago. If she had stayed patient and just stopped after arranging Marchand's fatal stabbing in prison, which she had been certain no one could trace back to her, there wouldn't be all this brouhaha with everybody and his brother protecting the target and having about a million guards surrounding her. Baker was an ex-cop, for God's sake. Her father was an ex-cop. Her buddies in blue would do whatever they had to do to protect her. For the first time in her life, she had made a major blunder. But there was no turning back now. She would have to wait until the target was easy pickings. And she would have to handle the details herself. She'd been called a killer before by her competitors. They had meant that to be a pejorative and not a literal label. Little did they know she relished the word and lived up to it whenever possible. Regardless, she was untouchable.

CHAPTER THREE

Homicide detectives Loshi and Mack were already seated in straight-backed chairs on either side of Rosemaria's bed when Josh walked into her room the next morning. Her eyes were still sunken in, and the black-and-blue bruises on her face were even more pronounced, but she was thoroughly enjoying the conversation. Her face lit up when she saw him. "Josh, pull up a chair and sit beside me." Loshi stood up, grabbed another chair by the window, and placed it next to the bed. Josh leaned down and gave Rosemaria a gentle peck on the cheek before easing into the chair.

"You guys have met before, right?" Rosemaria asked.

Josh acknowledged the cops with a nod.

"I've been filling them in on what happened. Thank God Raul was there and for the bulletproof glass. We would have been shot to pieces otherwise." She smiled as if she were talking about a football score. "They have no leads on who the shooters were, just that they were probably pros. I can't think of anybody I've put away who has that kind of money. Vick and Hernandez are destitute." She explained to the two detectives, "Two mutts who were given twenty to life a couple of months ago for armed robbery of a liquor store and for the attempted kidnapping of yours truly."

Loshi reacted. "They were fool enough to try to kidnap an officer of the court?"

Rosemaria laughed, "Apparently, I was a major annoyance. Anyway, I didn't even prosecute them. I was just a witness. No one I've put away since I moved back to L.A. would be able to afford to hire a couple of assassins, not even the crooked politicians I put in the federal pen." She suddenly stopped, took a deep breath, and looked down in shame. "I'm sorry. I'm so, so sorry. I don't mean to make light of the fact that a bullet meant for me ended up killing an innocent girl. That wasn't fair."

"We get it," Loshi said.

She looked up at the two cops and Josh. "No, no, you don't. I feel guilty that she died and yet relieved it wasn't me, and that's a terrible thing to feel. It should have been me."

Josh said, "I get it. I do."

Mack, clearly uncomfortable with the intimate direction the conversation was taking, interrupted. "I hate to break up this bare-it-all therapy session, but my partner and me better get back to the office and look over what we've got so far on these two dirtbags. The gym has cameras on every side of the building, and we collected ammo rounds up the yin-yang. The sniper left his rifle behind. Forensics will come up with something. There was a stolen car by the side of the road, apparently driven there by the sniper. That was his intended getaway vehicle until he missed his target, and everything went sideways.

"I want to help if I can," Rosemaria said.

Mack grimaced. "Hearing you say that sends chills up my spine, Ms. Baker. I've heard about you from your friends Larry and Vanessa. Larry told me about some of the close calls you had working with him at BHPD. Keep out of the line of fire. You're not a cop anymore. You stay home and let us do the investigating."

Rosemaria sighed heavily. "I still have a job to go to."

"Take leave until we get these guys," Loshi said.

"Can't do that."

The two cops stood up and shook hands with Josh. "I leave it to you to control this woman."

Josh shook his head. "Can't be done."

The cops headed for the door.

"And here I thought San Diego was just a quiet little beach town," Rosemaria called after them.

Mack snorted. "Yeah, like Hollywood is full of movie stars and Lamborghinis." And he was gone.

Rosemaria took Josh's hand. "Raul came to see me. I got to thank him for saving my life."

"I stopped in his room and did the same. He's just down the hall."

"If it hadn't been for him, the downpour, all the umbrellas"—She stopped. "The dog. What happened to the little dog?"

"He's fine. One of the uniformed officers took him home with her."

"I'm glad about that, but it's possible he could be a clue. Where did he come from? Does he have a chip? Maybe they can track down the real owner and ask—"

"Whoa. Let your cop brain rest for a few days. Mack and Loshi are on it."

"Yeah, but I'll call them and make sure."

Josh closed his eyes and rubbed his forehead. "Ah, maybe leave it to them, okay?"

"I don't know why they don't want to take advantage of my experience. I'm not just a victim; I was a homicide cop, for God's sake."

Josh puffed up his cheeks and blew out air. The woman *was* uncontrollable. "The doctor said you'll be here a day or two, and then I'll be able to take you home. I don't intend to leave you alone for a minute."

"You can't do that."

"Why not?"

"You'll be on your tour."

"I already told Joell I couldn't go."

She stared at him. "Why would you do that?"

"Somebody's trying to kill you. Do you really think I can get up on a stage and sing when all I'm doing is thinking about you?"

"I'll have police protection. I have a gun, and I know how to use it. You're not blowing the best chance you ever had because of me."

"It's already been decided. Joell understands, so let's not argue."

"You can't make a decision like this without talking it over with me. It's too important."

"Wow. This is a first." They both turned and saw Larry walking toward Rosemaria's bed. "I don't think I've ever heard the two of you argue before. I thought you guys were perfect together like pancakes and syrup, peaches and cream, Sonny and Cher—oh no, that didn't turn out too well. What seems to be the problem here? You're not even married yet."

"He told Joell he's not going on the tour and didn't even discuss it with me. I'm so pissed I could spit nails."

Josh was unmoved. "You can scream bloody murder, and I'm still not changing my mind."

Larry stood at the foot of the bed rubbing his palms together, a smug look on his face. "Being the great detective that I am, I foresaw this problem yesterday and already solved it."

"Josh studied him skeptically. "I'm not going."

"Oh, ye of little faith."

"Out with it, Larry," Rosemaria said. "I like it already."

"As you know, my parents are obscenely wealthy. Their house in Holmby Hills is practically an armed fortress with alarm systems up the wazoo. They have agreed to let Rosemaria stay there for as long as Josh is on tour. They will hire two more armed guards and put Rosemaria in a room deemed fit for foreign dignitaries. Rosemaria will be safer there than with you in your tiny apartment and will be waited on hand and foot. I await your humble expressions of gratitude."

Rosemaria stared at Larry for a moment then reached out to grab Josh's arm. "Say yes," she whispered.

Josh's skepticism slowly faded, and he looked like Christmas had arrived early. "She'd be guarded day and night?"

"A whole lot better than you could do, my friend."

Rosemaria was excited enough to run out of the hospital and join a marathon with her ass hanging out of her gown. "Call Joell, Josh. Find out if you can still change your mind about the tour, and you have to go to the premiere too. There's no reason for you not to."

Josh hesitated, then: "I'll call her out in the hallway. I don't want either of you to hear me beg." He took out his cell phone and headed out the door.

Rosemaria's bruised and battered face was shining. "Thank you, Larry. You've given us a wonderful gift."

He leaned over and made a move to hug her, then saw her cringe. "Sorry, I forgot. Am I still your favorite ex-partner?"

"No one even comes close."

"I'm going to stay in touch with the San Diego homicide detectives. Your old pals from BHPD, Jimmy Waite and Daryl Osborne want to be a part of the investigation as well. The lieutenant signed off on it."

"The killers are probably long gone. Who hired them is the question."

Josh walked back in. They looked at him in anticipation.

"Tell my secretary to clear my schedule. I'm off to Prague next week."

"Yes!" Rosemaria yelled, waving her good arm wildly in the air, winced in pain, then let it fall back on the bed and barely whispered, "Oh," closed her eyes, and sank back on her pillow as the guys hovered anxiously over her.

She opened one eye. "Just kidding." She smiled. "If whoever is doing this thinks they can turn me into a mass of quivering jelly, they better think again."

Josh patted her hand. "Not you, my fierce warrior. Never you. You can leave the quivering to me. Just label me strawberry rhubarb."

At that, Rosemaria and Larry guffawed in unison. It only hurt her side a little bit.

CHAPTER FOUR

The procession of cars headed for the magnificent Collins estate befitted a head of state. There were two police cars in front and two in back, and in one black Mercedes limousine sat the central figure of the protective convoy, the central figure's fiancé, the driver, and a personal bodyguard. All of them were traveling through the hallowed, tree-lined streets of Holmby Hills, where only the excessively wealthy could afford to live. As they neared their destination, the central figure in the Mercedes was displaying extreme discomfort.

"This is way over the top, Josh. I am so embarrassed."

Her fiancé felt otherwise. "Larry promised me you would be safely escorted to his parents' house, and he delivered."

"I feel like the head of a drug cartel with a hundred competitors looking to blow her up. I'm just a lowly prosecutor, and we get death threats all the time." She paused. "Not really."

The bodyguard, Cameron Buckley, a dark-haired man in his thirties who filled out his tailored black suit with muscle and not an ounce of fat, spoke up from the front passenger seat. "Ma'am, I don't know if the San Diego detectives told you, but the rifle the sniper used was a Barrett M82A1, extremely accurate and expensive. The shooter left it behind when he came after you, which means money is not a consideration for whoever hired them. No prints, though. You can safely assume they will try again."

Rosemaria shuddered. "Well, I can't live with Larry's parents forever. We're just going to have to track down this person who hates me and put him away. Of course, then he could come after me from behind bars."

"Your boss, the chief assistant prosecutor at the Airport Courthouse, promised after this monster is caught and convicted, he will make sure he's put away in super max and stripped of every dime he owns so he can't hire anybody." Buckley said.

"Wow," Rosemaria said. "I didn't know he thought I was that important."

"After I come back from the tour, we'll have round-the-clock protection for you until the killer is caught," Josh added.

"We can't possibly afford that."

Cameron cleared his throat. "Mr. Collins has already requested that I or another security guard from our agency be hired to protect you until the assassins are caught."

I'm sure you'll all do an excellent job, but, Josh, how are we ever going to pay Larry back? It will take the rest of our lives."

"We'll figure it out."

The procession paused in front of the gates to the mansion, and Rosemaria, who had promised herself she would never be impressed by awesome wealth, stared at the scene in front of her as the huge black wrought-iron gates slowly swung open, and they drove down the long drive to the house. They had passed some impressive mansions while they were driving through Holmby Hills, but this one was not only massive; it was beautiful, surrounded by lush green lawns and an abundance of magnificent landscaping. It was constructed in a three-storied California Mediterranean style, beige stucco with curvy, bright-white borders around the windows. At the top of the front stairs and portico was a double oak door that looked like the entrance to a medieval castle. She grabbed Josh's hand, and they grinned at each other. "I promise not to get used to it," she said.

The Mercedes stopped at the front entrance, and Larry stepped out of the police car that had led the procession and walked toward the Mercedes. He opened the door for Rosemaria. "Wait here."

The front door of the mansion opened, and a nurse with a wheelchair pushed it down a wooden ramp that had been constructed for Rosemaria. As the nurse, a thin and willowy, soft-voiced young lady introduced to them as Madelaine, helped Rosemaria into the wheelchair, every police officer stepped out of their cars and was scanning the area. She had worked with most of them at BHPD, and, holding back tears, she was overcome by their dedication to her safety. She allowed herself to be wheeled up the ramp to the front door.

Josh, Cameron, and Larry used the tiled steps and joined her. There would always be twinges of worry now and then, but as Josh observed the care and professionalism of Rosemaria's protectors, he felt tremendous relief knowing he would be able to enjoy performing, secure in the knowledge that she was a lot safer here than she would have been with him in their tiny apartment in West Hollywood.

"Welcome to our home." Larry's mother, Loretta, stepped into the doorway, accepted a hug from her son, and smiled graciously at the others. Her husband, Andrew Collins, Larry's stepfather, was right behind her. He ushered them into the foyer and led them down the hallway. Josh followed a few steps behind the group and surveyed the vast space of the Collins' living room where Rosemaria was being given a chance to rest and get her bearings before being moved up to her suite three stories above.

The walls were white; the dark wood beams were attached to high ceilings. The couches and chairs were covered in silken fabrics in various pastel blue and mint colors that matched the blue-and-white curtains hanging on either side of the tall windows. The end tables appeared to be slabs of marble, and glass-topped coffee tables were set in front of at least three conversation areas. A large wet bar with crystal glasses displayed in a pine cabinet covered half a wall. The view of the outside patio revealed an Olympic-size pool with guest houses on either side that were bigger than any house Josh had ever lived in. The scene in front of him was breathtaking—a green lawn surrounded the pool and stretched into the distance for a quarter mile where tall hedges with even taller black iron fences behind them guarded the property. Giant palm trees grew at both ends of the guesthouses. Smaller palm trees grew closer to the main house. Four sky-blue umbrellas rose out of thick glass tables surrounded by groupings of chairs and lounges on three sides of the pool.

As Josh stood in the midst of this incredible luxury and watched Rosemaria being wheeled toward the French doors that led outside to the pool area, he marveled at how far he had traveled since he met the woman who was now at the center of his life. From his younger days singing in nightclubs, then working on his musical when he could carve out a few minutes a day, while at the same time writing commercial jingles—all of it while meandering through an alcoholic daze that had he had accepted as necessary therapy to dull the ache in his broken heart. Years ago, when his father had murdered his younger son with a shotgun and Josh had been forced to kill him to protect himself and his mother, Josh figured that any kind of normal existence would never be an option for him. Then he met Rosemaria, and everything changed. This feisty, strong, independent woman refused to give up on him, shattered his dark and hopeless world, and gifted him with a lightness he never imagined he would ever experience. He watched her as she sat in her wheelchair, her arm in a sling, her face bruised, but she never acknowledged to the people around her that she was in pain. Larry, who never wavered in his loyalty, and Loretta and her husband, Andrew Collins, the police commissioner who had made the magnanimous offer of protecting Rosemaria's life with everything they had at their disposal, were all focused on her as she expressed her gratitude.

Larry's mother, a lovely lady in her sixties who had allowed age to settle on her easily with no visible signs of fighting off the inevitable with plastic surgery, poo-pooed Rosemaria's attempts to apologize for disrupting their lives. "My darling girl, don't give it a second thought. We've had some high-profile foreign luminaries stay in the suite where you'll be living for the next two weeks. Believe me, some of them actually *were* a bother." She looked over at her husband, who appeared to be a little older than she was, not classically handsome, but his confident bearing and obvious self-assurance made his mediocre looks irrelevant.

He shook his head and laughed. "Some of them had more body-guards than we had rooms. We had to put a few of them in the pool houses. And the endless demands for special diets threatened Lorretta's sanity. I would happily have allowed her to strangle them if not for the international repercussions."

Lorretta spoke confidentially, as if only to Rosemaria. "I came close, believe me, but there's too many cops in the family for me to get away with it."

"I would never have investigated you, mother dearest," Larry said. "You know that, but if you should feel the need, just try not to leave any obvious clues I'll have to ignore. Meanwhile, let's briefly go over the logistics so Rosemaria can go up to her suite and rest." He turned to where Cameron was standing next to the French doors, ever watchful. "Do you want to do the honors, my friend?"

Cameron walked over to the massive white-brick fireplace that stretched to the ceiling. He was all business as he faced the group. "Ms. Baker, the suite you'll be staying in is on the third floor. The windows cannot be accessed from the roof or the ground. The glass is impenetrable. There are cameras in the hall, over every doorway inside your suite, and in the living room and kitchen areas. You can turn the cameras that cover the bedroom, living area, and bathroom on and off. There is a video screen on the wall beside the door where you can see whoever is outside in the hallway. There is a safe room off the bedroom where, in case of emergency, you can lock yourself in, and it is impregnable.

"The suite next to yours will be occupied by a female guard who is due to arrive in a few minutes. She, like the guard in the main floor security office, will have access to videos from all the cameras in the house and on the grounds. Every square inch of the property is covered by cameras. The front gate cannot be opened by anyone other than a guard in the security office, and no one will be allowed to enter the grounds unless they have been prescreened and approved.

"Four guards will patrol the grounds day and night, and I will have personal responsibility for making sure you come to no harm. If you ever have any concerns, there is a walkie-talkie in your room with channels available only to you, me, and the other guards." He looked at her. "Do you have any questions?"

Rosemaria cast a worried glance at Josh. "I don't know what to say, and as everybody who knows me can attest to, that is highly unusual. I feel like I'm being treated like the president, like I'm someone who deserves all this, and I don't. It's overwhelming—all these people to protect just me?"

Commissioner Collins was standing at the bar sipping a drink. "Yes, I can see why you find it a bit overwhelming, but understand—all the security precautions were in place when we bought the house. We didn't have to do much to make it safe for you except hire two more guards recommended by Cameron. Loretta did love the house and the convenient location, but we also bought it as a favor to people we know who wanted a secure location for visiting dignitaries. Don't feel like you're putting us out, Rosemaria. We've done this many times before."

Josh stood up and moved behind Rosemaria. "Then, if everyone doesn't mind, I'd like to move my fiancée upstairs so she can lie down and rest."

The nurse, Madelaine, who had been quietly listening to the conversation while seated close to her patient, quickly stood. She glanced toward the doorway where the elevator was.

"Follow me," Larry said. He led them out into the hallway. Cameron had already disappeared. As Josh pushed Rosemaria's wheelchair toward the elevator, Larry looked at her with sympathy and understanding. "I know exactly how you feel, even though I spent a couple of years living here. My mother and stepfather are a part of the high echelons of LA society. It sounds quaint, but there it is. And this vast barn is a part of living in that stratosphere." The elevator door opened, and he held it as they went in.

A tall woman in her twenties with dark hair pulled back in a simple bun, who seemed to come out of nowhere, stepped in behind them. She addressed Rosemaria. "I'm Kirsten Lowell. I'll be your personal bodyguard for the duration of your stay here. I will be in the room adjoining yours and as unobtrusive as possible."

"Thank you," Rosemaria said and smiled at her.

Half an hour later, Josh and Rosemaria were finally alone in the bedroom. She was sitting up in the king-size bed while he munched on a red apple he had picked from the large fruit bowl sitting on the glossy round table that also held bananas, mangoes, and a variety of fruits he didn't recognize. As he chewed, he wandered around the room. looking at the fancy furnishings. Kirsten had shown them all the suite's security details—the cameras, the walkie-talkies, and the locks on the doors—and disappeared into her room. Madelaine was down the hall in her suite, and Rosemaria felt like she could finally breathe.

She looked around at all the cameras. "Do you think they can hear us talk?"

"I don't think so. I think he said there's a button you press on that pad on your nightstand and on the desk if you decide you want security to hear you."

They both jumped as a loud knock was heard. They looked at the screen by the door and saw that it was Cameron. Rosemaria clicked the unlock button, and Josh opened the door. "Welcome."

Cameron smiled and took a few steps into the room. "Thank you."

"Is everything okay?" Rosemaria asked.

"Yes, but if you don't mind, I have more logistical information regarding the running of the household that Loretta asked me to pass on to you. Is this a good time?"

"Absolutely," Rosemaria said as Josh made himself comfortable in a chair near her bed.

"I'll make this as succinct as possible."

"You have the floor, or have a seat. Take as long as you wish," Josh said.

Cameron chose to stand, took a breath, and began. "Most of the staff is now on paid leave. We have left in place only those who are absolutely necessary to running the household to cut down on the people coming in and out of the property. Mr. Crais, the pool man, who has been employed here for several years, will be coming onto the property on Mondays and Fridays. Max and Brent are part-time workers and students at UCLA. They will be doing light housework and other tasks as needed. They have undergone rigorous background checks. Mildred, who is the head of the household staff, lives in five days a week. Her room is off the kitchen. She does not work on Wednesdays and Saturdays and stays at her other residence on those days. Manuela the cook is a day worker, and her days off are Fridays and Sundays. She makes breakfast at eight a.m. for Mr. and Mrs. Collins, who notify her the day before if they will be eating breakfast in and if she is needed to make lunch and dinner. You can let her know by calling on the intercom what meals you would like, and they will be brought up to you. Because of their busy schedule, Mr. and Mrs. Collins are usually gone during the day and sometimes on weekends as well. Their suite is located on the second floor, as are three guest suites. The third floor has your suite and two other suites, which will be unoccupied except for the one your nurse is staying in. Any questions?"

Josh looked at Rosemaria, who looked a little shaken, and said, "Thank you, Cameron. Tell Loretta we appreciate her asking you to fill us in so thoroughly."

"My pleasure." And he was gone.

Josh turned to Rosemaria. "What's wrong?"

"Did you hear that? This is insane. I'm being treated like a delicate orchid who needs to be watched every minute, and I'm disrupting the entire household. Me being here is not fair to everyone who lives and works here. I don't know if I can do this."

"You will if you want me to go on tour."

She breathed out heavily, staring up at the ceiling and then at Josh. "You're right. I'm sorry. If living here gets you on that plane to Europe, then this is where I'll be." She smiled. "The sacrifices I make."

"Living in this kind of luxury would be difficult for anyone."

"You know what I'm saying. I've spent most of my adult life chasing and arresting violent criminals in treacherous neighborhoods. I'm not a helpless flower."

"Should I bring you a mirror so you can see what shape you're in, my delicate rosebud?"

"Yeah, there's that too. I really am messed up" She reached up and touched the butterfly bandages on her forehead. "I'm also going to have a scar here. Will it bother you that my face is flawed?"

He grabbed another apple from the bowl, and, pulling up a chair next to her, still munching on his, he handed her one. "Just a badge of courage. After this is over, you can regale our friends with stories about how you got it."

"I hope I still have a job when this is over."

"You told me Lattimer said you should take all the time you need."

"I'm no good at doing nothing." She took a big bite of the apple. "I'm happy you're staying the night."

"Just one night. Cameron said me coming and going all the time was too risky. I might be followed."

"I'm sorry I'm in such a sorry state that I can't make your stay worth your while."

"I'll figure out something."

"How could I doubt you?" They grinned and stared at each other as they chewed.

* * * * *

He stood in his office, dreading the fallout from the catastrophic bungling of what should have been a simple hit. It had been a perfect plan. He had followed the orders of the cold-blooded schemer just as precisely as if his life depended on it, and it did. The two shooters had been hired through reliable sources. The sniper on the hill would take care of the woman, and the shooter on the ground would finish off the driver if he moved too quickly and tried to take out the sniper. The stolen car was parked offroad. The sniper would take apart the rifle and scatter pieces of it along the highway, and drive the car to a vacant lot near the airport. The second shooter would pick him up, and they would get on a plane and fly out of the country.

The would-be assassins had prepared like the professionals they were: planting the listening device in the singer's house and the tracking device on the limousine; they knew exactly where the target would be, but they blew it anyway. They had underestimated the driver's skill, the main target's physical ability, and the torrential rain that the idiots who predict the weather didn't know was coming until it was too late. Now there were second thoughts. Was all this really necessary? He had argued they should have left sleeping dogs lie, and nothing would have happened. But it was too late to change course now that an innocent woman had been murdered, and he knew he would be blamed for the screwup. He also knew if there was a next time, the target better end up dead, or he needed to disappear to a place far away where that heartless monster could never find him.

CHAPTER FIVE

ndy Mack and David Loshi had been working homicide in the San Diego Sheriff's Department for over twenty years, ten of those years as partners. They were not easily provoked, shocked, or impressed. So, as they drove up to the Collins mansion, which was easily the most impressive house they had passed on the way to their destination, neither would admit to the other that they were slightly gobsmacked at the sight of the conspicuous symbol of wealth they were about to enter.

They had been told by their captain that Ms. Baker was in no shape to be moved and had to be interviewed in her suite at Los Angeles Police Commissioner Collins's house in Holmby Hills. As it turned out, the commissioner lived in opulence the internet had not even begun to adequately describe. Even though he was the police commissioner, they had checked him out thoroughly. The commissioner's vast wealth was clean, garnered from a family inheritance combined with hard work. Inside the house, they stood in the elevator next to Cameron Buckley after passing through intense security clearances and gaping at the palatial interior. Cops or no cops, no one was excluded from the strict rules set up by Buckley. He had ushered them to the entrance of Rosemaria's suite, and they waited while she checked the screen on the wall beside the door before she clicked the button on her desktop that unlocked it.

After being offered something to drink and accepting small bottles of Pellegrino, Mack and Loshi were seated in comfortable armchairs in the living room area, which probably cost more than the combined worth of their pensions, ready to proceed, determined to focus on the job and overcome their awe at their surroundings.

Ms. Baker, seated across from them in a wheelchair, acted as if she were recovering nicely, but the bruises on her face were startling in their variety of colorations—blue, red, green, black. They were bigger and brighter than when they had seen her in the hospital. Even her beautiful features and shiny auburn hair couldn't overcome the ugliness of those bruises.

"I know. I'm a sight, aren't I?" Rosemaria grinned. "A face even a mother can't love. And the scar on my forehead will be with me forever, I'm afraid." She leaned toward them slightly and spoke with a quiet intensity. "I've been thinking about what you said to me in the hospital, but I've decided I will help catch those bastards and whoever it was who hired them. And I won't let this wheelchair and a broken arm and sprained ankle stop me." Her determined gaze took them aback.

Mack spoke first. She was just as stubborn as he had been warned about. "It's going to take weeks, maybe more, for you to heal, so even if you still were on the force, there's nothing you can do."

"We know how you feel," Loshi said, "but have some faith in us. We're pretty good detectives and have been at it for a long time. So let's not waste any more time arguing about this. What can you tell us about people who might have grudges against you?"

He took out his recorder and pressed the button. She looked away for several seconds, and the detectives were afraid she was going to go off on another tangent, but she jumped right in. "Walter Atkins, a prosecutor I worked with, has a deep, pathological hatred toward me. He'd kill me if he could get away with it, but he's not rich and I doubt if he could afford to hire professionals to knock me off. Grover Vick, the armed robber I testified against, vowed to kill me, but again, he's in San Quentin and would have to rely on befriending a parolee and talking him into killing me for nothing. Last year, I cleaned up a mess of corrupt politicians who had kidnapped friends of mine, but they're all locked up in maximum security prisons with no chance of parole. I'd be willing to bet my life they're keeping their noses clean. Petty drug dealers and pimps I arrested in Hollywood who threatened me are probably dead by now or still in prison. You can check with Hollywood, and they can dig out the cases I worked on and give you some names."

"Anything more recent that rings a bell?" Mack asked.

"No, but there is one interesting case that might be a lead of some sort."

"What is that?" Loshi asked.

"Well, this is going back around ten years ago, but someone who was arrested for murder when I briefly worked the case as a uniformed officer in Hollywood was killed in Tehachapi Correctional Facility two weeks ago."

Loshi was confused. "How is this relevant?"

"Well, he called me a week before he was murdered, and he convinced me to come up and talk to him in person. He sounded so desperate I figured a visit couldn't hurt, and I was curious about what he had to say. I was never convinced that he was the guilty party anyway. But I was just a rookie cop and didn't have much input when it came to the investigation. I interviewed some of the kids who lived in the same apartment house as the victim and turned in my report. That was about it."

"I still don't get it," Loshi said.

"He had hoped to convince the Innocence Project to get involved with his case, but they turned him down. Even though he was in the youthful offender program and had a good chance of getting early parole, he wanted to prove his innocence and begged me to talk to Sherilyn Cosgrove, the murder victim's girlfriend. He said she would tell me she believed in his innocence. I agreed, but he was killed before I had a chance to do that."

Mack was puzzled. "Where are you going with this?"

"Detectives, this murderer or victim of a frame, David Marchand, was going around telling other inmates that he had one of the best detectives in LA who was now a prosecutor looking for the real killer of Ramin Hassan, his best friend who he supposedly killed. The case against him never made any sense to me. If David was innocent, maybe somebody got a little nervous and wanted to stop me."

"But after his death, the case must have been closed for good," Loshi said. "Why would they think you would investigate?"

"Because I'm known for hating loose ends. Because there was still the murder of Marchand to investigate. And another thing—Victor Marchand, David's father, had a vendetta against everyone involved in getting his son found guilty. He's super rich and influential and could hire anyone to kill whoever he wants."

"But you were going to help his son," Mack said. "Why have a hard-on for you?"

"His son is dead because we all did our job and put him in prison."

"That's a little bit of a stretch," Loshi said. "Not much point in risking everything you have to get back at a rookie cop just doing her job a lot of years ago."

"That's why I think it might be worth it to look at the other people in Ramin's life, especially the people he lived with. One of them might know something. I never thought the investigation was thorough enough. Once they settled on David, a rich, spoiled screwup about to flunk out of USC, the detectives pretty much stopped looking at anybody else."

"And how does this all lead back to you?" Mack asked.

"I'm not sure. You're the detectives. I'm just the poor victim stuck in a wheelchair."

Mack clicked off the recorder. "Uh-huh. Just stay a victim, okay? Let us do the digging. We'll follow up on these characters you gave us."

"Any leads I come up with, you'll be the first to know."

Mack and Loshi were not impressed by her expression of sincerity. "Uh-huh," Mack said again.

"Except for one thing."

"What?" Mack sighed.

"Any leads concerning the little dog?"

Mack's tightened his lips into a thin line. "Not yet. He didn't have a chip, and he's busy being spoiled and ain't talking."

"I guess that's about it for now," Loshi said.

"Rosemaria smiled. "I will have Cameron escort you out." She pressed a button on the arm of her wheelchair, and within a few seconds, there was a knock on the door. "Come in, please."

Cameron opened the door and held it open for the two detectives.

"Happy hunting, detectives. I wish you well," Rosemaria said.

"Uh-huh," Mack muttered on his way out.

* * * * *

Joell was in her element. Except for performing, which was what she had lived for since she sang at her first recital in grade school, organizing anything—a show, a tour, decorating her various houses—was her favorite pastime. She was in her office on Wilshire Boulevard, surrounded by some of the most important people in her life. She was especially happy to see Josh Sibley, her friend and musical discovery, sitting off to the side, lost in thought, probably thinking about Rosemaria, wondering how she was— well taken care of, thank God. Miranda Telfer, her PR person extraordinaire, with a spiky new purple-and-brown hairdo that was her attempt to stay hip with their younger fans, was seated in front of Joell's desk. Harvey Morgan, pudgy and balding and the best promoter in the business, who had been with her since her first hit single, was seated at a table in the back of the room working at his laptop. Next to Miranda was Joell's agent and most trusted adviser since she first set foot in a recording studio, A.J. Meisner, dressed conservatively in a gray Armani suit that nicely set off his short-cut silver hair.

Joell was bringing someone else with her who was getting a huge break by being on the tour. Angelo Mazziotta, lead singer in a band called Mad Dogs, was dressed in a black turtleneck and black jeans and affected a moody, intense attitude. He looked impatient for the meeting to begin. She was already having second thoughts about bringing him and his band onboard, but it was a favor to Harvey Morgan, and she couldn't back out now. Seated on the right side of her desk was Dag Olufsen, a blond Swede she had nabbed from ABBA years ago, who was the best logistics guy in the music industry when it came to organizing a tour. After they first began working together, she had hoped that maybe there might be the possibility of something personal developing between them. He was attractive, charming, hardworking, just her kind of guy. But alas, when she became a little too forward, he let it be known he had someone special back in Stockholm. Another strikeout for the most desirable woman on the planet—or so the gossip rags intimated. She was in no hurry to find someone. Her standards were high, and she was quite content with her life as it was, for the most part.

Joell put up a hand for the chatter to stop. "Attention, all my darlings who are going to make this tour, even though it is a short one, more fabulous than any other we've ever produced. We will have three weeks of sold-out arenas, and we can't disappoint our fans. But before we leave, on Saturday night, at Grauman's Chinese, as you all know, we will be attending the premiere of the movie for which yours truly recorded the theme song which my friend"—she gestured toward Josh, who nodded his head slightly in acknowledgement—"Josh Sibley wrote. Monday, we fly to Prague. We'll have one day to set up, rehearse, and soundcheck, then Thursday, Friday, and Saturday at the O2 Arena. Sunday, we fly to Budapest and have two days of rest. Wednesday, rehearse; Thursday, Friday, and Saturday at the Puskas Arena. Repeat in Stockholm and fly home on Sunday. Any questions before Dag gets into the details?"

Angelo raised his hand. "Will there be doctors on hand for when we collapse from exhaustion?"

Joell managed a smile, even though she found his question offensive. She was bringing him as a favor, and already he was acting like prima donna? "Hey, I'm a lot easier on you than some headliners and this tour is a real quickie. But yes, I'll have doctors on hand to resuscitate you if necessary."

Josh noted the easy banter between people who had toured together and were relaxed and even a little bored listening to Joell and Dag go into detail about the trip. But he was apprehensive. This would be his first tour. How would he fit in with the other musicians? How would jet lag affect him and his voice? He'd never flown out of the country let alone all over Europe. How would fans react to him, a no-name who had never had a hit in his life? He felt out of his depth, and a part of him wished he could change his mind and retreat to the recording studio, singing his five-second commercial jingles. The darkness of the unknown was beckoning. He wondered if they had AA in the towns where they were headed. At any rate, his sponsor was as close as his phone. He tried to concentrate on what Dag was saying, but he had to admit, he was afraid of failure.

CHAPTER SIX

Rosemaria was looking forward to her father's visit, even though she couldn't stand up to greet him. She was learning, with the help of Madelaine, to maneuver herself in and out of her bed, to do her bad arm finger exercises and leg lifts with her good leg, to get into the bathroom and on and off the toilet. Her broken arm and the non-life-threatening bodily injuries she had sustained were still too painful for her to be able to handle crutches. The good thing was that neither Madelaine nor Kirsten was hovering over her, which would have driven her mad. If she was going to be a prisoner, at least she needed some semblance of privacy.

She heard Cameron's buzz and gave him her quick two-buzz answer from the button on her wheelchair. The door opened, and her father quickly strode into the room to her side, a big smile on his face. He bent down and hugged her gently and sat in a chair next to her. She was very happy to see him but was perplexed at the still-open door. That was very unusual.

"I have a surprise for you," her dad said. "She had to go through a rigid security check, but she passed with flying colors."

Cameron came in holding Suzi the cockatoo in her cage. Rosemaria squealed like a teenager having been asked to the junior prom by the class stud. "Suzi!"

"Gilbert get down! Gilbert get down!" Suzi shouted and fluttered around her cage excitedly.

"Thank you, Dad. I'm so happy to see her." After Rosemaria made sure Cameron had closed the door behind him, she opened Suzi's cage, and the bird hopped out and flew around the room in several circles before finally landing on Rosemaria's shoulder.

Her dad explained, "Josh has been so busy finishing up recording a commercial campaign for Wilson's Furniture Stores and making plans for the tour and the premiere, he thought the two of you might like to keep each other company."

"And he didn't even tell me. I'm really sweet on that guy, Dad."

"Yeah, I noticed. Anyway, I felt like I was in a spy movie getting her out of there. Cameron made it clear I would not be able to pick her up in case I was being followed. So Mrs. Wilkes from next door took her to the vet, making it look like she needed treatment, and then my friend Sandy picked her up at the back door and drove her home, where I picked her up and drove her over here."

"Sandy, huh?"

"Nothing like that. Don't get any ideas."

"You'd tell me if there's anything there, right? It's been a lifetime since Mom died."

"Enough about that. With all this time on your hands, I know you haven't spent it watching Netflix."

"I love how you know me better than anybody, and yeah, I've been thinking about the case. You're the only person in my life besides Josh who truly gets me and accepts me as I am."

"I like what you are."

"Some find the way I am annoying."

"You have the instincts of a born detective. Enough said."

"Keeping that astute observation in mind, the more I go over it, the more I'm convinced this has to do with Ramin Hassan and David Marchand. It's just too coincidental that Marchand was killed two weeks after I went to see him about helping him clear his name, and you know how I hate coincidences."

"You also hate the obvious, and that seems too obvious, like a movie script convenience."

"Maybe the killer didn't care about being obvious. Maybe he just wanted David's story to die with him."

"Mack and Loshi are going through the records of everybody of any consequence who might have a grudge against you. You know very well that Walter Atkins is insane, and now that he's been permanently let go from the LA DA's office and is scrambling to make a living as an ambulance chaser, he just might come up with the money to hire a couple of pros to put you out of his misery."

"He'd never hire anybody, Dad. He wants to see the fear in my eyes as he strangles me to death." She snorted. "As if that could ever happen."

"Vick is another consideration. Cons make all kinds of deals in the pen. He could have made a deal with someone in exchange for something he could do for them in prison. The cops need to investigate killings in San Quentin and see if any can be traced to him."

"Cons killing each other is not unusual."

"Exactly my point. Someone inside might have wanted to kill David for reasons known only to his fellow inmates. We'll never find that out."

She sighed. "Dad, why do you have to make so much sense just when I get my mind set in one direction?"

"You never liked that the detectives on the Hassan case made up their minds early that Marchand was guilty. Jumping to conclusions is also something you hate, even back when you were in uniform. But you're doing it now."

"Doggone it. You always did pull me up short when I stampeded full steam ahead."

"You have a lot of time now. Not like when you were investigating the murder of Maria Ramirez and trying to find the people threatening Tiffany and Maryanne and working as a prosecutor at the same time."

"Yeah, that was a little sticky, but you're right. I just wish I could do a little leg work if I come up with something."

"This may surprise you a bit—I have agreed to work with Waite. Osborne is busy on other investigations, so he's okay with it, and so are the captain and the lieutenant."

"Holy horse feathers, Batman. When did you decide this?"

"Today. We'll work with you. We have a few ideas of our own and can travel anywhere. Sargeant Osborne is giving Waite plenty of space. Larry is the official liaison with the San Diego Sheriff's Department, but he has a full plate right now investigating the murder of the couple in Bel Air. But as soon as San Diego gives him any info, he'll be passing it on to us.

"Is Larry making progress on the Bel Air case?"

"Seems pretty cut and dried. The son and his girlfriend are the obvious suspects. Just plugging up the holes and looking at other people."

"To avoid the 'rush to judgement' accusation, I gather."

"You got it."

"Why didn't downtown take the case?"

"Larry and Harvey were first on the scene, and robbery homicide have their hands full with a string of unsolved murders downtown."

"I guess they'll try the case in Van Nuys."

"Probably. But let's get back to you."

"Investigating this could be dangerous for you, Dad."

"I was a cop for more years than you've been alive, daughter. And I've survived in one piece so far—of course, with a little help from you that one time."

"You probably would have gotten out of that scrape without me. But I did good, didn't I?"

"You did. Selfishly speaking, saving my life was absolutely a good thing. Now I intend to return the favor. I can't just sit on the sidelines when you're in danger. With all due respect to Mack and Loshi, I know that you, me, and Waite are just as highly qualified a team as they are. We'd like to have first crack at Atkins, but Mack and Loshi will beat us to it. If they eliminate him, we'll confab with you and decide on our next moves. Okay with you?"

"Confab, Dad? That is so Hollywood. I'm stunned."

He leaned over and gave her a peck on the cheek. "Buzz your bodyguard to get me out of here. Time's a wastin'.

* * * * *

Suzi settled in nicely with the help of Kirsten. One of Cameron's body-guards brought in a perch from God knows where to place on a side table, put newspapers down underneath to catch her droppings, and brought water and food. Suzi, being an extremely social bird who loved everyone, soon made friends with Kirsten, perching on her shoulder and talking up a storm with her limited vocabulary. "Let's win the lottery! Let's win the lottery!" After Rosemaria persuaded Suzi to leave Kirsten's shoulder and fly back to her perch, Kirsten went into the adjoining room, giving Rosemaria her privacy.

She called Josh, and he answered on the first ring, but before he even said hello, Rosemaria all but yelled, "Thank you, thank you, my love. What a nice surprise. Now I have a member of the family to keep me company. You couldn't bring Noor and Gilbert too, could you? There's plenty of room for them to roam around in the backyard."

"I'll have to leave them in the sanctuary. I don't think they're fond of car trips."

"I miss you so much, my love."

"We've never been apart for more than two days. I feel like a part of me is going to be ripped away."

"I feel exactly the same way. Isn't it wonderful? Never in my life did I think this kind of thing would happen for me."

"I guess that's one way of looking at it. A silver lining, for sure."

"You sound a little down, Josh. Is it worrying about me, or is it something else?"

"Oh, just a case of the jitters, I guess."

"Don't kid a kidder, mister. I know exactly what you're thinking. You're about to go on tour with the most famous singer on the planet, who has more hit records than anybody and millions of fans. You're feeling like you don't deserve to be on the same stage with her and her musicians and backup singers, like people in the audience will wonder why you're even up there."

"Yeah, well—"

"I'm going to tell you something; Joell is the best appraiser of talent in the business. She believes in you enough to put you in the show. And you wouldn't know this because you're not a woman, but just the sight of your handsome, manly self walking out on stage will make the females in the audience swoon, and half the battle is won already. Then the music will begin playing, you'll open your mouth, golden tones will issue forth, and everyone will be lost in what you're singing. On top of that, you have something few singers have—stage presence. Now, you listen to this because I'm talking to you like the daughter of an actress who taught me a thing or two. You, my sweet, have that rare innate acting talent that enables you to connect with the lyrics in an organic way that most singers are unable to do. Even a lot of famous singers don't have that talent. They just sing. They don't connect to their own real emotions. You connect. The audience will feel it. Trust me."

Rosemaria waited as there were several seconds of silence on the other end of the phone. "I wish I could come over there right now and thank you properly for that pep talk."

"Thank God you can't; that sounds like it might hurt a whole lot."

"I believe you've turned my mood around, daughter of an actress. Thank you for sharing your wisdom."

"Well, I pay attention. Always have. It's what makes me a good detective."

"And prosecutor."

"And that, unless they give my job to someone else while I'm gone."

"You're much too valuable."

"Okay, time to stop shoring up our fragile egos and get on with it. I'll bet you have a commercial to record."

"How'd you know?"

"You told me this morning."

"Oh yeah."

"Break a leg, sweetheart. Just pretend though, not for real like my arm."

"Will do. Love you."

"Forever." And she clicked off.

CHAPTER SEVEN

Walter Atkins, in his early thirties, with a weak chin disappearing in the folds of a chubby face, looked up from his laptop and over the stained particle board that separated his desk from the reception area of his storefront office. He saw two men in dark suits enter the front door and immediately spot his head and eyes visible over the board. He knew they were cops from the minute he laid eyes on them. He knew their look well from his years as a prosecutor in Van Nuys, then briefly after being transferred to the Airport Courthouse office. Cheap suits, entitled attitude, fake friendliness disguising a predatory purpose. He knew why they were here. He had never liked cops when he was a prosecutor, but they served a purpose, and he put up with them.

He stood up and walked around the particle board to where they were standing, next to the vacant desk where a receptionist should have been sitting could he afford one. "How can I help you gentlemen? I handle every kind of personal injury except dental. Too difficult to prove, you know."

The Asian showed Atkins his badge, as if it weren't already obvious. The middle-aged white guy said, "Detectives Loshi and Mack. We'd like to ask you a few questions if you don't mind."

Atkins used the voice he reserved for a friendly jury, charming but professional. "Have a seat." He gestured toward the orange plastic bowls on stainless steel that served as chairs. "What's this all about?" As if he didn't know.

The detectives sat and attempted to adjust their butts to the small, hard surface of the chairs. Mack took the lead. "It's about the attempted murder of one of your former colleagues, Rosemaria Baker."

Atkins settled his broad behind on a chair behind the receptionist's desk. He intended to show that he was the person in charge of this interview, indicated by his superior position seated behind a desk, however battered it might be. He was the master of this domain, by God, and nobody was going to intimidate him.

"Oh yes, I heard about that. Such a shame that happened to a dedicated prosecutor. But those are the risks we take as we put our lives on the line to uphold justice. How is she doing, by the way?"

"She's doing very well," Mack answered. "But it was a close call."

The cops waited. Atkins knew that was a ploy to get suspects to talk, but he wasn't falling for it. Thirty seconds passed, and no one said anything.

Loshi broke the silence. "I understand the two of you had some problems."

"Only the usual differences about how to handle a case. She worked for me and had a tendency to go her own way. As her boss, I had to set her straight from time to time. After all, that was my job."

"Of course," Loshi said. "Yet at some point, your differences became so great that your relationship became untenable, and you were let go."

It was all Atkins could do not to lash out in rage at being reminded by this two-bit detective of the injustice that had been done to him because of that pain in the ass, Baker. "It was for the best. I needed to move on in my career and establish my own practice. That had been my goal all along."

The eyes of both detectives swept the small storefront with its cracked linoleum tiles, paint flaking off the walls, and one peeling print of an Italian street scene hanging lopsided on the wall.

Atkins quickly added, "I know the office looks a little forlorn now, but I just moved in. Workers will be here next week to do a complete remodel. I'm looking forward to growing a booming practice here. It's so convenient, just down the street from the courthouse and the police station. This area of Van Nuys attracts a lot of people who need my services."

"Did you resent Baker for having you fired?" Mack asked bluntly.

Atkins was momentarily taken aback. "I . . . I was shocked when it happened, of course. I thought I had been fulfilling my duties properly, but the assistant attorney general thought otherwise."

"What exactly was it that got you fired?" Mack asked. "It would have had to have been pretty egregious. You almost lost your law license over it."

Atkins's patience had worn thin. "Where, may I ask, are you going with this? You obviously know what happened, and I don't care to relive it for the sake of your curiosity." He was livid.

Loshi pushed him to the brink. "Did you hate her enough to want her dead?"

Atkins stood up. "As a former prosecutor and officer of the court who respects the law above all else, I take that as an insult and a threat. The next time you talk to me, I will have my lawyer present. Time for you to leave, gentlemen."

The two detectives took their time getting to their feet, happy to be free of the torture inflicted on their rear ends by the tiny sixties-throwback chairs. As they sauntered toward the door, Mack said, without looking back, "Don't leave town."

"And don't you insult me with cliches," Atkins spit out, unable to contain his rage any longer. "Get the hell out of my office!"

He paced back and forth in the tiny reception area seething, glaring daggers at the cops as he eyed them walking away down the sidewalk. He lived and breathed for the day when that Baker bitch would get her punishment for what she had done to him. The humiliation he was forced to swallow every day was almost too much to bear.

The detectives' black Toyota sedan was only a few steps away, parked in front of a meter. "Think we rattled his cage enough?" Mack asked his partner.

"Maybe too much," Loshi said.

"No, I think it's best that he goes after her again while she's under the commissioner's protection. We'll know every move he makes. Having a guy like Collins on our side, with his clout, made our warrants sail through the system like a breeze. Even if Atkins waits until she's out of that fortress, we'll nail him before he gets to her."

"I hope you're right. I kind of like that girl, unpredictable though she may be."

"And maybe Atkins isn't the one. Let's check out Vick next and see where his head is at."

Loshi opened the driver's side of their sedan and looked up and down Van Nuys Boulevard at the crumbling storefronts, aging businesses, garbage on the sidewalks, and a homeless man sleeping under a filthy blanket in front of a vacant office. "From the sublime of the wealthy to the depths of misery. I think I prefer San Diego."

"Our motel in Sherman Oaks isn't bad. But I agree. Let's try to solve this fast so I can get back to my nice, ordinary house in Chula Vista."

"I have a feeling getting back home won't be that easy," Loshi said as they got in the car and strapped in.

* * * * *

It wasn't like Oscar night in Hollywood, but with Joell attending the premiere and various invited celebrities having made it known they would be there, there was a pretty good throng of people waiting to catch a glimpse of stars as they walked by them only a thrilling few inches away.

Joell and Josh sat resplendent in the back of a long black limousine as it rolled up Highland Avenue. Joell was in her element, ready to greet her fans as her limo driver turned left on Hollywood Boulevard, then waited in a line of limos in front of Grauman's Chinese Theater to pull up at the red carpet.

She looked at Josh sitting opposite her, striking in his black tuxedo, his unruly blond hair still long but fashionably tamed by her own hair stylist. He had balked at getting a haircut at first but gave in when Joell asked him to do it as a favor to her. After all, he was her escort, and the fact that she was a star with an image to uphold convinced him to accede to her request.

A page opened the door to the limo, and Josh emerged first, then extended his hand to help Joell step onto the sidewalk and the red carpet. Spotlights fanned the night sky. The fans were ecstatic as they pushed against the barricades. They cheered and called out her name, and she waved and smiled as she accepted Josh's arm. Her red dress was molded to her body, high in the front and, in the back, plunging below her waist. She emanated glamour and charisma and heated up the entire scene like a blazing fire on a wintry night. He led her past the onlookers, who gaped at her as if she were too unreal to touch, to a spot near the entrance where Mario Lopez was waiting, mike in hand, in front of a camera. The crowd quieted briefly as they waited for someone else who "was somebody" to step out of their limousine onto the red carpet.

"Mario, it's been forever," Joell said. "I haven't seen you since the opening of my restaurant Marvela on La Cienega. It's good to see you." Josh noted the plug for her restaurant seamlessly inserted into the interview.

"Have you seen the movie yet?" Mario asked.

"Only at a screening at Universal Studios, and it was fabulous. As you know, I sang the theme song, and my friend here, Josh Sibley"—she indicated Josh at her side— "wrote the lyrics and music."

Mario flashed his dimples at Josh. "It must have been exciting to have Joell record your song. I'm sure it will be a big hit for both of you."

"One can only hope," Josh said and wanted to kick himself for sounding so trite. But this whole interview wasn't going to win any contests for originality.

"Thank you for stopping by, Joell, Josh. Let's hope the audience loves *New York Nights*, and you have a hit on your hands."

Joell bussed him on the cheek. "Thanks, Mario."

A male usher appeared at Joell's side and led them into the theater.

At the Collins residence, Rosemaria, Kirsten, and Madelaine were in her living room watching the red-carpet show on a TV screen that took up a quarter of the wall. Rosemaria and Suzi, who was perched on her shoulder, had stared when Kirsten pressed a button on the control pad that was attached to the long wooden buffet. A huge original painting by a famous long-dead painter, which Rosemaria was sure must have cost a million bucks, slid aside, and the giant screen appeared.

Kirsten shook her head as the glamorous couple on TV disappeared from view. "Your guy's looking good, Rosemaria. Personally, I wouldn't let him out of my sight for a minute."

"I wasn't going to attend the premiere anyway. I'm not much for Hollywood glitz. And how am I not going let him out of my sight when I'm stuck in this wheelchair behind bars?"

"I'm sure she has nothing to worry about," the gentle Madelaine murmured.

Rosemaria pressed the TV off button on the pad of her wheelchair. "That's it for now. I'll have to wait for him to call me to find out how the audience liked it."

"Want us to play cards some more and keep you company until he calls?" Kirsten asked.

"No, I'm a little played out, even though both of you owe me at least two thousand dollars."

Kirsten stood up. "Okay, but remember, we're just lulling you into a false sense of security before we bring the hammer down."

"You're not supposed warn people of your strategy."

"I'm terrible at poker," Madelaine said. "And I'm still not sure what the winning hands are."

Kirsten stopped by the door to her room, and Madelaine waited by the front door of the suite. "Is there anything we can get you before we leave?" Madelaine asked.

"I'm good. I'll buzz if I need anything, or a prowler gets through security."

"Okay, boss." Kirsten gave a two-fingered salute, and they left.

Rosemaria grabbed her cell phone off her lap, clicked a number, and waited. "Dad? Tell me something I don't know."

Steven Baker was behind his desk, leaning back in his chair in a study that hadn't changed since Rosemaria was a baby. He had held on to the house in Simi Valley when he moved to Tahoe because, at one point, he had hoped she would want to live there. She'd made it clear that was not going to happen, but he'd started to second-guess putting the house up for sale because being near his daughter was becoming more and more important to him as the years crept up on him.

"I talked to Mack and Loshi after they interviewed Atkins."

"Yeah? Yeah?"

"And they said when they mentioned your name, steam practically came out of his ears. Honey, I think he hates you even more than you are willing to admit. And he's a psychopath who is fully capable of hurting you. I don't think you should dismiss him as a suspect."

"What else did they say?"

"His office is in the worst part of Van Nuys near the courthouse. It's no more than two hundred square feet and looks like the last jumping-off place before you want to put rocks in your pocket and wade into the LA River."

"It's not deep enough to drown in this time of year."

"Nevertheless, they got warrants to bug his phones, house, and office in case he should contact a hit man, excluding his chats with clients, of course."

"He's too poor, Dad. How could he pay anybody?"

"That may be true, but I don't think we can count him out. Jimmy managed to get ahold of the files from the Ramin Hassan case, and we're going to go through those tomorrow to see what pops up. He has to scan them first before he can email them to you. Most of the information was in hard copies, only some on the computer."

"Tell Waite to email them to me as soon as he can, Dad. Please. I want to get going on this."

"Will do. The detectives are going up to visit Vick in San Quentin tomorrow. That should be interesting."

"I wish I could go."

"How are you feeling?"

"My face still looks like I went ten rounds with Max Schmelling, but other than that, your daughter is still a mess of broken pieces."

"You're too young to know who that is."

"He got knocked out by Max Baer in thirty-three but beat Joe Louis in thirty-six and held the heavyweight title until the rematch, and Louis creamed him. My face looks like I was in every one of those fights."

" You're a wonder, daughter."

"I know. Talk to you tomorrow. Love you." Rosemaria grimaced and clicked off. She saw that Suzi was busy crunching on her nighttime snack in the big new cage Loretta had provided, but she sent a glance in Rosemaria's direction, instinctively knowing when she was in pain. Every so often, a sharp sting would stab her in the chest and leave her breathless. Madelaine had assured her she had no serious internal injuries, and the discomfort was caused by bruised muscles, but still, the stabs of pain were, at times, severe. Loretta had suggested she have an internist come to the house and examine her, but Rosemaria declined the offer. She already felt like enough of a wuss hiding out in a suffocating, albeit luxurious, cocoon. Only for the sake of Josh's career was she behaving like a sniveling coward.

Suddenly, feeling inexplicably depressed, she wondered how Noor and Gilbert were doing. She missed them terribly. At least every other weekend, they had visited the cat sanctuary north of Santa Barbara to spend time with their "kids." Noor, the glorious protective black panther who had been Josh's best friend when he worked at the LA Zoo, had saved Rosemaria's life when another assassin had been within seconds of killing her. She would have died if not for Noor. Gilbert, the mountain lion, had lived with Josh for a time as a baby. She had never asked how he managed to sneak little Gilbert out of the zoo so he could personally care for him when he was sick, but Jerry, the zoo vet, was undoubtedly in on the plot. Now both their kids were living a free and happy life in a place where they were protected and had the freedom to roam for miles. She briefly wondered if the same people who had wanted her dead back then could be involved in this latest attack but immediately dismissed the idea. They were all in prison, and their lives and political careers had been destroyed. They had nothing to gain by killing her except maybe revenge, and, if traced back to them, the attempts on her life would only result in longer sentences.

Suzi was feeling Rosemaria's despondency and flew out of her cage to land on Rosemaria's shoulder. She nuzzled her cheek with her own feathery one.

"Thank you, dear friend. It's good to have you here." Tomorrow, Cameron would be taking her downstairs so she could sit on the patio and enjoy the fresh air and sunshine after being cooped up in her suite for days. Loretta had visited her every day and was very concerned about Rosemaria's health. She insisted there was nothing like vitamin D to heal the body, and Rosemaria was looking forward to it. She decided she might as well wait in bed for Josh's phone call, which would be hours away, after the screening and then the party at Vitello's.

She wheeled herself over to the bed, which had been lowered for easy access. She braked the chair, used the lever that slightly lifted the seat, then, using one hand to push herself into the bed, she scooted to a comfortable position. She had a heavy wrap around her ankle, a bandage on her shoulder where a bullet had grazed her, and a cast on her broken arm. She had to follow instructions on how to move to avoid bumping her injured body parts against anything. Eager to get back on her feet, she was doing everything Madelaine told her to do. But still, it would be weeks before she was mobile. The sprained ankle would take two or three weeks to heal and maybe five to six weeks for the broken arm. To her, it seemed like a lifetime. As she had told Josh, she had always believed that self-pity was deplorable, much like envy, which she also hated, maybe because her mother had died longing with all her heart and soul to have the kind of career that other actresses, many of whom were no more beautiful and talented than she, had. Rosemaria was in danger of slipping into the same kind of swamp of despair if she didn't get ahold of herself. Josh would bring her around. She would just close her eyes for a bit and wait for his call.

* * * * *

Joell was hosting an exclusive after-party at Vitello's, her favorite Italian restaurant in the Valley. She had invited only cast and crew from

New York Nights and her inner circle, which meant at least twenty celebrities. It was a big crowd. As Joell swirled around the tables playing hostess, exuberant over the audience reaction to the movie, Josh; Ken Jordan, Josh's employer and the producer and director of the movie; and his wife, Marla, were at the same table. While Ken was speaking in private tones to their son Kevin, an assistant AD on the film, Marla was enjoying being in the same room with so many recognizable singers and actors. She thought the two leads in the movie seemed overwhelmed by the attention they were getting. They weren't famous yet, but Marla knew they soon would be. The girl was only nineteen, but her unique pixie quality, which reminded Marla of Leslie Caron, had made her urge Ken to cast her. She had not been wrong. The girl was wonderful. The boy playing opposite her was funny and had a quirkiness that was catchy. Because he wasn't classically handsome, she had thought he was wrong for the part, but she had to admit Ken had been right and had found a combination that clicked. She looked across the table at a subdued Josh. "You look glum, Josh. Are you thinking about leaving on Monday? You should be enjoying the moment. Everybody loves your song."

Josh smiled. Marla had always been one of his biggest fans. He knew he might not have lasted as a commercial writer and singer for Ken's company if not for her faith in him as well as the support Jenny, Ken's assistant, had given him. Smart and sassy with short brown hair, Marla didn't look old enough to have a teenage son. He told her, "Don't be fooled by my bland exterior. This is just me being happy about the movie but wishing Rosemaria could be here to enjoy all this."

"My dear, you know how she feels about Hollywood parties. She told us weeks ago she was trying to figure out a way to get out of going to the premiere. But that doesn't mean she's not supportive. Just think—she offered herself up as a prisoner for your sake. She never would have done that for anybody else. Be happy she's so well protected."

"I'm not worried about anybody breaking in. I'm more worried about her getting cabin fever and breaking out."

"Maybe you should call her and make sure she's still there." Marla laughed. "I think you've been social enough to make Joell happy." She nudged him on the arm. "Go ahead, call her. Let her know Ken's got a smash hit on his hands." She looked at her husband, who broke away from a conversation with a crew member and gave her a thumbs up.

Josh took a sip of his soda and pushed back his chair. "I'll be outside should Joell ask."

Rosemaria thought she had been asleep for just a few minutes when her cell phone rang. Three hours had gone by. Josh! She clicked on her phone. "How'd it go? Did they love the movie? Did they love your song?"

Josh was standing outside the entrance to Vitello's. "Yes, they loved the movie, but I don't think people single out the opening song as to why they like a movie."

"But it's Joell singing it. That's what's going to get you attention and boost your career."

"Forget all that. How are you dealing with being cooped up?"

"No worries. In two days you'll be flying across the Atlantic, and I'll be sitting by the pool in the sun on the patio."

"I'd rather be there with you."

"Come on. Don't you know that to be a star, you have to be selfish and self-centered and have a huge ego? Being so concerned about me when you're about to launch an international career will never do."

"I'll make you a deal. I'll develop the biggest ego you ever saw if you promise not to throw your wheelchair over the wall and climb over. I know you. You're itching to get involved in the investigation and are probably trying to figure out how to stand on crutches with one foot using one arm and hobble around talking to suspects."

"I promise I won't do that, but from you, I want to see a little swagger when you come home. I want to see star power, and maybe you can even act a little bit full of yourself. Not around me, of course, only around the paparazzi who will be swarming all over you."

"I can see I better get my career advice from a more reliable source."

"Okay, what do I know anyway? I'm just a law enforcement officer, working from my tiny office in the courthouse and trying to make the world a better place."

"I will do everything I can to live up to your expectations."

"Go back to your party and mingle. It's good for your career, and I'll talk to you tomorrow."

"I love you."

"Me too, more." They clicked off, and Rosemaria felt her mood lighten. There were so many failures in show business. Her very talented mother had died of what Rosemaria believed was a broken heart. She never was able to break through, and it destroyed her. Her mother had a husband and a daughter who admired her and loved her, but it wasn't enough. If Josh didn't succeed and had to settle for writing commercials the rest of his life, she wondered if he would perceive that as failure. Would her love be enough for him? With that troubling thought, she drifted off to sleep.

CHAPTER EIGHT

The drive from the San Francisco Airport to San Quentin was one Loshi and Mack were very familiar with. They had taken the same route several years before and always enjoyed the scenery on the way, if not the destination. Situated on a scenic point in Marin County, the dirty cement walls of the prison that loomed ahead contained 3,776 prisoners and counting. It had been established during the rough-and-tumble times of the gold rush days and had the biggest population of death row inmates of any prison in the country. For decades, Hollywood had featured the prison as the site of many of their crime and cop movies. In recent years, San Quentin had become practically like a college campus with accredited classes, sports, jobs, and opportunities to attend religious services and experience forgiveness for all their sins, including torture and serial murder. Come-to-Jesus moments were common among murderers. Mack and Loshi had nothing against rehabilitation and cutting down on recidivism, but personal experience had made them more than a little cynical. But perks, amenities, and classes aside, for the inmates, there was nothing glamorous about the reality of being locked up inside.

Loshi and Mack had driven up eight years earlier to interview a piece of trash they had arrested for the vicious murder of two adults and four children in Chula Vista. He had been put on trial, barely escaped the death penalty, and was given a life sentence, but, to no one's surprise, including his defense lawyer, once inside, he had proceeded to beat up a guard within an inch of his life. It was Loshi's and Mack's unfortunate job to interview him before his trial for assault, and, subsequently, another useless twenty years were tacked on to his sentence. A few weeks later, the two detectives were ordered to question him again after an apparent personality clash and too-close-for-comfort living quarters resulted in their felon sticking a shiv in his cellmate's right eye, resulting in immediate death. The facts were cut and dried, but procedure had to be followed before he once more went on trial, so they were assigned to drive up again and interview the psychotic bastard. He was given another life sentence by a bleeding-heart judge and jury, much to the dismay of the two detectives and making them wish they lived in Texas. Within three months of the second verdict, the felon ended up killing a psychiatrist who was treating him for depression. Society was saved from the expense of another trial, which would undoubtedly have resulted in another life sentence, when the felon unexpectedly hanged himself—some said under suspicious circumstances. But that was the way of the world when dealing with murderous predators, and Loshi and Mack had been only too happy to hear the news.

This time, their interviewee was a felon named Grover Vick with a rap sheet a mile long, not the least of which was the attempted kidnapping and murder of Rosemaria Baker. After going through the usual ID and security checks, they found themselves seated opposite him in a pleasant, newly painted beige room with a one-way window on one wall. Vick was a huge black man, even bigger than when he had first entered San Quentin a few months ago. He obviously was availing himself of the weightlifting equipment the prison offered. His hands and legs were secured in manacles.

He stared at the detectives, slightly bored. "I'm missing my computer class, and we're having a test tomorrow, so make this fast. I'm only talking to you because the warden says I have to." He cocked his head and waited, a hint of a snarl on his face.

Mack and Loshi quickly figured out that Vick had not taken advantage of opportunities to become "born again," and they wouldn't have to wade through all kinds of hypocritical BS. Nevertheless, it never hurt to try and establish some kind of rapport.

"Looks like you been working out a lot," Loshi said. "Amazing what you've done. The gym here must be fully equipped with anything you need."

"You guys up here to do a Chuck Norris commercial, or do you want to ask questions about that lying sack of shit prosecutor who leveled false charges against me and got me in here?"

"That kind of attitude doesn't do well at parole hearings, Grover."

"You let me worry about that. I had nothing to do with trying to blow her brains out, so if that's all you have, we can end this bullshit conversation right now."

"The warden says we can talk to you for half an hour," Mack told him. "You want to change your mind about having a lawyer present?"

He sighed and leaned back in his chair. "Don't need my lawyer because I don't know nothin'. In case you haven't noticed, I'm incarcerated, and the guards don't let me out during the day so I can kill people."

"Have you talked to anyone in here about hiring an assassin?"

"I'd have to be a total moron to answer that, wouldn't I? Do you interrogate people much, or is this your first time?"

"We'll be conducting interviews with people you've had contact with inside and outside prison, so lying won't help," Loshi said.

"Nobody snitches. They'd end up dead."

"I gather you're still resentful of Ms. Baker," Mack said.

"She wrecked my freakin' life. Other than that, I hope she's very happy until whoever's after her improves his aim."

"We'll be checking into any kind of access to money you might have, and we're talking to your partner Castro Hernandez and your family members," Loshi said. "You want to cause them trouble?"

"Nobody means diddly-squat to me." He leaned forward, and, with eyes as cold and black as the devil's heart, he spat out his words. "Talk to whoever you want, threaten them, burn their eyeballs out, and try and force them to make up some lie, but you will never pin this on me." He leaned back again. "You can sit here for another half hour. I don't give a damn, but I ain't sayin' another word."

The atmosphere in the car during the drive back to LA in a rental car was subdued. They were driving back so they could stop and talk to Hernandez who was incarcerated in Soledad in Salinas. Mack and Loshi had interviewed several other inmates who had contact with Vick, including his cellmate. They proclaimed they had never heard him speak a harsh word against Baker, let alone try to get somebody coming up for parole or somebody on the outside to kill her. They'd gotten nothing from Hernandez and Vick's only surviving relative, his mother, was a barely alive meth addict who lived in a tent under a freeway overpass in Santa Monica. It looked like Vick was a dead end. But, like Atkins, he had a deep and abiding hatred for Baker. Senator Haynes, who had conspired with gun manufacturer Harvey Dillon to kill two witnesses to their crime of murdering a third witness, was in Victorville, a high-security federal penitentiary, and hiding behind lawyers, refusing to talk. Mack and Loshi had been assured by Detective Coleman that, for reasons he couldn't disclose, Haynes would rather eat cut glass than go after Baker, whom he had wanted dead for reasons of pure revenge. That sounded to the detectives like an interesting story on its own.

They packed up their belongings at the motel and said goodbye to their temporary home in Sherman Oaks. They had a long drive back to San Diego, where they would find out if any leads had developed from the stolen car and search online for anything they could find on the Ramin Hassan murder case. They weren't ready to admit it, but Baker could be right in assuming that's where the answers might lie.

CHAPTER NINE

Rosemaria was enjoying the fresh air on the patio while reclining on a padded blue lounge chair. Despite Loretta's admonition that she needed vitamin D, she had chosen to be totally protected from the sun by a large umbrella in the same light-blue color. Her wheelchair was nowhere in sight. She didn't want to see it and just imagined she was enjoying the Collins' hospitality as countless other personages of importance had done before. She wondered if all of them had had a personal bodyguard seated across the pool in the shade of the guesthouse, undoubtedly staring at her from behind her aviator glasses.

The Olympic-size pool, only a few steps away, was sparkling and inviting. The temperature was in the high eighties, and her cotton blouse was already showing signs of sweat under her arms. If only she could take a running leap into the water and splash to her heart's content, she would be in heaven. Funny how even life's simplest pleasures were unappreciated until you couldn't indulge in them anymore. Suzi, sitting protected in the shade of a huge flowering lilac bush, was also enjoying the fresh air inside her cage, which had required two trusted guards to bring downstairs. She was happily pecking away at some special treats that Loretta had ordered for her.

Rosemaria had encouraged Madelaine to please take some time off today. She loved the sweet girl, but being fussed over was so against

Rosemaria's nature she felt suffocated by her ministrations. She was also looking forward to speaking with her father again in complete privacy. She lay back and breathed deeply, imagining the healing that was taking place inside her body and out. She felt no pain in her shoulder any longer, her broken arm was knitting together beautifully, and her sprained ankle was days away from being back to normal—if only. But she remembered that her assistant at the prosecutor's office, Karen, was a firm believer in visualization and said it really did help. Karen, a classy, young African American woman, always impeccably dressed, and a veteran of the political machinations of the DA's office, had helped guide Rosemaria through her first months as ADA at the Airport Courthouse.

That reminded Rosemaria she needed to call her today and catch up on what was going on at the office. Her fellow prosecutors, Reid Smith and Terrance O'Malley, were dividing up what would have been her cases, kindly volunteering to work extra hours to make sure her job was safe. They had all forbidden her to call in for a week, and the week was now up.

She thought of Josh landing in Prague today and all the new and wonderful sensations he would experience in finding himself in the capital of a European country as different from the familiar streets of LA as night from day. The tourists would be gaping in awe at the ancient architecture and the natives going about their business as if their beautiful and unique city was nothing out of the ordinary. He would drink it all in and enjoy every minute and then probably write a song about it. Or maybe he was focused on his first huge concert, in a foreign country no less, and willing himself not to feel intimidated by his lack of experience and the star power he would be sharing the stage with. Rosemaria had told him to concentrate on work and not feel he had to constantly call and update her. She hoped he would follow her advice. Meanwhile, she would relax and wait for her father and Jimmy to come so she could sink her teeth into the investigation.

* * * * *

Josh was grateful to have been assigned a window seat on the plane. The seat next to him was thankfully empty, but he could hear the muted conversations of Joell and the others discussing plans for their concert in Prague a few rows up. He had managed to sleep for almost half the trip, and his meal had consisted of an apple and two carrot slices. He would wait to eat when they arrived. There were sure to be restaurants near their hotel that would suit him. He had researched the city and the concert venue on his laptop, and now that they were within two hours of landing, his excitement at seeing a city and hearing a language completely unfamiliar to him made him feel like he was about to experience a great adventure. Maybe it was old hat to the rest of the people he was traveling with, but despite his fears and insecurities about how Joell's fans would welcome him, he was determined to enjoy himself. Rosemaria had said he needed to expand his ego, develop a sense of self-entitlement. He was confident in his talent. Did that count? He was looking forward to checking into the hotel and doing some exploring of the city by himself. He missed Rosemaria, and he missed Suzi, Noor, and Gilbert. He was still a provincial country boy at heart. He would have to do better regarding that ego thing.

* * * * *

Having almost nodded off by the pool, Rosemaria heard muted voices coming from inside the house and Loretta's pealing laughter. That meant her dad was there and had said something funny, probably about all the security being in place more to keep his daughter in than to keep killers out. Ha ha. If she heard that one more time, she'd throw her cell phone at somebody's head. Unfortunately, she was incapable of throwing anything. She looked through the French doors and saw Loretta leading her father to the patio from the garden room. The doors opened, and Loretta came out before her father.

"This man is too priceless to be living alone. I may have to go over my list of single friends and see if I can find a few candidates who are deserving of him."

"Oh, I wish you would," Rosemaria said. "He's long overdue for some female companionship."

Steven shrugged and placed the laptop he was carrying on the table. "I've never lacked female companionship but thank you both very much for your concern."

"He's commitment phobic, Loretta. We need to find him a keeper."

"Got it." She turned to go inside. "Mildred will be out in a minute with some lemonade."

After she left, Rosemaria could barely contain herself. "I looked over the records Waite sent me. I assume you have them on your laptop too?"

"I do, and I find it all very interesting. Let's talk it through, okay?"

"I was aware of a lot of the details, but, as you know, I wasn't involved in the investigation."

Steven opened his laptop and turned it on. He referred to his notes on the screen as he spoke. "Let's start with the bare-bones facts, okay? Ramin Hassan was an eighteen-year-old boy who worked part time in his father Adib's oriental rug store on Melrose. One day, his father had a business appointment and left Ramin in charge of the store. At the end of the day, Ramin was told to bring several thousand dollars in cash from the bank to the store for a transaction regarding a huge rug shipment coming in early the next morning and put it in the safe. The Iranians delivering the rugs liked being paid in cash. Ramin's father had decided to forgo an armored truck delivery because the bank was only a block away.

Business was slow, and Ramin was talking on the phone to his girl-friend Sherilyn that morning and made the stupid mistake of revealing his cash errand from the bank to the store to her. He also bragged he would be taking care of the Iranian shipment himself because his father had an important breakfast meeting where he was trying to close a deal on the biggest sale they'd ever had. Ramin took care of a few customers, then called Sherilyn back. They talked for so long he almost missed his chance to get to the bank before it closed. When Ramin's father called to make sure he had brought the money to the store, he couldn't reach him. Worried that something had gone wrong, he went to the store and found the back door wide open, his son shot dead, and David unconscious with a gun on the floor near him."

Mildred, a sweet-faced lady in her fifties, dressed as always in her gray maid's uniform, came out with a lemonade pitcher and two large plastic glasses and put them on the table. She poured lemonade into one glass and handed it to Rosemaria, who accepted gratefully. "Thank you, Mildred."

"If you need anything," Mildred said, "just wave at Cameron"—she indicated the bodyguard who was standing next to the guesthouse several feet behind Kirsten, his gaze focused on Rosemaria— "and he'll buzz me."

"Will do."

Mildred went inside, and they were alone again. Rosemaria, immersed in cop zone, focused on her father's narration.

"The bank bag Ramin had brought back to the store was found in the parking lot. There were several stories about what had happened: the two boys had had a fight; the whole thing was a setup between the two of them to give David the money. He was a rich, spoiled ne'er-do-well about to flunk out of USC, living with a bunch of drugged-out hippie types in a falling-down old house in Hollywood, and he hated his father, whom he wanted off his back. There was obviously a fight, staged or not. A falling shelf hit David on the back of his head and knocked him out. David's fingerprints were on the gun, but no residue could be found because floor wax from an overturned shelf had spilled all over his arm, hand, and chest. Security cameras inside and out were turned off, so there's no proof of what had actually happened or who saw the open door, came in, and took the money. David received a phone call some time before the killing from a phone that couldn't be traced."

Rosemaria had been listening intently and squinted into the distance as she tried to recall details of what had happened from ten years ago. "I remember David's father fought like crazy to keep him out of jail and hired the best defense lawyers in the state. The prosecution could only prove manslaughter. David insisted there were two people at the store who had knocked him unconscious and killed Ramin. But forensics could find no proof of anyone else being at the scene. Everyone I talked to at the house insisted Ramin and David were good friends, and the only thing that made sense was that it was an accident. When the detectives came to question them, everybody clammed up and didn't say much of anything except for Sherilyn, who insisted David would never have shot Ramin on purpose. None of the people in the house were asked to stick around as material witnesses, and they all left town except for Sherilyn."

"What were the reactions of Ramin's parents? Do you remember?"

"Yes, I do. Very clearly. The detectives who interviewed them at their house said they heard his mother wailing uncontrollably in the bedroom. Days later, she couldn't stop crying. In court, they sat behind the prosecution looking grim, staring at the back of David's head as if he were the devil. They believed he was guilty. After the verdict, they flew back to Marseilles, where they had originally immigrated after leaving Iran. I assume they're still there."

"I remember news cameras in front of the so-called hippie house in Hollywood."

"God, yes. But the kids only snuck out at night for food until they all left town, so there wasn't much to film, and none of them gave interviews. As you said, the house was portrayed in the media as a drug den filled with dropout losers who disappeared into thin air. And David was portrayed as being even worse."

"Tell me what David said when you went up to see him in Tehachapi."

"First of all, I asked him why he wanted so badly to talk to me about the case when he was on track to receive early parole. He was eligible under the youthful offender program."

"And?"

"He told me he couldn't admit his guilt when he didn't do it. I was his last shot before he would have to tell the parole board he killed his best friend in order to get out, and he didn't want to do that. He wanted everybody to know he was innocent. He said Ramin had called him and asked him to come by. He was positive somebody in the house overheard Ramin's conversation with Sherilyn and told some people he would be alone at the store that night with all that cash. He and Ramin never planned to steal the money."

"Why didn't he believe Sherilyn could have some part in setting up the robbery?"

"No reason, except for blind faith. He believed she truly loved Ramin and would never have taken part in a plan to kill him."

"First order of business is to talk to her in person. You set it up since David trusted you and you were going to help him. That might convince her you believed in him."

The afternoon sun was heating up the patio, and they both took long sips of their drinks.

"Hey." Jimmy Waite had opened the door to the patio and stepped outside.

"Get over here, you little mug," Rosemaria said. "I need to get a close look at you."

Jimmy nodded at Steven, then dutifully walked over to Rosemaria's lounge chair and gingerly gave her a hug. At six-one, the twenty-three-year-old redhead was hardly little. "Your face looks a lot better than when I saw you in the hospital," he said.

"Well, I didn't see you."

"You were a little bit under the weather."

"You've been going to the gym since I saw you last. Looking good, junior. I hear you're not just a computer geek anymore. Sargeant Osborne is letting you out in the field."

"You rescued me, and here I am, at your disposal." He made a face. "Until Lieutenant Eldridge changes his mind."

"Well," Steven said, "pull up a chair, and help us solve this mystery. Between the three of us, it shouldn't take long."

Jimmy grinned and sat next to Steven. "Mack and Loshi would have their feelings hurt if they heard you say that." He opened the black case he had slung over his shoulder and took out his laptop. "We'll make sure we don't get in their way and cooperate with them. Right now, they're headed in a different direction."

"How'd it go with Vick, Hernandez, and Atkins?" Rosemaria asked.

"In as few words as possible, they all hate your guts, wish you were dead, but don't have money to pay for hit men." He bit off his last words. "Maybe that was too blunt. Sorry."

"So, what's the next step for Mack and Loshi?"

"They don't exactly share their strategy with me, but I think you've almost swung them over to your side."

"Dang. I hoped they'd keep going down the wrong road so the three of us could have Sherilyn and the kids in the house all to ourselves. Now we'll have to dodge and parry so we don't get in their way, or they'll get pissed off, and you'll end up back in the computer room."

"Yeah, how do we do this exactly?"

"It's going to be touchy," Steven said, "but maybe if we figure out ways to finesse our interviews, we can avoid annoying them too much."

"There's a lot of me in you, Dad."

"Thank you, daughter. As Waite discovered, most of the kids who lived in the house have disappeared. I don't know how much effort San Diego is going to put into finding them. With Waite's expertise, he'll find their most likely location, and when he does, we'll track them down in person. Some we know have moved to other states, and we only have the address of one of those. Maybe Mack and Loshi will find everyone's exact location and fly to wherever to talk to them. In that case, Waite and I will follow up. We'll never get in the detectives' way. But we'll be more thorough."

"Dad, did I appreciate you enough when I was growing up? I know you solved a lot of cases, but did I ever appreciate how good you were?"

"You tell me. Now, Sherilyn needs to be the first interview. While Mack and Loshi are off on other tangents, we'll see what she has to say."

"I have her phone number," Waite said. Rosemaria grabbed her cell phone, and she dialed the number he gave her.

She let it ring for several seconds. "No answer. I'll try again later. As soon as she says yes, I'll call you, Dad."

They all looked up as the patio door opened. Loretta and Mildred, whom Rosemaria had noticed was treated more like a family friend than a servant, stepped outside, both holding heaping platters of hors d'oeuvres. "I know you and Josh are vegan, so everything on here is safe to eat," Loretta assured them. "Manuela put it together herself."

Rosemaria waved Cameron and Kirsten over. "This is fabulous, Mildred. Thank you so much. Dad, would you make a plate for me?"

The three men eyed the food hungrily as two of Loretta's servants, both Latinos in their early twenties—Brent, outgoing and buff like he worked out every day, and Max, who had a startling resemblance to a young Antonio Banderas—came out carrying trays holding plates, forks, knives, glasses, and other necessities. The food platters featured three kinds of bread, assorted crackers, sliced cheese, cheese spread, faux meat, tomatoes, onions, olives, pickles, mustard, vegan mayo, three kinds of chips, and chocolates and fruit tarts for dessert.

"Join us, Loretta, please," Rosemaria said.

"Sorry, can't. I have work to do. Which reminds me, Rosemaria, I have something to run by you later. We'll chat after you finish up your meeting." Mildred followed her through the French doors.

Brent surveyed the table and asked Rosemaria in a heavy Spanish accent. "Is there anything else we can bring you?"

"Are you kidding? This is more than enough."

The two young men grinned and went in the house.

Suzi, inspired by all the excitement around the food arrival, fluttered about her cage. "Who's at the door?" Who's at the door?" As always, her chatter was completely disconnected from reality.

Rosemaria bit into a piece of sourdough bread slathered with vegan cream cheese and watched her dad, Jimmy, Kirsten, and Cameron dig into their tasty treats. If only Josh were here to see her doing missionary work by possibly converting everyone in the house to eating plant-based food. He would be very pleased with her. She'd come a long way since her Pink's hot dogs and pepperoni pizza days before she met him. Except for being the target of a murderer and being intent on tracking the bastard down, she felt pretty damn good.

CHAPTER TEN

Andy Mack sat by himself in his house, staring at his laptop on his kitchen table. Not having a nagging wife or girlfriend to tell him things like go to bed, you've worked long enough, you don't pay enough attention to me, blah, blah, blah was worth the occasional bouts of loneliness. His second ex-wife had confirmed this beyond a shadow of a doubt. She had been a world-class nagger. Now, he could work all night if he felt like it or watch TV at two in the morning or do whatever else he felt like doing, like having a beer for breakfast, which he hardly ever did, but he could if the mood hit him. He'd only had five beautiful months of freedom, but he knew for a fact he'd never give it up again.

He and Loshi had combed through Baker's past cases, come up with a few who might bear a grudge strong enough to kill over, and found at least two that fit the bill—one was a famous actor who had hired a hit man to kill his wife when she threatened to divorce him and take their son away from him. Baker had been the lead detective on the case and built what Mack thought was an air-tight case for the prosecutor, but the jury had acquitted the SOB for reasons known only to that bunch of fawning dimwits. As was proven in the Simpson case, too often, juries don't give a crap about the facts; they only care about seeing their favorite celebrity escape justice. In the case of the actor, his career was destroyed, and his dead wife's relatives sued and won in civil court, but the actor had fore-seen this unfortunate turn of events and signed over most of his money to his grown daughter for safety's sake as soon as he was arrested. Mack was convinced the actor most certainly still had a few bucks salted away God knows where, so if the stone-cold guilty mug wanted to get revenge for his ruined life and career, he could probably afford to pay for someone to do the dirty work. Mack doubted if his boss would try to get the actor to come down to San Diego for an interview, so another trip up to LA was in his and Loshi's near future.

Dr. Albert Hecht, whom Baker had successfully prosecuted and put away for attempted murder, was another possibility. He was serving his sen-tence in medium security in the Richard J. Donovan Correctional Facility south of San Diego, which would make for a convenient trip for him and Loshi. Hecht had been chief of staff at Cedars-Sinai in Los Angeles before Baker brought him down—another high-and-mighty sleazebag whose life she had ruined. Lots of motivation there to seek revenge.

And there was always David Marchand's father, who had made a big stink after his son was killed. He hated the LA cops for pinning the murder of Ramin on him, as he saw it, and had threatened civil suits and all the rest before flying back to Atlanta to run his international corporations. But Mack could not see him hiring someone to kill the only person who had promised to help clear his son.

Mack and Loshi agreed that approaching the obvious suspects and eliminating them or finding their perp amongst them was the best way to go before running off on a wild goose chase trying to track down David Marchand's former roommates. Mack had his best computer guy trying to find most of them, but they had scattered all over the country and beyond. Baker being so set on believing the hit man was one of them just proved that the injuries to her head had affected her reasoning capacity. Her cop instincts were way off base this time. But if she and her pen-sioned-off detective father made any moves to get in the way of the real investigation, Mack would have no hesitation in cutting them off at the knees. He and Loshi had a stellar reputation to protect, and no one, not even the poor bruised and shot-up Rosemaria Baker, was going to tarnish it. Larry Coleman was his official liaison at the BHPD. Steven Baker and Waite were investigating on their own, and they better toe the line if they expected no interference from Mack and Loshi. As a prosecutor and former cop, no one knew better than Baker that "fruit from the poisonous tree" could sink a case faster than a ship's anchor, and he couldn't let anybody poison his witnesses or evidence. But Baker's reputation preceded her, and he knew in his heart she would be nothing but trouble.

* * * * *

Joell had chosen the five-star Carlo IV hotel as the home for her troops in Prague for four days. The hotel façade looked like a fairy tale palace, and the interior did not disappoint. The floors in the lobby were polished to a gloss finish, and the high ceilings; large vases with tall, blooming flowers; and elegant furniture arranged in conversational settings evoked an era of gentility and grace. Josh had been enthralled by the scenery as they drove through the city—the many bridges that crossed the Vltava River as it meandered through the city, a skyline of buildings that gave the impression he had been transported into another age. He vowed that someday he would come back and stroll hand in hand with Rosemaria across those bridges.

His room was small but impeccably furnished with the same ancient European flavor as the rest of the hotel. As soon as he entered, he sank into a comfortable chair and marveled at how he had ended up living a dream he had visualized when he was young but considered impossible his entire life. At the airport, the group had split up, some taking taxis, but Josh and Joell's conductor were invited to share her limo. Barely listening to Joell talking about charts and the local musicians they had hired, Josh intently gazed out the window at sights he had longed to see ever since he was a boy in his small hometown in Wisconsin. He had always thought of himself as worthy of success because of his innate musical talent, so why, now that his moment had arrived, did he have an overwhelming fear of failure bordering on all-out performance terror? He thought of calling Lenny, his AA sponsor but decided, after two years of sobriety, he had to prove he could handle the pressure alone. He didn't want to confide in Rosemaria either. She had enough to deal with. He'd call her tomorrow after rehearsal. He had two days to work with the local orchestra and shake off the self-doubt.

* * * * *

Kirsten had accompanied Rosemaria back to her suite then left her alone. The laptop was on her desk, and she needed to make notes while her discussion with her dad and Jimmy was fresh in her mind. She had tried calling Sherilyn again when they were all together on the patio but kept getting Sherilyn's message greeting. She clicked on her cell phone and tried again.

Sherilyn answered. "I'm not sure that it's a good idea that I talk to you." Her whispered voice was harsh."

"Sherilyn, this is Rosemaria Baker. I'm the detective who was going to help David Marchand prove his innocence."

"I know who it is."

"David was sure you would talk to me."

"I changed my mind."

"Why? I don't understand."

"Why? Are you kidding? That was before he was killed, and you were shot. Other people who lived in that house have disappeared. They could be dead for all I know."

"No one has to know you talked. And it won't be to me. It'll be my father, a former detective. He can arrange to meet you very discreetly." She hesitated before playing the sympathy card. "Don't you want to know who really killed Ramin—and David?"

There was silence for several seconds. "I'll think about it. But I'll call you. I'm at work now; I can't talk anymore." She clicked off.

Rosemaria looked at the phone in her hand. "That went well."

She heard a knock on the door and looked up at the video screen. It was Loretta. She buzzed her in.

As Loretta walked smiling into the room and closed the door behind her, Rosemaria wondered if the woman ever had a bad day. Then again, living like Queen Elizabeth with a husband who adored her didn't leave much wiggle room for misery.

"I told you I had something to run by you, dear." Loretta said.

"Please sit down. Whatever it is, whatever you want me to do, the answer is yes."

"Now you don't have to agree, and I can reschedule, "Loretta said as she sat on the loveseat opposite Rosemaria. "This is something that has been months in the planning, but still, your safety is more important than people being inconvenienced."

"I would love to be inconvenienced, Loretta."

Loretta glanced at her sideways and raised her eyebrows. "Your father said you'd say that. Anyway, the thing is, next Saturday evening, I have planned a gala for about two hundred people to raise money for a new wing of the Modern Art Museum on Wilshire. Quite a few people, including the mayor and some of Andrew's friends who are in the running for police commissioner of San Diego will be there as well and a few Hollywood celebrities. Does the thought of this disturb you?"

"Absolutely not. I will watch the festivities on the monitors in Kirsten's room."

"Wonderful! And I will have Cameron bring you up some food. We have an excellent caterer, whom I will instruct must make vegan food available to the guests." She smiled. "I'm learning, dear."

"I have no complaints." Rosemaria patted her belly. "As you can see by my expanding waistline. All the more reason to look forward to Saturday."

"The elevator and stairs will be closely guarded at all times, so you needn't have any worries in that regard." She stood up. "I'll leave you to your work. Your father filled me in on your latest pursuit, and I know you'll want to get back to it."

"You seemed to have gotten to know my dad pretty well already."

Loretta opened the door and turned back to her. "I promised to find him a keeper, didn't I? It's important to know what a man likes." She went out with a sly smile and closed the door.

Three years ago, that last statement would have initiated her gag reflex. "What a man likes? Who the hell cares?" she would have said. Now that she had become the semi-obedient fiancée of the man of her dreams, she was not averse to finding ways to make him happy. She hoped he would call today. Yes, she had told him not to feel like he had to check in all the time, but one little phone call couldn't hurt.

She shook off the longing to hear his voice and went back to her laptop. She looked at the names of the people who had lived in the house with Ramin. One of them, she was certain, was out to kill her. She couldn't explain why this was the road she was going down, but she felt that presentiment she always had in the past when she had been proven right. Let Mack and Loshi do whatever they might do. But she had to follow her gut.

She studied Waite's notes and photos on her screen. Twelve people had crowded into that three-story crumbling old house, now long gone, replaced with a ten-story apartment building. Those tenants had included Sherilyn Cosgrove, who only stayed there occasionally with Ramin; Keith Tomlin, who was the apartment manager and lived in the house with his wife, Maisie; Micco Stolz, who was half Native American on his mother's side and roomed with his girlfriend, Sarah Holcomb; and Clyde Hallet, a community college dropout, who was staying there with his girlfriend, Lorna Selverino. Mariah Venmore had a room to herself and was studying design at a school in Hollywood near Santa Monica Boulevard; Stacey Fields and her boyfriend, Sam Oliver, were straight arrows who never did drugs but, according to the report, lived there to save money so they could rent their own place after graduating from UCLA.

Sherilyn could be a wealth of information in helping them find all these people, but Rosemaria didn't want to press her and risk pissing her off for good. Three of the twelve were accounted for—David and Ramin because they were dead, and Sherilyn because she was still in LA. Mack and Loshi had not been kind enough to share with them yet the whereabouts of the other nine, if indeed they had that information, so Jimmy was tracking them down himself. Knowing Jimmy, it would take him less time than it would take the San Diego cops.

Rosemaria looked up at Suzi who was dozing in her cage after all the excitement of being outside and meeting new people. It caused her to repeat most of her vocabulary, over and over again, to everyone's dismay. Now that Rosemaria was not expecting any more visitors, she reached up and quietly opened the door to Suzi's cage. After experiencing what a cage-like existence felt like, she wouldn't wish it on any living creature. She had always understood why Josh had worked so hard to get Noor and Gilbert and then finally Sammy the elephant out of their prisons at the zoo and to a sanctuary, but now, even though she was living in a mansion, it was still unbearable to be confined. *I'm doing it for Josh*, she kept telling herself, *and he's worth it.*

At least she didn't have to have a nurse looking in on her all the time anymore. She liked Madelaine but the girl made her feel like she was eighty years old in assisted living. She had tested her ankle this morning, and it felt pretty good—not too much pain. Her femur was still broken, but she could still do a lot with her other arm. Being stuck in a wheelchair was the worst thing about all this. She felt herself starting to nod off and wheeled over to the bed, used the tiny elevator to get the wheelchair even with the mattress, and hauled herself in. Just a little nap while waiting for Josh to call.

*　*　*　*　*

After slamming down the phone of his landline, the desperate chump (which is what he called himself) who had blown the assignment to kill Baker raged around his living room. Every time he talked to the bitch, he felt like he had walked ten miles in a frigid snowstorm. He wanted to smash the mirror and swipe everything off the dining table in one angry swoop. But what was the point? He'd only have to clean it up sooner or later.

He couldn't stop obsessing over his predicament. He was terrified. The woman could tear him apart in sections without batting an eyelash. Who knew she was certifiable when they met years ago? He'd done his job, used his computer savvy to hire pros who were supposed to know what they were doing, and they cost plenty. Because they blew it and the ex-cop was still alive, he knew he would pay for it one way or another. He didn't know whether to lay low and ignore her; skip the country, which was his first thought after the attempt was blown; or wait until she gave him another assignment like the flunky he'd become. After arranging to have Marchand offed herself, she didn't really need him anymore, and they both knew it. But still she kept him hanging on, waiting for orders he knew were coming. He was tempted to pack up and leave immediately, but what she'd paid him so far wasn't worth the risk he'd taken or enough to enable him to completely disappear. He needed the rest of it, but now he was trapped in the deep end of the pool and drowning.

*   *   *   *   *

Suzi was sitting on Rosemaria's pillow, giving her gentle pecks on the cheek, rousing her out of a deep slumber. She grabbed her phone. Had she missed a call? Nothing. "What's up, Suzi?" she mumbled. "Why'd you wake?"

"Let's turn on the TV! Let's turn on the TV!"

"Do you really mean that, or are you just spouting your usual nonsense?" Suzi cocked her head and stared at her. "I'm sorry. I didn't mean to insult you. Okay, I'll turn on the TV." She clicked the TV button and Netflix. "There's got to be something on here somewhere," she mumbled. Finally, finding a British crime series she liked, she pressed another button, and the head of the bed raised up to a comfortable position. Suzi flew off to her perch where she could eat and watch TV at the same time—her favorite thing to do. Rosemaria loved British mysteries. Everybody sounded so intelligent just because they spoke in that great English accent. The detectives were just going over the crime scene when her cell rang. Josh!

"How are you doing, you wonderful man!?"

"You're always playing hard to get." Josh was reclining in his chair with his stockinged feet on the coffee table. "But I'm doing okay. We just had a great rehearsal. The local musicians had no problems with the charts, and they backed me up just fine. Everybody went out to some restaurant a few minutes ago."

"What do you mean, 'okay'? You're in one of the most beautiful cities in the world. You should be flying, and why didn't you go out with the others?"

"I'd be flying if you were here."

"You and that mushy stuff. But hey, what's the venue like?"

"It's the O2. Beyoncé killed it here last weekend."

"You'll kill it tomorrow night. I know it."

"Yeah, I hope you're right. I know Joell will. They love her here."

"You sound a little down."

"Just tired. Jet lag and all that. I think I'll go out and get something to eat or maybe order room service."

"Okay. Think of me the whole time."

"Nothing else, my love. Bye, sweetheart."

"Bye."

Josh clicked off and sat for a second before deciding to call room service. Rehearsal had gone well—he hadn't been lying about that—but he could sense Joell's unease at his failure to bond with the other musicians and choice to hang out by himself. She was used to his gregarious, easygoing nature. Truth to tell, Josh was not in a socializing mood, and he didn't feel like faking it. He would bring everything he had onstage, and Joell would not be disappointed. But offstage, he couldn't dredge up the will to express feelings that weren't there. It took every bit of energy he had to cover up his irrational sense of dread of being onstage. Acting like an ungrateful, petulant child was ridiculous, and he didn't like himself for it. Tonight, he would spend time alone in his room and tomorrow night make a herculean effort to live up to Joell's expectations of him.

* * * *

Sherilyn couldn't keep her mind on her receptionist job. The agents at William Morris Endeavor really respected her and had made her a part-time script analyst, which meant she could recommend scripts that were worth packaging. Twice, answering the phone, she had connected people to the wrong agents and once had disconnected an important client. Until yesterday, she had definitely decided not to talk to Rosemaria Baker. She wanted to forget the whole thing, even though not knowing who killed Ramin had been eating her up for all these years. She knew David didn't do it. And now he was dead. Police had put the wrong person in jail for killing Ramin and had barely investigated when David was killed, until somebody tried to assassinate a prosecutor who had nothing to do with the case. Now Sherilyn was worried the murderer would come after her, and the police would keep screwing up. She knew it was totally irrational, thinking that after all these years of going about her business, somebody would want to eliminate her. But other people had been threatened in the past, and she was sure that's why they had moved away. She needed to decide what to do and not keep Baker waiting. Did she want to find Ramin's killer enough to stop acting like a coward? She had to make her decision before her jittery nerves got her fired.

CHAPTER ELEVEN

Albert Hecht looked like a broken man. Even though he wasn't manacled, he shuffled slowly through the door of the interview room wearing blue denim pants and a chambray shirt, his eyes downcast as he sat opposite Mack and Loshi, who eyed each other, surprised at Hecht's demeanor. This was Cedars-Sinai's former chief of staff, a millionaire doctor who had lived on the same street as a member of the Kennedy family. Now, sitting at a table across from them in an interview room, he looked more like a school janitor.

"Dr. Hecht?" Mack tried to get his attention.

Hecht didn't change his expression. "I'm not a doctor. I'm a baker. Ironic isn't it, seeing as a woman named Baker got me here."

"What?" Loshi asked.

"That's what I do here. Bake bread. Day in and day out, I bake. And that's what I am."

The two detectives quickly ascertained that Hecht had lost the will to live and was merely existing.

Hecht looked up at them. "If you want to ask me questions about the Baker woman, all I have to say is this—she took my life, and when she was done shaking me like I was chicken parts in a paper bag filled with flour, everything came out mixed up, upside down, and unrecognizable.

There is nothing left of the life I knew, and nothing will ever be the same. Killing her would solve nothing. It would not make me happy. By the time I get out, I'll be old enough to live in an old folks' home. I'll exchange one prison for another. So, who cares, detectives? Who the hell cares?" His voice was as weary as if he'd walked ten miles to get there to talk to them.

Mack and Loshi shrugged and blew air out of their mouths practically in unison. This guy was a dead end.

"With all due respect, Hecht," Mack said, "you almost beat a man to death. Baker didn't do that. You did."

"I'm not the same man anymore."

Mack nodded. "We'll leave you to your baking then."

The guard appeared and led him away, and the detectives stood up and headed for the door.

"They all say they're different now," Loshi said. "You notice that? He almost killed his elderly driver two years ago, and now already, he's different."

As they walked to the parking lot, Loshi observed, "I read they have classes in manners and etiquette here to help the parolees fit in better on the outside."

Mack, ever cynical, snorted. "Hecht had manners and etiquette up the yin-yang. What was lacking was humanity. And you either got it, or you don't."

Loshi laughed as he opened the driver's side door. "People do change."

Mack opened the passenger door. "If you say so." And he got in.

* * * * *

"Whoo-hoo, Dad." Rosemaria was in her lounge chair on the patio talking into her cell phone while Suzi nodded off in her cage. "I had a call from Sherilyn. She'll see you, but I told her you would call her with time and place and tactical moves to get her to the meeting spot without anyone following her."

"What makes her think someone's following her?" Steven was at his desk in his study, his laptop in front of him.

"She's paranoid, Dad. She doesn't want to end up like me or worse. So keep her happy and give her some instructions. She's a font of information, and she could be the key to unraveling this whole mystery."

"I will do my best."

"I know you will. You taught me everything you know. That's why I was such a brilliant cop and now prosecutor."

"Apparently, I forgot to teach you modesty."

Rosemaria chuckled. "Totally useless in our line of work but, okay, I admit I'm not perfect."

"Concentrate on healing, daughter. I'll get back to you after I talk to Sherilyn. Love you."

"Same." She had barely clicked off when she glanced up to see Larry coming out the French doors. "My darling partner! I thought you had forgotten me."

He was at her chair in two long strides and bent down and kissed her cheek. "I don't think that's possible for anybody's who's met you, and unfortunately, that goes for the bad guys too."

"Yeah, I know." She gestured for him to pull up one of the metal table chairs next to her. "Hence my gilded cage."

His eyes swept over the broad expanse of green lawns, trees of every variety, the pool houses complete with ornate draperies and looked back at her. "Not bad digs for a girl on the run."

Suzi perked up at the sound of Larry's voice. "Can I get you anything? Can I get you anything?"

"Holy cow." Larry looked at the cockatoo. "She learned something new."

"Now you know how much everybody's hovering over me. You're used to all this because you grew up with it, but in time, I admit, I could be."

"If you remember, I did not grow up with it. I grew up in a big house before my father died, but it was nothing like this. How are you adjusting to being helpless and dependent?"

She tapped the wrapping on her ankle. "You're mean. If not for this darn thing, I could be a lot more mobile. Your mom is bringing me some kind of moving apparatus where I can stand up and steer myself to wherever I want to go."

"I know. It will suit you better than sitting all day. You can pace or glide as you mull things over."

"Speaking of mulling, is the report in yet from San Diego about where all the people in the murder house moved to?"

"The murder house?" He grinned and shook his head. "Uh, no, not yet. Jimmy may very well beat them to it." He laughed. "Murder house. Here you are, protected like a head of state against professional assassins who want your blood, and you make light of it."

"It's just that I know down to the marrow of my bones that the answers are in that house. And as soon as Dad reports back from talking to Sherilyn—"

"You dad is talking to Sherilyn?"

"Oh yeah, I set it up a few minutes ago."

"Mack and Loshi won't be happy about that."

"We'll coordinate perfectly. I promise you. It may seem complicated, considering all the witnesses who need to be interviewed, but we can do it without any hard feelings either way."

"If you say so. I'm only the middleman. I'll do my best to stay out of the way of flying objects."

"Never mind all that. I want to hear about Vanessa and the baby. That's what's really important. And by the way, Josh is doing great."

She barely gotten the words out of her mouth before Larry had his cell phone out, primed to display the new pictures of Melissa he'd taken just this morning.

She oohed and aahed while he proceeded to explain why his one-year-old daughter was the brightest, most beautiful little girl ever born and to describe in detail every delightful move she made. There was nothing left of the obnoxious ladies' man Rosemaria had met on her first day at BHPD. That annoying jackass had long departed and was not even a distant memory anymore.

* * * *

The woman whose main goal in life these days was seeing Rosemaria dead was flying down Wilshire in one of those rare moments when she allowed the driver to put the top down on her sky-blue Rolls Royce and let the wind blow her hair all to hell. She had been invited to the fabulous Collins mansion for the most exclusive, glamorous fundraiser of the year. The man she intended to marry had been detained out of town on business and apologized for not coming back in time. But once she heard rumors through her fiancé's law enforcement sources that a private protection service had been hired to guard the Collins mansion, she had launched an all-out campaign to get him to return home. Chances were good that the Baker woman was the person they were guarding, seeing as her hosts were the parents of Baker's ex-partner. Her fiancé was not a pushover like most of her conquests, so he had to be handled expertly. But he had proven to be as vulnerable to her machinations as most men, and he had agreed to cut short his meetings with two heads of state in DC and would be flying back to LA. Of course, she had no intention of taking a potshot at the well-guarded prosecutor at the party should she be there, but she could advance her agenda in other ways. She could hardly wait to find out if the target was really staying at the Collins mansion.

* * * *

Steven Baker sat in his unobtrusive dark blue Mazda in a parking lot underneath a freeway near LAX. He had given Sherilyn directions to the location, including how to ditch a tail. He doubted she was being followed, but if making her feel safe was what got her here, that was all that mattered. She was fifteen minutes late, and it would be dark soon, making it more difficult to find the location. He checked to see if she'd texted him but, so far, nothing. He was enjoying being back in the saddle, especially since it was for the benefit of his one and only daughter. Sitting and waiting was practically imbedded in his DNA after being a cop for so many years. He finally spotted the gray sedan she told him she would borrow from a friend approaching his car. He waved at her as she parked close by. She looked in every direction before getting out of the car.

He smiled as she opened the passenger door. "You made it. Good for you."

Sherilyn was attractive, thirty-one years old with short blonde hair, and she had made no enhancements to her face as he would have expected of someone who worked in the movie industry. William Morris Endeavor was a high-end agency that repped a lot of famous actors, directors, writers, and more. If you weren't famous, you were welcome to go elsewhere for representation. "I followed your directions explicitly," she said breathlessly. "I drove to an indoor parking lot in a shopping mall, called a cab to pick me up outside Macy's, had him take me to my friend Christina's house in a roundabout way, and then drove her car here."

"Perfect. I can see you were not followed. Good job."

"You can tell?"

"Absolutely."

"Okay, good. I'm ready to talk about everything if you want."

Sherilyn had a naïve quality that caught him off guard. She still had a country girl freshness for someone who had lived in a house where drugs and booze flowed freely and had two of her friends end up murder victims. But she was clearly disturbed and frightened by being a part of the investigation.

"Don't worry, Sherilyn," Steven said. "You're perfectly safe here, and I would never do anything to put your life in danger. So, you can relax, okay?"

She was hesitant. "Okay."

"Set the stage for me, if you will," Steven said. "Tell me about the house, the layout, who lived where, if there were couples, who was in charge of the house, your friends Ramin and David. Whatever you want to share, just feel free to say whatever comes into your head."

"You don't seem like a cop. I thought you'd grill me or something, ask direct questions."

"I'm leaving it up to you. Any feelings, impressions, dislikes, fears, whatever. I'm going to turn on my phone to record what you're saying." Steven picked up his cell phone and clicked record.

"Well . . ." She looked at the phone as if it might bite her but dove into her monologue. "You might think it was weird that Ramin was living in that house when he had a rich dad, but he was the kind of guy who didn't want to be set apart from people he went to school with. He wanted to fit in with everybody who had a lot less, even though it was an illusion. He always had a safety net the rest of us didn't. I met him because whenever he used to work for his dad, he would get his coffee at the same place I did on Melrose. I worked at a dress shop nearby. We kept seeing each other, one thing led to another, and you know how it is." She stopped, her eyes tearing up. "I'm sorry."

"You can cry. Perfectly normal."

"It's been so long since I talked about this." She grabbed a tissue out of her purse and gripped it hard in her hand as she spoke. "I was living with a roommate, but sometimes I'd stay with Ramin at the house. I kept trying to get him to move to someplace better, but he wouldn't. Living on the wild side, you know? But smoking weed was about as wild as he got. Stacey and Sam were mostly straight, though, and I think Mariah was. Clyde was the guy who everybody got their drugs from. I think he bought and sold on the street too. His girlfriend Lorna was shy and smoked some weed but wasn't into other drugs, I don't think.

"Was anybody else living there at the time?"

"The apartment managers. They lived there—Keith and his wife, Maisie. They were in their thirties, and I don't think Keith was much into drugs, but Maisie, yeah. They'd managed a bar before, but it closed, and I guess they were desperate for any job they could get. Micco was the nicest of them all and really good looking. He was part Native American and wanted to move to Arizona where he said his roots were and paint or something. He and his girlfriend Sarah used to paint murals on school walls in the Valley. Really beautiful. They made some money that way."

"And David? What was his story?"

"He was really messed up. He had grown up totally protected, and after his parents moved to Atlanta, he kept going to USC but was blowing off most of his classes. If he hadn't gone to jail, he would have been kicked out for sure. Weed, cocaine, sometimes meth—he wanted to try everything. His parents had been really strict, and it was like he wanted to break free of them."

"Do you know how he ended up at the house?"

"He and Ramin met at a club downtown and hit it off. You know, both rich kids pretending to be like everybody else."

"Do you know where any of them are now?"

"Well, it was kind of strange."

"Oh?"

"After Ramin was killed and the police were talking to everybody, and the press was trying to interview us, none of them except me hung around town. They all left the house and moved somewhere else. After David was arrested, I ran into Keith when I came to get some of my things out of the house. He barely looked at me. He acted like he could hardly wait to get out of there. I think I'm the only one who stayed in LA. I called Sarah, who'd always been so nice to me, but she acted scared too."

"Do you think they had been threatened?"

"You mean by the person who really killed Ramin?"

"Yes."

"I think it's possible, but why hadn't I been? I'm the one who had been on the phone with Ramin when he told me about the money he was getting from the bank. I told that to the police."

"You were already set to testify at the trial. Possibly, the murderer wanted everybody else gone before they could share what they knew with the cops."

"But nobody knew anything."

"Nobody but the murderer."

"I know. And that's what scares me now. What if he or she thinks I'll remember something?"

"After what you've told me, I owe you an apology. I may be a bit paranoid, but you might possibly be in harm's way."

"What do you mean?"

"Detectives from the San Diego Sheriff's Department are going to want to talk to you sooner or later. Insist that they take the same safety measures that we did. I may be overreacting, but I don't want to you to take any chances."

"Aren't you working together?"

"We have the same goal but different theories on the case."

"You're the father of the ex-cop."

He nodded. "Yeah, I'm her dad. And because her life is in danger, we want to work harder and faster. Understand?"

"Yeah, I do. I hope you find him or her."

"We will."

She opened the car door. "I'll help if you need me, but I hope you don't. Call me in the evening, okay? When I'm not at work."

He nodded and watched as she shut the door, quickly ran to her car, and drove off.

* * * * *

At least eighteen thousand people in the O2 arena were cheering and stomping their approval. After three encores, Joell waved her final goodbye at the fans, and the stage lights went black. She rushed backstage where Josh, the backup singers, and the musicians were waiting to congratulate her. She hugged Harvey and headed toward the stage door. As she passed by Josh, she said, "Meet me in my trailer. We need to talk."

Josh was taken aback by her tone. He thought he had given a good performance—one ballad and an R&B number that rocked the house. He was her lead in and was determined not to let her down, so he had left his crappy attitude at the hotel and come out onstage with every ounce of energy he could muster. Was she going to send him home? Now he had to worry about on top of everything else.

He knocked on the trailer door, and Miranda came out. She patted him on the arm as she went by. "Good show, Josh."

Joell was alone, seated at the small banquette drinking a soda. "Have a seat."

"Is something wrong?"

"You tell me."

"I thought it went well."

"'Well' is not why I brought you here. 'Well' is not why I recorded your song. 'Well' is not what I expect from you."

"I'm sorry."

"Something is distracting you. I thought with Rosemaria locked up tight in the Collins mansion, you'd be able to concentrate without worrying. Is her situation what's going on with you?"

"No, it's not Rosemaria."

"Okay then. Whatever it is, I don't want to know. Just deal with it. Tomorrow, our movie's being released worldwide. The music video for "New York Nights" is all over social media. Soon you'll be famous. This tour is supposed to put all that into overdrive, but your head is somewhere else, and I don't know where it is. Tonight, we're all having a late-night snack in the hotel restaurant to go over some of the glitches in the show. Be there. No more hiding."

"I'll be there."

Her voice softened. "In case you didn't know, you're one of my favorite people on the planet. You made it possible for me to do something really good for an animal that was suffering horribly when we got Sammy out of the zoo. You have a heart of gold and deserve every chance I'm giving you. Whatever is keeping you from realizing that, get over it." She was almost pleading with him.

It was all Josh could do to keep from breaking down. He pinched his mouth closed, gave her a brief nod, and almost ran out the door. He needed to talk to Lenny.

Lenny Mortensen, Josh's AA sponsor, was in the driver's seat of his shiny fire engine–red sixteen-wheeler, tooling down a Texas freeway just as the sun was going down. Independent and loving it, forty-five years old, with a solid body from regular workouts and a craggy face with a lot of character that (he felt) was irresistible to women. He punched the phone screen button on the dashboard. "Yo."

Josh was standing outside the hotel in a deserted restaurant area near the entrance. "It's me."

"I know that."

"I'm in need of some words of wisdom."

"What's going on?"

"Black thoughts. Bad feelings. Can't get into the music."

"And the dogs are howling and the demons circling?"

"No, not that bad. Don't feel like raiding the mini fridge either. If I drank one drop and lost my way, I'd lose Rosemaria. I won't let that happen."

"You know what's going on as well as I do."

"Do I?"

"Yeah, you do. So, let's spell it out here and now. For years, you drank because of what happened with your father when you were no more than a kid. He murdered your little brother and was threatening you and your mother with a shotgun. So you shot him. Not an easy thing for anybody to have to deal with. Afterward, you hated his guts and hated your mother for not protecting your brother. It ate you up alive, and you drank to drown it out. But your drinking was also making sure your God-given talent stayed buried because you figured you didn't deserve anything good."

Lenny waited but heard nothing but silence on the other end, so he barreled on. He had no intention of tiptoeing around the obvious at this point.

"For two years, you've worked through this in AA, asking for forgiveness from your higher power and working on forgiving your parents. Obviously, you have a long way to go. But I'm going to tell you this right now. You damn well better not blow this chance you've been given. You owe it to everybody involved in this tour to pull yourself together right now and stop feeling sorry for yourself and drowning in your own self-centered bullshit.

"From everything you've told me about Rosemaria, she has faced serious situations more than once and come through them just fine. But she volunteered to be locked up and not do the work she loves, just to relieve your worried mind. She's making a huge sacrifice for you, and you have no right to wallow in the past and make her sacrifice be for nothing. The only way to win this battle is to act like the man you are and make all this worthwhile. You owe your lady that much."

Josh said nothing for several seconds, then: "Wait a minute. I'm picking myself off the floor."

"I slapped you good upside the head because that's what you deserve."

Josh began slowly pacing back and forth. "Maybe so but I'm still a little wobbly from your vicious right cross."

"You'll live."

"How come truck drivers know so much?'

"Because we learned life on the road, man. We're not like those people with advanced degrees who are educated beyond their intelligence."

"Thanks for having my back."

"You're welcome. I'm heading into Fort Worth with a load of cement bags right now, so I'll have to sign off. You good?"

"Never better."

"See you in LA."

Josh clicked off the phone and headed for his meeting with Joell and the others. He didn't want to be late.

CHAPTER TWELVE

The kitchen in the Collins mansion was twice as big as her dad's entire house in Simi. Plus, they had a butler's pantry that Rosemaria was never sure what exactly it was for. This was the first time she'd seen one in person. She was standing near the sink on her new stand-up electric contraption with a knee rest to keep weight off her ankle, handles to hang on to, and controls by her right hand. It had taken a bit of practice, but now she could move around the first floor and fix her own food instead of being waited on all the time, which had made her feel like a total schlub. But the kitchen was so huge, she couldn't remember where everything was after Manuela, a grandmotherly Latina, had given her the complete tour yesterday.

She'd start with something simple, like a sandwich. All she needed was a plate and a knife; everything else should be in the refrigerator. She was about to open the refrigerator door when she felt a tap on her shoulder and almost fell off her contraption. She swung her head around and saw it was her former partner. "Larry! What are you doing here? Why sneak up on me like that?"

He gave her a chaste kiss on the cheek. "I used to live here, remember? I get to come and go as I please. Cameron doesn't even pat me down."

"Mildred gave me the run of the kitchen, and I was going to fix myself something to eat. Want something?"

"No, but I have information regarding the case if you're interested. Of course, if you'd rather eat . . ."

"Are you kidding? Lay it on me."

"You want to sit or keep standing on that thing?"

She managed to remove herself from the standing wheelchair and settle herself on a tall stool next to the massive granite-topped center island. "Go ahead."

"Even though I'm buried in work investigating the Bel Air murders—"

"Yeah, I've been reading about that. Really brutal. I'll help you with it as soon as I figure out who's after me."

He stared at her in disbelief. "Are you—?"

"Yes, I'm kidding. Sort of. Now open up that laptop you're holding, and let's hear your news."

Larry did as he was told and booted up his laptop. "As I was saying, even though I'm buried in work, I volunteered to be liaison between San Diego and us so I could be of some help to you."

"Get on with it, please."

"Okay." He did some typing. "I read your father's notes on his interview with Sherilyn, and I think she may be helpful as we go forward. There's a lot she can fill in on what went on in that house. As far as where most of those characters are now, San Diego and Jimmy don't yet have a clue. But I'll tell you what I do have: The last known residence for Micco Stolz is a low-end residential motel in New Mexico in a small tourist town called Red River. He grew up on a reservation in New Mexico near lots of galleries and artists, which is what probably made him decide to move back since Sherilyn said he liked to paint. Jimmy and the San Diego computer guys are tracking him down to wherever he moved to from the motel. His girlfriend, Sarah Holcomb, apparently did not like life in the desert and headed for Seattle, where she married a dentist and moved to a suburb called Issaquah. The only effort she made to hide her whereabouts was changing her first name to her middle name, Denise, and she is going by her married name, Lawson. Still, easy to find.

"Keith and his wife, Maisie, the managers, have disappeared. Clyde Hallet and Lorna Selverino were both born in Fort Worth Texas, spent time in Reno, now totally off the grid. Mariah Venmore left the house as soon as David was arrested, and we don't have a clue where she's from or where she's gone. There's literally no record that she ever existed."

Rosemaria's eyes opened wide. "I'm liking her for this right off the bat."

"I agree. But let's not have tunnel vision. That's what got David Marchand in hot water."

"Just like Dad, you don't trust my gut. Nevertheless, I'd love to talk to Sherilyn myself before Mack and Loshi get to her. Any chance of that happening?"

"You leaving the house and interrogating a witness? Are you kidding me?"

"Doggone it. I'd like us to get to these witnesses first, and I'll bet Sherilyn can give us more info on how to find these people. I'll see if she'll do an interview with me on Zoom, okay?"

"Jeez, you are one impossible—"

"What?"

"Never mind. Okay, moving on—as soon as our friends from San Diego get finished talking to that actor whose career you destroyed, they'll probably head on up to Issaquah. But Clyde and Lorna really interest me. I'd like to know where they ended up and how deep he was into dealing drugs. Drug dealing and murder are like a matched set, you know what I mean?"

Rosemaria stared off into the distance. "Yeah . . . what about Stacey Fields and Sam Oliver, the straight Goody Two-Shoes who never touched drugs? Do they sound too good to be true or what?"

"Oh yeah, I forgot to say—they took off for Oregon just before the trial but moved out of their studio apartment in Bend after living there for two months and are off the grid like Mariah."

"Mack and Loshi are sharing their notes with you, aren't they?"

"So far, but the jailhouse interviews led nowhere."

"Well, I'm going to call Sherilyn tonight after she gets home from work. Maybe I can get her to confide a few secrets in me, woman to woman, you know?"

"If she can help lead us to Clyde and Lorna, who have managed to completely disappear, I will be forever grateful."

Rosemaria slipped off the tall stool and adjusted herself into the electric glide. "Meanwhile, I'm starving. Can I make you a sandwich?"

"I've heard about your culinary talents."

"So that's a no?"

"Oh, what the hell? Tomato and lettuce on rye, please, mustard, no mayo."

She glided over to the refrigerator. "And I expect your wife, my best friend, to visit me soon."

"She's been busy with Melissa, but I'll tell her."

"She doesn't want to be around somebody with a target on her back. I get it."

"Don't be hurt. It's only been a few days."

She took a package of bread and some veggies out of the refrigerator. "The trouble with you Colemans is you don't know when I'm joking. Now stand back and get ready for the best sandwich you ever tasted." She began spreading too much mustard on the bread, and Larry inadvertently cringed, but Rosemaria caught it. "And stop believing Josh's lies about my cooking. I'll have to talk to him about that when he gets home." She grinned. "Only two and a half weeks to go."

*　*　*　*　*

This was not the kind of sunny day in Seattle when tourists took one look at the lovely city situated between the bay and Lake Washington, saw the ferries crossing Puget Sound to the islands, and longed to be on them as wispy white clouds floated above in the blue sky. When a day like that happened, visitors from California tended to immediately call their real estate agents and put their houses in the San Fernando Valley up for sale so they could move to the emerald city surrounded by bodies of water. Not today. As Loshi drove himself and his partner toward Seattle from the airport, a low-hanging gray-and-black cloud layer felt downright claustrophobic and covered the windshield in drizzle. Even though it was June, there was a chill in the air, and the atmosphere was depressing as hell. Just before they got to downtown Seattle, they realized they had taken the wrong freeway and now had to go over a floating bridge across Lake Washington to get to Issaquah. But it was worth it. The lake was huge. Beautiful houses were situated all around it, with lush green lawns leading down to the shore. Incredible views in all directions, even with the drizzle.

"Beaucoup bucks to live here," Mack said.

"Couldn't do it anyway. Have to have sun."

"I hear ya."

They drove across the bridge toward Issaquah.

"We're headed into Ted Bundy territory, you know," Mack observed.

"No, I didn't."

"Yeah. Dr. and Mrs. Lawson live near Lake Sammamish. He scouted for victims there."

"He was too good looking to resist."

"Never had that problem," Mack said.

They took their exit and looked for street signs.

"Being too good looking has its drawbacks," Loshi insisted.

"Name one."

"I'll think about it."

Loshi pulled up in front of a dark wooden split-level house situated on a block with other split levels. The woods behind the houses were mostly tall evergreens, and the ground was choked with lots of thick greenery. It looked as if nature was slowly creeping up on the houses and any minute would surround and swallow them. Beach lovers Mack and Loshi shuddered at the sight.

They walked up two flights of pebbly, mold-stained stairs and knocked on the red-painted wooden front door. The lady who opened the door looked like any everyday housewife, slightly plump, with brown hair touched by slivers of gray.

"Denise Lawson?" Mack asked, holding up his badge.

"I am. Please come in, detectives."

Fifteen minutes later, the detectives and Mrs. Lawson were seated at her modest dining room table with mugs of hot tea in front of them.

"You're sure you wouldn't like some sandwiches or cookies or something?" Denise asked.

"No, we're fine, thank you," Mack answered.

Loshi took out his cell phone and made a move to turn on the recorder.

Denise frowned. "Would you mind not doing that?"

Loshi nodded, put away his phone, and took a pad and pen out of his inner jacket pocket.

She shifted around in her chair, then stared out the window. "It was a time in my life I regret, you know?"

The detectives retained their passive, congenial facial expressions and said nothing.

"There were a lot of drugs floating around the house all the time. I hated it, but Micco was friends with Sam, and he talked him into living there. They both liked hiking and being out in nature, and the rent was low, so we could afford it. I stayed in my room a lot and avoided most of those people. I told Micco I was leaving LA after I graduated from college, and he said he was okay with that. Then"—she hesitated— "after the murder, we all got the warning calls."

"Could you be more specific?" Loshi asked.

"I thought somebody would have told the police back then, but I guess they didn't." She looked expectantly at the two detectives, but they didn't say anything, so she sighed and continued. "Right after David was arrested, we all got phone calls from someone with a distorted voice, you know, like mechanical, that said leave town, or we'd all end up dead. Some of us were scared, like Sam and Stacey, but Keith said it was a crackpot, and we should ignore it."

"But you didn't ignore it," Mack said.

"At first, we did; then things started happening."

"Such as?"

She looked at Mack. "Well, the brakes on Micco's car failed when he was driving down Mulholland after a hike, and he almost went over a cliff. When Stacey was coming back from the beach in Santa Monica and was standing at the curb with a big crowd of people, she was shoved into traffic and hit by a car. She was only bruised because somebody grabbed her and prevented her from being run over. As soon as that happened, we all got another call telling us we weren't safe if we stayed. Clyde and Lorna were the first to leave, then Micco and me."

"You were all being interviewed by the police at the time," Loshi said. "Why not tell them about the warnings and the accidents?"

"We didn't know who to trust. Everybody knew David didn't kill Ramin, but the police arrested him anyway. Nothing made any sense. We were afraid of the police and afraid of whoever had killed Ramin. We were just kids. We didn't want to die."

Mack blew out a mouthful of air in frustration. The detectives on the case had blown it. They should have been more patient and insistent in talking to the kids in the house and possibly gotten the truth out of them. But David was too convenient a patsy and ended up dead because of it. "We absolutely understand, Mrs. Lawson. You were scared kids. But let me ask you this: Do you think someone else in the house killed Ramin? Someone who was capable of threatening the rest of you and almost killing Micco and Stacey?"

"Only Clyde. He could be really nasty when he was snorting cocaine. He had a terrible temper. Every once in a while, I'd see him on the street outside the house with one of his suppliers, and they were all tatted up like him, like criminals in gangs, you know."

"How about Mariah? Mack asked. "She seems like a real mystery. Did you talk to her much? Do you know anything about her background? Where she's from?"

"She was a real hard worker. I know that. But there were rumors she was having a thing with some of the guys. She avoided the women but went out of her way to flirt with the men. She went after Micco, but he seemed oblivious. She attended design school in West Hollywood and was determined to make something of herself even though she didn't have much money and was living in that dump with the rest of us."

"Did she ever give you a hint of where she might run to after the threats started coming in?"

"Well, after I told Keith the manager that we were moving out, he said the house was due to be condemned and torn down anyway. It was just as well. I asked him if anybody else had given notice, and he said Clyde and Lorna had already, and just before I talked to him, Mariah told him she was leaving the next day. Keith said she seemed very concerned but didn't say where she was going."

"I guess you don't know what happened to Keith and Maisie?" Loshi asked.

"No. I don't know what happened to anybody after we left. I had a big fight with Micco, and I decided to move back home to Seattle."

"It turned out well for you," Mack observed.

"Yeah, I finally met a really nice guy when I was going to the U Dub, and he just set up his own dental practice here in Issaquah."

"Why did you and Micco fight?' Loshi asked.

"He was set on going to New Mexico and finding his roots." She made air quotes with her fingers. "He was ambitious. I liked that about him, but how was he going to get rich painting? You have to be in New York and have connections to make that happen. Besides, I did not want to live in the desert. It's not for me."

"So where did he move to?"

"Taos, I think. I haven't talked to him since we went our separate ways."

Mack took out his card and put it on the table while Loshi put away his pad and pen. "We appreciate how helpful you've been Mrs. Lawson. If you think of anything at all that could help us, please call, okay?"

Denise took the card and bent it back and forth nervously. "You don't think that after all these years, Ramin's killer can still track me down, do you? With that cop getting shot at and everything, you don't think that has anything to do with me?"

Mack was as reassuring as he could be, considering the fact that he didn't have a clue what the killer's intentions were. "I don't think the killer will come after you. Just take all the normal precautions you would no matter what."

They all stood, and Denise walked them to the front door. "I'm sorry you came on such a gloomy day. It's really quite beautiful here when it's sunny."

Mack grinned as they went out the door. "I hear you don't get a lot of that in Seattle."

"We get more than you think, but don't tell anybody," she whispered.

The detectives gave her a friendly wave before driving off, Loshi again behind the wheel. "Want to take a look at Ted Bundy Drive?' Mack asked. "It's a piece of history."

"Get outta here."

"Last chance. We might never be up here again."

"I'm headed to Pike's Market and getting me some of that fish they like to throw around."

"Don't come cryin' to me with regrets when we get home."

"I'll hold back the tears. The only memory I'm taking home is the best seafood in Seattle.

Mack took out his cell and started typing. "I'm on it."

CHAPTER THIRTEEN

The Wynn in Las Vegas is a five-star hotel that caters to those who wish to gamble, eat, drink, and celebrate special occasions in spectacular surroundings. Repeat customers say they enjoy their time at the Wynn so much they never stay anywhere else when visiting Las Vegas. The rooms are maintained in pristine fashion, the dining is superb and sitting poolside while sipping drinks brought to you by friendly, efficient waitresses is the ultimate in enjoying the desert sunshine. Lorna Selverino loved being one of those waitresses. She didn't mind one bit dropping out of college and fleeing LA since it meant ending up here. Although, at the time, she had been plenty scared.

At thirty-one, she still had her perfect figure, a pretty if not beautiful face, and an outgoing personality that resulted in hundreds of dollars in tips every day or night, depending on what hours she was assigned to work. She was on the day shift today and enjoyed going down the elevator to the pool where most people seemed to be in a good mood, taking a break from losing at the tables or slots. Small or devastating losses were all forgotten while splashing in the pool and baking one's skin to a golden tan.

She was walking down the hallway from the pool to the elevator when she felt her phone vibrate in her pocket. She slid into an alcove and saw an unfamiliar number on her cell. She purposely didn't have a lot of friends, and all of them were in her phone, but not this one. Maybe it was a spam call. "Hello?" She almost dropped the phone when she heard the familiar voice and stepped farther into the alcove and turned her back. "Clyde?"

"Yeah, it's me." He was sitting in a battered jeep in a parking lot next to a gas station and convenience store. The letters on the store were in Spanish, and time and weather had made them almost illegible. "Lorna, you need to leave and go somewhere else, like right now."

"What do you mean? Where are you?"

"I'm out of the country. You don't need to know where, but it's somewhere safe. I told you to come with me, but you insisted on going to Las Vegas, and things don't look good. You have to get out of Las Vegas and take the bus somewhere far away from there."

"Why? I'm finally happy now. I don't want to go anywhere else."

"It's not safe. I told you. I think that the same person who killed Ramin and David just tried to kill a cop that supposedly talked to us years ago. I'm telling you for your own good; you need to leave." He was becoming frustrated and angry.

"You think it's Mariah. But she doesn't know you told me anything. Why come after me?"

"Stop asking questions. If you won't leave, then you need to be extra careful. Get a security system, don't walk alone in the dark, buy a gun, things like that."

She was hesitant. Her whole life had just been upended again. "No one knows my real name. I use the Social Security number you got me in Reno. I used that woman's name to have my credit checked. I've done everything like you told me to do. No one can find me."

Clyde shook his head in disgust. "All right, Lorna, I warned you. And you can't call me back on this phone. I'm getting rid of it as soon as I hang up." He clicked off and jumped out of the jeep. He ground the cell phone into the gravel, picked up the pieces, and threw them into the jungle vegetation a few yards away. He backed the jeep out into the road and drove through the dusty town where the only cell phone coverage within a hundred miles of where he lived could be found. He headed back to his shack in the jungle.

Lorna was devastated. She loved her job and the few friends she had made who never asked questions and loved her for who she was. She earned enough to live in a nice apartment, go to shows once in a while, and maybe soon even learn to play golf. There was no way she was running away. She'd be more careful, though, and maybe one of the security men could help her buy a gun. Her goal was to meet and marry a nice man with a lot of money and never have to worry about anything again. No way was anybody derailing her plans.

* * * * *

After Larry had put dishes in the dishwasher and driven back to BHPD to work on his own case, Rosemaria had taken time to familiarize herself with where everything was in the kitchen in case she ever wanted a midnight snack. She glided across the floor, out of the kitchen, through the huge dining room, then through the living room, over polished wooden floors and pastel oriental carpets, carefully making her way around the chairs, couches, and tables scattered throughout the rooms in perfect decorative symmetry. She was getting the hang of her standup wheelchair and confidently headed toward the hallway and the elevator. She almost collided with a coffee table when Andrew Collins stepped out of his study and startled her.

"You got a minute?"

He turned around and went back into his room. Rosemaria steered her way through the furniture arrangement and glided into the vast study where Andrew spent most of his time when he was home. "Yes, sir. What's up?"

Collins had seated himself behind his desk and was holding several sheets of paper in his hands. "I see you've learned to navigate on that thing."

"Yeah, I could get spoiled and never walk again."

"God forbid." He looked at her in consternation.

"I was just kidding." Boy, him and Larry both. "I think my ankle is healing fast. Madelaine is taking the compression wrap off tomorrow and putting a softer one around it. I'll keep testing it and see what happens."

He looked down at the paper. "Well, don't put weight on it too soon. Meanwhile, I want you to take these with you and look over these names and see if you recognize anyone. There's short bios and pictures as well." He stood up and handed them to her.

"Thank you." Rosemaria stuck the papers in the basket that hung on the front of the glider.

"I don't think you're going to find anyone dangerous on there," Andrew said, "but Cameron and Kirsten insisted that you have plenty of time to study the pictures and see if you recognize anyone."

"I appreciate that." Her cell phone rang, and she fished it out of her pocket and glanced down. Her face lit up. "It's Josh."

Andrew stood up. "You stay here. I have to talk to Loretta. Tell him hello from us."

"I will." Rosemaria was grinning from ear to ear as she clicked her phone on. "Josh! What are you doing right now?"

"I'm up early. Couldn't sleep. I'm about to go down to breakfast."

"How was your European debut? Did you knock their socks off? Did they demand encores?"

"Encores are only for Joell, and yes, they seemed to appreciate me."

"You are so modest. By the time you get home, that'll totally change. You'll have a swelled head and fans chasing you up and down Rodeo Drive."

"Why Rodeo, pray tell?"

"That's where we'll be doing all of our shopping once you're famous."

"Okay."

"Boy, you're easy."

"Only when it comes to you."

"Well, you need to go eat and get plenty of rest today before the show. What will you sing tonight?"

"I'll be singing the ballad I wrote about my brother."

Her face softened. "I love that song."

"I hope it's not too down."

"You'll kill it, my sweet."

"I haven't asked about you."

"I'm living in the lap of luxury, getting accustomed to the life you'll be providing me within a year or two."

"Maybe more like three or four. Stay out of trouble."

"Never."

"Call if you need me. Love you."

"You better."

They clicked off. Rosemaria heaved a big sigh of contentment as she surveyed the impossibly beautiful room she was standing in.

* * * *

Larry was at this desk on the landline, his voice getting louder the more frustrated he got. "We've shared everything we've got so far. We need to know if Denise Lawson had anything useful to tell you. Quid pro quo, remember?"

Mack was driving his own car, headed for home on a surface street. "I don't remember anything about quid pro quo. We told you if you learned anything, you have to share it with us, and if we think you're interfering or getting in our way, we're shutting you down."

Larry sucked in air and tried to stay calm. "Look, there's a lot of people to track down and talk to. We can divide up the work. Why can't we pretend we're all on the same team instead of you guys being the bosses and only sharing what you see fit? That's not the best way to proceed. You tell me who you intend to talk to, and Baker and Waite can take someone else. Why not? This isn't about taking credit. This is about saving the life of an ex-cop who happens to mean a lot to me."

Mack stopped at a red light and mulled this over. "Let me think about it."

"Can you think fast? We need to make plans."

"Okay."

"Okay, what?"

"Loshi and me are going to New Mexico tomorrow to see if we can find Micco Stolz. Meanwhile, if your guys can find Fields and Oliver and have a little chat with them, we wouldn't mind.

"Well, no one even knows where to look."

"You're the one who told us they headed to Oregon after the murder, maybe near Bend. Our guys found out Fields had an aunt up there somewhere. Maybe she's still in Oregon. So follow up." The light turned green, and Mack started moving again. "Don't complain. I just gave you a gift."

"Okay, okay. We're on it."

"And full report if your guys find them."

"It may take a while."

"This is their chance to show off their superior detecting skills."

"This isn't mano a mano between two police departments."

"Could've fooled me," Mack said.

"All right then. Game on."

"And if we have questions for Sherilyn, we'll be calling her."

"I think she's shared just about everything she knows."

"I doubt that."

"Right. I'll be in touch."

Larry hung up and dialed another number. After a moment he left a message. "Steven, pack your bags. I'm making plane reservations for you and Waite to fly to Portland tomorrow. You're officially retired, Baker, so don't look for a paycheck in the mail." He hung up and stared at his computer, contemplating his next move regarding the Bel Air murder case. He had hit a dead end, his two best suspects had taken off, and he wondered briefly if Rosemaria had meant it about getting involved. Then he shook off that nutty idea two seconds after it reached his brain. Things were complicated enough.

* * * * *

Rosemaria was back in her sit-down wheelchair in front of her desk in her room. She was typing on her laptop until Sherilyn came into view via Zoom. "Ah, there you are. Forgive the delay. I'm not used to interviewing like this."

"That's okay. I've eaten dinner already and was just sitting here waiting." Sherilyn sounded less than enthusiastic, and the expression on her face as she stared at the screen was downcast.

"What's wrong, Sherilyn? You don't look happy."

"I'd like you to ask me all the questions you have so I don't have to do this anymore. I want to go back to my life with my boyfriend and not have to worry if somebody's going to find out I'm talking to you."

"I'm afraid that the detectives from San Diego will be calling you soon. If we want to avoid that, let's try to see if you remember anything that might be important."

"Like what?"

"For instance, about Stacey and Sam. Apparently, they took off for Oregon and were last heard of in Bend. Did they know anybody up there? Have family and friends?"

"I didn't talk to them all that much. I guess if you like nature, that's as good a place as any to wonder around."

"Were they a tight couple? Do you think they would have stayed together?"

"She was really hung up on him. I think he might have cheated on her, though. I heard them fighting about somebody once in the backyard. They were trying to whisper, but Stacey was really mad."

"You don't know who they were fighting about?"

"I don't."

"Do you think Keith and Maisie would have stayed together?"

"I doubt it. She was kind of a dingbat. She was pretty, but I think Keith was ready to dump her. He thought he was hot stuff having owned a bar, even though it went bust. He had a high opinion of himself for reasons I couldn't see. She seemed like a space cadet. A boat with no rudder. He seemed ready to move on even before Ramin was murdered."

"And idea of where he wanted to move on to?"

"Sorry."

"For a group of people who lived so close together, everybody seemed to have kept a lot of secrets."

"Maybe if you can find some of the others, they'll know more. I never wanted to be in that house in the first place. They weren't the kind of people I wanted to hang around with."

"What kind of people were they?"

"Losers with empty dreams working half assed at getting degrees but who'd rather sit around and wait for somebody to come along and give them whatever they wanted. Ramin wasn't like that. He was working even though he knew that eventually, yeah, his parents would hand him a fortune." She sniffled. "The only worthwhile guy in the whole house, and he gets killed."

"I'm sorry."

"I've told you as much as I know. Please, can I just try to forget all this and not talk to anybody anymore?"

"I'll try to make that happen, Sherilyn, but I can't promise."

"Okay. Thanks. Goodbye then."

"Bye."

Rosemaria ended the call and screwed up her face in frustration. She'd write up a report about her talk with Sherilyn and send it to Larry, who would send it to the San Diego detectives. It was obvious they were beating their heads against the wall with her. Why annoy the poor woman any further when she had nothing more to add to what she'd already said?

Meanwhile, she had looked over the list of attendees of the gala next Saturday and seen nothing that raised an alarm. Everybody's history had been checked, and nobody's face looked familiar, except the mayor and some of the actors and actresses she'd only seen on screen, and she doubted if they were after her. According to Mack and Loshi, even the actor she'd investigated had moved on. He was making a fortune doing commercial voiceovers under a different name and had even managed to shed a tear or two in front of the detectives over the wife he murdered but still insisted he didn't. His daughter had transferred all his money back into his bank account, and he was living the good life. Making trouble for Rosemaria was the last thing on his mind. He was the one who got away, and there wasn't a damn thing she could do about it.

She knew she had to stay upstairs on Saturday evening, but at least she could look at the celebration on the monitors in Kirsten's room. It was like going to a party and not having to get dressed up but still getting to eat the best food a Beverly Hills caterer had to offer. One thing that hadn't changed throughout this entire ordeal was her appetite. Through thick and thin, she could count on that. She wondered briefly if there was anything at all that would make her not want to eat. The only thing she could think of was losing Josh, and that was never going to happen.

* * * * *

Every one of the three local bands nailed their numbers. Joell had recognized talent even from halfway across the planet. She had chosen them after watching their live performances on YouTube and had judged audience reactions. She allowed each of them no more than two numbers because she didn't like her fans getting too impatient. A little bit of anticipation was good, but too much made them weary of waiting.

As she watched Josh from backstage settling on his stool holding his guitar, she felt a little bit of a nervous flutter in her stomach. Whatever had been bothering him yesterday seemed to have lifted, and he had been his usual self all day, even reaching out to Angelo, who could be a jerk, more so when he was nervous. Josh noticed and helped Angelo relax by telling him stories about crazy things that had happened when he was singing in bars and fights got out of hand. Not that Angelo was appreciative, but Joell was. The orchestra began the intro to Josh's song, and she held her breath. She wished him well with all her heart.

The crowd at O2 stadium was so loud it sounded like the Rams had scored a touchdown at the Super Bowl. It was the biggest venue Josh had ever set foot in, and momentary stage fright made his stomach tighten. He shook off his anxiety and focused on his breathing. *In out, in out, relax, you can do this.* As the orchestra began to play, he wasn't sure if he had been wise to choose a ballad after Angelo and the local bands had worked the audience into a state of frenzy.

The noise from the audience hadn't lessened as he sat down on his stool on the darkened stage and strapped on his guitar. He wondered if he had made the right choice of song to sing. He had decided the best way to celebrate his recent ascent out of darkness was to share the same feelings that had reawakened his demons. If Joell wanted him to rip open his soul on stage, he would do just that.

The orchestra was vamping his intro, waiting for the audience to settle down, and as the spotlight hit him, the announcer said his name. Josh was surprised that he got any reaction at all. Apparently, the videos had garnered him some name recognition, and the audience clapped and cheered. He smiled out into the darkness and began to strum the strings of his guitar. For the second time in front of an audience, he sang about his brother and hoped the crowd would stay with him.

I'm walkin' down a road to nowhere.
I lost you long ago.
And dreams of tangled memories
Whisper soft and low.
I wander down the path where only
Fading secrets sing
Wondering how I'll face the night
And what the dark will bring.
The road to nowhere,
The road to nowhere,
Why can't it bring . . .
Why can't it bring . . .
Why can't it bring me back to you?

The times we had together were precious
but too few.
I still remember every moment
when our world was new.
You chased away the darkness
and taught me a new song.

We'd find a place the two of us
Where we'd both belong.
The road to nowhere
The road to nowhere
Why can't it bring . . .
Why can't it bring . . .
Why can't it bring me back to you?

As he sang the bridge, his voice increased in emotion and volume.

I'll find you somewhere. I'll do my best,
to let the sadness go and keep the rest.
You're everything that's good and I can see
You never really left your special place with me.

The orchestra swelled and filled in with a repeat of the bridge. Then he sang the chorus again.

The times we had together were precious
but too few.
I still remember every moment
when our world was new.
You chased away the darkness
and taught me a new song.
We'd find a place the two of us
Where we'd both belong.
The road to nowhere
The road to nowhere
Why can't it bring me back to you?
Why can't it bring me back to you?

As the orchestra faded with the final guitar chord, he felt like his whole future was riding on the reaction of this audience. Some of them probably hadn't even understood the lyrics of the song. But he hoped the feelings he had tried to share had reached a few of them, even though they were young and hadn't yet experienced the tragedies of life. A deadly silence seemed to last for an eternity, and then a wave of noise swept over him as the crowd expressed their approval in whistles and cheers. He sighed in tremendous relief. He wouldn't be leaving the tour after all. He grinned and waved to the audience as he walked off the stage, holding his guitar.

Joell was waiting for him in the wings along with Angelo and Miranda. Angelo nodded his approval, and Miranda put a hand over her heart. Joell took a step toward Josh and enveloped him in a hug that seemed to last for minutes. He stepped back, held her at arm's length, and saw, for the first time since he had known her, tears in her eyes.

CHAPTER FOURTEEN

On the two-hour flight from Burbank to Portland, Oregon, Jimmy wasted no time getting on his laptop to keep searching for information about Stacey Fields's aunt who lived in a suburb of Portland. After searching every database at his disposal at BHPD, he had finally tracked down one of Stacey's cousins through motor vehicles. He had found his name in records from the same school high Stacy went to, and he still lived in her hometown near Kansas City, Missouri. He had been willing to talk to Jimmy over the phone the day before. Fortunately, there was no love lost between him and Sam Oliver, and he was more than willing to provide Jimmy with any information he could to find the SOB. According to the cousin, Sam was not worthy of a beautiful, kindhearted girl like Stacey. All Sam ever talked about was moving to the West Coast and making it big. He acted like a bigshot because he lived in LA and fell in with a bunch of pot-smoking hippie types who weren't worth shit. He bragged to everybody back home that he was going to make a lot of money and would end up living in Bel Air someday.

Jimmy had asked him about Sam's love of nature and the outdoors. All crap, the cousin had said. It was Stacey who loved the mountains and hiking. She'd always been a vegetarian and loved animals. Couldn't stand to see any of them hurt. She'd fallen for Sam the minute he transferred to their high school because he was so good looking. She couldn't see what everybody else could: that he was a godless liar and as phony as a plastic corn cob.

After the cousin had exhausted his entire repertoire of Oliver's shortcomings, he had finally volunteered that Stacey had an aunt on her mother's side who lived alone in Portland, Oregon, a fact Jimmy already knew. That's where Stacey had really wanted to move to, he told Jimmy, not LA. Her dream was to live near the ocean but close to the mountains too. She looked at pictures of Oregon all the time. It was her Shangri-La, but Sam had dragged her to Sin City instead, the bastard. It had taken a few more minutes of venting to drag the aunt's name out of the cousin. He couldn't provide an address, but, according to him, they were detectives; they could find it. By this time, the cousin was in a foul mood and could hardly wait to hang up. "Let me know what happens when you find them. I hope she wakes up and dumps that two-bit loser." And with that he had hung up.

"You confirmed her address?" Steven asked. He had the seat back with his eyes closed.

Jimmy was studying the screen. "Yeah, at least according to the DMV. Her record's clean except for two moving violations. Our Norma Peters lives just about twenty minutes from downtown Portland. She's sixty-five but still works as a secretary for a construction firm where she's been for twenty years." He looked over at Steven who still had his eyes closed. "We're lucky Stacey's cousin talked to us, or we might have gone on a wild-goose chase to Bend."

"We might end up there anyway since that's the last place they were before disappearing."

"Ah." Jimmy leaned back and stretched his arms ahead of him as far as the space would allow. He smiled and shook his head. "This feels good."

Steven opened one eye and looked at him. "What feels good?"

"I'm finally out in the field instead of being trapped in the computer room. And I owe it all to your daughter."

"I should be offended, but I understand. If she hadn't been shot at, we wouldn't be here."

"Sorry, I didn't mean it like that. I wouldn't want anything to happen to Rosemaria."

Steven laughed. "I know that. And now you get a chance to make sure her would-be killer is caught. Nothing wrong with that."

Jimmy patted his laptop. "But for me, a Glock will never replace the internet."

Steven moved his seat back up. "I moved to Tahoe after I retired because I needed time to enjoy a peaceful existence for a while and indulge in a bit of Texas Hold'em in the casinos at the same time. But a peaceful existence is highly overrated. I missed the job—dirty, dangerous, and boring as it may have been at times. I did love being a cop."

"Rosemaria's just like you."

"For better or worse. She may solve this puzzle before we do."

"We're working together, just like the old days."

"She may have a new job, but I can guarantee you one thing: she'll never stop being a cop."

* * * * *

Steven called Norma Peters as soon as they landed in Portland, and she asked that they meet her at a restaurant near her job. It turned out to be a small café in a quaint, touristy area of town where the streets were lined with boutiques and gift shops. They sat at a table in the back corner, ordered their coffee, and waited. Fifteen minutes later, Norma Peters, thin, with gray hair, her deeply lined face looking troubled, walked through the door. They recognized her from her DMV photo. She looked around hesitantly at the few customers seated at the other tables before finally noticing Steven's wave. She wove her way through the tables and introduced herself.

"I'm sorry I'm late," she said breathlessly as Steven stood and pulled out a chair for her. "My boss is going on a trip to Seattle, and there was a lot to do before I finally got him out the door."

Steven slid his badge unobtrusively toward her, and she quickly said, "Yes, thank you. I have no doubt you are who you say. I just don't know how I can help you."

"Would you like something to eat?" Jimmy asked when he saw the waitress heading their way.

"No, I can't eat. This whole thing is a little upsetting."

Steven shook his head at the waitress, who turned away and spoke to another customer.

"From what you said on the phone, Stacey could be running from someone who wants to hurt her."

"We don't know that for sure, but we need to talk to her and make sure she's safe. Has she contacted you recently?"

"No. she hasn't. Ten years ago, she and Sam stopped by and asked if they could stay at my house for a while. I lost contact with her side of the family years ago after my sister died when I moved out here. She said they had to move away from Hollywood, but they hadn't decided where. Then one day, they were gone. She left a note and thanked me but didn't say where they had gone to. That's all I can tell you."

"She didn't contact you after that?" Jimmy asked.

"No. Not a word."

"Do you live alone?"

"I'm a widow. I lost my husband twelve years ago to cancer."

"I'm sorry." Jimmy said.

"I'm used to being by myself. I have my job and my friends, so I'm never lonely."

Steven handed Norma his card. "Will you call us if you hear anything?"

She picked it up. "Of course." She hesitated. "Is there anything more?"

"No, if we think of anything we'll call you."

Norma, seeming slightly relieved, gave them a nervous smile and walked to the door. She gave a brief nod to the cashier as she walked by.

The detectives watched her go out the door. "She was lying," Steven said.

"We have no grounds to get a warrant to check her phone records or tap her phone."

"We have friends in high places. Maybe Collins could help."

They stood and walked up to the cashier at the front of the restaurant. She took Mack's credit card, made the transaction, and handed it back without a word, not even the usual thank you.

After they stepped outside, Mack said, "That cashier was acting funny."

"Maybe she just hates her job."

They started walking toward their rental and heard a woman's voice behind them. They turned around to see the cashier following them. The woman looked to be in her thirties, somewhat homely with brown hair down to her shoulders and wearing a flowered summer dress.

"I couldn't help overhearing what you were talking about."

"You have information for us, miss—?" Jimmy asked.

"Veronica. I don't know if it's something helpful, but it's obvious you're detectives looking for information . . . and I couldn't help overhearing part of your conversation."

There were benches in front of the gift shop next door. "Why don't we sit, and you take your time telling us what you know," Loshi suggested.

Veronica slumped down onto one of the benches, and the detectives shared the other one.

"I'm sorry, and I know it's none of my business, but you will never find a woman kinder than Norma."

"She struck me as being a little tense and not too happy," Mack said.

"She was devastated when her husband died. When my parents ran this place before they left it to me, my mom used to bring her food because Norma was so unhappy, she didn't want to face anyone. She didn't ask my mom to go to the trouble, but Mom is just like her, generous to a fault. They've stayed friends, even after my parents retired."

She paused and looked as if she had just smelled a carton of sour milk. "Then, ten years ago, Stacey, a long-lost niece she hadn't seen since childhood, popped up with her boyfriend and asked to move in. Norma, being who she is, said of course, and in they came. They stayed for three months. Neither one of them ever looked for a job. They just sponged off Norma, and she took it, probably grateful she had people to take care of. Then, after three months, they left. Norma told my mother that they were headed for Bend."

"We tracked them to Bend. They haven't been there for years."

"Right. Norma let it slip to my mom that Stacey called a few weeks ago to say they were in Redmond, and could she send them money. She was embarrassed. Unbelievable that some people are just takers. Obviously, they're on the run from something or someone."

"And did she send them money?"

"Mom thinks she wired it through Western Union. She tried to talk Norma out of it, but she wouldn't listen."

Jimmy was typing on his laptop. "Redmond, that's up in the Deschutes National Forest."

"Practically," Veronica said. "If they were in Redmond two weeks ago, maybe they're still there."

Steven looked at her thoughtfully. "Do you have any idea why they would be headed there? Is there anybody in the area who might take them in?"

Veronica reached in the pocket of her dress and pulled out a silver bracelet with colored stone settings. "Apparently, Stacey spent her time at Norma's fooling around making jewelry." She handed the bracelet to Steven. "She gave that piece to Norma, and Norma gave it to my mom as a gift for helping her out."

"Your point being?" Steven asked.

"The town of Sisters is a few minutes down the 126 from Redmond. It's an artsy-craftsy town where somebody with a bit of talent could make money."

"Why are you so eager for us to find them?" Jimmy asked.

"They're just the kind of people who would drain a nice old lady dry, and I don't want that to happen to Norma." She stood up. "They must really be scared to hide out all these years in dumps like Bend and Redmond."

"Maybe they like those towns. Maybe they're nice towns," Steven said.

"And maybe whoever is after them is really good at finding people." She stood up. "You can keep the bracelet."

The detectives watched her walk back inside the restaurant and through the window saw her take over from the waitress who had been taking care of customers at the cash register.

Jimmy was typing on his cell phone. "Redmond is twenty-eight minutes from Portland. The Ponderosa Best Western looks like a good place to stay. We can scout around for a bit, and then we can head for Sisters if we don't come up with anything."

"First," Steven said, "we better shop for a different wardrobe and get out of these suits so we don't stick out like sore thumbs."

Jimmy scrolled through his phone. "There's a sporting goods store two blocks from here. It looks like they sell the right kind of apparel."

"Let's find a restaurant and eat first. I doubt if they'll have anything decent on the plane."

* * * *

Cameron and his crew had been keeping impeccable track of the comings and goings of every person who had a part in making the preparations for the evening's event—extra waitstaff, caterers from three different restaurants, liquor store truck drivers, florists, cleaning crew to keep everything tidy throughout the evening in an unobtrusive way, and others—Rosemaria had no idea who they were. State-of-the-art metal detectors had been set up at the front and back entrances with guards on either side. Everyone had to pass through them. No exceptions. The whole security apparatus arranged to keep Rosemaria safe was making her feel even more unworthy. At times, she felt like she needed to spend the rest of her life working with needy people in India to make up for these efforts to protect her.

Cameron had suggested that Rosemaria sit in Kirsten's room and study every face on every screen in case she recognized someone who might do her harm. Kirsten was downstairs helping the rest of the guards keep their eye on the arriving hired staff but would be back upstairs soon. Rosemaria caught herself nodding off every few minutes, bored out of her mind. She was stuck here while her father and Jimmy followed Stacey and Sam's trail to a place called Sisters in Oregon and were showing her picture around the arts and crafts stores. They were hoping Stacey was still making jewelry and would show up during the big crafts fair coming up in a week. It was a slim hope, but so far, it was all they had.

Mack and Loshi would be heading to New Mexico in a couple of days to talk to Micco Stolz, who was living in Taos as Denise had told them, even though Micco seemed like the person least likely to kill any-body. Keith, Maisie, and Mariah had completely disappeared. Jimmy hadn't been able to find a trace of Mariah. She was like a shadow person with no past or present. As for Clyde, she suspected he was somewhere south of the border living rough and maybe had taken Lorna with him.

* * * * *

Standing in her immense walk-in closet trying to narrow down what dress she would be wearing that night, a thrill ran though the killer's body. After hearing about all the security precautions, she was certain the target might very well end up being a few yards away from where she, her signif-icant other, and a few hundred other people would be mingling, trying to impress each other, and forking over thousands of dollars for the museum fund. The message to anyone who aspired to attend these events was clear: don't bother coming unless you're rich enough to write a big check, and her guy certainly was that, as was she.

The killer was certain she wouldn't actually see the soon-to-be-dead cop, but just knowing the bitch was close by gave her immense satis-faction—all those security precautions, and she would be walking right through the door, free as you please, on the arm of a man who could afford to own his own impressive mansion, which she would encourage him to buy as soon as she found the one she wanted. Spending time with real estate agents looking was half the fun. They were so disgustingly eager for a big commission. She had never debased herself like that, even when she was young and poor.

She admired herself in the full-length mirror as she held up one gown after another and then discarded them on the loveseat. The closet was twice as big as the entire room of the Motel 6 she had first stayed in when she moved to New Orleans. She remembered every smelly, sticky square inch of that room. Twelve years later, she was a long way from the Lafourche Bayou country and the shack she had grown up in. She, Leonie Gautreau—half Cajun, half Choctaw, a scrawny brat forced to wear dirty rags to school because her father wouldn't give her money to buy new clothes, and her mother didn't have the energy to do any washing—had come further than anyone could have imagined.

Her pathetic, beaten-down mother, who let herself be smacked around and treated like crap until the day she disappeared, never bothered to dream of any other kind of life. She just accepted what was. Leonie smiled when she remembered the probable cause of her disappearance. The first time she had felt power over another person was when she scared the daylights out of her mother. It was addictive. She never knew if the woman had managed to run off with another man or if she was nothing but a pile of bones in a swamp somewhere. But Leonie couldn't care less: not then, not now. The woman was a waste of mind space.

At the age of ten, Leonie became determined to earn enough money to move to New Orleans and fight for a better life. Since the bayou didn't offer a lot of ways for a Cajun girl to make money, she learned how to fix things like her father. He had a natural knack for anything to do with carpentry, and he was a self-taught electrician. Because he was a perfectionist, he was much in demand, and when he needed a helper to keep up with all the work, she filled in just fine. Her father never dared smack her around like he had his wife. He sensed that his daughter would never put up with it. He had nicknames for her—*dur ange*, which meant tough angel, or he'd call her *entêté*, stubborn, and her favorite, *glacé*, ice. When she turned fourteen and was showing signs of becoming a beauty, sometimes he called her *joli*, which meant pretty. But she always liked *glacé* the best because it suited her.

When she was young, most of the time, she felt nothing but the driving need to escape the bayous. Later, in New Orleans, she learned how to enjoy the fruits of her labor, and she found great pleasure in devising foolproof plans to rid herself of anyone or anything she no longer needed. Ever since her father had called her by nicknames, she had come to like them. Resentful competitors whom she stepped over with no regret called her every filthy name in the book behind her back. She considered them compliments. On the other hand, coworkers, whom she treated well because she needed them in order to be successful, thought she was classy and nice. In unguarded moments, she told some of them about her father's nicknames for her, but none of them ever stuck. So *glacé* remained her secret nickname for herself. She was ice down to the bone.

* * * * *

The invitation had said nine p.m., but since no one ever wanted to be the first to arrive, the guests didn't begin showing up until nine-thirty. Rosemaria was staring at the monitors, searching every face for even a hint that she might recognize them. Kirsten had been ordered by Cameron to stick to Rosemaria like glue after the guests arrived, so she sat silently in a chair beside her and watched the monitors as well. Rosemaria had made it clear she needed to concentrate in silence. She had told Kirsten that noticing things other people overlooked was something she had been known for as a cop. It was her specialty, except for the time Vanessa had pointed out that one of the murder suspects Rosemaria was looking for was wearing a hairpiece. It was the last piece in a puzzle that had helped Rosemaria track down the killer. She really missed seeing her best friend and her little goddaughter. All the more reason to focus on finding whoever was determined to kill her.

She kept watching the video screens even as Mildred brought her the most scrumptious food she had ever tasted and several pots of coffee to keep her awake. There was no sound from the monitors, but when Loretta announced the amount raised, everyone cheered, glasses of champagne were raised, and Rosemaria could hear the celebratory noise as it traveled three floors up to her suite. Several times, she had seen on the monitors that guards were preventing people from entering the elevator or going up the stairs, but none of them looked familiar to her. They were nothing more than curious lookie-loos, she imagined. Even rich people wanted to explore a mansion this lush and laden with priceless works of art that belonged in a museum.

Later, lying in bed and trying to sleep, Rosemaria had a feeling of unease that wouldn't let her relax and nod off. Her gut told her she had missed something, something small that would have led her further along in the investigation. She would look at the footage again after her mind was clear. All those hours of staring at screens had given her a huge headache and made her eyes sting. She would wait a couple of days. She was grateful that Kirsten had understood her need for quiet during the party and her need for privacy during the day. She imagined Kirsten had had more interesting assignments as a bodyguard. Oh well, in about a week and a half, Rosemaria would be released from captivity, and Kirsten could move on to more challenging guard duties.

Tomorrow she would call the sanctuary and find out how Noor and Gilbert were doing. Hearing Jason's descriptions of how they were making new friends, splashing in pools, and running through the hills had to satisfy her until she and Josh could drive up and visit them again. And maybe stay a few days in the small cabin they leased across the road from the sanctuary. But not until the killer was caught. She wouldn't bring her troubles to the sanctuary and endanger their lives as she had done the year before. Noor and Gilbert were safe from harm now, and they would stay that way.

*　*　*　*　*

The underground parking lot of the hotel was well lit, and there were a few people walking to their cars at one in the morning, but still, Lorna felt a little nervous. That dickwad Clyde had called again and had managed to put enough of a scare into her that she had felt the need to park near the elevator so her walk to and from her car was shorter. He was stupid to think anybody wanted to kill them after all these years, but it couldn't hurt to be a little careful. Parking garages were where a lot of murders took place in the movies.

She got in her car and hurriedly locked the door just in case. She couldn't wait to get home to her little apartment, take a bath, and fall asleep to a series she was watching on Amazon—a French spy story in which most of the spies were women. She wondered how courageous she would be if her life were put in mortal danger, or, God forbid, she was tortured to reveal information on her fellow spies. She hoped she would be brave, but how could anyone know until it happened? She drove through the middle-class neighborhood of modest houses and apartment buildings and pulled into her carport. Safe at home. She sighed with relief, then cursed Clyde again for bringing all this tension into her carefree life. She walked up to the second floor of her building then down the hall to her door and hesitated before putting in her key. Clyde had talked her into putting half a match from a matchbook in the door jamb almost at the top where no one would notice it. Ever since, she had been checking to see if it was still there when she came home. She figured he must be into spy movies too, if he could even watch movies wherever he had run to. He was so over the top. She decided she was not going to talk to him anymore.

Nevertheless, she checked to see if the match was still there. Her body went rigid as she stared at the door. The match was gone. Someone was inside her apartment. She slowly took off her high heels, backed away, and ran down the hall and down the stairs. When she reached the ground, she heard her door open and knew she didn't have time to get to the carport. She ran as fast as she could through the backyard of the house next door and looked for lights on. There was no time to bang on doors and hope somebody would get up and answer before the person chasing her caught her.

There were no lights on anywhere she could see. She threw her shoes as far as she could down the side of one house, ran in the other direction into a backyard, and dived underneath a dying rhododendron bush. It was all she could do, but it gave her cover. She stopped breathing and waited, hoping the person following her had missed seeing her dive into the underbrush. The neighbors' German Shepherd started barking inside the house, and a light came on. She lay frozen in fear, not knowing if the person chasing her was still standing in the backyard, had noticed her shoes and gone off in that direction, or had given up and taken off. In one of her spy movies, she had learned that when you were hiding after being chased, you didn't move for hours. No matter how uncomfortable or frightened you might be, you stayed put. She might not be the bravest girl in the world, but she could outwait anybody.

* * * * *

The man in the black jeans and black hoodie who had been chasing Lorna was swearing under his breath as he walked quickly down the sidewalk to his car three blocks away. Now that he had failed another assignment, a simple one of killing a complete nitwit, he knew his own life wasn't worth two cents. How the hell had the girl known he was in the apartment waiting for her? It should have been an easy kill, out of the public eye, quiet, fast. But somehow, she had sensed his presence and taken off running. When the dog started barking and lights went on, he had no choice but to get the hell out of there.

Now he had to face the long drive home. And then what? Tell the psycho he had partnered with that he wanted out and hope she'd forget about him? That would never happen. Hide? He had come to the realization that running away was hopeless. She could track him down anywhere. She knew where every one of those clowns she'd terrified ten years ago was hiding, except maybe for one. Her unpredictability was the thing that scared him the most. She could smile one second and stab him in the heart the next. He had to convince her to give him another chance. She had bought and paid for him, and he had come cheap. Now, one way or another, he had to pay for his stupidity and greed.

CHAPTER FIFTEEN

It had taken two days to find the exact whereabouts of Micco Stolz. San Diego forensic computer staff had tracked him to an apartment in Taos where he had lived for a few years, then to a house in town where he was currently living. His art gallery, Stolen Sky, was located in the heart of the art district on Kit Carson Road. Wearing their newly bought "Western" duds—jeans and checked shirts—Mack and Loshi walked from their rented car to the gallery. Mack couldn't help stopping and admiring the paintings displayed in the large picture windows, forcing his partner to wait for him impatiently as they slowly made their way toward Stolz's gallery. This was art that Mack could appreciate, not a bunch of lines and squiggles that a third grader could draw with his eyes closed. These were real paintings of real people and scenery you could recognize.

"I didn't realize you were such an art lover." Loshi nudged Mack to move along.

"If I could afford it, maybe I'd buy one and take it home." Mack peered in one of the windows, looked closer at a price tag attached to a painting of a river flowing through a lush green valley, and drew back. "Or maybe not."

They walked the few steps to the Stolen Sky gallery where they hoped to find Micco amenable to talking with them. They rarely called ahead of time before an interview. They liked catching people unaware so they didn't decide to flee or have time to cook up some cockamamie storyline. They stepped inside and saw Micco, a dark-haired, good-looking guy whom they recognized from his driver's license photo, seated at a desk close to the entrance, speaking on a landline. One middle-aged couple was in the gallery, seemingly entranced by the paintings, mainly Native American portraits and a few delicate pastel watercolors depicting the scenery of desert and mountains, as they slowly moved from one to the next. Micco waved and indicated for Loshi and Mac to approach as he finished up his call.

There was no place to sit, so the detectives stood staring at the paintings, Loshi shuffling his feet in boredom while Mack enjoyed every minute.

Micco hung up the phone and offered them a pleasant smile. It quickly disappeared when Loshi handed him his card. "Let me see if I can find my assistant, and we can go into my office."

The detectives hoped he wouldn't make a run for it out the back door but figured with all this money invested in the art gallery, he'd probably stick around.

Micco came back with a svelte blonde in her twenties trailing behind him. She gave them a curious look and kept walking toward the couple who seemed like they might be potential customers.

"Follow me," Micco said and led the way to the back of the gallery and into his office. They followed him inside, and after Micco shut the door and sat behind his desk, he indicated two chairs close to his desk. "Please, have a seat." He looked at Loshi's card. "So, it's Detective Loshi and . . ." He looked at Mack.

"Mack."

"From San Diego. May I ask why you've come all the way here to talk to me?"

"Well," Mack said, "actually, this is about something that happened years ago but now has come back to slap us in the face like a greedy ex-wife who's hell bent on vengeance, if you know what I mean."

Micco looked genuinely confused.

"Did you hear about the ex-cop who got shot in San Diego two weeks ago?" Loshi asked him.

"Can't say that I did."

Mack decided to hit him right off with the million-dollar question. "Why did you leave LA after David Marchand got indicted for manslaughter in the middle of the school semester?"

If Micco's reaction was fake, Mack decided, he was a really good actor.

"Why are you asking me about that now? What does that have to do with the cop that was shot?"

"Ex-cop," Loshi said. "You met her about ten years ago when she interviewed you after Ramin Hassan's murder."

"I'm sorry. I don't remember her. It was such a crazy time."

The detectives said nothing, just waited for Micco to fill in the empty air.

"She was shot last week? Did they catch the guy? What's that got to do with me?"

"*Does* it have anything to do with you?" Mack asked him.

Micco put his head in his hands. "Okay, can we slow down a bit? Why was a cop I talked to years ago shot, and why did you come all the way here to ask me about it? A light went on behind his eyes. "Oh, I get it. This has to do with David being murdered in jail. I heard about that. He was trying to get a new trial. Was this the cop who was going to help him?"

"So you knew about all that, huh?" Loshi asked.

"Yeah, the Innocence Project people came here to talk to me about a year ago. I told them everything I knew, but I guess they dropped the case."

"How'd you know about the cop who was going to help him?"

Micco hesitated. "I'm not an idiot. They said something on the news about a cop having been to see him just before he was killed. I didn't know it was the same cop who had come to the house ten years ago. Why would I?"

Mack stared at him for a few seconds before commenting, "You've done well for yourself." He looked around at the stacks of unpacked paintings on the floor. "This must be a costly piece of real estate."

"I've only had it for three years. I sold some of my paintings, worked in other art galleries, and saved up until I could open my own."

Mack looked skeptical. "That doesn't seem like enough money to open a place like this.

"I qualified for a federal grant because I'm half Native American. My mother's from here; she's from Picuris Pueblo. It's where I grew up."

Mack nodded slowly. "For a guy on the run, you don't seem too worried about being found."

Micco's demeaner changed abruptly, and he scowled at the detectives. "Do I need a lawyer?"

"Do you think you need one?" Loshi asked.

"No, I don't. It's obvious you've talked to somebody else who lived in the house and found out we were getting threatening phone calls. After the so-called accidents I'm sure you heard about, I don't think any of us planned on sticking around."

"Yeah," Loshi said, "most of them have outright disappeared, and others have been difficult to find. You, however, didn't make much of an effort to hide."

"I figured since I didn't know anything and wasn't any kind of a threat, I would just move to another state and go on living my life. It's worked out so far. I hope you coming here doesn't change that."

"Where were you on July nineteenth of this year?"

"July nineteenth?" He tapped on his desktop computer. "I was"— the detectives assumed he was studying his schedule— "right here. I wrote up two sales that morning." He looked up at them. "Why would I want to kill a cop I don't even know?"

"Ex-cop," Mack said. "She believed in David and was going to investigate what really happened. That couldn't have been good news to whoever killed Ramin."

"I wish her well because the detectives who talked to us back then just zeroed in on David without even trying to find who really did it."

"We've come to that conclusion," Loshi agreed.

Mack fixed a hard gaze on Micco's face. "Is there anything you want to tell us about the other people in the house—anybody acting strangely before or after the murder?"

Micco shuffled papers around his desk and avoided looking at the detectives. "It was a long time ago. How can you expect me to remember?"

"Not so long," Loshi said.

Micco picked up a pen and began doodling on one of the papers, pressing down hard. "Uhm, okay, let's see. Clyde was a drug dealer who was around a lot of scuzzy people. He wasn't close to anybody except his girlfriend Lorna. They took off together for parts unknown. Everybody else acted like normal potheads and went to classes whenever they weren't high. Stacey and Sam were pretty straight, and I can't see them murdering anybody."

"And Mariah?" Loshi asked.

"A little weird. No drugs. Not bad looking and usually kept to herself. I sensed a lot of underlying currents in her. She kind of gave me the creeps."

Loshi stood up, and Mack followed suit. "You have my card. We may stick around for a couple of days. Call us if you think of anything."

Micco looked stricken. "You're sticking around? You're not going to go around asking questions about me, are you? Like, do I seem like I could murder somebody?"

"Absolutely not," Loshi said. "Mack's become quite the art connoisseur. And Taos is a great town. We're giving ourselves a few days off. Giving the gray cells a little rest, as Poirot might have said."

"Is he your boss?"

"No," Mack said. "Just kind of like a mentor."

"If you buy, consider some of the paintings here. I'll give you a good deal."

"I might do that." Mack smiled, and Loshi followed him out the door.

An hour later, sitting in a Mexican restaurant over steaming hot dishes of beans, rice, and burritos, they pondered Micco and his reaction to the news of Baker being shot at.

Loshi scooped a huge helping of salsa onto a chip. "He was nervous but seemed genuine to me."

Mack bit down on a forkful of burrito and chewed. "Yeah, but you can't really tell. We've run across some great liars in our day. And how did he know about Baker going up to see Marchand?"

"Maybe it was on the news, like he said. After he was shot, a lot of things came out. For some reason, I keep coming back to Mariah. Maybe it's because she was perceived as a loner and a little weird."

"And because she doesn't have a past or present that anybody can find. How can somebody not exist in this day and age of computers and search engines?

"That too."

They enjoyed their meal in silence for a few minutes until Loshi wondered, "Do you think our compadres from Beverly Hills are making any headway tracking down Fields and Oliver?"

"Who knows?" Mack managed to say with a mouthful of rice.

"Think they look as genuine as we do in our new clothes?"

"We can take pictures and compare."

"Nobody likes a wise ass."

Mack took a gulp of his soda. "Now you tell me."

"Sometimes it takes years to build up to the truth." Loshi wiped a trail of salsa off his chin.

"You're just mad because you didn't take me up on my offer to go by Ted Bundy Drive. You missed seeing an important piece of homicide history."

"That is so gory and politically incorrect."

"But I'm right, aren't I?"

"I'll regret it to my dying day."

Mack smiled. "See? When I'm right, I'm right."

They continued to eat in comfortable silence.

* * * * *

The Redmond Inn was clean, and it was also close to the Redmond Airport, where Steven and Jimmy had rented a car to drive to Sisters, twenty miles southeast of where they were. They checked into their respective rooms, changed from their suits to something more casual, and met downstairs to decide where to eat dinner. Jimmy had found a Chinese restaurant just two miles away, and he volunteered to drive. It turned out to be an excellent choice, and they concentrated on their ramen soup as they shared occasional thoughts about the case and waited for their pad Thai and various other dishes.

"How soon do you want to head out in the morning?" Steven asked between bites.

"Not too early. It's a half hour drive and no sense in getting there before stores open."

"We have a lot of ground to cover, so we'll split up, okay?"

"I hope the pictures we have of them from ten years ago bear some resemblance to what they look like now."

"The age progression photos look pretty good. We'll show both."

The waitress brought over a large tray of food, and the detectives looked over the steaming array hungrily as she set the plates on the table. They hadn't eaten since the packets of dried nuts and pretzels they had on the plane from Portland to Redmond. Jimmy started scooping rice onto his plate and heaping spoonfuls of shrimp, fish, veggies, pad Thai, and more on top of the rice.

Steven did the same after Jimmy was finished taking hefty portions. "My daughter has been nagging me to eat healthy."

"She's a tough cookie, your daughter."

"You noticed."

"You seem plenty healthy to me. You're skinny as a rail. You look ten years younger than you are, and your mind doesn't seem to be slowing down."

"I think she wants me to live forever."

"She'd approve of this, I'm sure," Jimmy said, a forkful of noodles headed for his mouth. "Sorry, but I've never mastered chopsticks."

"Me neither. I hope we're on the right track coming here."

"We'll find out tomorrow."

"I'm wondering how long we should stay until we find something."

"It's a small town. Two to three days, I'd say. If Veronica heard right, the two of them probably live in this area, and odds are good that Stacey will come in for the arts and crafts festival. It's the best time to sell whatever she's been working on."

"If we see her, we follow her back to wherever the two of them live. I don't want to catch just her."

"We better rent a four-wheel drive in Sisters in case we end up on some rough roads."

"We'll carry our Glocks into town every day. You never know where we could end up."

Jimmy put down his chopsticks and frowned.

"What's wrong? Eat something bad?"

"I've never been shot at."

"There's always that risk," Steven said, "But remember this: most people have really bad aim."

"That's comforting."

Steven laughed. "We're not tracking hardened criminals here, just witnesses on the run. I'm fairly certain they won't shoot you."

"'Fairly certain' doesn't inspire confidence."

The next morning, they had some muffins, orange juice, and coffee at the motel and drove the thirty minutes to Sisters. Having spent a lot of time in Tahoe, to Steven, driving through this kind of scenery was like coming home. But Waite, who had known nothing but city life, felt like they were up in the middle of nowhere. The town was a lot bigger than he had expected. For hikers and outdoor lovers, the Deschutes National Forest was a mecca. Surrounded by mountains with views of the Three Sisters volcanoes from whence the town got its name, they had to admit it was not a bad place to spend time.

There were a lot of shops and restaurants to cover, so they didn't waste any time sightseeing. They checked in with the Deschutes County Sheriff's Substation first to let them know what they were doing in town and who they were looking for. Sheriff Sid Macklemore, who ran the station, wasn't in the office, but the deputies were helpful, even though they had never heard of Stacey Fields or Sam Oliver. They advised them not to approach the couple directly if they found out where they were but to allow them to assist with bringing them in for questioning. The detectives agreed and armed with ten-year-old photographs and age progressions, they separated and began their search. Jimmy had the bracelet Veronica had given them in case someone recognized the work.

Going door to door, showing pictures, asking questions are always grueling chores for cops, but sometimes, it's the only way to track people down. Because the couple had gone off the grid, the only reason the detectives had ended up here was Veronica's tip. For all they knew, Veronica could be full of hot air or could have heard wrong, and the detectives could be on a wild goose chase. But this was the best lead they had, and people were pleasant enough and seemed to have plenty of time to talk. By noon, the two detectives were ready for lunch and reconnoitered at a pizza joint, ordered their pizza, poured themselves sodas at the machine, and compared notes as they waited at a table for their order to arrive.

"Two people in a quilt store told me they'd seen somebody who looked like her, but they couldn't be sure." Jimmy said. "Other than that, I've come up empty."

"Same here. And we don't know if she's selling her jewelry to any of these shops, or maybe she's making and selling something else."

"Or maybe she's not selling anything, and she and Oliver just come into town for supplies. They don't seem the type to eat what they grow."

"We have to check with all the car repair shops as well."

"I found no car registration for them online, and he might be fixing his car himself."

The waiter brought their pizza and plates, and they each grabbed a slice. "I couldn't live like that." Jimmy said. "Off the grid, I mean."

They chewed their pizzas in silence as they followed their own thoughts.

"When they run out of cash, they'll hit the old lady up for more," Jimmy said. "Maybe we could get them then. But how do we get her to cooperate?"

"My daughter can't wait that long. We have to find these two now, get whatever information they have, and move on."

"Right." Jimmy nodded. "You're right. I want the same for Rosemaria. I hope we're the ones who get to nail the bastards."

"You have no idea of how much I want that." Steven said.

They finished their pizza, split up, and once again went about the boring but necessary chore of talking to people.

CHAPTER SIXTEEN

Josh leaned against the mirrored wall of the elevator, exhausted but euphoric. Budapest fans had shown them as much love as Prague. The Puskas Arena had been packed that night with thousands of enthusiastic Joell fans, and the love had generously spilled over to the rest of them. Yeah, the other bands knew they were fill-in until Joell came on, but while they were on stage, it didn't feel like that. Josh had rocked the place with a rockabilly number that seemed to last for ten minutes because the audience refused to let him go. The local musicians had read the charts and played the music like they'd been rehearsing for weeks instead of just two days. Every night of the tour had been fantastic, but tonight, everything had clicked into place like never before. He hadn't talked to Rosemaria in two days and felt an overwhelming need to hear her voice. He'd take a shower, fall into bed, and call.

The showerheads sprayed hot water on his head and body from every angle. He loved feeling the nervous energy and tension dissipate; they were good things when he performed but not so good when he was offstage and just wanted to relax and get back to being the person he used to be. There was nothing wrong with fame and money, but he loved the process of writing and creating and spending time with someone who had loved him when he didn't have a penny in his pocket. He wondered if he would be able to balance his two personas. He had a mentor who showed him every day it was possible. No one was more famous than Joell. No one had the adulation she had enjoyed for years. And yet, she was, for the most part, down to earth and caring.

He stepped out of the shower, wrapped himself in the thick towel supplied by the Ritz Carlton, and located his cell phone. He was about to click Rosemaria's number when he heard a knock on the door. "What the—?" he mumbled to himself. It was two-thirty in the morning. He grabbed a bathrobe, put it on, and went to the door. He looked through the peephole and saw a girl, maybe around nineteen, waiting for the door to open. He opened the door an inch.

"Yes? What can I do for you?"

The girl's face broke into a smile. "Oh, good, you're still up." She spoke with a heavy Hungarian accent.

"I think you have the wrong room. You need to go downstairs to the desk and—"

"No. I need to talk to you, Josh."

"Why?"

"Well, I work for a newspaper here in Budapest and have some papers for you to fill out so I could give them to my boss tomorrow morning, and I thought, since I won't be able to come by in a few hours, that you could fill them out now."

"Papers about what?"

"Just stuff about your availability for publicity interviews tomorrow, stuff like that."

This did not pass the smell test. "Wait here," Josh said. He left the door ajar, went back inside, and dialed Joell's room on the landline. "Hi, it's Josh. Did you send someone to my room from a newspaper?"

Joell, wearing comfortable gray sweats, was seated at her desk in her suite working on her laptop." What are you talking about?"

"A girl is outside my room—" He saw the girl enter his room and close the door. "Make that inside my room, saying something about publicity interviews."

Joell's voice went into high alert. "Josh, don't go near her. I don't care if she starts tearing her clothes off. Go into the bathroom and lock the door. I'm sending security to your room."

The girl, with a seductive smile, sat down on the couch, not a paper to sign in site. As she started to take off her jacket, Josh followed Joell's orders and went into the bathroom. He hoped the girl was not in the process of taking off all her clothes. How great would it be to be accused of rape on his first tour? It seemed like less than two minutes when he heard talking outside the bathroom. He opened the door and saw a security guard escorting the girl out of his room. He came out and was about the close the door when Joell appeared. She brushed by him and turned around, livid.

"Hey," Josh protested. "I didn't know she was going to force her way in here."

"I'm not mad at you. I'm furious that she managed to somehow find out your room number and get up here. I'm a stickler for security and keeping my people safe from stalkers and scam artists."

"Scam artists?"

"Male-female teams who prey on unwitting victims. The woman rips off her clothes, screams rape, then the boyfriend comes in and threatens to call the cops, et cetera, et cetera."

"Why me? I'm not rich. How much blackmail money could I afford to pay?"

"You're new. You have no experience with this kind of thing, and you're vulnerable because you have no clout and have everything to lose. They'll get what they can from you then do it to someone else. But don't worry. If she's a scam artist, I will nail this girl to the wall. She and whoever she's working with will regret the day they messed with one of mine." She headed for the door.

"So, this is the price of success, eh?"

"Not on my watch." She turned and walked out the door.

Josh followed her and stood in the doorway, watching her stomp down the hall toward the elevator. He had never seen her this angry, but he could appreciate the lengths she went to to protect her people. He reached into his bathrobe pocket for his cell phone and dialed.

"Hey, missy, what's going on in la-la land?"

"Josh!" Rosemaria broke into a gleeful smile. She was seated at her desk in the sitting room, her laptop open in front of her. She glanced down at the time. "What are you doing up? It's the middle of the night over there."

"I just had an adventure." He settled down on the loveseat.

"What do you mean, adventure?"

"A girl broke into my room and tried to seduce me, then Joell and the security guard rescued me before she had a chance to tear her clothes off, scream rape, and blackmail me."

Rosemaria chuckled. "You are funny."

"I'm serious. They just left. I think Joell is going to have the girl strung up by her thumbs."

Rosemaria's jaw dropped open. "No way."

"Mouth to God. And I wouldn't dare lie to you. But enough about my close call with scary Hungarians. Are you making any headway finding out who's after you?"

Rosemaria's face scrunched up in a scowl. "If I were there, that woman would be black and blue all over and floating down the Danube with nothing to hold on to but a rubber ducky."

"I find comfort in knowing nobody is scarier than you are."

"I can't be scary until my ankle heals—around the time you get home. Get ready to be attacked, my friend."

"You want to frighten me into staying away?"

"I happen to know you don't frighten easily."

"You happen to be right about that, and we'll just see who scares whom when I get home."

Rosemaria sighed dramatically, then abruptly sat up. "Actions, not words, buddy. But in answer to your question, we've made no headway in the quest for my would-be assassin, and everybody but me is out in the field talking to suspects and witnesses and doing their best to find the no-good son of a gun. But my dad is on the case. He'll find her or him. Of that I have no doubt."

"I like hearing that."

"I'd rather hear about you and your musical triumphs. My life is boring."

"That should only be the case. I'll fill you in on everything when I get home. I want to run something by you next time we talk, but right now, it's almost three a.m., and I need to get some sleep after all the excitement of almost being a blackmail victim."

"Can't you tell me now?"

"Can't. I'm walking toward my bed now. I'll call in a few days, or you can call me."

"Okay, have a good rest."

"Love you."

"Love you too."

Rosemaria almost melted into her chair. Her backbone disappeared, and she felt limp as a dishrag. That's what he did to her every time she heard his voice. She needed to block all that out and concentrate on the footage of the fund raiser. She'd been through it twice and hadn't seen anything unusual. It was probably her imagination that there was something to find.

Kirsten knocked on her side of the room-divider door, opened it, and stuck her head in. "Are you and Suzi about ready to go downstairs?"

"In a second." Rosemaria wheeled herself over to her electric glide and maneuvered into position. Kirsten waited patiently, knowing Rosemaria liked to do it herself. They went into the hallway, left the door open, and waited by the elevator.

"Are you expecting any visitors today?" Kirsten asked.

"Not as far as I know. Maybe someone will surprise me."

The elevator door opened, and two guards assigned to wheel Suzi's cage downstairs and onto the patio stepped out. As they headed inside Rosemaria's suite, one of them said, "Suzi will be down in a minute. Last time she chewed us out all the way downstairs, telling us to get off the couch."

Rosemaria and Kirsten took their places in the elevator. "I'm trying to teach her something new and useful besides 'Can I get you anything,' but it's not working," Rosemaria said. "The last one to teach her anything before that was one of Josh's old girlfriends. She must have said 'I want to win the lottery' about a million times for it to sink into Suzi's memory bank."

The doors closed, and Kirsten whispered, "I think you're the one who's won the lottery."

Rosemaria agreed.

Alone out on the patio, Rosemaria settled in on her favorite cozy lounge chair in the shade with her laptop, cell phone, and lemonade on the table beside her. Suzi fluffed her wings, enjoying the fresh air, and chipped away at a treat attached to the cage. "This is the life, huh, girl? Don't get used to it."

"Don't get used to what?" Larry stepped through the open French doors and swooped down to plant a kiss on her forehead.

"To what do I owe the pleasure?" she asked as he sat opposite her.

"You know. I was in the neighborhood—"

"Yeah, right. Lay it on me. Is the news good or bad? Full report."

"No 'hello, how are you, how's the family?'"

"Now you've made me feel bad. Yes, how are Vanessa and your darling baby girl, Melissa?"

"They are excellent, and you'll be seeing Vanessa soon. She's now part of Loretta's women's group that meets here every month."

"I believe Loretta did mention that. I may even be able to come downstairs since the odds of finding my killer among a group of young Beverly Hills matrons who are dedicating their lives to charity is rather small."

"I'm totally in favor of that. Now, my report as you requested."

"Yes?" Rosemaria said impatiently.

"Your father and Jimmy struck gold their second day in in Sisters. Someone recognized Stacey as a jewelry maker who has a bimonthly concession stand at the arts and crafts fair where she sells her jewelry. Somebody else said she also comes into town occasionally for supplies with someone they assume is her husband. So, the question is, do they wait a few more days to see if one of them shows up, or do they give up for now and wait for the fair? I told them to stay a couple more days, and then they can leave and concentrate on finding Keith, Maisie, and Mariah. What do you think."

"I agree. What about the other team? Are they on to anybody else after talking to Micco?"

"They did. And there's good news and bad news. They found Lorna working at the Wynn Hotel in Las Vegas by looking at the security cameras and using facial recognition software to see if they could find a match. It took over a week, but there she was, working as a cocktail waitress in the casino under a new name and looking very happy."

"And the bad news?"

"Before Mack and Loshi got to Vegas, she had disappeared."

"Oh no."

"Her purse is gone, but her car is still in the carport, and it doesn't look like she took any clothes with her."

"Maybe she's shacked up somewhere with a boyfriend," Rosemaria suggested, not believing a word of it.

"Her boss says she's as reliable as clockwork, but she hasn't been to work for a couple of days and didn't call in sick. She has friends and coworkers who care about her, and they're very worried. They say this is not like her. They think something must have happened to her."

"Damn. Do you think she's still alive?"

"She hasn't shown up in the morgue or any hospital yet. So that's a good thing."

"And she looked happy?"

"Very. Barely making it, but she's settled in, making something of her life. But if the bad guys are after her, they think she knows something."

"There's something else. Sherilyn is refusing to talk to Mack and Loshi. They called her at the agency and wanted to ask her more questions over the phone. She said she's done answering questions and hung up on them."

"Will they bring her in as a material witness and question her?"

"On what grounds? We can't prove she has any useful information."

"Maybe she was threatened. I'll call her and see if she'll talk to me."

"You can try." He stood up. "Well, it was good seeing you and Suzi are getting acclimated to the good life, but I have to get back to work. I'm sorry I didn't have better news. With any luck, sounds like your dad and Jimmy are close to finding the nature lovers."

After he left, Rosemaria tried to concentrate on reading the cases Karen had sent her. She wouldn't be prosecuting any of them—her friends and colleagues Reid and Terrance would—but maybe she could find some bit of incriminating evidence they had overlooked. She knew perfectly well, of course, that would be interfering, and even though they would act polite and patient, they wouldn't appreciate it one iota. Nevertheless, pretending to be helpful gave her something to do. She blew out a mouthful of air in frustration. In a little over a week, Josh would be home, and her ankle should be healed. She would be able to ease her way back into the courthouse work schedule, and life would be back to normal, albeit with a bodyguard hovering over her at all times. It wouldn't be Kirsten or Cameron but a male already handpicked by Cameron—a big, burly, dangerous-looking man named Abe Gwaltney, according to the photo and description Cameron had shown her. Rosemaria thought that was a little sexist, but Josh didn't care. He had talked to Cameron, unbeknownst to her, and said he wanted the best and the biggest guard for Rosemaria. So that was that. No use arguing. If it was only her life in danger, she would have protested, but since she was with Josh so much of the time, his life might be in danger as well. She'd go to the ends of the earth and agree to anything to protect him.

The heat made her sleepy, and she found herself nodding off while composing an opening statement to one of her cases that was now Reid's, which would never be heard in court. She fumbled for her cell phone when it rang.

"This is Rosemaria."

"Is this Rosemaria Baker?" The voice was deep with a Latino accent.

"Yes, this is she."

"This is Santiago Medina. I work security at the Wynn and Encore Hotels in Las Vegas."

Rosemaria's entire body went on high alert. "Yes?"

"I have someone here who would like to talk to you."

Rosemaria waited, holding her breath.

"Hello? Am I talking to Rosemaria Baker?" The soft voice quavered.

"Yes. Whom do I have the pleasure of talking to?"

"This is Lorna Selverino."

Rosemaria almost dropped her phone. She took a moment to compose herself. "Lorna, it's so good to hear your voice. Are you okay?"

"Yes, I'm with my friend Santiago. He works at the Wynn where I was working up until two days ago." She began to sniffle.

"I'm so sorry you lost your job. How can I help?"

"I remember you from years ago. You seemed so nice and like you really cared about finding out who killed Ramin. And then you were going to help David."

"Where have you been for the past two days?"

"Well—"

"Go ahead. You can tell me."

She spoke nonstop in one long desperate narration. "Two nights ago, someone was waiting for me inside my apartment. I knew someone was there because the match I put in the door was gone. So I ran and hid in my neighbor's backyard. The dog started barking and woke everybody up. Then I went inside, and they let me call Santiago, and he came and got me. But he lives with his mom, and I can't stay here, and I don't know where to go."

"First of all, putting the match there was very smart. Second, you need to have Santiago take you to the police station and report this."

"I can't do that. If I go, I can't prove anything happened or who did it or tell them why. Then whoever is trying to kill me will know where I am if I go back home, and I can't stay with Santiago any longer."

"The police will put you in protective custody."

"They won't because they won't believe me. I'll have Santiago and his mom go get my car, and then I'll just drive as far away from Vegas as I can get."

"No. You can't do that. I'll help you. Don't worry. Let me talk to Santiago again."

He got on the phone. "Hello."

"Listen, Santiago, I'm going to ask you some questions about Lorna. You can answer yes or no. Have you known her for the entire time she's worked at the Wynn, and do you trust her?"

"Yes, and yes. Very much so."

"You think she's honest?"

"Of course. My mom likes her very much and is very worried about her. She's even a better judge of character than me."

"Do you have feelings for this girl?"

"Yes, but I haven't told her."

"Would you be able to get a couple of days off and drive Lorna to LA? If you do, I have a place where she can stay."

"I will do that. Where is it?"

"It's my father's house in Simi Valley. Let me call him and make sure it's okay. He might not be home when you get there, but if it's okay with him, I'll tell you where the key is. My dad's a cop. She might be alone for a couple of days before he comes home, but no one will guess she's there."

"I will be happy to do all that for Lorna."

"Good. If my dad says okay, I'll call you as soon as I hear from him and text you the address."

"This is very kind of you, Ms. Baker."

"How did you get my cell phone number?"

"Your landline is listed, and I guess you have it forwarded to this number."

"Oh. Okay."

"Tell Lorna she's going to be safe very soon."

She hung up and wondered how she was going to break it to her dad that one of the witnesses he was looking for was going to be a houseguest. She thought he might think it was rather convenient. If she knew her father, he would get Lorna to open up about everything she knew as kindly and effortlessly as convincing a kitten to eat her gourmet dinner. She also thought she'd better tell Cameron she had forwarded her phone to her cell weeks ago, and maybe, security wise, it was not such a good idea anymore.

* * * * *

It was the third and last day of the Sisters stakeout, and the intrepid detectives were beginning to lose hope of ever catching sight of Stacey and Sam. They were seated side by side on a bench in a small park across from a souvenir store drinking cold drinks from Starbucks.

"I don't want to admit defeat, do you?" Jimmy said.

"We may be at the point of diminishing returns, my friend."

Jimmy sucked on his straw. "You may be right."

"You know what cops used to say in old 1930s movies when their feet hurt?" Steven asked.

"No."

"My dogs are barking. I've always wanted to say that."

"You can say it now."

"Well, they used to say it in that New York accent cops had in those old movies. But anyway, my dogs are barking."

"Mine too. Every dog and puppy in my feet is barking."

Jimmy looked around lazily. "Let's sit here for a while. Maybe she'll walk by."

Steven jumped to his feet and was staring straight ahead. "She just did. Or, I mean, drove. That's her in that broken-down Chevy. I'm sure of it. She's hardly changed. Go get the car. I'll keep following on foot."

Jimmy was startled into inaction.

"Hurry!"

Jimmy leaped off the bench and ran down the block and around the corner to where they were parked on the street. Steven walked quickly, trying to be unobtrusive in case she looked in the rearview mirror. Jimmy pulled up in the car beside him, Steven jumped in the car, and the chase or, considering the slow traffic, the crawl was on.

"Stay a couple of car lengths behind."

"She doesn't' know who we are," Jimmy reminded him.

"You're right. Just don't lose her."

They came to another red traffic light, and Stacey and the traffic stopped outright. Steven's phone rang.

"Yes, daughter. You caught me at a really bad time."

Rosemaria was still on her lounge chair on the patio. "Sorry, but I have a question for you. Lorna was in Vegas, was chased by someone who was waiting for her in her apartment, now she's on the run, and I told her she could stay in your house for a few days."

"Say again?"

"Lorna Selverino. One of the people we've been looking for. She's a nice girl. I'll vouch for her. If she steals the silverware, I'll pay for it. And I need an answer now."

The light turned green, and cars started moving. "All my valuables are in the Reno house. The only things of importance to me are some of your school mementos. If she takes those, you don't have to pay me."

"Does that mean the answer is yes?"

"Yes, now let me get back to my high-speed chase through the mountains." He clicked off.

Rosemaria looked puzzled, then dialed Santiago and told him the good news.

Lorna came on, crying. "Thank you so much, Ms. Baker. We will leave right now."

"The spare key is hidden under a fake rock just to the left of the stairs. I'll text you the address. Call me when you get there."

"I will."

Rosemaria clicked off and smiled. It was so good to be in on the action. But what was that about her dad being involved in a high-speed chase? Probably hyperbole considering the small town he was staked out in. Nevertheless, she wondered what the heck was going on. She wouldn't tell Larry about Lorna just yet. If he didn't know where Lorna was, he couldn't be blamed for not reporting it to Loshi and Mack. She wanted her dad to have a crack at Lorna first.

Jimmy was managing to stay two cars behind Stacey even though traffic was speeding up.

"I'll call the sheriff's office and let them know we're following her," he said. He punched buttons on the dashboard screen and waited a couple of seconds. "Yeah, this is Detective Jimmy Waite of the Beverly

Hills Police Department and my associate Steven Baker. We're following Stacey Fields in a gray Chevy right now. We're almost to the south end of town heading for Three Creeks Road, I think."

A female voice answered. "The sheriff is out of the office."

"Okay, tell him when you reach him. He can call us on this number." Jimmy clicked off. "This is exciting. Think they'll shoot at us when we get to wherever?"

"I hope not. Is your gun loaded, Barney?"

"Make fun all you want. I practice once a week and hit the target every time."

"Better unlock the glove compartment so we're ready just in case she starts firing."

"You forgot to remind me to bring the bulletproof vests."

"I'll use you as cover."

Stacey turned right off Three Creeks Road onto a two-lane highway, then left up a hill that ran alongside a narrow creek. There were no longer any other cars in front of them, so Steven slowed down, staying far behind Stacey. They drove for another half hour, and he couldn't see any more road signs. He looked over at Jimmy who had the GPS on the screen. "Do you know where we are?"

"Up shit's creek, I would say. No, really, I'll let the sheriff know where to meet us."

Steven was afraid to fall too far behind Stacey in case she made another turn, and he asked Jimmy to speed up to be closer. If she saw them, so be it. If they had her in custody, they could get Sam. She turned right on a bumpy road that must be shaking the daylights out of Stacey's old Chevy. Jimmy stayed close. By now, she was sure to have seen them. "Call the sheriff again and let them know we may be following on foot soon."

Jimmy dialed the number, and again, the sheriff wasn't there. "Okay," he said. "We are near something called Malone's Point. The road is now almost nonexistent. She knows we're behind her but hasn't acknowledged us. If she starts hiking, we'll follow"

The female voice answered. "I'll let the sheriff and the deputies know where you are."

"Thanks, no problem." He clicked off and looked at the GPS. "It looks like there aren't any roads around here. We're in the wilderness now, city boy."

"Look who's talking."

"They were half a city block behind Stacey as her truck disappeared behind trees and brush. Her brake lights told them she had stopped and was probably getting out. They grabbed their Glocks from the glove compartment, ready to follow her. Jimmy felt his cell phone vibrate. It was the sheriff; the text message said something about being at a traffic accident on the 20. Jimmy gave him their coordinates and assured him they wouldn't try to apprehend the subjects themselves.

As they got closer to Stacey, they could hear her breathing heavily. She was wearing clothes and shoes fit for a mountain climb, carrying a backpack. She kept walking as fast as she could, never looking behind her. The detectives stayed several yards back.

Stacey and the detectives kept walking. Stacey was showing no signs of slowing down.

"She's in better shape than we are," Jimmy whispered.

"She's been doing this for a few years, if Veronica is correct."

"Bless that Veronica. She got us this far."

"She's leading us straight to her boyfriend. Where's the loyalty?"

"Maybe she's leading us on a wild goose chase while he does a runner."

They came to a clearing, and Stacey made a beeline for the far end where the forest began again on an incline. The detectives let her gain some ground until she reached the trees, then half ran to catch up. They lost her, then spied a small cabin halfway up the hill. Stacey had disappeared.

"What if they both take off in the other direction before the sheriff gets here?" Jimmy said. "We can't let them get away when we're this close."

"You're right. I'll move around to the side to make sure they don't go out the back through a window. You stay here." Steven stepped away from Jimmy, moving from tree to tree, doing his best to stay hidden. A rifle shot rang out, and the detectives hit the ground. The bullet hit a tree inches away from Steven's face.

"Stay down!" Steven said. "Don't fire."

Another shot rang out, and they saw Stacey and Oliver running from the back of the cabin up the hill.

"Let's go!" Steven was up and running, and Jimmy was not far behind.

They lost sight of the couple, then saw, a split second early, that Sam had stopped and was about to fire again. The detectives dove in front of a rock as bullets passed over their heads. Steven got out his Glock and saw Jimmy had done the same, "Fire to warn, not hit!" Then he yelled at the fleeing witnesses, "Stop shooting! We're police officers. We're not here to harm you!"

Sam ran higher up the hill. They saw Stacey, exhausted from the climb, barely able to keep up. They heard boots crashing through the underbrush and suddenly found themselves in the company of three young sheriff's deputies. "What's all the shooting about, gentlemen?" one of them asked.

"The guy is running, leaving his girlfriend behind, and firing on us every chance he gets."

"Wait here," one of the other deputies said. "We'll catch his ass."

Only too happy to comply, the detectives watched as the deputies easily caught up to Stacey, said something to her, and kept going after Sam. Neither detective gave him much of a chance to escape. They took the time to catch their breath and watched as Stacey came stumbling down the hill toward them. "I'm supposed to stay with you or be arrested for fleeing the scene of a crime," she said, her face crumpled in defeat.

The three of them looked up the hill as they listened to a volley of gunfire, then total silence. "I don't think we'll have to wait long," Jimmy said. He found himself a comfortable tree stump, sat down, and took out his phone. "Cell phone coverage ended a long ways back," he said to Stacey. "I guess you couldn't warn him we were coming."

"We have CB radios in the car and cabin, but they're broken," Stacey said. "That's part of the reason I was in town." She walked away from them and sat on the stairs going up to the front porch, not in the mood to talk.

After several minutes, the detectives saw the deputies through the trees at the top of the hill with Sam, his hands cuffed behind him. One of the deputies was carrying Sam's rifle. When they reached the cabin, Stacey stood up and tried to move close to Sam. A deputy stopped her.

He addressed the detectives. "We'll process these two and lock them up at the station. Why don't you come by in about three hours, and you can have your chat? Meanwhile, this guy is looking at being charged with attempted murder of police officers. He won't be getting out for a while. The girl faces charges of aiding and abetting and failure to cooperate with law enforcement. She'll get bail tomorrow if she can afford it." Sam kept his mouth shut as the deputy shoved him past the detectives, and Stacey, sulking, trailed behind them.

The detectives looked at each other.

"That went well," Jimmy said.

"It looks like manhunts are your forte. I will write you up a commendation."

"It won't mean a whole lot coming from a pensioner, but thanks anyway."

Steven shrugged. "I offered. At least we can now finally enjoy a relaxing meal knowing the escapees are locked up."

"Sounds good," Jimmy said. "Lead the way, buddy."

"It may be slow going back to the car. Don't tell Rosemaria my bad knee is acting up."

* * * * *

Maisie Tomlin had been under their noses the entire time. She was a broken, toothless crone at age forty-two. Meth, heroine, crack, and whatever else had taken their toll. She was barely alive and had been sleeping in a small tent on an overpass above the Hollywood Freeway. A good Samaritan had found her collapsed on the street and taken her to a shelter on Hollywood Boulevard, where a volunteer had persuaded her to give him her real name. In short order, the cops were notified, and her presence at the shelter reported to Larry and the BHPD, and then he called Andy

Mack. Mack and Loshi had driven up from San Diego to question her, but when they saw her lying in her bed at County Hospital, they knew she was beyond being questioned and probably not long for this world. She had an IV in her arm, wires taped to her chest, and an oxygen tube in her nose. Nevertheless, the nurse gave them permission to sit by her bedside and attempt to get something out of her before she passed.

Maisie looked up at them with rheumy eyes and seemed confused, as if she was trying to place them. "Keith?" she whispered, looking at Mack.

He decided to play the card he was dealt. "I'm here to make sure they treat you right, Maisie."

She attempted a feeble smile and strained to speak. "I always knew you'd come back. Where did you go?" Saying just a few sentences exhausted her, and she closed her eyes, then stared up at the ceiling for a few seconds before looking back at Mack.

"I went where I usually used to go, Maisie. You remember where."

She struggled to come back from the blackness that was slowly creeping down from the ceiling to her bedside. She tried to back away from the advancing shadow. "No. No. Not now." Her eyes filled with tears.

"I'm here now, Maisie. I won't leave you again."

She peered at him through tortured eyes. "I don't believe you. You promised that before."

"But I always came back."

"Were you with her?" Pain deeper than the pain of her addiction clawed its way to the surface.

"No, I wasn't with her."

"You were. I know it."

"Who do you think I was with, Maisie?"

"That-that, scary woman I hated. You know who." She closed her eyes and seemed to stop breathing. The detectives were afraid they had lost her, but she opened her eyes again. Hate and anger were keeping her going.

"She was mean to me, but you liked her. I know you did. You gave her free rent. Don't think I don't know because I do." Betrayal, hurt, and loathing shone on her face and emanated from her like a poisonous cloud.

"Who are you talking about, Maisie?"

"That awful woman, that's who. She stole you and sent me away. And you didn't care."

"I'm sorry. I didn't mean to do that."

Maisie was gasping for air. The detectives wondered if they should call the nurse. But she was making a supreme effort to reach out to Mack. "Hold my hand, Keith. Please? I'm sorry. I need you. Don't go away again."

Mack took her hand, which felt as if it was made of chicken bones and parchment paper. "I'm here, Maisie. Just rest. We'll talk later. I'll be here."

Mack wanted to cry. Forty-two years old and she was dying of old age. She squeezed his hand hard and gazed at him with all the love she could muster. In a split second, her eyes filled with dread, she began gasping for air, and her entire body shuddered. A sound came out of her mouth, and then her body relaxed, and she stared sightlessly up at the ceiling. Her grip on Mack's hand loosened, and he knew she was gone. The heart monitor flatlined. He sat there, still holding her hand, not having the will to let go. Loshi didn't say a word and bowed his head.

They sat there like that for five minutes, even as the nurse came in and turned off the monitors. There was no point in taking extraordinary measures to bring her back. She had no life, even when she was alive, and no family to make demands on her behalf. Mack slowly let go of Maisie's hand and wiped his face. He was surprised to find it wet. He stood up and nodded at the nurse, then at Loshi, and the two of them headed for the door, but they couldn't help but look back one more time at Maisie who, they hoped, had finally found peace.

They were seated in a booth in a dark but clean bar on Hollywood Boulevard. Glasses of beer were on the table in front of them, but they weren't drinking and weren't talking. Loshi knew Mack had taken Maisie's death hard. She had needed someone to hold on to when she passed, and Mack had made himself available, not just as a cop hoping to get answers but as a human being. He'd never look at Mack the same way again. He waited patiently. He'd let Mack speak when he felt like it.

After several minutes of staring into their beers, Mack finally spoke.

"That was hard."

"It was."

I felt like a chump tricking her like that."

"She needed Keith, and you were him. You gave her comfort."

"I hope there's heaven."

"Yeah. She'll be there."

"I guess we need to talk about what she said."

"When you're ready."

"I am."

"I wonder who the scary woman is. Has to be somebody in the house. She got free rent."

"And she hung out with that cheating bastard, Keith."

"We really need to talk to Sherilyn."

Loshi's phone buzzed. He answered. "Loshi. . . . Yeah? . . . Wow. . . . I'm with him now. I'll tell him. He looked at Mack and clicked off. "That was Coleman. Baker and Waite found Oliver and Fields in Oregon and got shot at for their trouble. They're going to question them in about an hour."

"Good on them."

"You're not envious?"

"Not at all. Maisie, bless her dear heart, gave us a lead and we didn't even have to get shot at."

CHAPTER SEVENTEEN

The interrogation room in the sheriff's station was small, painted a dingy gray, with enough room for a table and three or four chairs and not much else. It was not meant to be comfortable. It was meant to encourage people to spill their guts so everybody could leave the room as soon as possible. Steven and Jimmy aimed to make Stacey's stay as uncomfortable as they could. They decided to talk to her first because they figured she was likely to give them something to compare with what Sam might say and undermine his credibility if he chose to talk. She sat across the table from Steven with Jimmy and Sheriff Macklemore, a gray-haired, granite-faced man in his 50s, sitting a few feet back. She had her head bowed, and her mouth was set in a tight straight line. Her attitude hadn't changed since she stopped talking to them up at the cabin.

Looking at her closely, Steven saw that even though she had the same short brown hair and pretty face as in the old photograph, the years had taken their toll. Shadows under her blue eyes and deep lines etched on either side of her mouth spoke of ten years spent on the run, rarely free of fear. He sat quietly and waited until Stacey registered acute discomfort at the silence and spoke, looking at Steven defiantly. "I know I don't have to say anything and can ask for a lawyer."

"Yes, you have that right. Would you like to call your lawyer now?"

"You'd have to be pretty stupid not to know I don't have one."

"In that case, if you ask for a lawyer, you will remain incarcerated here until such time as we can transport you to Bend, where you will be arraigned in court and have the opportunity to request a court-appointed attorney. If you choose to talk to us now, we will evaluate your part in your boyfriend's attempted murder of law enforcement officers, not charge you with any crime, and allow you to go free, but you must remain in the area as a material witness." Steven sat back and waited, showing little interest in her choice. Jimmy and the sheriff remained impassive as well.

Stacey fidgeted in her chair and looked on the verge of tears. "You mean, if I agree to testify against Sam, I can go free?"

"Possibly. Depending on what you tell us."

"But I didn't know he was going to shoot at anybody. And he had no intention of hitting you."

"If you are giving up your right to a lawyer, we have Miranda papers for you to sign confirming your decision. If you are not giving up that right, you need not say another word." He stared at her with a face set in granite. The gravitas of all three men aimed in her direction was having an effect.

"I-I . . . want to talk," she stuttered. "No lawyer."

The sheriff was ready with the papers for her to sign. He leaned forward and placed them on the table along with a pen. She pulled them close to her, looked them over briefly, and signed. Steven handed them back to the sheriff.

"I'd like to go back to the beginning, Stacey." Steven's voice had not softened. "You left Los Angeles in the middle of a semester, changed your name, and ended up in a cabin in the woods. Why?"

Stacey was hesitating, looking for answers to give, but Steven wasn't having any of it.

"Answer my questions truthfully, or you are on your way to Bend."

Stacey's resolve crumbled. Her will was no match for the three men staring at her, devoid of any sympathy. "The beginning," she said. "I guess I'll start with moving into that filthy house, where I never wanted to live."

"Go on," Steven said. "Tell us what happened."

"It was cheap, and we were working at menial jobs to pay for school—just community college, but we figured that somehow, we'd get scholarships to a four-year school. We were doing well and avoiding the drugs that were all over the house. Ramin wasn't into drugs, and Sherilyn, who used to stay with him, wasn't either, but everybody else was. I just tried to avoid them all."

"What changed?"

"Mariah moved in."

"How did that change things?"

"She was weird." Stacey was searching for the right words. "She was pretty but very cold. She avoided the women, but if she needed or wanted something, she knew how to play a man to get it." Her mouth turned down in disgust. "I'm pretty sure Keith didn't make her pay rent, and because Micco was so good looking, she went after him in the most blatant way. And I think he caved in, but she'd never stick with someone poor like him. The funny thing is the two men who were rich, Ramin and David, didn't want anything to do with her. I heard her tell Clyde that she was going to make it big in the design business and make a lot of money. It was her goal to be incredibly wealthy."

"Is there anything else you can tell us about her?"

"She just had a presence. It's hard to explain. She could be friendly one minute and the next minute act like you didn't exist. The whole atmosphere in the house was like there was a demon living there."

"That demon wasn't Clyde and his drug dealing?'

"Not even close. It was her."

"Then Ramin was killed."

"Yeah. Finding David there was pretty incriminating, but none of us believed he was guilty. After he was arrested, we all got phone calls warning us to leave. Micco left right after he had a suspicious car accident, and we took off after I got shoved into traffic. It was obvious whoever was threatening us wasn't kidding around."

"What do you think the killer thinks you know?"

"That's what's so strange. None of us know anything about the murder. We told the first female cop who talked to us, who was in uniform, that we didn't think it was David, but the detectives didn't care. If the first cop had come back before I left, I might have told her I suspected Mariah, but after the phone calls, I was too scared."

"How soon did Mariah leave?"

"Right after the female policewoman talked to us. She left the house the next day, and I never saw her again."

"Sam seems desperate not to talk to us. Do you know why?"

"You have to ask him. He avoids talking about anything that happened in that house. He'll have to tell you himself if he knows anything."

Steven turned to the other men. "Is there anything you'd like to ask Stacey?"

Jimmy nodded. "When the two of you ran from the cabin and he grabbed his rifle, didn't you suspect that he was going to use it?"

"No! I promise you. I'd never seen him shoot at a human being before ever. I never thought he'd do that. You have to believe me."

Steven looked at the sheriff, who shook his head.

"Stacey, as a material witness, you'll have to stay in the Sisters area. If you flee, there will be a warrant issued for your arrest, and you'll be immediately incarcerated."

"I won't run. I'm done with that."

"All right. You can go. We'll be talking to Sam next, but he's facing charges of attempted murder. If he asks for a lawyer, we'll be taking him to Bend for arraignment. Do you have money to stay in town? The cabin may not be safe."

"I have money."

"All right." Steven put his card on the table, and she picked it up. "Detective Waite and I will be leaving town tomorrow, but we'll be back for Sam's trial, which may not happen for several months. Call me or call the sheriff if you feel like you're in danger."

Stacey made a move to stand up. "So, I can go?"

"You can."

She quickly walked out the door without another glance at the men in the room.

"Interesting stuff about Mariah. I don't think Stacey knows anything, but I have a feeling Sam does," Jimmy said. "Let's see if he has anything to say."

"Let him sit and stew overnight, shall we?" Sheriff Macklemore said. "I know of a great place to have lunch." He smiled. "It's on the department."

That sounded agreeable to everyone, and they were more than happy to leave the claustrophobic but productive room behind.

* * * *

"I'm sorry I haven't come sooner, and I have no good excuse."

Vanessa and Rosemaria were seated facing each other across the coffee table in the sunroom. Much of the furniture was white wicker, which might have seemed dated in an ordinary house, but here, in this expansive room, filled with light from several floor-to-ceiling windows framed on either side by exquisite tall blue drapes with gold threads woven through the fabric, tied back with gold ties, the effect was the height of fashionable decor. There were a variety of palms planted in large blue pots reaching toward the light shining down from the glass ceiling. Flowers spilling from large vases added to the effect of well-being and comfort. They were sipping lemonade from crystal glasses.

"You've called several times to check up on me. That's good enough. I know you were keeping your distance in case you might catch a stray bullet aimed in my direction."

"I know it's crazy, and I'm over it now." Vanessa shook her head. "When you first got shot and I thought you weren't going to make it, I was devastated. I thought what if you died, and what if I had been with you? What if my daughter had lost her mother? All I wanted to do was stay at home with Melissa and shut out the world and all the violence, which is highly impractical when you're married to a cop. For not the first time since I married Larry, it hit me how close all of you are every day to losing your lives. And I didn't dare share any of this with him. What was he going to do—quit his job because I was having a prolonged panic attack? I just kept it to myself and pretended nothing was happening in my screwed-up brain."

"That's some confession, girlfriend." Rosemaria smiled. "And Larry is not close to death every time he goes to work. Most cops retire without ever having used their gun except at the shooting range and never get shot at. Some of us just seem to attract nut cases even when we're not cops anymore. But, trust me, I am an exception, okay?"

"I'm so sorry. I was a terrible friend."

"You weren't," Rosemaria assured her. "So now you ventured out to visit me in my fortress?"

"Well, as you know, Loretta is having a meeting Wednesday of the junior board of the Beverly Hills Charity Guild, which was partly responsible for the fundraiser that raised several million dollars for the art museum. And now, wonder of wonders, this one-time poverty-stricken actress finds herself a part of that illustrious group, so I'll be here Wednesday." She smiled. "First you don't see me at all. Now you can't get rid of me."

Rosemaria rubbed her hands together gleefully. "And it looks like Cameron, my chief bodyguard, is going to allow me to come down for the meeting. I'm not a rich Beverly Hills matron, of course, but I get to listen and eat all the great food."

"I know. Loretta told me. I'm so happy you'll be there. I still feel a little out of place."

"You do know how rich you are, right? Larry would happily move you into a house three times the size of the one you live in if you asked him."

"Oh God, no!" Vanessa was horrified. "The one we're in now is big enough for a family of ten. I don't know how people live in houses like this one. I prefer cozy to grand."

Rosemaria pointed her forefinger at her. "And that is why Larry loves you so much. But I'm sure there's a lot of other things he likes about you."

"I don't kiss and tell."

"Get your mind out of the bedroom, and let's talk about what fun we're going to have after we catch the evildoer. And I hope it's soon because I'm running out of names for the creep."

"Speaking of which, Josh and Larry have been making plans to keep you safe after he comes home, and I've been helping. He said it was okay to tell you, by the way."

"And what kind of mischief is being planned behind my back?"

Josh wants the two of you to move into a doorman building with a lot of security, so Larry and I have been looking online for the perfect place."

"A doorman building? Isn't that a little pricey?

"The song he wrote for Joell is going to reach number one any minute, and he's getting a lot of money for the tour. Am I paying more attention to your swelling bank account than you?"

"I guess you are. Josh forwarded our mail to Ken's office, and Jenny's been taking care of the paychecks and bills. And where is this building we're supposedly moving into?"

It's on Burton Way in Beverly Hills. There's at least three we're looking at. I'm going to send you pictures so you can decide which one you like after I narrow it down a little and go in person for a look-see."

"I'd be living a few blocks from the police station."

"Is that a problem?"

"Are you kidding? I love it. It will only take me a couple of minutes to drive over there to bother them in person if I need their help with a case . . . or to offer to help them."

Vanessa hesitated a moment too long. "I'm sure they'll appreciate that."

"I caught that. But we only have Salvation Army furniture. Will we be allowed to move in?"

"Don't be silly. I'm looking at furniture as well. Not a lot, just a few necessary pieces. I'll help you decorate later. So, are you happy? You're not mad we planned all this behind your back?"

"You and Josh figured I'd make a fuss and say we couldn't afford it, didn't you? Well, I'll wait and see what you come up with and just how much our back account has swelled. Okay?"

"Okay. I thought I'd soften you up before Josh tells you."

"Things are changing in our lives. I know that. I'm not going to hold him back. I just would like to live to see him win his first Grammy."

Vanessa shuddered. "Don't talk like that. You'll force me back into my shell."

"I'm sorry. I'm kidding." Rosemaria lifted her glass up in a toast, and they clinked glasses. "Just wait until this scuzzball has to face off with a *real* Beverly Hills housewife. He or she won't know what hit him or her."

CHAPTER EIGHTEEN

The self-described ice woman loved going to Sade's salon on Rodeo Drive. She could easily afford to pay the most exclusive hairdresser in town to come to her condo and do her hair. But her home was her sanctuary. No one was invited there, ever. Except, of course, her fiancé and her servants. She never had to wait at Sade's. She was always treated like a queen, and why not? She doubted if anyone tipped as exorbitantly as she did.

As soon as the lady ice walked through the door, the sycophants showed her to her chair in the back of the salon, fetched her tea, placed her handbag in a small safe under the counter, and led her to the shampoo area. Then Sade, a tall, thin, woman in her thirties with a heavy French accent and a bit of an attitude, which was acceptable since she was so talented, would do her magic, snipping and combing until the ice woman's layers were trimmed to perfection. Then the famous Sade blowout. No one could wield a blow dryer like Sade. When ice lady walked out of the salon, ready to meet one of her business contacts in one of the many trendy indoor/outdoor restaurants on Rodeo or Beverly, she felt like a million bucks, which she was easily worth.

Today, the lady was doing a little shopping in preparation for her committee meeting on Wednesday. She had to look the part of a modest young woman who was overwhelmed at once more visiting the Collins mansion. The first time she was there, along with over two hundred guests and almost as many waitstaff, the target had been nowhere in sight. But it was obvious from the strictly guarded elevator and stairs that she was somewhere in the house.

This time, she had a feeling that, because only a few successful young female entrepreneurs would be in attendance, the curious Ms. Baker might very well make an appearance. What could be less threatening than a meeting of Mrs. Collins' fellow committee board members? If she was right, she would be up close and personal with the target and would immediately see in her eyes if there was a hint of recognition. But it didn't really matter if the target didn't know her from Adam. Now that Baker and the other detectives were determined to track her down, this one had to go. Being educated in the ways of the internet and learning every detail of a person's life, she knew Baker was driven and would never let go of the case until she solved it. After Baker was dead, the rest of them she could easily handle. Four bumbling detectives and a wannabe. Child's play. She would lead them down the garden path with so many false clues they'd never figure things out. But Baker—she was trouble. She was also on track to become very dead.

* * * * *

"You look beautiful," Kirsten exclaimed. "Wow! All I've ever seen you in are sweatpants and a T-shirt. And you actually put on makeup. I can't even see your bruises."

Rosemaria was standing in her glide, wearing the dress Vanessa had sent over and insisted she wear. Since they were the same size, it fit perfectly.

"I couldn't let all those rich women show me up, could I? Too bad you have to wear a uniform and pack a gun."

"I'm not a guest; I'm on the job. I have been ordered by my boss to be as unobtrusive as possible but close by. I don't want to put a damper on the proceedings."

"I have no doubt that Cameron will have his eye on me every minute, seeing as all these dangerous females are invading the mansion."

"One never knows, does one?" Kirsten asked, lifting her eyebrows. "You know that as well as I do."

"Yes, I do, but it would be nice to pretend to have a good time at a glamorous function. It may never happen again."

"My confidential report on you said you hate glamorous functions."

Rosemaria brought her hand to her heart. "Yikes, you found me out. Your dossier is correct, but after being locked away for two weeks, even a plebian such as I find myself longing for some human interaction."

"I won't take that as an insult, and I totally understand. Do you wish to go down now or be fashionably late?"

"I'm always early. It's my fatal flaw."

"Then put your glide in gear, and let's do it."

The meeting was to take place in the massive Collins living room. It consisted of several separate conversational areas, and Rosemaria and Vanessa made themselves comfortable, sipping their drinks by the fireplace. Kirsten stood several feet away near the French doors, seemingly relaxed but always on alert, ready for the unexpected. Rosemaria and Vanessa had come early, and two ladies—Drew Peterson, who looked to be in her twenties with free-swinging, long black hair, and Sophia Infanti, a zaftig dark-haired lady in her thirties—were seated in the other chairs around a coffee table. They had come only a few minutes late, not at all fashionable, almost on time in their world, which was probably why Rosemaria immediately took a liking to them.

Drew was staring at the paintings on the wall near the fireplace with awe. "Can you imagine owning paintings that belong in a museum?"

Vanessa studied the paintings. "I think prints are just as nice. And you can buy whatever you like and not worry about anything happening to them."

"What business are you in, Drew?" Rosemaria asked.

"My best friend and I started an internet site when we were sixteen that was taking business away from Facebook, so they bought us out for ten million dollars a couple of years later. We'd gotten bored with it by then and started working on something else, so selling it was okay."

Rosemaria just about choked on her lemonade. "Sixteen?"

"Yeah, but people a lot younger than us are doing the same kind of thing."

Trying not to be gauche by uttering a loud exclamation, Rosemaria changed the subject. "Are you married?"

Sophia chimed in, "She's being pursued by Alain Gerard, one of the most sought-after interior designers in the country. You'd be lucky to get him if you're looking for someone."

"Uh, we're not in the market for someone right now"—Rosemaria gave Vanessa a look— "but when we're ready, we'll keep him in mind."

"Yeah, but the problem is," Drew complained, "that he gave me hardly any say whatsoever in designing my own house, which was a drag. That's how I met him. He's a few years older than me and treats me like a kid."

"I think you can afford to buy a few nice paintings, though, Drew." Vanessa said. "You should indulge yourself."

Drew laughed. "Yes, I could hang them in my computer room where they wouldn't distract from the overall color scheme of the house."

"At least he cares," Vanessa said. "I could decorate our house with drawings done by grade school kids, and Larry would believe me if I said they were Picassos."

"Let's face it," Rosemaria said. "Some of his paintings look like they were painted by five-year-olds."

Sophia agreed. "So true. I don't understand most of the stuff displayed at the Museum of Modern Art. Crushed soup cans spray-painted purple sitting on pedestals? I mean, really, what is that?"

"Don't let some of the ladies on the committee hear you," Drew said with a twinkle in her eyes. "They love Jackson Pollock, who threw paint on canvases and squished it around with brooms and stuff. We might be thrown off the committee for expressing our true feelings instead of being arbiters of good taste."

Within an hour, most of the ladies on the committee had arrived, and Loretta was standing in front of the fireplace calling everyone to order.

The chatter stopped, and Loretta began to go through the agenda. First, she complimented everyone on the great job they had done organizing the successful fundraiser for the museum, enabling them to acquire several more valuable paintings: including a Jackson Pollock. The four ladies sitting right in front of her had to choke back giggles at hearing that.

Loretta then brought up the next fundraiser, which would take place at the Beverly Wilshire Hotel and would raise money for the various homeless shelters sponsored by the committee. The junior members would be in complete charge of that one, and Loretta said they would all be getting emails asking for ideas on the invitation list, what politicians could be counted on to be there, should it be sit-down or buffet, and a list of other decisions that needed to be made. She would leave it to them to decide who would be the head of the committee.

A PowerPoint presentation had been prepared, and Brent and Max quickly set up a screen in front of the fireplace. The presentation was a montage showing battered women, children with torn clothes and bruises, the shelters that were being sponsored, a list of needs that must be supplied to accommodate the ever-growing number of endangered homeless women, and the cost of building more shelters. The PowerPoint presentation ended, and the mood in the room was somber.

Loretta addressed the group. "Now you know, if you didn't already, that this committee is not about glamour and getting our pictures in the paper; we are about making a difference in the lives of these women and children."

Rosemaria thought to herself, *Why not just have everyone here donate a few million dollars? They'd reach their goal today, here and now, without the necessity of a fundraiser.*

As if she'd read Rosemaria's mind, Loretta continued. "The reason we hold these fundraisers is not only to invite hundreds of wealthy individuals to contribute to our cause but also to get them involved enough to keep giving year after year. We have to make them feel like they are an integral part of our program. Yes, most of us here can afford to give and give generously, and we do, but we need more than that. We need to have the community involved by accepting donations no matter how small to make sure these shelters are maintained long after we are gone."

Everyone applauded enthusiastically, inspired by Loretta's passion for the project. And Rosemaria felt slightly guilty for her doubts about the sincerity of rich people.

When it was finally time for dinner, the dining room was large enough to accommodate half the crowd. Tables had also been set up in the sunroom and outdoors on the patio. Rosemaria glided from the living room to the buffet, then to the sunroom, with Vanessa following, holding two plates of food. Vanessa put the plates down and helped Rosemaria get settled in a chair. She made herself comfortable, chatted with Vanessa about Melissa, and thoroughly enjoyed their dinner.

After the meal and several drinks, everyone was up and mingling, catching up on gossip and welcoming a few new young ladies on the committee. Rosemaria attracted curiosity and attention because of her cast and wrapped ankle, not to mention her interesting mode of transportation. She avoided any explanations except to say she was a houseguest of Loretta. Drew and Sophia stayed close in case anyone might even hint that Rosemaria didn't fit in. She was oddly comforted by their concern. She couldn't help noticing they were both treated with obsequiousness by the other committee members.

At one point during the evening, Vanessa stood close to Rosemaria and whispered, "Drew's boyfriend is not just a famous decorator; he owns twenty design firms all over the US, Europe, and Dubai. Sophia's husband is chairman of Roanoke Pictures."

Rosemaria's mouth hung open. "No way," she whispered back. "But they're so nice."

"Don't look now, but your prejudice is showing."

"I love you and Larry."

"True, but we were friends when I was a poor actress, and you didn't know Larry was loaded when he was your partner."

"I like Loretta and Andrew very much."

"I'll tell you something else. Josh is going to become very successful. The two of you will end up eating in fancy restaurants, and you'll have to join committees like this one just like me."

"That is a cruel thing to say, Vanessa. I'll never be a joiner, and Josh will always rather eat at Veggie Grill."

Rosemaria's cell rang, and she fished it out of her tiny shoulder bag. Vanessa gestured for her to take the call and moved away to mingle. "Yes, Larry."

Larry was in his well-appointed mostly white kitchen holding Melissa while speaking on his cell. "I just wanted you to know that Stacey and Sam were tracked down by your dad and Jimmy. They're both in custody, but Stacey has been named as a material witness and is on her own for now. Mack called and said that they found Maisie in USC County Hospital where she died while they were trying to question her. Mack said her body was riddled with disease from all the drugs she'd been taking. He sounded choked up as he described her."

"It must have been bad. Mack's not the type."

"Must have. Enjoy the party. I've got my hands full here with Vanessa leaving me alone with the daughter."

"You're a good dad, Larry. Bye." She clicked off and mulled over what Larry had told her. It seemed as if the people in the house were being tracked down and maybe eliminated as suspects one by one. Micco was living the good life doing what he dreamed of doing, Sarah was a housewife married to a dentist, Lorna was at that moment headed for her dad's house, and Maisie was dead from abusing her body with drugs. Stacey and Sam were question marks. The others were yet to be found. She had to block it all out of her mind until after the party. For now, she would act the part of a houseguest with nothing on her mind except the women and children who were the focus of this get-together.

By the end of the evening, Rosemaria had met a woman who owned her own real estate company, a woman who insisted Rosemaria must come visit her in her homes in Cannes and Switzerland, someone else who had built her own worldwide import-export business, a woman who was partnered with her husband in a multibillion-dollar hedge fund, and a few wives and girlfriends of political candidates. After saying goodbye to Vanessa and her new best friends Drew and Sophia and expressing her thanks to Loretta, Rosemaria was escorted back to her room by Kirsten and gratefully helped into her wheelchair, where she sat, exhausted and overwhelmed by the display of an overabundance of riches and entitlement. For Rosemaria, the evening had been like entering another world where everything people desired was attainable. There was no want, no need that could not be filled.

You're wrong Loretta, she thought. *If all those women gave only a small portion of their money, the shelters could be funded forever.*

* * * * *

As the ice queen waited for one of Loretta's valets to bring her Mercedes around, she considered what a fun evening it had been. She had several friends on the committee, and her fiancé would be delighted with all the new relationships she was establishing to help him further his career. She had been introduced to the target, who didn't show a glimmer of recognition. After several plastic surgeries, the picture on her driver license showed a much different face than the one the Baker woman had talked to ten years ago and contacts had changed her eye color. If she had been certain the ex-cop would not recognize her when she began this fateful journey, she might never have hired the assassins and left well enough alone. Too late now. She had to chuckle when she saw Baker navigating through the rooms with her injuries on display in her stand-up wheelchair. Next time, Glacé would hire someone who wouldn't miss.

For one brief moment during the evening, she had felt a stab of anxiety as she studied the target. In Baker, she perceived something undefinable—a toughness, an underlying energy force that made her an able opponent. But the ex-cop was working at a disadvantage—she didn't know who she was looking for. On the other hand, the ice queen knew exactly where her target was and that she would most certainly die as soon as she moved out of the Collins mansion. Then she would send the other detectives on a wild-goose chase that would result in dead ends. Those incompetent idiots would never find her. After she had killed Ramin, she'd left clues that led straight to poor, hapless David Marchand, and they'd never bothered to look at anyone else.

Most cops were easily manipulated, but instinctively, she knew the Baker woman did not fall into that category. Glacé had known early in life to leave no clues, have no pictures taken that would come back to bite her. If, in a rare moment of weakness, she felt she had revealed too much to someone, they had been eliminated with no regrets. There was nothing and no one for the cops to find. She knew where the possible witnesses were, and she would take care of them one by one before they could be induced to talk, which was unlikely. But why take a chance? Lorna had somehow escaped, but she would use her contacts to find her. That brainless boob didn't know anything, but she might have been in contact with Clyde, who was the one person she had failed to locate. He was a loose end she couldn't afford to have running around free. With her luck, his drug-dealing pals had killed him a long time ago.

As she tipped the valet, got in her car, and buckled up, the rage that was never too far from the surface began to overtake her good mood. Damn that Baker woman! The ice queen's life had been moving along so beautifully. She was at the pinnacle of her success, and then that pain in the ass Baker had to talk to David and promise she would find the real killer. Why couldn't she just have left well enough alone? Why did she force her to kill the pathetic little twit?

She could still back away, let Baker live, and stop drawing any more attention to herself. That would be the rational thing to do. But she saved her rational decisions for her business dealings. This was different. Suddenly, she was consumed with hatred for that redheaded bitch and all the people in the house in Hollywood who had never believed in her and her dreams. There was no turning back now. She drove through the open gates and onto the streets of Holmby Hills, seething. All enjoyment of the evening had vanished.

CHAPTER NINETEEN

The interrogation room was stifling hot and so small it felt like the walls were closing in on him. Sam Oliver knew he was stuck like a rat in a glue trap. But a rat was the last thing he wanted to be. If he said anything to the cops about Mariah, it was over with him and Stacey, and Mariah would find out, and he was a dead man. If he said nothing, he would end up in jail, and Mariah would find him and have him killed like she did with David. He ran his fingers through his hair and pulled at it hard. How did the cops find them? If they could, so could Mariah.

When he'd met Mariah at age nineteen, he didn't have the brains to recognize a psychopath when he saw one. She was so good at hiding her true nature, she was right up there with Ted Bundy in the charm department. And yet, if he met her for the first time now, he still wouldn't recognize the pure evil she hid underneath layers of beauty and sex. She had all the men enthralled, except for Ramin and David. For some reason, they had been immune and never showed the slightest interest in her. He wondered where the other suckers were: Clyde, Keith, and Micco. They were either dead or in hiding so deep the cops and Mariah would never find them. He looked up as three men walked into the room and the only thought on his mind and the only thing he would say was *lawyer*. But they showed little interest in him as they came through the door. They chatted about their lunch, the weather, the crowds of tourists, and everything but him. What were they playing at?

"I'm not saying anything, and I want a lawyer." Sam said. "I know my rights."

Jimmy sat down at the table in front of Sam, put his laptop down, and opened it. "Okay, that's fine." He clicked on some keys for a few minutes.

"What are you doing?" Sam asked.

"Sorry, I can't talk to you," Jimmy said as Steven whispered something in Sheriff Macklemore's ear.

"What's the timeline on getting Oliver to Bend?" Steven asked.

"We can get him there by five-fifteen tomorrow," Jimmy answered, "which means the court will be closed, and he'll spend the night in jail. He'll be arraigned the next morning on attempted murder charges, at which time he can ask for a court-appointed lawyer. He'll be held with no bail. Then we'll—"

"I didn't try to murder anybody! I was just protecting myself!" Sam sounded desperate.

The sheriff was firm. "Do not speak, Mr. Oliver. Don't say a word until you have spoken with a lawyer." Then, to Jimmy: "We'll question Stacey again tomorrow and see what more she knows about this Mariah character. She can help with the drawing, and then we can do an age progression from that drawing." He chuckled. "Lord knows we have enough artists up here who are up to the task."

"Stacey doesn't know anything. You can't talk to her," Sam insisted.

"If I could talk to you, Mr. Oliver," the sheriff said, "I'd tell you that Stacey has been advised of her right to an attorney and has given up that right. No charges will be filed against her, and she will be staying in an apartment in Sisters until we need her to testify against you in court."

"No, she wouldn't do that."

Steven, his impatience growing, took some folded-up papers out of his jacket pocket and pushed them and a pen across the table at Sam. "If you want to talk, you'll have to sign these Miranda papers. Otherwise, shut up." He stared at Sam, who had sweat beading on his forehead.

Sam grabbed the papers and signed. He pushed the papers back at Steven, who reached over and picked them up.

Sam wiped his brow with the back of his hand. "Please, you can't let her be out there on her own."

"Why?" Jimmy asked.

"Why, why, why?" Sam repeated hysterically. "Because I'm a moron, a jackass, a bonehead, the biggest idiot of all time, that's why!"

"Very descriptive," Jimmy observed.

Steven continued to stare at him and said quietly, "If you're going to get yourself out of this mess and stay out of jail, you're going to have to come clean, right here, right now and hold nothing back. That's the deal, Sam. All of it, now."

Sam put his elbows on the table and his face in his hands and moaned. Then he sat up and looked off into the distance. "Okay, I'll tell you everything, from the beginning. Then you have to help us, or I can tell you for sure, we are dead."

Four hours later, Steven was in his hotel room lying on the couch and reflecting on what Sam Oliver had told them. After Sam had finished making his statement, they drove him to the apartment where Stacey was staying and arranged for one of the sheriffs to park outside. Tomorrow, they would fly them both to San Diego where Mack and Loshi could figure out where and how to make sure they were safely ensconced in a secure place. At first, as Sam began his recitation, Steven had thought Sam's fear had been unreasonable, a product of an overactive imagination. Halfway through Sam's story he changed his mind.

Sam and Stacey had been doing fine before Mariah came along. They were taking their classes in community college, working at various jobs to earn money to pay the rent to Keith. They weren't into drugs except for a little pot now and then and stayed to themselves. When Mariah Venmore moved in, Sam said it was like an icy breeze came through the door that cast a pall over the whole house—at least that's how he remembered it now. She was pale with eyes so light blue the irises almost looked white. She was thin and of medium height but had a presence that set her apart from the others. She was, for the most part, quiet and stayed in her room when she wasn't at school but would occasionally come upon the men in the house when they were alone and have quiet conversations on the ratty back porch or in her room. Once Sam was surprised to see Keith coming out of her room at two in the morning. Keith was older than the rest of them, maybe in his mid-thirties, and with his average looks and flabby body, he wondered what the attraction was for Mariah. He found out later from a bitter Maisie that Keith was not charging her rent.

Mariah never talked about where she was from but had what Sam thought was a way of moving and talking at times that made him think she was from the South. But, some days, after coming back from her design classes, she was all business with an entitled attitude and would let anyone present know her teachers considered her extremely talented. According to her, they had all told her that she would be a major success in her field. Those were the times she came to life, when she talked about making it big. Everyone in the house, especially the women, had differing opinions of her, but what everyone agreed on was that she loved money.

Sam admitted he had been one of Mariah's conquests. But he was too paranoid to do anything about it anywhere near the house. When Stacey was in class, Sam used to drive them in his old Toyota to a parking lot in Griffith Park and lead Mariah to a place in the hills, sheltered by trees, where they would have sex on the grass. He always finished early because he was terrified of being caught doing it in public but being naked out in the open air excited her, and she wouldn't let him go until she was sated. He always felt guilty afterward and had to make an effort to not seem as if he was hiding anything from Stacey. But he couldn't stop his crazy obsession with Mariah. If Mariah insisted on having sex, he would say yes, even after he found out he wasn't the only one. The open secret among the men in the house that she was sharing herself with all of them made her seem even more exciting. For nineteen-year-olds, she was everything their parents had warned them about and that was irresistible. Except for David who found her to be strange and off-putting and Ramin, who only had eyes for Sherilyn.

The morning after the night Ramin was shot, Mariah had left the house early, around five a.m. Sam had gotten up because he had promised a friend he would drive him to the airport. When she saw him standing in the hallway looking at her, she was at first surprised, then gave him a piercing look with those light eyes that made his blood run cold. She fumbled with her keys as she tried to lock her door, and the large canvas bag she was carrying slipped off her shoulder. He made a move to help her and got a glimpse of a plastic bag inside wrapped around a bundle of something that looked like it could be stacks of papers or books. He remembered her saying one word that froze him in his tracks: "Don't." That was it. That was all she had to say. She walked down the hall, out the front door, and he never talked to her again.

When he heard Ramin had been shot and robbed, he instinctively thought back on that moment with Mariah. He buried his suspicions at first—an unsophisticated teenage girl capable of such an act? He didn't want to believe it. Was she carrying the robbery money in her bag? Did she have something incriminating in there? Had she gone out the night before? He didn't know. He'd been in his room with Stacey all night. His imagination was running away with him.

When the young, uniformed policewoman came to talk to them, he said nothing to her about his suspicions. He didn't want to implicate Mariah if she was innocent, and if she wasn't and had killed Ramin, he didn't want to be next on her list. The women in the house knew nothing about Mariah's conquests, or, if they did, they weren't talking. Everyone said as little as possible about the other housemates, not willing to point the finger at anyone. Sam got the feeling that everyone was frightened and distrustful but trying hard to act normal. After David was charged with the murder, Sam did not relax. He never thought David was capable of killing and robbing anyone. Why would he do it? Ramin was his friend; they both had families with a lot of money. There wouldn't have been any point.

Sam couldn't remember who left first after Mariah disappeared. Sam, Stacey, and the others decided to stay. They had classes to attend and a future to think about. But then the warning phone calls came in, Micco was almost killed, and Stacey was shoved into traffic. It was time for them all to get as far away from Los Angeles as possible. Keith said he and Maisie already had another management gig, and Micco wanted to move back home anyway. Every one of them knew that David was not capable of killing Ramin, and all had their suspicions about who might have, but they shared nothing with the lady cop who came around first or the detectives they talked to later. They just wanted to leave, Sam was ashamed to say, allowing David to take the fall. He didn't tell Stacey until they were at her aunt's house in Oregon whom he suspected and why they needed to get as far away as possible. She became so angry at his betrayal she almost left him, but after she calmed down, she decided she didn't want to be on the run alone.

When asked by Jimmy if there was anything, no matter how small, that Sam remembered about Mariah, he said he never found out where she was from but once, during sex, she used words he'd never heard before. He asked her later what they meant, and she said they were endearing terms she made up. He'd believed her and never felt so completely under someone's spell. He was young and vulnerable, so maybe that was it. But because of his foolish weakness, he and Stacey would never be safe.

*　*　*　*　*

Madelaine was carefully unwrapping Rosemaria's ankle. "It looks good. There's no swelling whatsoever. But when I help you stand, don't put all your weight on that foot."

Rosemaria was seated in her wheelchair, mentally crossing her fingers and hoping with all her heart that her ankle had healed, and she no longer needed any mechanical assistance to get anywhere. Not being physically whole was killing her. The broken arm she could deal with, but not being able to walk had been torture.

Madelaine took her arm and helped her up from her wheelchair. "Okay, step on it lightly, and tell me how it feels."

Rosemaria stood up on one leg and carefully placed her other foot on the floor.

"Okay, go ahead and put weight on it."

Rosemaria did as she was told.

"Feel any pain?"

Rosemaria grinned at Madelaine. "I don't."

Madelaine still hung on to her arm. "All right. Take a couple of steps."

Rosemaria took one step and then tentatively took another. Not even a twinge.

Madelaine released her arm. "It's amazing you're healing this fast but take it slow."

Rosemaria took a few more steps around the room and looked at Madelaine. "I don't think I'm ready for a marathon, but can I please go downstairs and show off to Mildred and the others?"

"As long as you rest after you get down there. You said you wanted to go to the library and find some books to read. Let's head there, and then you can sit for a while, just to make sure you don't overdo."

"You got it."

A few minutes later, Rosemaria was sitting alone in the immense library, which was next to Andrew's office and totally apart from his own library. That room also had a huge selection of books, but nothing like this. This looked like a reading room at the New York City library with a couple of much smaller reading tables. She wondered if they had any beach-read thrillers on the shelves or if they were considered unworthy of being part of this collection. Her phone rang, and she reached into her pocket, looked at the screen, and answered.

"Hi, sweetheart. Where are you?

"I'm at a sidewalk café with Miranda. We're admiring the view of the water in Stockholm."

"Say hi to Miranda for me. Tell her to sign you as a client now, or she'll miss the boat if you go with someone else."

The sun was shining on the narrow street with a glut of tourists walking by, and small boats were floating on the nearby canal. Josh and Miranda were seated opposite each other, both with salad plates in front of them. Josh grinned and handed the phone to Miranda.

"Hi, girl. Josh tells me you're really enjoying the good life. I think I'd better get him a lot of publicity so his career takes off, and you don't leave him for some rich dude."

"So far, no rich dude I've met is even slightly tempting."

"He's a big hit over here, but I think he's ready to come home. Take care of yourself, okay?"

Josh took his phone back. "I have her eating salads, my love. Soon she'll be stepping over from the dark side and joining us."

Miranda took a bite of her salad, waved him off, and yelled at the phone. "I'm still having fish for my main course. I'm in Sweden, for Pete's sake."

"She's close, though, really close." Josh gave a thumbs up to Miranda.

"Well, don't nag her," Rosemaria said. "Remember how you used to annoy me when I was trying to enjoy my pizza?"

"It worked, didn't it?"

"It wasn't the nagging that did it. I left the dark side because I had designs on you. And now that you're mine, I have no regrets."

"Did you look at the pictures of condos that Vanessa sent you?"

"I did. I gather that's what you wanted to talk to me about."

"It was."

"I like the one that's closest to Rexford. What do you think?"

"You're the decider. Tell Vanessa, and she'll get right on it. Whatever it is, we can afford it, so don't worry."

"I'm just a girl from Simi Valley who decorated our apartment with a few choice pieces from a thrift store, but I'm ready to take the plunge."

"Our Salvation Army days are over. But if we crash and burn, remember, Martha is saving my apartment on Cherokee for us."

Martha was a homeless woman that Josh befriended and convinced to move into his old apartment.

"Maybe she won't let us back. I think she likes it there."

She looked up and saw Cameron standing in the doorway with a grim look on his face.

"My bodyguard is here and apparently has something to tell me, so I must hang up now."

"Call me later and tell me nothing's wrong."

"I'll text. Love you." And she clicked off.

Cameron came in and stood next to her. "Something's come up."

"What's wrong?"

"A woman showed up at your apartment when one of my men was there to make sure your mail was being forwarded. She says she's your fiancé's mother, a Mrs. Ellie Sibley from Marysville, Wisconsin."

Rosemaria would have fallen over if she had been standing. She stared at Cameron, unable to speak the words that were trying to form in her brain.

"We checked her out, and she is definitely who she says she is," Cameron said, making note of Rosemaria's curious reaction. Since he didn't get a response, he went on. "I told her you were both presently unavailable, which made her very upset. Do you want to talk to her?"

Rosemaria had regained her composure but was still shocked at Ellie showing up unannounced after all these years. She hadn't seen Josh since he left Wisconsin when he was nineteen. "Where is she?"

"My man took her to Starbucks down the street from your apartment. He's waiting to hear from me."

Rosemaria thought for a minute, took her phone out of her pocket, and dialed. "The number for the Beverly Wilshire Hotel, please." She waited and dialed again. "Yes, this is Rosemaria Baker, and I'd like to make a reservation for Mrs. Ellie Sibley, a single, for a week, checking in today." She looked up at Cameron and waited. "Wonderful. Can I call you in ten minutes with my credit card number? Great. She'll be there within the hour. Ellie Sibley." She hung up and shook her head.

"You picked a nice place for her."

"She's his mother. What could I do?"

"You don't want to talk to her?"

"I do. It's just that . . . I don't know what to say to her. We've never spoken before, and things are a little difficult between her and her son. . . . Tell her to call me after she's checked in."

"All right. I'll have my man drive her to the hotel."

"Thank you, Cameron."

"No problem." He clicked a key on his phone as he walked out the door.

Ten minutes later, Rosemaria was back in her room, proudly having made it up the elevator without any hint of pain in her ankle. She gave the hotel her card number and had a small anxiety attack. What was she going to say to Ellie? But an even bigger question was whether she should tell Josh his mother was here. He might get so upset it would affect his performance, and she couldn't let that happen. She'd never lied to him ever, and now she was keeping something big from him. Was that a lie? Would he understand and forgive her? Now she had to sit and wait for Ellie to call.

Her phone rang, and she jumped, then relaxed when she saw it was her dad. "What's up, Detective. Did you catch the unsub yet?"

He laughed. "Unsub indeed. You've been watching too many cop shows. Well, I think we've made some headway. Jimmy and I are on a flight to San Diego with Stacey and Sam. We talked to Mack and Loshi, and we've pretty much agreed that Mariah Venmore is our number one suspect."

"I gather Stacey and Sam were what the high-speed chase was all about."

"More like a sluggish drive through traffic. But forget that. Sam came up with a pretty good picture of who this Mariah woman is. If we can talk to Clyde and Keith and coax more info out of Sherilyn, I think we may be able to get somewhere."

"Larry told me about Maisie."

"She OD'd in the hospital yesterday. Mack said she was so ravaged by drugs that she looked ninety years old. She thought Mack was Keith and accused him of leaving her for Mariah. She said something about a place they used to go. I don't know if any of that is useful or not, but apparently, Mariah had a go at every man in the house except David and Ramin."

"And they're dead."

"I wonder if that had anything to do with why they are. Maybe she's the vindictive type and singled them out for punishment."

"She killed Ramin, stole fifty thousand dollars, and framed David. And now she's getting rid of anybody who knew her in her past life, including me."

"That's about it."

Well, Lorna is waiting at your house. Are you going to take a crack at her before telling Mack and Loshi? You guys seem to be getting along so well right now."

"We're flying into San Diego, delivering our witnesses to the sheriffs, driving a rental to Burbank airport to get our cars, then driving home. I'll be very surprised to find Lorna at my house and will say you arranged it behind my back in a moment of desperation."

"Dad, you're getting to be way too much like me."

"That could be, but it's just that I think I'll have a better rapport with her than those two. And as long as she stays at my house, I think she'll be okay."

"Thanks for catching me up on everything."

"You're a part of this investigation. And you practically dumped an important witness right in my lap. I'll bet Lorna knows a lot about Clyde that will prove to be very useful."

"Let me know."

"Will do."

After she hung up, Rosemaria buzzed Kirsten's room. "Could you have a couple of the guys come here and take the wheelchair and glide away? I won't be needing them anymore." She fist-pumped with her good arm and walked back and forth across the room a couple of times just for the heck of it.

CHAPTER TWENTY

Ellie Sibley was ecstatic over her room at the Beverly Wilshire—the most glamorous and famous hotel in all of Beverly Hills. She had just talked to Josh's fiancée, Rosemaria. She told Ellie that Josh was touring in Europe and would be home in a couple of days and that she herself was rehabbing at a friend's house after an accident. Her son must be doing extremely well to be able to afford putting her up at the Beverly Wilshire. It was the same hotel where Julia Roberts had stayed in *Pretty Woman*, for heaven's sake. She never dreamed she'd end up in the same hotel as Julia.

Rosemaria had told her to sightsee in downtown Beverly Hills, take herself to lunch, or eat at the hotel and charge it to the room. Ellie thought she might do that once or twice, but she didn't want to take advantage of their goodwill. She'd find a grocery store, buy herself some sandwich fixings, and happily eat in her room watching cable TV. Only a few more days and she'd finally see Josh after more than twenty years of estrangement. She hoped he had forgiven her by now for failing her boys so terribly, even though it was impossible for her to forgive herself. She would live with the shame of what she had done for the rest of her life. But it was important to see Josh now and share her news with him.

She knew she didn't deserve to have him back as her son, but she wanted it so badly she had decided to come out and ask him in person.

One of her coworkers had helped her track down Josh's address. Everything was so easy for young people to find out on the internet these days. And she wanted to show up in person instead of giving him a chance to reject her over the phone. She had decided to be brave this time, something she had never been her whole life. If he turned her away, she could accept that she had tried.

* * * * *

Lorna sat alone in the dark and waited for Mr. Baker to come home. She had insisted that Santiago head back to Las Vegas right away, stop halfway, and spend the night in a hotel. That way, he could be back for work the next night and not lose any more time on her account. She didn't know it would be so hard to say goodbye. She might never see him again, and it caused an unexpected painful twinge in her heart. He had a hard time leaving her too. She could tell. She hadn't realized until then how strong his feelings for her were because she had been so set on meeting a high roller and had never even considered a life with a lowly security guard. Now it was too late to tell him she cared for him, and it wouldn't have mattered at all if he wasn't rich.

She hadn't wanted to leave him, but she couldn't have stayed at his house and put his life and his mother's in danger. He kissed her gently on the cheek before he opened the door to leave, but she drew him back and kissed him fully on the mouth, unable to resist letting him know what her heart was saying. He kissed her back, and they clung to each other for several moments before he broke it off. She saw he had tears in his eyes. "Take care of yourself," he said, and then he was gone.

She had never felt this way with Clyde. With him, she was a convenience, a possession, sometimes a sounding board, and a sex partner. That was about it. But he must have some concern for her. Otherwise, why would he keep calling to ask if she was okay? Maybe he wanted to make sure she didn't share anything she had told him with anyone. Yes, that must be it. If Mr. Baker was as nice as his daughter, she would tell him everything. She was through being a convenience.

Steven saw that the house was dark when he pulled up the driveway and into the garage. He wondered if Lorna had arrived. He walked into the kitchen, turned on the light, and saw her in the living room sitting on the couch in the dark. She jumped to her feet as he walked into the room.

"I knew it must be you when you drove into the garage." Her words came out fast as if her nerves were frayed. "Who else would have the clicker? I didn't want to turn on the light until you came in case your neighbors wondered who might be here when you were gone." She heard herself babbling and didn't know how to stop. "I didn't go into any other room or—"

Steven calmly put his keys on a tray on a bookshelf, turned on a lamp beside the couch, and said kindly, "You must be Lorna." He approached her slowly and put out his hand. "I'm Steven."

She shook his hand and said, "Yes, I'm Lorna."

He gestured for her to sit back down and made himself comfortable in his favorite easy chair.

"I see you made it here from Vegas in one piece. I'm grateful to Santiago for taking such good care of you."

"He's a good friend."

"Everybody needs those."

"Are you hungry? Would you like something to eat?"

"No, we stopped at Burger King on the way here."

"Then why don't I make you comfortable in Rosemaria's old room, and you can get some rest. You must be tired."

"Okay." She picked up her overnight bag, but Steven took it from her and led her down the hall into a small bedroom. She noticed that some high school mementos had been left on bookshelves from when Rosemaria lived here. They were mostly basketball and softball trophies and pictures of her when she was young. Only a few years later, she had become a cop and was investigating criminals, including Lorna herself and everybody else who'd lived at the house.

"I think you'll be comfortable here. You have your own bathroom, and there's plenty of towels. If you need anything, just give a holler. I'll be up for a while, right down the hall in my study."

"Thank you." She felt like crying and didn't know why.

"We'll talk tomorrow. For now, just rest and know you're safe here."

"Okay."

He smiled at her and shut the door, and for the first time since she had hidden in the rhododendron bushes, terrified of being found, she felt like she could finally close her eyes and not be afraid.

The images on the computer blurred, and Steven closed his eyes, dead tired from the events of the past two days. As the investigation seemed to be moving inexorably to the woman who called herself Mariah Venmore, he wondered how anyone could be as effective in erasing her past as she had been. She was a ghost, and, lord knows, Jimmy had done his best to find the smallest trace of her, but there was nothing. If Lorna was trusting enough of him and Jimmy to reveal all she knew, then maybe she could help them reach Clyde, who was in deep hiding for a damn good reason. He must know something that had put the fear of God in him, and Steven wanted to know what that was. He clicked off his computer and decided it was time to call it a day.

Lorna had awakened at six a.m., at first alarmed at finding herself in a strange bed in unfamiliar surroundings. It took a minute for her to remember where she was and to feel ready to face whatever was in store for her. How bad could it be? She was living in a house with an ex-cop who treated her like gold. He wanted to get information from her, that was true, but still, he was very kind. She had taken a very short shower and didn't blow-dry her hair for fear it would make noise and wake up Mr. Baker. She had dressed and sat at Rosemaria's desk until she heard him rustling about in the kitchen, and the aroma of coffee wafted into her room. She walked down the hall and saw him standing over the stove, making pancakes. The kitchen table was set with three placemats, plates, forks, and knives. Butter and syrup were in the middle.

"I'm making pancakes this morning. I hope you like them. My daughter loved pancakes when she was growing up, especially before playing in an important basketball game. She said she needed her carbs."

"I love pancakes too. It's been a while since I had them."

"Jimmy Waite is going to join us. He's my partner in trying to track down this person who is coming after Rosemaria. I think you'll like him. Go ahead, have a seat. He'll be here any minute."

She nodded and sat down. "So, your daughter was into playing sports?"

"That she was. Her favorite was basketball. She was good at it too but never tall enough to try for a scholarship. She was a fierce competitor since she was in grade school; winning was everything."

"I like her already."

"Did you sleep okay?"

"It was fine. I didn't wake up once till morning."

He picked up a plate, heaped a stack of pancakes on it, and placed it in front of her. "Eat it all, or you'll hurt my feelings."

"It looks good."

They heard a knock on the front door. Steven put down his spatula, walked to the door, and unlocked it. Jimmy came in, all smiles and positive energy.

"What's gotten into you today?" Steven asked. "What are you so happy about?"

Jimmy headed for the kitchen where Lorna was sitting in front of her heaping place of pancakes. "I got to sleep in my own bed, that's what, and I get a chance to eat your famous pancakes. What's not to be happy about?" He stuck out his hand to Lorna. "Hi, I'm Jimmy Waite." He shook her hand, walked over the coffee maker, and poured himself a cup.

"Nice meeting you," Lorna said shyly.

"Would you like some?" he asked her.

"Yes, please."

Steven took another plate, filled it with pancakes, and set it down on the table as Jimmy poured coffee for Lorna and Steven. "Sorry. I should have asked."

He made himself a plate, and before long, they were gorging themselves on pancakes drenched in syrup and asking for seconds. After they were thoroughly stuffed, everyone helped with clearing dishes and cleaning

up; then they took their coffee cups into the living room and made themselves comfortable.

By this time, Lorna had forgotten her nervousness and had warmed
up to both Jimmy and Steven. "Those really were the best pancakes I ever
had. Do you make them from scratch?"

"Yes, ma'am. Got the recipe out of an ancient but still reliable Betty
Crocker cookbook."

"She must be a really good cook."

He was reminded how young she was. "She's the best." And he took
a sip of coffee.

"So . . . I guess you have some questions for me."

"You up for it?" Jimmy asked.

"Well, I'm as ready as I'll ever be."

"Say whatever comes into your mind." Steven said. "We can ask questions later if we have any."

"If you've talked to some of the others, I guess you know Clyde was
into dealing drugs a little. He just did it for his own use and for the other
people in the house. It wasn't like he was a criminal or anything."

Jimmy was all understanding. "We get that. Totally. It was just for
recreational use."

"Exactly. I didn't really do any drugs until I met him. We were both
hanging out at the same coffee shop on Melrose after work, and he and I
became friendly. After a couple of weeks, he told me about a place I could
live for almost nothing, which sounded great to me, so I moved in. I started
out smoking weed, then he had me do some ecstasy once in a while but
mostly weed. I was still able to do my cocktail waitress job. I'm really good
at it. Customers like me." She looked at them for approval, and she saw
them nod encouragingly.

"After a while, Clyde started making more and more money off dealing drugs, and I told him it worried me. He hated that. Told me to eff off,
if you know what I mean. He became very distant, and I knew there had to
be somebody else. Sometimes I'd see him sneak off in the car with Mariah
and not come back for hours. I'd cry by myself in our room, but I didn't say
anything. I knew he'd just get angry, and I didn't want him to kick me out.

I had nowhere else to go just then." She took a sip of her coffee and set it down on the table. "I guess you must think I'm a terrible person."

"Absolutely not," Steven said. "You were making the best of a bad situation."

She puffed out her cheeks and blew out air. "Yeah, it was bad, all right. Just before Ramin was killed, Clyde and Mariah were always off in the backyard, talking and arguing. I don't know about what. I think Mariah wanted in on his business from what I could hear. She didn't seem to have any visible means of support, and I wondered where she was getting her money. After Ramin was killed, the two of them acted like they didn't know each other. Something was going on, but I didn't know what until later."

"What did you find out?" Steven asked.

"We took off for Reno after Mariah disappeared, and Clyde acted like he was really scared. I kept asking him why, and he finally told me it was Mariah who had killed Ramin. I said we had to go back and clear David, but he went crazy, saying we couldn't do that. I asked him what he was so afraid of, and he said he had found out about the money that would be in the store the next morning. And, like an idiot, he had told Mariah. She knew he knew she had killed Ramin and would kill us both if she felt like it. He wanted to go to South America or Mexico, and I said no way, that I was going to go to Vegas and get a job. Instead, we went to Reno, where he helped me get a new social security number from somebody who had died and gave me some money and disappeared. Then I went to Vegas, and the rest you know."

Steven stared into space. "I'm wondering how the hell she found you."

"How did you find me?"

"Through the security cameras at the Wynn," Jimmy answered.

"Then she found me the same way. She knew I'd always worked as a cocktail waitress, and Clyde didn't get a new cell until we were in Reno. She probably checked out every bar and casino in Reno and Vegas until she found me at the Wynn."

"Excellent deduction, Lorna. If you want a job at BHPD, I'll vouch for you."

She scrunched up her face in embarrassment. "I'm not smart enough to work for you. And they'd never hire someone like me anyway."

"When this is over, we'll find you a job somewhere where you can use your brains."

"I kind of like being a cocktail waitress, until I get married, that is."

"Good girl. You know what you want." Steven said. "Are you sure Clyde wasn't involved in the murder somehow? He didn't go out that night to possibly take out the security cameras in the back of the store, help her get the code to open the door, anything like that?"

"I don't remember. He might have. Looking back on it, I'm not sure of anything. I just know he was scared out of his wits. And I don't think she shared any of the money with him. But I have to tell you, I was carrying a load of guilt the whole time we were hiding out in Reno. I kept thinking about David in jail for something he didn't do, and I didn't help him. When I heard he was killed in prison, I couldn't go to work that day. I just cried myself to sleep and hated myself."

"Yeah, but you weren't the only one that knew," Jimmy said. "And the detectives failed to do their job. There's a lot of blame to go around."

"Do you think Clyde will call you again?" Steven asked.

"Wherever he's living he has no cell phone coverage, so he has to drive somewhere else to call me. He only does that every few weeks. He'll probably call in about a week to find out where I am and who I'm with. I used to think it was because he cared. Now I think he calls to find out if I've kept my mouth shut and if I've heard anything about Mariah."

"Since you're staying here, maybe he'll call when I'm home, and I can talk to him."

"He'd never talk to you. He'd just hang up."

"We can try."

"Knowing that Mariah was getting it on with every guy in the house except Ramin and David, you must think we're all a bunch of pathetic losers, me included."

"We're not here to judge," Steven said quietly. "Just to get to the truth."

Jimmy stood up, took his coffee cup into the kitchen, rinsed it out, and put it on the drainboard. Then he came back into the living room, looked at Lorna, and said, "Don't worry about what other people think of you anymore. You're doing the right thing now and facing everything you did in the past that was wrong. You have the rest of your life to make better decisions, and I know you will." He opened the front door. "I'm going home and get back to work." And with a wave and a smile, he went out.

"I'll be on the phone and on my computer for a few hours," Steven said. "Go ahead and watch TV in here or in your room. Consider this your safe house for now. We'll take it one day at a time, okay?"

"There's still a lot of books in Rosemaria's room, a lot of thrillers I haven't read. I think I'll read and maybe think of something else to help you."

Steven stood up. "Sounds like a plan. Knock on my door if you need anything."

He left her there, went into his study, and dialed Rosemaria.

"How'd it go?" she asked as soon as she clicked on. She was already in bed reading a David Baldacci book she had discovered amid all the more sophisticated literary tomes in the Collins library.

"She doesn't think Clyde had anything to do with the murder, and she doesn't know where he is. Maybe South America, maybe Mexico. The next time he calls her, hopefully, I'll be there and try to talk to him."

"If Mariah wants me so badly, I know she's staying close. She's undoubtedly waiting until I'm out of my fortress and exposing myself as a target again."

"Do you know how it chills my bones to hear that?"

"It's not doing wonders for my own bones either, Dad. And Josh is exposed as well. He's scheduled to play San Francisco and Seattle after he comes home from Sweden. I have to make sure he goes and doesn't cancel because of me. Let's catch this scary broad so we can go back to normal."

"I'll do my best."

"Me too, Dad. Sleep tight."

She hung up and put the Baldacci book aside. If Mariah actually was the killer, what if she had decided to kill Rosemaria because she thought she might recognize her after all these years? Apparently, the people who had lived in the murder house who might still be able to identify her were too frightened to talk. That meant she'd either become some sort of high-profile person, and Rosemaria might be able to recognize her from the media or someone Rosemaria might come into close contact with. Considering Mariah's obsession with money, she could have become very successful by now. Rosemaria knew it was a huge stretch, but what if Mariah had become a part of the Beverly Hills inner circle and had actually attended the fundraiser at the Collins mansion? She shivered. Rosemaria's paranoia was now running full bore.

Tomorrow she would ask Elmira, Loretta's secretary, for a list of every woman who was a member of her charity. She would email that list to Jimmy so he could have his people check out the history of all the women in the late-twenties-to-mid-thirties age range. She would have to be more proactive as soon as Josh came home and would say nothing to him, her dad, or Vanessa about what she was thinking. After she had moved into her new apartment, she intended to go to every committee meeting she was invited to. Somewhere among those wealthy women could be lurking the money-hungry psychopath who had spent the last ten years building her fortune.

The only other reason Mariah would want Rosemaria dead is that she knew of Rosemaria's reputation as a homicide investigator and was afraid she would not stop digging until she found David's killer. That was probably the most likely scenario. Kicking up dust in Vanessa's inner circle might be a complete dead end and only serve to annoy her best friend. But if Mariah had become hugely successful and wanted to get near Rosemaria, she would make it easy for her. At the same time, she couldn't let Josh be put in harm's way because he was close to her. Rosemaria was running blind, grasping at straws. But her life was on the line, and she had to follow her instincts, no matter how farfetched her theories might sound to anyone else.

The next morning, still in bed, she called Ellie at the Beverly Wilshire to ask how she was doing and if she needed anything. Ellie was leaning back in a comfortable upholstered chair, noshing on snacks from a mini mart a few blocks away and drinking coffee she had brought up from the café downstairs. Rosemaria told her it was perfectly okay to order from room service, but Ellie insisted she didn't want to be a bother. When Rosemaria told her that Josh would be home that Monday Ellie expressed her excitement at seeing him again, but Rosemaria guessed she was probably a bit apprehensive as well, not knowing what Josh's reaction would be. Rosemaria again told Ellie she was happy she was here and that she finally would have a chance to meet her fiancé's mother. She made Ellie promise she would splurge on some of the hotel's amenities and not worry about the cost.

They said their goodbyes, and Rosemaria tossed aside her blanket and looked down on her now-healed foot. She wiggled her toes and luxuriated in the knowledge she could walk normally again. She grabbed her scratcher from the night table and stuck it down between her arm cast and her skin and scratched an itch. In a few weeks, the cast would be gone, and no remnant of the ill-fated hit would remain. Unfortunately, Amy was not so lucky. She placed a plastic bag over the cast, swung out of bed, and headed for the shower. As the water cascaded over her in gentle sheets, she was reminded that after Josh's last concert in Stockholm, she would have to face the unenviable task of calling and telling him that his mother would be waiting for him when he came home. She predicted that might be an unpleasant conversation but nothing she couldn't handle.

CHAPTER TWENTY-ONE

Rosemaria's four self-appointed godfathers were having a meeting at the last standing Du-pars in Los Angeles at the Farmers Market near Fairfax. Du-par's had been founded back in 1938 and, through the decades, had been the favorite meeting place for hundreds of thousands of Los Angelinos. While other Du-pars had tragically closed, this one was always available for good food, a comfortable booth, and pleasant waitresses. Steven, Jimmy, Larry, and Darryl Osborne, who was head of robbery homicide now that Rosemaria had left the department, were enjoying omelets, hash browns, and toast while updating each other on the progress of the investigation.

Steven bit into his toast and chewed thoughtfully before asking Larry, "What's new with Mack and Loshi? Is there anything more from Stacey and Sam? And have they been tracking Atkins or found any connection to a woman who could be Mariah? She's working with someone, could be him."

Larry was sipping and enjoying the unparalleled Du-pars coffee. "I will answer all your questions in due time, but may I savor my cheese and avocado omelet for a few minutes first? He put a forkful of omelet into his mouth, closed his eyes, and smiled. "This is the best." He took another sip of coffee. "Stacey and Sam are in a safe house in San Diego and haven't added much to what they already said. San Diego has looked into Atkins's financial records, and he is as poor as he claims to be. He could never afford to hire any hitmen. His career is on a one-way trip to nowheresville, and if his hatred of Rosemaria is as burning hot as I think it is, he's emotionally unbalanced enough to take her out himself without any help from anybody. He also has a concealed carry permit for a Colt 911 he's had since he started out as a prosecutor."

Osborne put down his fork, wiped his mouth with a napkin, and said to Steven, "That worries me. Rosemaria could have two individuals coming after her, maybe three. I think her idea that the killer is a young Beverly Hills matron is completely off the mark. That she's going to go forward with that cockamamy theory is not like her." He turned to Jimmy. "We wouldn't even know about it unless you had told us."

"She only agreed to me telling you because I told her I couldn't check the names on her list otherwise," Jimmy said. "She was pissed. She didn't want all of you thinking that suspecting a Beverly Hills housewife or self-made businesswoman was a stupid idea."

"We all agree that Rosemaria has always had good instincts," Osborne said. "But after everything that's happened and who she's been hanging out with the past few weeks, it could have made her go off on the wrong tangent."

Jimmy agreed. "For this girl Mariah to have gone from living in a dump in Hollywood to leaving for parts unknown and then coming back to LA wealthy and successful enough to fit into the Beverly Hills social scene is a stretch."

"Not if she killed Ramin and stole his money," Steven said.

Larry looked surprised. "You're going along with her on this?"

"Not necessarily. But I know my daughter."

Osborne stared thoughtfully out the window. "The more I think about it, Rosemaria was the only cop who interviewed Mariah up close and personal after the murder. After that, all eyes were on David. It's possible that Mariah thinks Rosemaria can identify her."

"But why would she put herself in a position where Rosemaria might recognize her?" Steven asked.

"So, we're back to the unlikely theory that Mariah has reinvented herself and is entrenched in the Beverly Hills scene or on the periphery of some sort of political or celebrity spotlight where Rosemaria could possibly identify her if she happened to see her in the media," Larry said.

"We don't even know that she is the killer. All we have are the suspicions of other people in the house," Osborne said.

"True. But there's no harm in considering that Rosemaria may have a point," Steven said. "Jimmy, what did you find?"

"We've narrowed the names down to a hundred and fifty who are in the right age range as Mariah. We're a quarter of the way through, but so far, they all check out. I couldn't find any red flags on any of them."

Osborne shook his head. "Give what you have to Rosemaria, and maybe she can find something. She has time on her hands right now, so you never know." He looked at the others. "What else?"

"Mack told me that Victor Marchand has been calling asking about the progress of the investigation into the death of their son," Larry said. "He's fuming that David was killed shortly after Rosemaria paid him a visit and inferring that somehow she's to blame, as crazy as that may be."

"Where do the Marchands live?" Larry asked.

"Atlanta. And they have homes in Bel Air, Big Sur, and San Francisco."

"Is there any chance Marchand is in LA now?" Steven asked.

"He's rich. He has his own jet. He can be anywhere he wants to be whenever he wants."

The other three all looked at Steven, and Jimmy spoke up. "There's no chance that Marchand is after Rosemaria, and he certainly is not connected to Mariah, who, if she's a killer, might have had his son murdered."

"He doesn't know that," Steven said. "And this woman, if Rosemaria is correct and from what the people in the house have told us, is a manipulator extraordinaire."

"What about this guy, Keith, Maisie's husband, who used to meet Mariah at some unknown location? Any idea of where he might be or where they met?" Osborne asked.

Larry smiled at his colleague, "I didn't know you were paying such close attention, boss. But in answer to your question, all our attempts to find Keith have gone nowhere. He and Mariah have vanished off the face of the earth. Everyone else is accounted for except the illusive Clyde, who may be residing somewhere south of the border."

"Thank you for that update," Osborne responded. "And yes, Larry, I am paying attention to this and all the other cases we're working on, because Rosemaria is special to me. I also tracked down the two detectives who investigated Ramin's death and decided to focus on David as the shooter. They both have retired and moved away: one to Idaho and the other one to Montana. Neither one of them is interested in rehashing an old case, said they gave the prosecutor what they had, and if we have a problem with David being convicted take it up with him."

Larry put down his fork, and sat back in the booth. "Nice."

"So who needs them?" Steven said. "But I want you to know how much I appreciate all your efforts on behalf of my daughter."

"Now, now," Jimmy said. "Let's not get sappy. You know Rosemaria wouldn't approve."

"She'd be pissed is what she'd be," Larry said. "She'd tell us to get back on track. Unfortunately, since our tracks are all leading to dead ends, I'm hoping our intrepid partners in San Diego are having better luck."

"Our computer guys aren't anything to sniff at," Osborne said. "They'll be finished going through Rosemaria's list in a couple of days. Maybe we'll find the devil woman in there."

"And I'm going to stick close to home so if Clyde calls Lorna, maybe I can talk to him." Steven addressed Jimmy. "Is there any way to trace his cell phone?"

"If I were there and could attempt a trace on my laptop while he's on the phone, yeah, there's a chance. He probably buys a new phone every time he calls and throws away the old one."

"I can't expect you to live at my house on that slim possibility," Steven said. "And I know you have other work to do."

"So, let's look at what we have," Osborne said. "Mack and Loshi will continue to deal with Marchand, but he's probably just an annoyance they'll have to put up with. They will continue to search for Keith, who has to be somewhere close if he's working with Mariah. Our computer guys will go over Rosemaria's list with a fine-tooth comb. Sherilyn still isn't talking to Mack and Loshi, and there's no way to force her."

Larry interrupted. "I didn't tell you that Stacey and Sam helped San Diego create a likeness of Mariah as she looked at age nineteen, and they used age progression software to create a new likeness of what she might look like now. They put that in the facial recognition database to see if they get any hits. They're also using the facial recognition software to see if they get any hits off the list we gave to Rosemaria."

"Mack and Loshi haven't shared any forensics they found in the car the shooter left on the road or on the rifle?" Osborne asked Larry.

"As of now, they've found nothing. The car was clean. No fingerprints on the rifle. They were pros. The blood traces they found on the ground they're putting through CODIS."

"We have to expect they'll come after her again," Steven said. "Next week, Rosemaria will be moving out of the Collins mansion and into a condo that has decent security. She'll have a bodyguard wherever she goes, courtesy of the Collins family." He acknowledged Larry. "Loretta and Andrew insisted. We can expect my daughter to take a proactive interest in this case. And if she acts true to form, we may not always know in what direction that may take her."

"How about the cast on her arm?" Jimmy asked.

"It won't come off for another two or three weeks, which makes her more vulnerable."

The guys had been digging enthusiastically into their meals as they talked, and now their plates were clean as a whistle. The waitress stopped by and asked them if they needed more coffee. They shook their heads no, and she laid the check on the table. Steven grabbed it.

"No arguments. I'm paying," he said.

"Let's meet here again," Osborne said. "We'll take turns paying."

They slid out of the booth and headed out the door to the parking lot. Before they went their separate ways, Larry had one final word. "So far, we're working surprisingly well with our pals in San Diego. Mack and Loshi didn't even get upset over us having the first shot at Lorna. So keep sharing everything you get with me, and I'll share with them, and we'll keep everybody happy. Rosemaria, who we know likes to fly off the reservation more often than not, will have to be more cooperative in this respect."

"Seriously?" Jimmy asked.

"Okay, forget that last part." He grinned and headed for his car. And the others weren't far behind.

* * * * *

Vanessa was swimming laps in the Collins' Olympic-size pool as Rosemaria, submersed up to her waist in the water, hung on to the side of the pool with one arm and kicked her legs. Not being able to exercise had put on a few inches on her waistline, and she didn't like it, especially now that Josh would be home in a couple of days, and she would be displaying her naked body to someone besides the full-length mirror in her room. The extra blubber was not the least bit attractive. She could insist on making love in the dark, but he would still feel the burgeoning love handles. He always said he loved to have something to hang on to, but she didn't believe a word of it. With a lot of work at the gym and eating less, she had become lithe and limber by the time he left on the tour. Now he was coming home to a blob.

"Is it possible to lose five pounds in two days?" she asked Vanessa when she finally came up for air beside her.

"Yeah, if you chop off a leg."

I'm not doing that."

Vanessa heaved herself up on the side of the pool and grabbed a towel. "You don't need to lose five pounds. I've never known anybody who was so adept at body shaming herself as you. You've gained maybe three pounds since the . . . unfortunate event. It will come off just living life normally now that you can walk again."

Rosemaria kept kicking her legs for all she was worth. "I don't want him to be disappointed. Especially since he might be mad at me for not telling him his mother is here."

"Yeah, that is a rather sensitive topic for him."

"I'm going to tell him tonight and just take my punishment."

"You did it for his own good. When he calms down, he'll see that."

"You think he'll get angry?"

"He might, but you did the right thing." Vanessa stood up, grabbed a terry cloth robe off a chair, and sat down. "I always feel like I'm at a twenty-million-dollar spa when I come here. And my own husband spent his childhood living in a house almost as big as this one and then here. Why isn't he an insufferable jerk?"

"He was when we were first partners, but I engineered a massive makeover before I handed him over to you. And it wasn't easy."

Vanessa looked around at the grounds, which reminded her of the Bel Air Hotel, and at the incredible pool/guesthouses that were bigger than the house she grew up in. "You did an amazing job. He's just about perfect now."

"Speaking of money, I've been thinking of something. All these people who have fundraisers for this and that cause—if the committee members got together and just donated their own money, they wouldn't need to waste huge amounts of money on fundraisers. They could just fund the museums or battered women shelters or whatever themselves."

"I used to ask myself that in the beginning, but after getting to know some of these people, I figured it out."

"And the *Jeopardy* question is—?"

"Why just give when you can get publicity and praise for giving and have an excuse to buy new gowns and be photographed at glittery events and feel superior to all the little people who are unable to give. I don't put everyone, especially my mother-in-law, in that category, of course."

"Wow. You're still able to say it like it is."

"My mother was a nurse, and my father was a tax accountant. We lived in a humble home and took a week's vacation in the summer. But we were happy. Then I became a starving actor until I got a few parts. I married a rich husband, but I remember my roots."

"So why are you doing all this committee work?"

"Because, like Loretta, I will help my husband in his career ambitions, and part of that is networking with people with money. Besides, there are people like Drew and Sophia who are really down to earth and nice."

Rosemaria reached up, and Vanessa stood, grabbed her good arm, and pulled her out of the pool. Rosemaria sat next to her friend, and Vanessa put Rosemaria's robe over her shoulders.

"So, tell me which of the women I met you really like. The ones who are close to you and the ones who work the hardest." Rosemaria asked.

"Okay." She pondered the question. "I haven't known Drew and Sophia very long, but already, they are high on my list of likes. There's Isolde Garwood, who is an executive at the Maitland Corporation and is dating the heir to the Mindell banking fortune. Nancy Winfield, who is on the UC board of directors and is going out with or engaged to—I forget which—an executive at Disney. Sally Mankowitz is another one who's high on my list, very unassuming and a hard worker, one of the top real estate agents in Beverly Hills and married to the owner of Mangrove Petrochemical. Jackie Radcliff is CEO of Delmar Imports, which has a few other offshoots, and is another one who gives her all to every cause. She's engaged to Henry Greenwood, who inherited some sort of company that I forget now and, from what Jackie said, has political aspirations. Hortensia Sarturo owns a nationwide janitorial service that she built from scratch and is married to the mayor of Beverly Hills, who has his mind set on running for higher political office."

"Listening to that list of accomplishments could make a girl feel inadequate. Could you please email all of that to me when you get home?"

"Why? What are you up to? You're not going to interrogate my friends, are you?"

"Absolutely not. I want to get to know them all. Now that I live in the 90210 zip code, I want to get involved a little in your committees. My husband-to-be could be famous any day now, and he may want to go to some charity events."

"You hate with a passion any event where people have to get dressed up. I know you. You have an ulterior motive." She sat up, shocked. "You don't think any of my friends are out to kill you, do you?"

"Of course not. Don't be silly. I'm just expanding my comfort zone. I don't want to be a lowly ADA forever. I may run for a higher office too someday."

"Oh my God. Now I know you're up to something. But don't tell me what it is. I don't want to know. I'm going to the pool house to dress." She stood up. "You know, being your friend is a real challenge sometimes."

"I've heard that said before."

Vanessa shook her head and walked away, muttering to herself.

Rosemaria needed to have Jimmy do a deep dive into the women on the list of Vanessa's closest friends. And she needed him to email their pictures to the available housemates and see if any of the women's faces stirred a glimmer of recognition in Mariah's former cohabitants. She had probably gone through a lot of plastic surgery and changed her look completely, but maybe there was some sort of oddity on her face that couldn't be changed that one of the housemates might remember. Now that it was possible to get plastic surgery that could even fool facial recognition software, it was a longshot.

She had a feeling that Clyde had fled the country and headed as far south as his money would take him. Where else would he go when most of his drug-dealing scumbag friends came from south of the border? She thought of asking Malcolm Curtis, the marine who had rescued her friends Tiffany and Maryanne from corrupt politicians and the hitmen they hired to kill the girls. Allowing the girls to live and possibly reveal the politicians' dirty secrets had not been an option for those denizens of the DC swamp. Rosemaria wondered how they were enjoying their new digs in the federal pen.

At any rate, she had nothing to lose by asking Curtis if he had any way of getting a lead on Clyde's whereabouts. Maybe he could take a couple of his marine buddies, now freelancers, south of the border and coax some information out of Clyde if they found him. It was doubtful that Clyde was Mariah's helper, but he wasn't this frightened of the woman for no reason.

Rosemaria knew she was getting way ahead of herself, and Clyde could be anywhere from Southeast Asia to Timbuktu. Besides, she hated to take Curtis away from Melody and Tiffany, even for a short amount of time. He had adopted both girls who now considered him their father. For the first time since Rosemaria pulled them off the streets, they had found security and a sense of purpose. They were both in college at Ohio State University and working toward degrees in business. She was so proud of those girls her heart swelled just thinking about them. After they saw on the news that she had been shot, they immediately called while she was still in the hospital. She made light of the whole situation and calmed their hysteria. She insisted it wasn't necessary for them to fly out. Until they had a more substantial lead on Clyde's whereabouts, she didn't want to do anything to unnecessarily upend their lives. She would wait a while, and if they still were making no progress, she would call Curtis. But only as a last resort.

* * * * *

The ice woman was furious. She was alone in her twentieth-floor office in Century City, sitting behind her desk with the door closed. That meant no one was allowed to knock or call, even in case of emergency. She hadn't been able reach her dimwit partner for two days. He was supposed to be at her disposal twenty-four seven. He had some brass cajónes to ignore her like this. It was unacceptable, and when she reached him, she would excoriate him up one side and down the other. She had just called him again for the fifth time today and got nothing but the outgoing message. And he knew full well she would not leave a message.

She clicked her long nails on the mahogany desktop, realized she was doing "The William Tell Overture," and stopped. How proletarian. Where the hell was he? Even before the debacle with Lorna, she had come to the conclusion that she had to rid herself once and for all of the idiots she had shared the house with. She could skip Maisie because she was dead and Sarah who was so clueless it was a wonder she'd found her way up to Seattle. How the hell had the harebrained cocktail waitress gotten away? And how could her partner blow a job that easy? The others knew too much and were a threat to her well-being. She should have killed them all years ago instead of just scaring them into running away and hiding. Even if they didn't know enough to help the idiot cops, she was sick of having to track them and worry about where they were and who they were talking to. She'd been doing it for ten years and that was long enough. She had told the pinhead what she wanted when she ordered him to kill Lorna. Now he was getting cold feet. But there was no escape for him. He was in too deep to confess to the cops. The two of them were in this together. He knew if he didn't do as he was told, she'd kill him herself.

* * * * *

Meanwhile, the pinhead was sweating bullets. He sat at his kitchen table and wondered how he could have gotten himself into such a mess. He hadn't been a bad person. He just had dreams of a better life, success, money, and everything that went with it. He had been enchanted by Mariah and her strange aura. She was beautiful in a haunting way that appealed to his darker nature. First, she seduced him, then talked him into helping her rob Ramin. How could he have known she was capable of killing him? He had been horrified, but she wouldn't let him go and solidified her hold on him by paying him part of what he had been promised. She had reminded him as only she could of how deeply he was involved and that she needed him to keep track of the others.

From one end of the country to the other, as her fortunes grew, he was the one who always had to know where all the housemates were, if they were hiding, if they were talking, which none of them were. Then, after David talked to Baker about investigating his case and proving him innocent, David had been murdered in jail. He knew then that her money could buy anything.

Why did she have to ask him to find snipers to kill the cop when she could have done it herself? He asked her that, and she said flat out she needed several degrees of separation between herself and the deed. He took that to mean he was expendable. He almost went to the cops at that point, but instead, he chickened out and found the assassins, who ended up bungling the job, online. That had brought her wrath down on him something fierce. And since the failure with Lorna, she was so out-of-her-mind mad he didn't understand why she hadn't just killed him by now. But she had made it clear she wanted all of the housemates dead, except maybe

Sarah and possibly Sherilyn, and he was the one who would have to do it. He desperately wanted to back out and go to the cops. What could he be found guilty of? Only hiring killers to kill the ex-cop. And the ex-cop was still alive, and Lorna was still alive. But Amy the receptionist had died, and that was murder for hire. He could get the needle for that one. Wherever Clyde was, he wished he were with him.

CHAPTER TWENTY-TWO

Saturday night in Tele2 Arena in Stockholm would be the last concert on the tour, and Josh was ready to go home. He walked down the hallway from his room and pressed the elevator button. As he waited, he knew for certain that being away from Rosemaria, his daily routine, and Noor and Gilbert was not something he would want to repeat often. The excitement of playing his songs in front of thousands of people and sharing the bill with fantastic musicians was even better than he had imagined, but being on tour for months at a time would never be for him. Nothing could compare with the life he already had with Rosemaria. Joell had sent his career to a whole new level, which would make possible, if he could keep writing and recording his own songs, a future Rosemaria deserved. She would never stop him from going on the road. She gave him her trust and the freedom to build his career, wherever that might take him. The truth was that he felt much freer with her than he ever had when he was alone. The elevator doors opened, and he strode out confidently. His life was finally headed in the right direction, and he was determined to enjoy every minute.

A few minutes later, he was having with lunch with Joell and Miranda at the Operakälleren restaurant, a short walk from the Grand Hotel. It was a high-end restaurant filled with light from tall windows overlooking the

Stockholm Stream, the waterway that separated the restaurant from the Royal Palace. He sipped his water and stared out at the impossible view. It was light years away from where he had grown up.

"Eat up, Josh," Joell said between bites. "You better like the food here. The only reason I'm paying for us all to stay at the Grand is because it's near the best restaurant in Stockholm."

"I appreciate that, and yes, the food is delicious."

"Don't let her guilt-trip you," Miranda said. "She always stays at the Grand. Dag gets her the best rates in town. He books all his big acts there."

Josh dug into his celeriac with mushrooms and juniper. "I knew that."

"Huh. You did not," Joell proclaimed. "I'm the decider. I decide where to stay. Not Dag."

Miranda smiled. "I'll tell him you said that."

"You will not. If Dag ever left me, I'd have to stop going on tour."

"But, more importantly," Miranda said, "we need to talk about Josh and his choices when he gets home."

"Absolutely," Joell agreed. "The man is hot, and we have to take advantage of that."

"I'm in your hands, ladies. You know a lot more about that side of the business than I do."

Miranda liked hearing that—a pliable artist—and she was filled with enthusiasm. "First of all, you need your own publicist, and I have someone in mind for you from our agency. She's young, she's new, and I am mentoring her every step of the way. You'll love her."

"We have to make the most of your appearance on this tour and the fact that the "New York Nights" single has hit number one, and the movie is number five in grosses in the US. No one knows how long that will last." Joell's passion was evident. "I'm going to speak with my people at Universal Media and sign you on my label. You'll need a manager, of course, and I'll give you a list of ones that you can trust. Meanwhile, we have to get you into the studio as soon as possible to record an album and release that within three months."

"That all sounds great," Josh said, "but you have to remember one thing."

Joell looked at him expectantly. "What's that?"

"Somebody has made an attempt on Rosemaria's life, and she's going to have twenty-four-hour protection. The cops are investigating and doing their best to find the killer, but so far, they've gotten nowhere. We have no way of knowing how long that will take. How do we fit in publicity for me and protecting her, not letting the public know where we live or where we're going?"

"You're right," Miranda said. "We have two different things going on here. Josh needs to get as much press and attention as he can get while Rosemaria needs to be protected. I think we can do both."

"Yes," Joell said. "We'll work on that and figure out the best plan of action."

The waiter came and laid down the check. Joell handed him her credit card, and he quickly did the honors with his portable scanner.

They stood up and walked to the exit.

"I'm going to walk for a while," Josh said. "Think things out."

Joell and Miranda took turns giving him a hug, and they watched him walk away and go down the stairs.

"You're going all out with this guy," Miranda said, "and you're not even sleeping with him."

"Sue me."

"Okay, I'll never mention it again."

As they headed toward the elevator, Joell had to stop herself from laughing out loud. She was one of the biggest singing stars in the world, men threw themselves at her feet on a regular basis, but the man she admired most and wanted to be with was unavailable. First Dag and now Josh. At any rate, she would do whatever she could do for him, but her true feelings she would keep to herself. She had at least that much pride.

Several hours later, Josh stood on stage with Joell and the other bands in the show as thirty thousand fans voiced their approval with screams, stomps, and hands waving in the hair. The finale had been their biggest blow-out—a loud, garage band–type rock-and-roll number that shook the foundations of the Tele2 Arena. The backup singers, dancers, orchestra, and two local bands besides Josh and Angelo went all out. It was their last night on the tour, and everyone wanted to end with something so memorable fans wouldn't be able to stop talking about it. And it was Dag's hometown. He wanted to make a statement, and so did Joell.

Drenched in sweat, everyone poured off stage and found their way into the air-conditioned dressing rooms. Josh headed straight for the parking lot and checked the time in LA. He took out his phone and dialed.

Rosemaria had been expecting the call, grabbed her phone, and heard a joyous voice. "We're done. I'm coming home!" He sounded like he was flooded with adrenaline.

"I take it the concert went well."

His words ran together. "It was incredible. I wish you could have been there. It was like nothing I've ever experienced. Way over the top of anything that happened on the tour. I'm so wrung out all I want to do is fall into bed and sleep until it's time to go to the airport."

"Where are you now?"

"I'm outside to find a car that will take me to the Grand before the others come out. I didn't feel like waiting."

"Well, then, thanks for checking in, but find a car and get to the hotel and into bed. I'm happy for you, Josh. And so proud you have no idea."

"I know you are. And that makes everything a thousand times better."

"Call me tomorrow, and tell me when you'll be home."

"Will do. Love you."

"Love you too."

She clicked off the phone. Tomorrow, she would have to tell him his mother was here. She couldn't do that tonight and ruin his incredible high after such a triumphant performance. But she had to tell him before he arrived home.

* * * * *

By noon, the temperature in Simi Valley was in the triple digits. Lorna had been told by Steven it was okay to sit out on the patio and read, but it was just too hot. She had found a twenty-year-old thriller on Rosemaria's shelf that was pretty good except technologically, it was a little behind.

The cell phones were really primitive. How could any detective function without all the apps they needed to do their jobs? Sometimes they were actually forced to use pay phones and landlines.

She heard a knock and Steven saying lunch was ready. She realized how hungry she was and put down her book, remembering to take her cell phone with her.

Steven was standing by the kitchen table, pouring himself coffee. "Would you like some?"

She nodded, and he poured her a cup as well before sitting down opposite her. "It's just sandwiches, pickles, and chips, but I hope you like it."

She sat and smiled shyly. "It looks wonderful."

"Find anything on TV worth watching?"

"No, I've been reading one of Rosemaria's books."

"Must be ancient. We need to find you something more recent. You can use my Kindle too."

They ate in silence for a few minutes.

"How long will you let me stay here?"

"Until we find the person who's trying to kill you. This is the last place they'd look for you."

"That could take a long time."

"Once Rosemaria moves to her own apartment, you'll have five people working the case. Stopping Rosemaria from investigating a crime is like stopping a cattle stampede. You can try, but you might get hurt doing it."

"You sound proud of her."

"That I am."

She pointed at him and giggled. "You have a glob of mayo on your chin."

"Oops." He grabbed his napkin and wiped. "Is that better?"

She nodded. "This is a good sandwich. Filling."

"When you're single, you have to learn how to make your own food."

"What happened to Rosemaria's mom?"

"Something went wrong with her heart. It was fast. She didn't suffer."

"I'm sorry."

"It was a long time ago."

They were both startled when Lorna's cell phone rang. She looked down at the screen then up at Steven. "I think it's him."

"Keep him talking." He texted Jimmy to let him know on the slim chance he could trace it just by having Lorna's number. Then he pressed the record button on his phone and placed it near Lorna's.

Lorna clicked her phone and put it on speaker. "Hello."

Clyde was standing by his jeep outside the hovel that passed for a convenience store and gas station in whatever third-world country he was in. "Why'd you put me on speaker?"

"Because I'm doing the dishes, and I need to dry my hands."

"Okay. What have you heard? What's going on up there?"

"Someone tried to kill me, and I had to leave Vegas. I'm hiding out at a friend's house."

"What? Mariah sent someone after you? That bitch."

"You think it was her?"

"Who else? Stop being so naïve."

"She must think I know something, like where you are or something like that."

"She should know I wouldn't have told you anything."

"Like what? What didn't you tell me?"

"I know stuff."

"Why? What did you do?"

"Never mind what I did. Listen, now that you're out of Vegas, just stay wherever you are. Mariah is stone-cold scary, and after she failed the first time, she'll want to kill you whether you know anything or not just because you got the better of her. She'll try to find you using all her resources, and believe me, she gets whatever she wants because she can twist people around until they don't know which way is up."

Lorna read a note that Steven scribbled and put down in front of her.

"Listen, Clyde. I hear that the cops are closing in on her, and when they arrest her, they'll find out what you did. Why don't you come home and tell them everything? You can testify against her and get off."

"You think I'd live that long? Forget it."

"Please come home. You can stay with me."

"Gotta go. I won't be calling you for a while." He clicked off, destroyed his phone, and heaved it into the brush.

Steven's phone rang, and he answered. "Anything? . . . Okay, I recorded the call on my phone. I'm sending it to you so you can have one of your forensic experts listen for ambient noises the human ear may not be able to hear." He pressed a few buttons and sent the recording.

"Good job." Steven said to Lorna. "You kept him on as long as you could. Maybe the lab can pick up noises, especially animal, car, industrial, or other sounds in the background that might tell us where he is. It's a long shot, but you never know."

"I wish I could have done better."

"It was plenty good."

"I'll do the dishes."

"We'll do them together. You can wash, and I'll dry."

They cleared the table and felt pretty good about moving at least a millimeter closer to finding the killer.

* * * * *

Jimmy was working on his home computer in his studio apartment in West Hollywood. He had access to most of the BHPD database and was searching for information on some of the people on the list Rosemaria had given him. He had divided the rest of the list between two other computer geeks in the department. At least when he worked at home, he was comfortable and could take snack and drink breaks whenever he felt like it, unlike when he had been trapped in the computer room for the last three years. He wondered how long Loo and the captain would let him work on Rosemaria's case. They did care for her like she was their own daughter, but there were a few other cases that demanded attention. He was doing the best he could keeping track of them, but his focus was on finding the elusive Mariah.

Now, as he worked on the list, he was waiting to hear from his colleagues if they had caught any ambient noises off Clyde's phone call. He wanted to be a part of making all the pieces fit.

His cell rang, and he saw it was the main character in this drama herself. "Hi, Rosemaria."

"Did you learn anything interesting from the list yet?" She was slowly walking back and forth in her room to condition her ankle to handle more stressful walking and possibly running if it came to that.

"I've thoroughly checked out six on the list so far—Isolde Garwood, Sally Mankowitz, Nancy Winfield, Hortensia Sarturo, Jackie Radcliff, and Drew Peterson. I can't find anything suspicious about any of them."

"Okay. Remember anything that seems even a little bit off, let me know, okay?"

"I assume your father told you about Clyde's call? I haven't heard back from the lab yet. It would be nice if we heard the mating call of a cockatoo that only lives in one small corner of a South American jungle."

"I can only dream of such a clue. But let me run something by you. What do you think of asking Curtis to use his connections to find Clyde? His tentacles reach far and wide, including some slightly clandestine government agencies."

"I like it."

"Yeah? Okay, well, I was thinking of Melody and Tiffany. I don't want to do anything to upset their lives."

"What's to upset? Curtis can make some calls, and his former marine buddies who are still in the field can make the trip to wherever Clyde is and persuade him to come in from the cold."

"Actually, there's no such thing as a *former* marine."

"I stand corrected, ma'am. Right now, I need to get back to my work."

They both clicked off.

Rosemaria sat at her desk wondering what the heck to do. She needed to find Clyde. It was obvious from what he said that he had been involved with Ramin's murder and that he, like everyone else except maybe Sarah and Micco, was terrified of Mariah. It was hard to imagine either one of them involved in killing David. She made up her mind that as soon as Josh came home and they straightened this thing out between him and his mother, she would call Curtis. Rosemaria had admitted before—she was like a shark. She had to keep moving forward or die.

Meanwhile, she would call her office and find out if her boss had changed his mind about letting her come back earlier. She was worried if she stayed out any longer, she'd lose her job. Karen had reminded her last time she called that both women and men were allowed to stay out longer than this on parental leave. She should just relax, pretend that she was having a baby, and know her job was waiting for her when she came back. Karen would tell her if there was any bad news. But relax? That just wasn't in her DNA.

* * * *

The next morning in Stockholm, Josh's overnight bag was on the bed. Both his other suitcases and his guitar had been taken downstairs by porters and would be delivered to the airport separately, along with everyone else's luggage. He still had half an hour before he had to leave. He hit the speed dial on his phone and sat on the love seat at the foot of his bed.

"Yes?" Rosemaria answered, keeping her eye on Suzi, who was flying around the room as if she knew something was up.

"I'm leaving for the airport in a few minutes and will be arriving at LAX at eight a.m. your time. Will you be there?"

"Need you ask?"

"I figured. After all, you are at my beck and call."

"Always and forever. . . . Josh . . ." She sounded hesitant.

"What's wrong? Are you all right? Was there another attempt?"

"No, nothing like that."

"Then what is it?"

"Someone came here to see you."

"To see me? Who?"

"Your mother."

There was dead air between them.

"Did you hear what I said? Your mother showed up at our apartment, and one of Cameron's men took her to the Beverly Wilshire, where she has been staying ever since." She waited, not daring to say another word.

Josh stared at the blank TV screen on the wall. *Why now? What did she want?* He needed to call Lenny before he said something stupid.

"I don't know why she's here, but I'll deal with it. Don't worry about it." His words came out harsh and abrupt.

"I would have told you right away, but I didn't want her presence here to affect your performance. I'm sorry."

"It's okay. I'm fine."

"I'll see you tomorrow morning. I love you."

"Yeah." And he clicked off.

Rosemaria fought back tears. This was the first time he had ever talked to her in that tone of voice since they had become a couple. Josh coming home from a tour, moving into a new home, seeing his mother for the first time in fifteen years—all of it happening tomorrow. Rosemaria figured if she got shot at, it would be a welcome diversion.

She heard a knock on the door and Vanessa's voice. "I'm coming in, ready or not." Rosemaria pressed the buzzer to unlock the door. As soon as Vanessa walked in, she saw the look on Rosemaria's face. She sat down next to her as Suzi fluttered about and landed on her shoulder. "Hi, Suzi. What's wrong with your mom?"

"I just told Josh about his mother."

"Did he get angry?"

"No. His voice turned stone cold, as if I were a stranger."

"Oh boy." She sat staring at Rosemaria at a total loss. "You're not used to that from him."

Tears poured unbidden down Rosemaria's cheeks. Vanessa put her arms around her as Rosemaria tried her best not to cry. "Never. He's never spoken to me like that ever."

"He was in shock. You have to remember that he's held on to the trauma of that day for all these years. You told me he's just starting to work it out. This is not about you; it's about him."

Rosemaria sat up while Vanessa grabbed a tissue from the night table and handed it to her. She blew her nose and wiped her face. "I wanted to do what was best for him. Do you think he'll forgive me?"

"Of course, and there's nothing to forgive."

"We've never been like this."

"I know. But it happens, and it'll happen again. We're human."

The tears were welling up again. "It's hard."

"I know, but let's talk about something that will cheer you up for sure."

"Okay."

"I had a few pieces moved into your condo, and I think you're going to love how it looks. It has a huge living room, a nice view of trees and a courtyard below, two bedrooms, one guest bath and an en suite, and a fabulous kitchen. Open concept with a fireplace in the family room and a sweet little parlor. I can't wait for you to see it."

"Thank you for all your hard work." Rosemaria grabbed more tissues to wipe her nose.

"It wasn't work. When all the unpleasantness is over, I'll help you decorate. Not fun to do that now when you're worried about some nutcase."

"Rosemaria dabbed at her eyes. "Josh and I always had this special connection, you know. It's been unbreakable, no matter what. The thought of that being gone tears at my heart."

"Will you stop? Nothing is broken. Nothing has changed. His mother, who he has hated all these years, is here to see him. He'll deal with it. It has nothing to do with you."

"But I want to help him."

"If you want my advice, which you probably don't, just butt out. Let him do this on his own."

"You're harsh."

"Well, when you act like a child, I must deal with you as one. No more kvetching."

"I feel better."

Vanessa looked at her. "You do?"

"Yes. I have a mother-in-law problem. So what else is new? Who doesn't?"

"Vanessa laughed. "Look what I have to live up to in Loretta. It's impossible."

"Let's go down and take a dip in the pool and give Suzi some fresh air. Then I will act like a diva one last time and ask Manuela to make us everything our hearts desire and have that handsome duo Max and Brent serve us as the royal sisters we are."

"Sounds like a plan. Grab me a suit from your closet."

CHAPTER TWENTY-THREE

The FASTEN SEATBELTS sign went on, and Josh buckled up and felt the plane lose altitude to prepare for landing at LAX. He was in the aisle seat, so he couldn't look out the window to see how close they were. He had tried to sleep during the eleven-hour flight to make time go by faster, but the thoughts tumbling through his brain wouldn't allow it. He and a few of the other musicians had taken the early flight. Others had chosen later flights or to stay in Stockholm for a few more days. Joell had friends in Sweden and would be enjoying a few days of relaxed country living before heading home.

He shook his head remembering Lenny's reaction when Josh had called him immediately after his conversation with Rosemaria. Although Josh was expecting a little bit of understanding and kind words, Lenny had instead torn him a new one. He had ripped him up one side and down the other, accusing him of making Rosemaria pay for his inability to get past ancient history with his childish, petulant behavior. He reminded Josh again that she had sacrificed her freedom for him so he could wander around Europe living his dream while she faced a life-or-death situation. It was time to stop whining about the past and move on.

When Lenny went on a rant, there was no stopping him, so Josh didn't even try. He also knew he deserved everything Lenny was throwing at him and felt a deep sense of shame for making Rosemaria feel he had rejected her. He sat impatiently, willing the plane to fly faster. He had wanted to call her back and apologize over the phone, but that wouldn't have been good enough. He wanted her to see his face as he said he was sorry and know without a shadow of a doubt that that no one and nothing was as important as what they shared. The plane descended, and he could finally see the city below. She was down there waiting for him, and that was the only thing in the world that mattered.

Traffic at LAX was busy as usual, but Rosemaria barely noticed. Cameron was driving a black SUV, and Kirsten was in the front seat while Rosemaria sat in the back, alone with her thoughts. Cameron had a sticker on the windshield that allowed him to park right outside the door where Josh would be coming out after going through customs. Josh had texted Rosemaria his every move since he deplaned.

When he texted that he had passed through customs, even though she had been ordered to stay in the car, she jumped out, intending to run to the door. But Kirsten was out of the car in an instant, grabbed her, and kept her from moving. She finally saw Josh inside, several yards away, pushing a cart loaded with his overnight bag, two suitcases and a guitar case. She waved excitedly even though she had been given explicit instructions not to call attention to herself. As he came out the door and walked toward her, she felt as if he were moving in slow motion. The look on his face told her all was forgiven.

She threw herself into his arms, and Josh, avoiding her cast, managed to wrap her in an embrace so tight she could hardly breathe. Her face was pressed against his chest, and he bent down, his mouth next to her ear, whispering over and over again, "I'm sorry, I'm so very, very sorry."

And she was whispering back, "No, It's okay. It's okay."

They stayed tight together for several seconds, then he held her at arm's length and said, "I love you, will always love you, and if I ever hurt you again, you can take that gun out of your purse and shoot me."

Rosemaria touched his cheek with her hand to brush away his tears. "Don't worry. I understand. And I won't shoot you, no matter what you do."

He took her face in his hands and kissed her. She could have stayed like that forever. But Cameron had grown concerned, stepped out of the SUV, and helped Kirsten usher the couple into the back seat. They grabbed the overnight bag, suitcases, and guitar off the cart and placed them in the rear. Cameron's eyes continuously searched the crowd for anything untoward. He and Kirsten got back in the car, and they pulled out into traffic.

Rosemaria leaned her good side against Josh, and their fingers tangled together. She whispered, "That was quite a PDA there, big guy."

"A preview of coming attractions."

"Can't wait."

"I called my mom after I landed."

"And?"

"I told her I'd come see her later at the hotel. We had a short conversation. She sounded happy."

"That does it."

"Does what?"

"I want to be president of your fan club."

"There's a lot of competition for that position."

"I can take on all of 'em with one arm in a cast."

"You're hired." He sealed the deal with a kiss as Cameron and Kirsten stared straight ahead.

* * * * *

The twenty-five staff members filtered out the door of the glassed-in conference room and walked back to their offices, a few on the same floor, others waiting for the elevators to take them to floors below, higher floors being the most desirable and sought after. Competition was stiff in the company, but the pay was high, based on performance, and fair. That's how the ice woman attracted the best in the business and kept them happy.

She stayed in her chair in the conference room, smiling at the last person to leave, who closed the glass door behind her. It had been a fruitful meeting, everyone eager to report their successes of the week. But her mind was elsewhere. She operated on two levels, always had. One was the world of business and high society, and the other one that had needed an ever-watchful eye since she began her journey to ensure everything stayed on track. It was imperative that nothing could be traced back to the beginning, and her secrets stayed safe. In this world of internet technology, where people could investigate every nook and cranny of everyone else's lives, she had needed to foresee possibilities that would keep her one step ahead of anyone poking their nose into her business. So far, so good. She was becoming quite the tech geek herself.

Her steady rise in fortune had gone along uninterrupted until David Marchand had decided to prove he was innocent. Approaching the Innocence Project had failed. But then David had decided to involve the pain-in-the-ass ex-cop who had a nose for trouble and never let up. Online, the ice queen had found an ex-con who might be willing to break parole and get himself sent back to prison for the right price. She found his number and, using a burner phone, sent him a text with a brief explanation of what needed to be done. The price—twenty thousand dollars. Easily worth the two and a half years he'd have to spend in prison to finish his sentence. She had left him a bag of money at a drop-off place, with the other half to be paid when David was dead. The money would go into a numbered account he would set up.

As expected, after he committed a misdemeanor theft, and his parole was revoked, he was sent back to the same prison he had been in, where David was serving time for murder. A month later, David was found dead with no suspects and no leads. The money had been quickly dispatched into the con's account.

Her one huge mistake had been involving another person in her plan to rob and kill Ramin. The boy had been so damn sexy and good looking. All the other males in her life, she had used and thrown away with no remorse; some she'd had to make disappear for good. But this one had gotten under her skin, if only briefly. When she looked back and wondered how she could have been so stupid, she excused her gross misstep by telling herself she had only been nineteen and vulnerable to someone with immense physical appeal. However, after a while, she realized he was not worthy of being anything more than a tool. She was in too deep when she came to that conclusion, but he could be useful when she needed him. And he would never be able to say no.

Now the ex-cop's singer boyfriend was home, and she would be released from her secure existence and be on her own, vulnerable to attack. How well she would be guarded remained to be seen. But before ending the annoying bitch's life, she had decided the others would be eliminated first. All of them knew too much. She had blamed the ex-cop for derailing her perfect plan, but she now realized she had to rid herself of everyone who had the slightest ability to destroy what she had worked so hard to build. And that was the fun part. This is what had brought her pleasure since she was eight years old. Money and murder. And getting away with it. There was absolutely nothing else in life that could compete with that thrilling combination. Her partner would do one more job, and then she wouldn't need any hired assassins or degrees of separation. She would do the rest herself.

* * * * *

The black SUV drove through the gates, after a brief confirmation into the intercom that they were who they said they were and continued on to the Collins mansion. There were several cars parked in the area at the side of the house, but Josh didn't notice that some of them might be familiar. Cameron and his man opened the door, and Josh helped Rosemaria out. The front door of the mansion opened, and Loretta walked down the few stone steps to welcome them. She stretched out her hand to Josh but decided to envelope him in a hug instead as a smiling Rosemaria stood back and watched.

"Welcome home, Josh. So, you're going to take our girl away from us tomorrow?"

"I'm afraid so. She'll have to go back to living the simple life with me."

"Well, until then, why don't the two of you come in and relax? We'll feed you a great meal later."

Josh grabbed his suitcases from Cameron's man, and Loretta led Josh and Rosemaria into the hallway.

"Put your suitcases down, Josh. Brent will take them up to Rosemaria's room. Let's go into the sunroom, and Mildred will bring you some lemonade."

As soon as Josh and Rosemaria rounded the corner into the sunroom, a crowd of at least ten people yelled, "Welcome home!"

Josh and Rosemaria were stunned. They looked at the happy faces of their friends crowding around them, giving hugs and laughing at the looks on the couple's faces—Steven, Larry, Vanessa, Jimmy, Madelaine, Kirsten, Raul, and Rosemaria's colleagues from the prosecutor's office; her assistant Karen, and her fellow prosecutors Terrence and Reid. Andrew and Loretta stood together near the French doors, enjoying the spectacle.

Mildred handed Josh and Rosemaria their drinks, and Larry and Vanessa ushered them to the wicker love seat.

"I'm going to kill whoever organized this whole thing," Rosemaria sputtered.

"Not everything is about you, girlfriend," Vanessa said. "Let's all raise our glasses and toast the man whose single has been number one on the pop charts for two and a half weeks. Here's to Josh Sibley."

Josh shook his head, speechless, while everyone lifted their glasses and drank.

"Thank you, everyone," he finally managed to say. "Remember, fame can be fleeting, and I will be back in the studio in a couple of days singing jingles for furniture stores just in case I'm a dim memory by next month." He lifted his glass. "And here's to the incredible Joell, who made all this possible"

"To Joell," they all shouted.

Rosemaria lifted her glass and looked at Raul. "And here's to Raul Sentoro, whose extreme courage saved my life. He's the reason I'm here, and I will always be grateful to him for risking his own life to save mine."

As everyone lifted their glasses, Rosemaria walked over to Raul and hugged him with her good arm. She knew that because of the insane, death-defying roller-coaster ride they had shared and Raul risking his own life to save her, they had forged a bond that would last a lifetime.

Mildred, Brent, and Max carried in plates of scrumptious-looking sides and main dishes and set them on the sideboard, and everyone grabbed a plate and took generous helpings of the offerings. Steven handed Rosemaria a plate, and Larry brought one for Josh. They dived in, both starving, having been too excited and anxious at the thought of seeing each other to eat that morning. Steven pulled up a chair next to Rosemaria.

"Are you ready to be out in the world again, daughter?"

"I can't wait, Dad. I'll be safe; don't worry. I know how to take care of myself, and I will have the best bodyguard the Collins can afford."

They were interrupted by Karen, who was joined by Rosemaria's fellow prosecutors Reid and Terrance in assuring Rosemaria that her job was safe. Terrance and Reid were dividing up her caseload and, so far, had handled everything fine, ratcheting up Rosemaria's insecurities that she might not be needed at all, provoking more needed reassurance from her colleagues. Conversations swirled around them, and Rosemaria noticed the strained expression on Josh's face as he smiled and answered questions.

She leaned over and whispered to Josh, "Excuse me for a minute. I'll be right back."

He watched her walk away, grateful for the surprise party their friends had sprung on them but wishing they were already alone in Rosemaria's room. He could barely concentrate on what Larry was saying when, in two minutes, she was back. She leaned over and whispered in his ear. "I called your mom. I told her you were too exhausted from your trip to come over tonight, and you would take her to breakfast tomorrow. We can move to our condo when you get back from breakfast. Then, while Vannessa and I are setting things up, you can go visit Noor and Gilbert."

She pecked his cheek, and he could only stare at her as she was grabbed by her good arm by Vanessa, who took her outside to the patio where Loretta and Andrew were talking to Karen and Reid. She had read his mind even in the midst of all this chaos and set everything right. As he watched Rosemaria greet her hosts and easily chatter away, he felt more satisfaction than he had felt that last night in Stockholm. The euphoria of having thousands of fans enveloping him in foot-stomping adoration was intoxicating but fleeting. He vowed no matter what happened in his career, no matter how often he was away from her, he would never forget what was really important.

* * * *

The "safe house" where Sam and Stacey were staying was really a second-floor one-bedroom apartment in the Cortez Hill section of San Diego. The neighborhood boasted upscale retail and restaurant options and high rises that had views of the Pacific, but so far, Sam and Stacey had seen little of it. Their safety was in the hands of cops who sat in cars in eight-hour shifts outside the building. The couple wondered how long that would last before they were left to their own devices and at the mercy of Mariah, who they knew would eventually find them. Meanwhile, they were bored out of their skulls. Up in the mountains, they had been free to live their lives outdoors and make occasional trips into town. Now they were prisoners and who knew for how long.

They were busy preparing sandwiches for lunch when they heard a knock on the door and froze. Sam walked toward the door and looked through the peephole. It was the cop on duty. He opened the door.

"Everything okay in here?" Officer Trawley asked. He was a slightly pudgy, balding, fiftyish man who treated them kindly.

"Fine. What's up?"

"I'll be coming back up in about an hour. They want you to go downtown for an interview. Shouldn't take too long. I'll have you back here in no time."

Stacey had moved up beside Sam. "They can have us as long as they want. And can we come back by way of Pacific Beach or the Gaslamp District or somewhere interesting? Maybe stop and have dinner? Anything to get out of here and feel human again."

Officer Trawley laughed. "Not much fun sitting in the patrol car either. I'll see what I can arrange."

He left, and Sam closed the door. "I keep thinking about the day we decided to save money by renting a room in that shitty house in the worst part of Hollywood. We should have kept looking and paid a little more.

Now we'll be paying for the rest of our lives." He sank down on the couch, drowning in his own misery.

Stacey went back into the kitchen nook and resumed preparing their lunch. "Stop feeling sorry for yourself. And it won't be for the rest of our lives. They'll catch her. I believe that. Some of those cops seem really smart, and they're motivated because of Baker. Even if they don't give a damn about us, she's got them all worked up to protect her."

Sam stood up, and Stacey offered him a plate. He picked up the TV clicker. "What do you want to eat to?"

"No more cop shows, okay? They're starting to make me feel creepy. Too close to home, if you know what I mean." She sat down on the couch next to him and took a bite of her sandwich.

He browsed through a few channels in the guide, found *Seinfeld*, and put down the clicker. "I remember when this show used to make me laugh."

"Stop with the boo-hooing and eat your lunch."

He chewed on his sandwich. "Hey, I never saw this one."

She smiled. "See, every day offers new and wonderful opportunities."

"You got it babe. A *Seinfeld* I never saw, a drive by the ocean. Life is good." He chewed and stared glumly at the screen.

* * * * *

The atmosphere in the interrogation room was relaxed and friendly. Stacey and Sam were sipping cans of pop, and Mack was drinking coffee from Starbucks. Loshi leaned back in his chair and looked as if he were about to fall asleep.

"We think," Mack said, "there is something, maybe something very small, in the back of your mind that could help us get a lead on this Mariah woman. What can you tell us about her that set her apart from everybody else in the house?"

"Well—" Sam began.

"Oh, for heaven's sake," Stacey interrupted. "The girl slept with every man in the house, except Ramin and David."

Sam looked at her in astonishment.

"You thought I didn't know? Give me a break. I never said anything because what was the point? If I'd given you a choice, you would have picked her over me in a second. On the run and ten years later, who gives a flying poop?" She looked at Mack and Loshi. "I think she's capable of killing as easily as she breathes. The men were too enraptured by her to notice she was a pure psycho. Unfortunately, now they're paying the price. If you manage to find Keith, I'd be shocked. He's the one who was most head over heels for her and probably knew some secrets. I have no doubt he's six feet under somewhere."

Loshi sat up straight. "Whoa, where's all this coming from all of a sudden?"

"I'm just sick of the subterfuge that's been going on for too long. I'm sure Sam knows a lot more than he's admitting to. So just tell them what you know, Sam. What's the use of hiding anything anymore? Any minute, we could end up dead."

Mack sipped his coffee leisurely. "We'll do everything we can to prevent that from happening, but if there's anything you want to share, Sam, we're listening."

Sam hesitated, and Stacey stared him down. "I didn't know she was going to rob the carpet store. I swear, I didn't know anything about it. But afterward, I suspected. She changed. Stayed to herself. I never touched her after that. After Stacey was almost killed, I was afraid she thought I knew something I could tell the cops, but there was nothing. Anyway, all I knew was Stacey and I had better get the hell out of there."

"She gave you no indication of what she was planning?"

"No, there was nothing."

"But you just said she robbed the carpet store," Mack said.

"I said I suspected she did, that she had money in the bag I saw. Why else jump down my throat?"

Loshi was getting frustrated. "You spent a lot of time with her—when you were eating, having sex, when nobody else was around. Did she ever say anything, talk about her past? She can't have been in total control of her words and actions every minute of every day."

"Well, I guess the only time she kind of let go was when we had sex, when nobody could hear us. She kind of threw herself into it, if you know what I mean." He looked apologetically at Stacey, who kept her expression neutral. "She used to yell out the usual, 'Oh God!' and that."

"That's it? That's Mariah out of control? 'Oh, God'?" Loshi turned away in disgust.

"Do you want Stacey to leave the room for a minute?" Mack asked.

Stacey's voice was hard. "I'm not going anywhere."

Sam looked at her and shook his head. "I'm sorry."

"Forget it." Stacey said. "If there's anything more, just say it."

Sam looked at Loshi. "She was like a lot of different people. She could be charming and sweet when she had to be, when we were walking by ourselves to the store, and affectionate when she wanted something from me. When she was in a good mood, she would laugh and talk in an accent that sounded like maybe she was from Brooklyn or maybe somewhere in the South, and she'd call me names like *cher,* and sometimes she'd call me Andy somebody."

"Andy?" Loshi asked.

"Yeah, something like that. She would yell out foreign-sounding names when she came."

"You knew she was having sex with the other guys," Mack said.

"Not at first. Even after we all found out, we couldn't stop. She was like a drug."

"Anything else?"

"Money. Mostly she talked about getting rich."

Mack nodded. This was going nowhere.

"We were still teenagers. The hormones were raging. What the hell did we know about anything?"

"I'd have to agree with that," Mack said.

Loshi pushed back his chair. "Thank you for coming in. Sorry you have to stay cooped up, but we'll do our best to find Mariah and get your lives back to normal as soon as possible."

They all stood, and Mack opened the door and ushered the couple into the hallway. A sheriff's deputy led them toward the exit. Mack and Loshi watched as they disappeared around a corner.

"That was less than illuminating," Loshi said.

"Well, she mentioned this guy Andy. That's something. Maybe an old boyfriend from her nonexistent childhood. Send the report to Larry. Maybe they can dig something useful out of what he said."

"You're getting very generous in your old age."

"I want this thing off my plate so I can retire with a clear conscience and take my vacation in Baha next month. I don't care who solves it, who gets the credit, or who takes her down. I just want it over with."

CHAPTER TWENTY-FOUR

With Trawley's sincere apologies, Sam and Stacey's beachfront dinner turned out to be takeout from a fast-food drive-in eaten in the car while watching the ocean waves lapping at the surf in Pacific Beach. But it was better than yet another microwaved dinner.

Later, back in their apartment, as Sam changed from his jeans into sweatpants and a T-shirt, he glanced over at Stacey tearing off her clothes and pulling on a loose, flowered shift. He had expected her to give him grief by yelling and calling him names, but she was being downright surly and hadn't spoken a word to him since the interview.

He tried to pull her close, but she pushed him away and stalked into the kitchen nook.

"Come on. It was ten years ago."

He followed her as she grabbed a Coke out of the refrigerator.

"Not the silent treatment, okay? We're all we've got right now. No boo-hooing, remember?"

She stopped sipping her Coke and studied the can for a few seconds.

"I'm not boo-hooing. I'm engaged in self-absorbed seething."

She saw him stare past her at the front door. "What's that?" he said.

She followed his glance. "It looks like a piece of paper was shoved under our door when we were gone."

They exchanged apprehensive glances.

Sam slowly walked over and picked up the paper. He unfolded it, and they both read what was written: "Mariah knows where you are. Meet me in the back of the market three blocks up. You're not safe. Burn this note. Geek boy."

They stared wide eyed at each other. Geek boy was what Sam had called Micco in a fit of jealousy over Mariah because he always had his head in his computer. No one else knew the name.

"It's Micco."

"What's he doing here?"

"I don't know. He's supposed to be in New Mexico somewhere."

"Maybe she decided to go after him."

She grabbed Sam and held on tight. "She's going to get us all, Sam. I swear she is!" She let go of him and grabbed her cell phone. "We have to tell Officer Trawley."

"But what if it's true? What if Mariah knows where we are? How do we know we can trust him?"

"He's a good guy. You can tell."

"Can we take that chance?" He paced the length of the living room and stared out the window at the lights down the hill. "I don't know what to do."

"I don't trust anybody who lived in that house."

"But what if he's right? Nobody can protect us from her."

"We call the cops. The detectives need to know this."

"Let's see what he has to say, and we'll sneak back in."

"You mean go out the window?"

"We can tie a sheet to the bedpost and come back the same way. We'll call whoever's on duty outside and tell them we're going to bed."

"This doesn't feel right." Stacey said. "Okay, we'll hear him out and come right back."

Five minutes later, they were on the ground at the side of the building, making their way between cars in the parking lot, behind the next building, and up the block. They found the market and walked to the back parking lot. They saw Micco sitting in the driver's seat of a black sedan. He waved them over. Stacey got in the back and Sam walked around to the passenger seat.

"What the hell, man?" Sam demanded as soon as he closed the door.

Micco started the car and drove out of the parking lot down the alley and, seeing that no cars were coming, drove down the hill. "She found out where you were."

"How?"

"She has a fiancé who's connected to the sheriff's department. If you remember, she can wangle anything out of anybody before they even know they've done something stupid."

"And she told you?"

"I kept track of most of you so she'd know where everybody was and make sure you weren't doing anything idiotic like going to the cops."

Sam looked back at Stacey, who was listening wide eyed.

"You were working with her all this time?" Sam asked.

"Until a year ago. Now I live on a boat and move from place to place so she can't find me."

"Then how do you know what she knows?"

"She kept the old laptop I set up for her with all the old codes. I hacked into it yesterday. She sent a message to someone and told them you were here."

"Who?"

"I don't know. Someone who is helping her like I did. Maybe the person who helped her with the robbery like I did."

Sam and Stacey looked at each other. He helped her with the robbery? They sped down the hill in silence, along Harbor, past the Sheraton, and parked by the marina. Micco opened the door. "Come on. My boat's in here." He unlocked the gate, and they followed him down the pier to a thirty-foot motorboat. Stacey and Sam stepped on board and followed Micco into the stateroom.

"What do you mean you helped her?" Sam asked.

"Have a seat." Micco gestured to the two bunks on either side of the stateroom. "I disabled the cameras by the gate and at the apartment building as well. The cops won't know you were here."

"Why?" Stacey exploded. "Why would you help her?"

"I didn't know she was going to kill him. After that, I was in too deep. I was an accessory to murder." He stood up. "Stay here." He went out on deck.

"This is insane." Stacey said. "We need to leave."

"We said we'd hear him out."

They heard soft thumping noises and Micco walking around.

Sam started to get up, but Stacey grabbed his arm. "We can't trust him. He's dangerous."

They heard the boat's engine start up and hurried outside. The boat was no longer roped to the dock. They saw Micco standing by the wheel. "I feel safer out on the water. If someone comes after us, we'll know."

Sam was torn with indecision. He and Stacey looked up and down the waterway and at the slowly receding parking lot. "I don't know about this." He was shaking his head.

Micco guided the boat out into the open water, passing warehouses and the navy yard, and headed south. The lights of downtown San Diego faded in the distance. "Don't worry. I learned a lot about boats in the past year. I know what I'm doing. You're safe."

Stacey wasn't having it. An ominous feeling of dread came over her. "I want to go back," she stammered. "We have to go back."

"You can't." Micco was suddenly cold and abrupt. "Sit down and shut up."

Stacey and Sam did as they were told as the boat moved farther down the coast. When only a few lights were visible on shore, he cut the engine, and they sat still in the water. "You can't go back to that apartment. The cops won't be able to keep you there forever. Mariah will get to you sooner or later."

"I don't believe that," Stacey said, her voice shaking. "Take us back. I don't want to be out here."

"That's not going to happen. I'm going to make sure she doesn't find you. I'm taking you to Mexico. There's a little town called Santa Lucia where we can pull in close to the beach." He reached into the cabinet under the steering wheel and took out a satchel. "There's ten thousand dollars in there and a change of clothes for both of you. You can disappear. Start a new life."

Sam had found his bearings. "That's crazy. We're not survivalists. We don't know how to live in the jungle or the desert or whatever's down there. To find work anywhere, we'd need ID, we'd need passports. Neither one of us speaks Spanish. We'd never make it."

Sweat was forming on Micco's brow. He began to sound desperate. "With that money, you can find a place to live, get to know people. They won't care who you are down there. At least you'll be alive!"

"What's with you, man?" Sam asked. "Why does this matter so much to you? We'll stay in the apartment as long as they let us and take our chances with whoever Mariah sends. It's a hell of a lot better than living in some shack in Mexico."

Micco shook his head. "No, no, no!"

Stacey was adamant. "Start the damn boat, Micco, and take us back. Now!"

"Do it, Micco," Sam said. "We're not going to Mexico."

Micco bent down, picked up a roll of masking tape and threw it at Stacey. She caught it and watched in horror as he reached around his back and pulled an automatic pistol out of his waistband and pointed it at her. "Tape his hands behind his back. I'm taking you down to Mexico and dumping you on the beach, and you will disappear. Because if you don't, we are all dead. Do you understand that? We are all dead."

Stacey stepped around behind Sam and started to unroll the tape.

"You're Mariah's partner." Sam said. "You messed with the brakes on your car to make them fail; you tried to kill Stacey. You hired the hit men to kill the cop. What have you done to Keith and Clyde?"

"Keith is dead, but I didn't kill him. I don't know where Clyde is, and neither does she."

"This isn't your boat. You don't live on it. She set this up so you could take us out here and dump us in the water."

"No. That's not what I wanted. I want you to go to Mexico and disappear so she'll think I killed you and let me live."

Sam put his hands up. "Okay, okay, calm down. We'll go down to Mexico. Put down the gun."

Micco kept the gun pointed at Sam and Stacey as he stood at the wheel. They sat down together on one of the bunks as Micco steered the boat farther down the coast.

No one spoke for several minutes until Sam asked, "Where will you go after you drop us off?"

"Not your worry."

"You don't have to kill us," Stacey said. "We won't tell anybody what you've done."

Micco looked at them, weighing his options. They both knew he was not going to let them go.

Micco spoke quietly. "Stacey, tape Sam's hands together."

Stacey looked questioningly at Sam.

Micco's face darkened. "Do it."

Sam jumped to his feet, lunged at Micco, and screamed, "Stacey, jump off the boat!" Sam grappled with Micco for control of the gun. "Get off the boat!" Stacey hesitated for a few seconds, then she heard the gun go off and saw a red bullet wound blossoming on Sam's chest. She dove in and swam to the other side of the boat. She heard Micco swearing as he fired the pistol into the water where she had gone in. He kept firing until the gun clicked empty.

Stacey was strong, but she was terrified she'd never make it to shore. She swam, knowing her life depended on her getting as far from the boat as possible. She knew she had about thirty seconds to escape. Micco would need to reload his gun and start firing blindly into the water. He would have to find something to weigh Sam's body before throwing him overboard and turning the boat around to come after her. She came to the surface on her back, letting only her mouth appear above the waterline. She took a deep breath, turned over, and went under again.

On the boat, Micco was panicking. He reloaded and fired into the water until he emptied his gun again. Then he picked up one of the fifty-pound dumbbells attached to a long chain that had been on the boat when he first checked it out. Mariah had thought of everything. Had she brought them aboard herself? Probably. She loved being close to the action if not quite part of it. He wrapped the dumbbell around Sam's waist with the chain and dragged him to the opening in the aft of the boat. He shoved Sam and the weight into the water and ran from one side of the boat to the other staring out at the dark water. Stacey was gone. He turned the boat around but couldn't go much farther toward shore. The water was shallow, the ground was rocky, and he needed to get back to the marina and then home. He had hours of driving to do. He kept firing into the water until he ran out of bullets. Her chances of surviving were slim to nonexistent.

Stacey had heard the splash of Sam's body hitting the water and knew Micco couldn't steer the boat and fire accurately. Even though she couldn't see the traces of the bullets, she knew they were coming close. Only luck would keep them from hitting her. Suddenly, the firing stopped. She wanted to shoot to the surface and scream and mourn Sam's death, but all she could do was keep swimming and coming to the top and breathing when she needed to.

Micco worried about her body showing up in a few days or weeks. But there was nothing he could do about it now. He could tell Mariah he had done as she asked and then take every penny he owned and disappear. Clyde had gone south of the border. That he knew. Wherever he was, he had stayed gone. That's what Micco needed to do.

CHAPTER TWENTY-FIVE

Josh was waiting for Rosemaria when she came out of the bathroom, one towel wrapped around her shampooed hair and another wrapped around her body. He was wearing his sweatsuit bottoms and had placed a pillowcase over Suzi's cage. He removed both towels and the plastic wrap around her cast, and she ran her hand through her hair to smooth out the tangles. He led her over to the bed where the covers were already turned down and gently laid her down. Their eyes never left each other's as he stepped out of his sweatpants.

"I guess you'd like me to tell you everything that's been happening with the investigation," Rosemaria whispered.

He lay down next to her and ran a finger down her bare arm. "Later."

"You know you can't get too rambunctious with me. I'm slightly imperfect right now."

"Injured, yes; imperfect, never."

He brought his lips close to hers, and she thought she'd die waiting for his mouth to touch hers. He teased her by holding back, and the anticipation was unbearable. When, finally, the softness of his lips met hers, she felt as if her entire body were set on fire. He pulled her to him, avoiding crushing the injured arm.

"Let me do everything. You just relax," he said.

She gave a slight nod, too overcome with desire to speak. She opened herself up to his expert ministrations and fell into an abyss of pure pleasure. All her apprehension, worries, and fears evaporated, and she surrendered control of her senses.

Later, they lay together, stroking each other lazily wherever there was exposed skin.

"I don't think I said I missed you since I came home."

"If this is what I can expect every time you come back from a tour, I may consider allowing you to leave me more often."

"I'd rather you go with me."

"How can I keep the city free of dangerous criminals if I'm tagging along after you? But maybe, in a year or two, after I've proven myself irreplaceable to Latimer. Meanwhile, my sweet, we'll just have to settle for these pleasant little reunions after you come back from your tours."

"Pleasant?"

"Okay, earth shattering, mind numbing, cataclysmic."

He shrugged. "Better."

"I'm good with words. That's why my closings to the jury are so effective."

"Are you thirsty?"

"Parched."

Josh got out of bed, walked to the bathroom, grabbed two plush terry cloth robes, and tossed her one. "Let's see what you've got in this state-of-the-art refrigerator of yours." Rosemaria wrapped herself in her robe and followed him as he went into the kitchen area, looked inside, and whistled. "Lots of fruits, veggies, vegan noshes, and even some nonalcoholic bubbly. I think that must be Vanessa's doing." He took out a bottle and unscrewed the top while she found glasses in the cabinet above the refrigerator.

"What do we drink to?" she asked as he poured.

"Now that I've had my way with you, the one thing I want more than anything in the world. Solving this confounded mystery of who is after you and making sure they can never try to hurt you again."

They lifted their glasses. "Hear, hear," she said. "Now that all the fun's over, want to watch some TV?"

"Yeah, why not watch a movie? Unless you want to catch me up on the investigation for real."

They moved to the living area, and she picked up the TV remote and clicked it on. He was in awe as the painting slid aside, and the massive screen was revealed.

"Wow."

"Now you see what I've had to deal with all this time."

"Don't worry. I'm here to rescue you."

"Maybe we can find excuses to visit."

They slumped together on the loveseat.

"Well, Rosemaria said. "Before we see what Netflix or Amazon has to offer, I'll briefly fill you in. We're pretty sure the killer is this woman named Mariah who lived in the house with all the college students. But nobody knows who or where she is. One person has disappeared and may be dead, another one is somewhere south of the border, one lady is in Washington State living a normal life, one guy is in New Mexico running an art gallery, and one couple is now in a safe house in San Diego. One lady is living with my dad in our Simi house and another one is here in LA working for an actors' agency. Oh yeah, one died of an overdose in the hospital a few days ago."

"One is living with your dad?"

"It's a long story. I'll tell you later."

"And what is your gut telling you about where this woman is?"

"My gut is telling me she's close by, and she hates me for messing up her perfect plans by getting involved with David. I think she thinks I'll remember her face even if she's had plastic surgery. That means she's someone I would come into contact with or is a public personality. She knew I was at the gym that day. She had it all set up for someone to kill me, but the rain, the umbrellas, and poor Amy who ran up to me and ended up getting shot messed up her plans. It stands to reason she has to be close to know all that and know the lay of the land by the gym."

"Makes sense."

"Everyone says she's ambitious and in love with money. There must be a lot at stake for her to have David killed in jail and then go after me."

"You could have seen her already and not recognized her. You'd think that would make her back off."

"I think she's a stone-cold killer, and she's cleaning house."

"Your gut is making a lot of assumptions."

"I know. But it has a mind of its own, and sometimes I just have to go with it."

Her cell phone rang, and she picked it up from the coffee table and clicked it on. "Hi, Larry. Is something wrong?"

"Sam and Stacey are missing."

She grabbed Josh's hand. "What happened?"

Larry was in his home office seated behind his desk, looking disheveled, and running his fingers through his hair. "They used a bedsheet to get down to the ground. They left everything—all their IDs, money, clothes, everything. Officer Trawley says they were perfectly happy in the apartment, just a little bored. He thinks they left of their own accord but is afraid something bad happened to them. Mack and Loshi are there now, looking for some hint as to why they left." He heard a click, looked at his phone, and said, "Let me call you back."

Rosemaria stood up and rubbed at her face. "Stacey and Sam are gone. They left everything behind. That makes no sense. My dad said they were happy to be off the mountain and living in civilization again. Even if they were getting cabin fever, they wouldn't have left and taken nothing with them. It's that woman. I know it." Her cell phone rang, and she grabbed it. "Yes?"

It was Larry. "They found a half-burned note in the garbage disposal. The only words they could make out were *meet me*, *safe*, and *gek bo*. The camera over the door was disabled."

"What the hell is *gek bo*?"

"Who knows?"

"They wouldn't trust a stranger or go anywhere with him. It was someone they knew."

"Somebody in the house?"

"Clyde, Keith?"

"Micco is in New Mexico. They just called him."

"On a landline?"

"Yeah. He doesn't know who could have taken them."

"I have a horrible feeling we'll never see them again."

"Sorry to interrupt your reunion."

"Don't worry. Your timing was fine. Are they looking at cameras all over the neighborhood?"

"The one over the apartment building front entrance was disabled, the one over the parking lot showed them sliding down on a sheet and disappearing behind a building. They're waking people up as we speak to see what other cameras show."

"Do my dad and Jimmy know?"

"Yeah, I called them first."

"They must be devastated. They're the ones who found them."

"They can't blame themselves."

"But they will. Oh well, I'll talk to them tomorrow. Thanks for the heads-up."

She sank down on the couch next to Josh, and he put his arm around her.

"Do you have any idea of how important you are to me?" she asked.

"I do."

"It makes me feel invincible."

"You promised me a while back you were going to cut down on your adventures now that you're a prosecutor."

"I'm trying, my love. I'm really trying."

*　*　*　*

Micco's hands were shaking as he wiped down every surface of the boat with a rag. Thank God the shore patrol hadn't been anywhere near the area that night. The boat was rented under a fake name, so no one could trace it to him. It would stay moored here until it was rented again. The police had already discovered Stacey and Sam were gone and called him. He had had the foresight to forward his landline to his cell phone. But who knew how long it would take for them to figure that out? He was having second thoughts about his escape plan. Should he go home and make definite plans on where to run or disappear now and not take any chances on the police finding him? If Stacey's body popped up, he wouldn't stand a chance if Mariah could track him down. *Think, think, think,* he told himself as he finished wiping down the boat. But he couldn't think. He'd just killed a friend in cold blood, and he knew he couldn't keep juggling the pieces of his life in the air anymore. Everything would come crashing down soon and it would be a relief.

* * * * *

The next morning, waves lapped against the pilings as Stacey lay half submerged in the water. She tried to keep her head up so she could breathe. The pier above her was old and rotten. No boats nearby, just a rocky beach, and no houses that she could see. After reaching the shore, she had discovered that the pain in her side was probably from a bullet that had gone straight through muscle and flesh. The salt water had helped keep the wound from becoming infected. She had not one ounce of energy to lift herself out of the water and thought it ironic that after swimming all that way she would die alone on a forgotten beach. She closed her eyes, hoping that if she just rested for a few minutes, she could regain her strength and go for help. But where? She couldn't go back to the apartment. She couldn't trust the police to keep her safe anymore. Micco was probably on the run with Mariah. Sam was gone, and she had no one.

She was overwhelmed with hopelessness and despair. Why had she swum so hard, beyond any kind of will and endurance she ever dreamed she had in her? What was all that effort for? The evil that was Mariah was waiting out there for her, and against that kind of satanic force, she didn't stand a chance. She opened her eyes and saw a figure walking toward her in the distance. As he came closer, she could see he was dressed in dirty rags with his pants tattered around his knees. He spotted her and looked confused and curious. She didn't fear him. How could anything or anybody be worse than lying here alone?

He bent down and spoke gently. "Don't worry. I'll take care of you."
She passed out.

CHAPTER TWENTY-SIX

THE Blvd Restaurant in the Beverly Wilshire Hotel was crowded even at nine o'clock in the morning. Josh had never given any thought to eating there before and noted the expensive furnishings, the touches of art deco, and the tall windows facing Wilshire Boulevard and Rodeo Drive. After letting the hostess know he was meeting someone, he stood at the entrance and scanned the room, looking for his mother.

He saw her seated at a table by a window, looking out at the boulevard, lost in thought. He was surprised to see how beautiful she was, looking ten years younger than her sixty-two years. Her blonde hair was expertly cut, and she wore a silky white blouse under a light-blue suit. She was as thin as ever. The haunted expression he had always associated with his mother was gone, replaced by contentment but still with a hint of sadness in her eyes. She smiled up at the waitress who came by to refill her coffee then suddenly spotted Josh.

Her smile faded as she watched him walking toward her table, and the sadness in her eyes was replaced with fear. She was afraid he would reject her. *No.* He reproached himself for being the cause of that fear and felt an overwhelming need to reassure her that he loved her still. He walked quickly toward her as she stood up to greet him, grabbing the edge of the table to steady herself. He wasted no time in putting his arms around her, hoping that holding her close would drive away her distress. He could feel her slight, small body shaking as he held her, then he pulled away to look at her to discover her face was drenched in tears. She was swallowing hard, trying not to sob out loud. He helped her sit down, and she fumbled to grab a tissue out of her purse. "I'm sorry, Josh," she managed. "I'm sorry for making a scene. Please forgive me."

He pulled his chair up next to her. "You have to stop this crying, or everybody's going to think I'm being mean to you."

She wiped her tears and studied his face. "Do you forgive me, my boy? Do you forgive me?"

Now Josh was fighting back tears. "Mom, I forgive you. None of that matters. We have our lives to live, so let's not worry about hard feelings anymore. I mean it, Mom. I want us to forgive each other and move on." He took her hand. "Can we do that?"

She leaned toward him, her face bathed in relief. "Oh yes. I want to do that."

He held her hand for a moment longer, then slid his chair back across from her and picked up the menu. "But there's something else very important I need to know."

Her eyes widened. "Yes?"

"Is there anything in this fancy restaurant I can eat?"

"There is, son, honest. Rosemaria told me you're vegan, which, of course, doesn't surprise me, seeing how much you've loved animals since you were little, so I made sure there are things on the menu you can eat."

He laughed. "I'm kidding, Mom."

He waved the waitress over, and Ellie, already having studied the menu up one side and down the other during the half hour she had been waiting, ordered the steel-cut oatmeal Brulé, and he ordered the pitaya fruit bowl for himself. He leaned back and studied her face, which was now glowing with happiness, and he felt the weight of the world lift off him. Lenny was right. He'd been a selfish SOB long enough. "You look beautiful, Mom. Radiant as a schoolgirl, as a matter of fact. What's been going on that's brought about this change from country girl to sophisticated lady?" He noticed his mother was blushing. "Wait a minute. There's a guy in the picture, isn't there? Has someone finally won your heart after all these years?"

"Well, actually, there is someone."

"Tell me."

"He's the manager of a bank in the town I live in now, a little bigger than Marysville, called Caanan, and we met when he came into the beauty shop where I work to get a haircut. I cut hair now, Josh. I went to beauty school and saved up to buy my own chair." She saw that he looked confused. "That's what you do. You rent a place in the shop, see?"

"Aha, I get it. And you cut his hair and now . . ."

"Well, he kept coming in to have his hair cut and finally asked me out. He's a widower. And he was so easy to talk to. I could talk to him about anything. It was so wonderful to be with someone like that, kind and thoughtful. So, after three years of dating, he's asked me to marry him."

"A whirlwind romance."

She laughed. "Old people take a little longer to make up their minds."

"Should be the other way around."

"You mean because we have less time?" She laughed.

"If you want my blessing, you got it, and Rosemaria and I want to be invited to the wedding."

"You mean it? We would love that."

"Do I get to meet him on Zoom before the big day?"

"As soon as I get home, we'll have his grandson show us how to set that up."

The waitress brought the food, and they dug into their meals. He noticed his mom enjoying her food and eating heartily, just like Rosemaria. Maybe that's why he loved that trait so much in her. A bit of something special in his mom that had always been with him, and he never realized it until now.

"Mom, you know I'd like you to stay for a few more days, but that's not going to be possible."

"Why is that, son?"

"Someone's trying to cause harm to Rosemaria, and as long as you're anywhere near us, your life could be in danger."

That perked her ears up, but she didn't show any signs of acting hysterically. Just the opposite. She listened quietly as he filled her in on the details.

"I will regretfully do as you say, Josh, but could we do one thing before I leave? Two things actually. Could you take my picture in front of the Hollywood sign and then the three of us have dinner?"

"Let me speak to the people who guard Rosemaria, and I'll see what can be arranged."

She leaned over and grabbed his arm. "I know nothing terrible is going to happen to either one of you. Do you know why?"

"Why, Mom?"

Because God would not take you away from me just when we found each other again. And not Rosemaria either. God would not do that."

He squeezed her hand. "I believe you're right, Mom. God wouldn't do that."

* * * * *

Stacey woke up and saw she was lying on top of a sleeping bag in a medium-size tent. The tent was filled with plastic storage bins, neatly stacked, and the canvas floor was clean. Her side had been wrapped with a clean bandage, but when she tried to move even slightly, it hurt like hell. She called out, "Hello? Hello? Anyone out there?"

The flap of the tent opened, and the face of her rescuer was smiling down on her. "So, you finally woke up, huh?" He took a bottle of water off a small wooden table, opened it up, and handed it to her. "You need to drink. You're dehydrated."

His hair was blond and shaggy with gray sprinkled throughout. He had the two-day-old beard that was in fashion these days. She could tell he had been good looking when he was young—thin straight nose, high cheekbones, light-blue eyes, and a wiry physique.

"Who are you?" she asked. Surprisingly, she felt no fear of him.

"My name's Randy. I live here."

"Why?"

"I used to be a surfer back in the day. All up and down the coast. I waited on tables to eat and surfed every day. Then life happened. I met someone. She wanted me to settle down and get a real job, so I did—managed to get a low-level position in an insurance office. I hated feeling like a prisoner, hated having a regular job, and we ended it. But nothing was the same anymore. I was older than all the other surfers; I became impatient with customers when I worked as a waiter. My parents died and left me a bit of money. So I moved down here, pitched a tent far away from everybody, worked part time in the stock room of a shoe store. I saved all my money so when the shoe store closed, I had a good little bundle in savings and don't have to ask for handouts."

"That's quite a history. Don't the cops hassle you?"

"They used to. They thought I'd attract more transients. But it's too far away from the fruitful panhandling areas, and the beach is too rocky and too inconvenient for tourists to search it out. There's nothing here but me and the seagulls."

"Thank you for wrapping my side."

"That was a bullet wound. Anybody could see that. You want to tell me what happened?"

Stacey saw no reason to hold back. Her instincts told her she could trust this person. "Someone took my boyfriend and me out in a boat to kill us. He shot my boyfriend, but I escaped and swam to shore. That's where you found me."

"Why'd he want to kill you?"

"He was hired by a woman more evil than you can imagine who wants to murder everyone she thinks can expose her horrible crimes. I don't know anything that could help the cops, but she's not taking any chances. She's relentless, and anyone who helps me is in danger. I'll leave as soon as I can figure out where to go."

"Why not go to the cops?"

"You actually believe me? What I told you is pretty crazy."

"I do believe you."

"Thank you. Cops can't protect me. Her tentacles reach everywhere. She can manipulate men and make them do anything."

"I've met scary bitches like that in my lifetime. I always ran the other way."

"She's worse, Randy—much, much worse."

"What's your name?"

"I can't tell you. It's better for you that way."

"Okay, then, I'll think I'll call you Gidget."

She laughed. "Like Gidget and Moondoggie?"

"Yeah, but I'm too old for you, so don't get any ideas."

"I can tell you were a good-looking dude back in the day. I would have gone for you, for sure."

She stopped and stared at Randy, not seeing him or the tent or anything in it. Everything disappeared from view. Out of nowhere, the horror of what had happened hit her like a freight train, and her entire body heaved as she cried—for the life she had planned that never came to fruition; for the lost serenity of the mountains; for Sam, whom she had once loved. It was all gone, and she had nothing left.

Randy sat quietly watching until her sobs became hiccups and slowly died away. He handed her a clean hanky. "I'm going to go out and buy you something to eat. What would you like?"

She sniffled and blew her nose. "That's all you can say after me telling you that horror story and breaking down like a pathetic demented sob sister? Don't you know what you've gotten yourself into?"

"What would you like? McDonald's, Veggie Grill, Plant Power? In-N-Out Burger, Shakey's Pizza? We've got it all down here."

She studied his kind, tan, wrinkled face for several seconds. "Randy, I do believe you're the best thing that ever happened to me."

"As I said, I'm too old for you. I'm fifty-eight, and you look like you're in your twenties. I'm no cradle robber, so keep your hands to yourself, missy."

She couldn't help laughing, but the harder she laughed, the more her side hurt, and she forced herself to stop. He waited patiently.

"What's it going to be? It's early, but I feel like a pizza myself."

"Yes, please, a pizza. I would like that very much."

"Turn around then, please. I have to change. I only wear these clothes when I pick up the trash that washes in off the ocean." He took a few minutes to change, and then she turned and saw a different human being. He actually looked presentable.

"Where do you do your laundry?"

"Fluff and fold, about a mile from here. The greatest invention in the world."

He opened up the flap and turned. "No one will bother you, Gidget. Don't worry. I'll bring you back some clothes and personal articles too." He went out, then the flap went up again. "By the way, the john is up the hill behind the stand of trees. It has a sanitized bowl I change three times a week." The flap went down again, and his footsteps in the sand were too quiet for her to hear him walk away.

*   *   *   *   *

It was almost ten-thirty in the morning and Rosemaria was waiting in her suite for Josh to come back from his breakfast with his mom so they could move into their condo. All her bags and Suzi in her cage had been moved downstairs by Loretta's staff. Abe Gwaltney, her new protector, was downstairs in the kitchen with Cameron, probably having to listen to some final instructions. She had chosen to wait upstairs so she could speak privately to Josh about his meeting. She was hoping for the best. She was not looking forward to saying goodbye to everyone in the house who had been so kind to her—Loretta, Andrew, Mildred, and her two main helpers, Max and Brent, who were working their way through college. What a great gig they had landed. Cameron and Kirsten, her protectors, had her gratitude forever. Madelaine, who had so lovingly nursed her back to health, would be coming by their new home in two weeks to cut her cast off, so she would see her again. It would be hard to leave these kind and thoughtful people, but she vowed that it would not be for good. She would see them all again when the murderer was behind bars.

Her dad was due to call her as soon as he went over Mack's and Loshi's reports. They were incredibly generous in sharing details and their own perceptions with Larry, which he passed on to Steven and Jimmy. So much had changed since they all butted heads in the beginning. Mack and Loshi had grown to appreciate their LA colleagues.

She picked up her cell phone and stared at it, willing it to ring. When that didn't work, she speed-dialed a number as familiar to her as her own. "Curtis? It's Rosemaria. I need to ask you for a huge favor, and if you decide not to do it, no hard feelings, okay? . . . It's a long story; do you have time to listen? . . . Okay, here goes. . . . Remember, you can say no . . ."

Twenty minutes later, she clicked off the phone and felt like a weight had lifted off her shoulders. Why had she been so worried? Curtis didn't hesitate. He was onboard.

She was checking the medicine cabinets for anything she might have forgotten when her phone rang, and she was happy to see it was her father. "Anything new, Dad?"

"A produce guy working at a market three blocks away from the apartment happened to go out back to throw some rotten groceries in the dumpster and saw three people get into a black sedan. One of them was a woman. They weren't being forced."

"Any cameras?"

"The car was too far away, but the guy looked at pictures of Sam and Stacey and said it could be them."

"Any cameras on the other buildings catch a black sedan going by at that hour?"

"Yeah, one at the ATM on the corner opposite the market. The black sedan was going down the hill. They're checking the traffic cameras right now."

"Did Mack and Loshi get anything more out of our two runaways before they took off?"

"Sam admitted when they lived in the house he was having wild and crazy sex with Mariah which pissed Stacey off mightily during the interview. Apparently, she knew about their relationship but not how hot and heavy it was. Sam told us something that might be helpful—sometimes Mariah would talk in a Brooklyn accent or Southern accent—he couldn't really tell which—and in her unrestrained moments of love she would call Sam *cher* and yell out for somebody named Andy."

"There were and are about a million Andys living in LA."

"Maybe he was a classmate. They're checking it out."

"Andy? That's it?"

"Those two had given up on running. I can tell you that. And I could kick myself for being the one who blew open their comfortable nest and let this happen."

"You couldn't have known, Dad."

"I want to help Jimmy track down this Andy. If he exists, we'll find him."

Rosemaria hung up and pondered if she knew anybody who was good with accents. Who would know about something like that? It came to her in a shot. Vanessa! Who knew more about accents than actors? She tapped some numbers on her cell and waited.

"Vanessa."

"Is Josh there yet?"

"Not yet."

"Listen, Rosemaria, I'm sorry I have to tell you this, but Larry won't let me be in your apartment while you're there. Delivering the furniture and other stuff was okay, but he's nervous about me being in the line of fire."

"I don't blame him. He's being sensible."

"I wanted to help you decorate. It's something I love to do, especially for friends."

"I need your help in another way, Vanessa. It's more important than decorating."

Vanessa sounded excited. "You mean like I helped you find that man who ended up almost killing you? Didn't do much good, did I?"

"Yes, you did. It was an important clue. But listen, do you know much about accents? Have you ever had to use any in your work?"

"Of course. Do you need me to call someone and fake an accent?"

"Nothing like that. Answer me this—what kind of an accent sounds a little bit like Brooklyn and a maybe a little bit Southern?"

"It might be Cajun. Some people might think it sounds like the combination of the two."

"You don't need to think about it? You just know this?"

"You're always surprised I know things you ask me about."

"Well, that makes me a colossal idiot because you're always right. You don't know any Cajun words do you? Is *cher* a Cajun word?"

"I don't know any Cajun, but I faked the accent once on a TV show. It's extremely difficult to do correctly. You can go online and find out if *cher* is a Cajun word, or it could be French."

"Let me do that, Vanessa. I have to hang up now."

"No problem. Let me know if I can give you any more help."

Rosemaria ran to her laptop and began to search. Yes! *Cher* wasn't just the name of a singer; it was a Cajun expression for a loved one. Maybe a word sounding like Andy was Cajun as well. The list of words was long, but she might as well make herself useful until Josh came back. So Mariah might very well be from Louisiana, huh? Very interesting. If she grew up in the swamps, probably killing helpless animals, why not progress to killing humans? She imagined the crumbling shack Mariah had grown up in, the mangrove trees, the thick roots crawling along the wet ground, and insects the size of her palm. Rosemaria's imagination was running away with her, and she was still in the *B*s with a few hundred more words to go. She was up to the *H*s when she heard the buzzer, saw Josh outside her door, and buzzed him in.

She ran to him and kissed him hard. "It went well. I can tell."

"She was beautiful, my love, and so sweet and understanding she about broke my heart. I told her what was going on with you, but she wants to stay another day and have her picture taken by the Hollywood sign and have at least one dinner with us. We have to check it out with Abe and Cameron to make sure it's okay."

"Let's make it happen for her then. Meanwhile, let's blow this popsicle stand and go home."

A few hours later, Josh was on his way to the cat sanctuary to see Noor and Gilbert, and Abe was comfortably ensconced in his room across the hall from Josh and Rosemaria's condo with his video screens of the front door, elevator, and third-floor hallway. Rosemaria had hung every picture, arranged every tchotchke Vanessa had brought over. Then she had made the bed, put away the china and utensils, and was treating herself to a bowl of bagged popcorn. She sat down at her new desk in the guest room, for which Vanessa had bought a double bed, dresser, desk, and bookshelves. She had also bought accoutrements for the bathroom next to the guest room, which would double as an office since they weren't about to have anyone staying there, risking having their brains blown out by a crazy lady.

She resumed her search for Cajun names, got to the end, and decided to start again. She began at the top and stopped almost as soon as she started. She hadn't seen it the first time around—andouille, a spicy sausage—which could be a term used during the height of passion. She looked up the pronunciation and said it out loud. Andouille. *An-du-e*—that could sound to Sam like Andy. Yes. Mariah was Cajun. No doubt about it. She grabbed her cell phone and tapped her dad's number. He answered immediately.

"You found out something."

"Mariah is Cajun. She wasn't saying *Andy*. Tell everybody to stop looking for him. She was saying *andouille*—hot sausage—an endearment she apparently used in the throes of passion."

"Cajun country takes up a lot of square miles. We'll need something more to go on before we go down to Louisiana and start snooping around."

"I'll find it, Dad, or you will. We're closing in on her."

She hung up, willing her brain to remember something one of the roommates had said that might give her a thread to follow. The only ones left to interrogate further were Sarah, whose life they absolutely would not disrupt, and Sherilyn, who was stonewalling them and wouldn't meet with anybody. Material witness? Not enough for a warrant to bring her in. But Rosemaria had an idea of how to get her to talk.

* * * * *

The ground on the hills in the cat sanctuary was hard and brown. It had been months since the rains had given them the much-needed moisture to turn the grasses and the small bushes green. Josh was lying flat on his back looking up at the sky with Noor on one side and Gilbert on the other, the two of them napping off and on. When Josh had arrived two hours earlier and opened the gate to the special enclosure where he could spend time with his cats, the two of them had come running. Usually Gilbert, the mountain lion, would hang back and allow Noor, the more aggressive female black panther, to roughhouse with Josh before he nuzzled his way in. But today, after three weeks of being apart from Josh, both cats took a flying leap at him, knocked him down, and engaged in unrestrained expressions of love. When he tried to sit up, they wouldn't let him. They smothered him with their bodies and their heavy paws. He finally gave up and laughed uncontrollably. This is what he had dreamed of when he worked as a part-time caregiver at the zoo and raised them from the time they were babies—that they should be this happy and free and never have to live in a cage again.

Soon, Rosemaria would be able to join him here, but she wouldn't come until Mariah was caught. She was determined that never again would she endanger Noor and Gilbert because of what was happening in her life. The year before, Noor had almost been shot while saving Rosemaria's life. She would wait until the danger had passed. Noor and Gilbert were as important to her as they were to him, and he hoped she was prepared for the greeting they would give her when they finally saw her again.

CHAPTER TWENTY-SEVEN

Abe Gwaltney, forty-one years old, curly salt-and-pepper hair, six feet four, 280 pounds, and somewhat rough spoken, was not usually asked to look at paint chips and try to decide what color should go on what wall as part of his job. Nevertheless, Rosemaria had engaged his help in making those important decisions. They were seated at the new antique pine dining table Vanessa had picked out and had delivered along with everything else in the apartment. Vanessa had also insisted that the walls in the entire place needed painting, even though Rosemaria protested that white on every wall was fine.

Abe and Rosemaria were sliding the chips around on the tabletop in a desultory manner, neither seeming too interested.

"Vanessa says that we have to paint before she can have shelves put up and buy more artwork for the walls. I grew up with off-white everywhere, and it's always seemed fine to me."

Abe shrugged. "She's a classy lady and into this kind of stuff. Besides, rich people always feel the need to 'update' because they can afford it."

"I hope you're not implying I have no class because I'm not into 'updating,' Abe. And whatever happened to that old fashioned word *remodel*? Nobody remodels anymore they 'update.'"

"Can I be honest with you?"

Rosemaria frowned. "Yeah?"

"Every one of us who has been assigned to you in the last three weeks thinks you're in a class by yourself, and it's got nothing to do with living in a fancy house."

She smiled. "I will take that as a compliment, Abe. What say we let Vanessa keep on making all the decorating decisions? My heart's not in it anyway. All I can think about is this case."

Her cell phone rang, and she grabbed it off the table. "I hope that's Vanessa." She looked at the screen and clicked on. "Ask and ye shall receive."

"Am I interrupting something?" Vanessa asked.

"Just the opposite. You are the person I need at this very moment."

"Uh-oh. A question or another acting chore? Who do I have to pretend to be now?"

"No one this time. I have a question for you. Do you know any famous or kind of famous actors who are represented by the William Morris Endeavor Agency?"

"Sure. A couple of them."

"Do you know either one of them well enough to do you a favor?"

Vanessa sounded wary. "Like what?"

"I need to get Sherilyn Cosgrove, a receptionist-slash-script analyst at the agency, over to one of their houses under false pretenses."

"For what reason?"

"We want this actor to tell Sherilyn he is interested in a script she read and recommended, and he wants her to bring the script over to his house so they can discuss it."

"And then what happens?"

"I will be there in my role as ex-cop to ask questions regarding what more she knows about the Ramin Hassan murder. She's refusing to talk to any of us, and I'm going to corner her like a rat in a box and get her to squeal."

"What?"

"You know I'm kidding. But seriously, I need to talk to her.

"Why not just have her come to the police station?"

"She's dug in her heels and won't budge. We don't want to go bang on her door or corner her at lunch. If she's being watched or followed, we don't want the killer to think she's cooperating with us."

"All right. Let me see what I can do. I'll get back to you in a couple of days."

"Two days works. We can wait until Josh's mom leaves town. She really wants to see the Hollywood sign, and I wish I knew where she could see it up close and away from other people. Actually going up to the sign is too open."

"I think I may know of a place."

"You can't possibly know of a place that fast. That's impossible."

"I may."

"If you weren't Melissa's mother and she didn't need you to be in one piece, I'd put you in charge of this investigation."

"Please. I'm good but not that good. There's a house on Macapa Drive up in the hills where the backyard has a view straight across the Cahuenga Pass to the Hollywood sign."

"Who lives in the house?"

"No one. It's up for sale. One of my friends looked at it."

"Is the realtor someone in your inner circle?"

"No."

"Good. Do not tell anyone you know about this. Tell the realtor you have some people from out of town who want to look at the house. Hopefully, they won't expect out-of-towners to be prequalified."

"I can do that."

"It's really important, Vanessa; no one can know."

"I'm married to a detective. I can connect the dots."

"Sorry."

"I presume you'd like to see it tomorrow?"

"That would be great. Thank you."

"I'll give your goddaughter a kiss from you."

"Tell her I love her. Bye." She hung up feeling slightly guilty for not asking about Melissa.

Abe had been listening attentively. "I'll get a driver tomorrow so we can cover the three of you. We'll have someone clear the area around the Hollywood sign so nobody can take a sniper shot from there. Shouldn't be a problem."

"I will be very much relieved when Josh's mom is safely back home."

* * * * *

A few hours later, Rosemaria and Josh were seated on the couch in front of the coffee table, and Abe had pulled up a dining chair facing them.

"McAdams, who will also be on night shift here, will pick up Mrs. Sibley at the hotel at ten a.m. with all her luggage," Abe said. "He should be here around ten-twenty. We'll take the half-hour drive to Macapa, where you'll meet the realtor, pretend you're looking at the house and take pictures in the backyard that have the Hollywood sign in the background. After ten minutes, you'll come back out the front door, enter the SUV, and we'll take Mrs. Sibley and the two of you to the airport. There won't be any time to stop for dinner. We'll escort her to her gate, but you'll have to say your goodbyes in the car."

"She's so excited, Abe," Rosemaria said. "Thank you for making this possible."

"You can't come to Hollywood and not see the sign. It looks better from far off than up close, anyway."

"Would you like to stay and eat with us?" Josh asked. "Vanessa loaded the refrigerator with every kind of frozen vegan meal you could possibly want."

"Uh, no, that's okay. McAdams is coming by shortly and bringing me some takeout. We'll be going over the plans for tomorrow."

He stood up and moved toward the door. "I appreciate the invitation."

Rosemaria's eyes narrowed. "Don't tell me false rumors of my cooking have penetrated my bodyguard team?"

"I plead the fifth," Abe said. "Seriously, McAdams should be here any minute. Lock the door behind me." And he left.

Rosemaria leaned back against Josh's shoulder. "I'm not that bad."

"Absolutely not. How about I make us a nice big salad?"
She jumped up. "I'll heat the rolls."
He followed her into the kitchen. "No one does it better."

* * * * *

Darkness enveloped the beach as the waves lapped lazily on the shore. Lights from homes and businesses were at least a mile away. Stacey sat on a makeshift bench made from driftwood and planks and watched Randy make a small campfire near the tent. A big fire might bring the cops running, but even a small one made Stacey nervous. Randy assured her cops were not roaming around the beach during this time of night. He proceeded to make old-fashioned coffee in an ancient metal coffeepot over the fire, poured them each a cup, and brought them over. She accepted one, and he sat next to her on the bench.

She sipped and registered surprise. "This is delicious."

"Just like they used to make it in the old days."

"Thank you for a wonderful dinner of pizza and salad."

"My pleasure."

She found herself sighing a surprisingly peaceful sigh considering her circumstance and stared out over the dark water for several minutes. Randy did the same.

"Don't you get lonely out here?"

"I don't stay here all the time. I'll go into town when I feel like it, maybe see a movie now and then, visit the library, go on the internet and check up on my money. As far as world events go, I have zero interest."

"Someone hurt you badly."

"That she did."

"But you'll never talk about it."

"Nope."

"I was hurt too. But I can't hate him anymore because he's dead."

"How long are you going to wait before you report what happened?"

"I don't know who to report to."

"I'll bet you know someone."

"I may know one cop or, rather, an ex-cop. The one who found me."

"So, what are you waiting for?"

"As long as I don't report it, I'm safe."

"You don't seem the type who would want to live in a tent forever."

"Maybe not, but as long as you'll have me, can we take it day to day?"

"I don't mind. I'm getting kind of used to having you here."

* * * * *

The next morning Ellie Sibley was waiting in the lobby of the Beverly Wilshire and ready to go as soon as McAdams pulled up to the curb. Josh had checked her out of the hotel over the phone and paid the bill. He had assured her again and again that he could afford it, and he was happy to do it, but still, she felt kind of bad she had stayed at such an expensive place. She could hardly wait to see the Hollywood Hills she had heard so much about and have her picture taken with the Hollywood sign in the distance. Her heart burst with pride at what her son had accomplished, coming to Hollywood with nothing but his talent and attracting a wonderful girl like Rosemaria, who, she could tell, loved him very much. As they drove through the touristy business district of Beverly Hills, she looked at the store windows along Rodeo Drive, where she had walked more than once during the past week and window-shopped just like Julia Roberts, except she could never actually go inside and buy anything. She didn't need to anyway. Just being right there in zip code 90210 was thrilling.

When they arrived at Josh and Rosemaria's condo building, the driver called up, and within two minutes, Josh and Rosemaria came down to the lobby accompanied by Abe, their bodyguard. Ellie knew that nothing could ever happen to them with somebody as fierce looking as Abe to protect them.

Abe got in the front passenger seat, and Josh and Rosemaria hopped in the back on either side of Ellie, out of breath and full of energy.

"Are you excited, Mom? You're going to see where a lot of big stars live today."

"Do they all live in mansions?"

"There are some big ones up there, but many are small and ordinary looking. It's the view they pay for."

"I'm sorry you have to leave so soon," Rosemaria said, "or you could have visited a couple of my friends who live in mansions in the flats that are so big you'd think they were hotels."

"What are the flats?"

"They're neighborhoods that are below Sunset and the houses look like palaces."

"You have friends who live like that?"

Josh winked at Rosemaria. "Not many, Mom, but we're hoping their luck rubs off on us."

Ellie laughed. "You don't need luck. Just keep singing, and you'll get there."

Rosemaria gently prodded Ellie's arm. "Funny, that's what I keep saying."

They drove east on Santa Monica, turned left past the Hollywood Bowl, then up Cahuenga and left toward Macapa Drive. On Macapa, the houses and driveways were built close together, and the street was narrow with a line of parked cars on both sides. Two of Cameron's men were already outside the house. One was seated in a construction company truck on Macapa facing Mulholland; the other was dressed in a gardening company uniform and was casually trimming hedges in the backyard of the house next to the one for sale.

They pulled into the driveway where trees partially shielded them from mansions on top of the hill a quarter of a mile away. The house was one-story stucco with large framed windows in the front. Ellie hugged Josh's arm, eager to get out and see a real Hollywood house with a backyard overlooking the whole city.

Despite the several armed protectors, Josh looked around warily. He saw the realtor, a fortyish blonde with lips that rivaled those of any woman on the "housewife shows", come out the front door and stop short when she saw the large black SUV. To Josh, it seemed as if her mind began racing when she saw several people getting out of the car with both a driver and what was obviously a bodyguard. She was undoubtedly figuring out her sales commission as she greeted Ellie, the prospective owner.

"Hello, Mrs. Sibley, I'm so happy to meet you. I'm Laura Mulrooney, and this must be your son and daughter-in-law."

"Almost daughter-in-law." Ellie laughed. "Not quite there yet. But soon."

They all shook hands. Josh introduced Abe as a family friend, a fact that no one, including Laura, would ever believe, and they went into the house. Ellie was wide eyed as she took in the kitchen with its gleaming appliances and granite counter tops. Then, as they walked down the hallway to the living room, the view of the backyard and pool through the floor-to-ceiling windows of the far wall took her breath away.

Laura sat on a stool at the bar. "Feel free to wander around and look in every room. If you have any questions, I'll be here."

Ellie was eager to step outside and see the view and the sign, but she allowed herself to be led from one room to the next by Josh and Rosemaria. As Abe waited outside by the pool, they viewed the high-end furniture, expensive rugs, wall hangings, and sculptures situated on dark wood tables waxed to a shiny finish. They stuck their heads in the three bathrooms that looked like they belonged in a five-star hotel. Ellie was enjoying herself but was happy when they finally slid open the back door and walked outside. The view of the city past the neighbors' backyards was just like she imagined it would be. Then she walked past the pool, looked through the tall trees, and saw the Hollywood sign in the distance.

"Well, Mom, ready to have your picture taken?"

She turned around and smiled. "I wouldn't mind living here," she whispered. "Think I could afford it?"

"We'll tell Laura you'll be in touch."

She punched him. "You're so bad."

Abe moved close to them, his eyes on his man next door clipping hedges. "Okay, folks, let's move this party along."

Rosemaria, even knowing the area had been cleared, had been searching for any spot that could hide a sniper. Not seeing any high ground, she joined Ellie and Josh. "Abe, you have to take the picture of the three of us."

Ellie took a camera out of her purse and handed it to him. "I guess you know how to use that?"

He reluctantly took the camera. "Yes, ma'am. I shouldn't be doing this."

"Let us know when we're in the right position for you to see the sign in the background," Ellie instructed.

Abe held up the camera. "A little to the left. Stay tight together so I get everything in the frame."

They put their arms around each other and shuffled to the left.

"That's better." He clicked once. "All right, a couple more." He took two more pictures and handed the camera to Ellie. "Should have a good one there."

"Thank you, Abe, and thank you for protecting my son and Rosemaria."

"I'll do my best, ma'am."

"We'd better go," Josh said, "before the realtor figures out we're just lookie-loos."

Ellie's eyes twinkled mischievously. "I have a driver and bodyguard. I'm sure she thinks I'm someone very important."

Rosemaria stepped up behind her and whispered, "You are important, Ellie. Put on a show. You're the mother of a big star."

They went back inside, and Laura looked at them hopefully. "It's an amazing view out there, isn't it? And the roses are lovely. Did you like the house?"

Ellie straightened her suit jacket and sniffed. "It's a little small, and I don't know if there's room for my entire staff, but I do love the location very much."

"She'll get back to you," Josh added.

Laura brightened. "If this one doesn't suit your purposes, I have others in the area you might like."

Ellie led the others to the front door. "I'll keep that in mind, young lady."

A third security guard seated by a window in an unoccupied house on Mulholland looking through high-powered binoculars spied movement next to the large boulders on top of the hill above him. He spoke urgently into his mike. "This is alpha one. Get everyone into the car now.

Possible sniper on the hill." His warnings became more urgent when he saw the butt of a rifle being pushed forward close to the ground through the opening in the underbrush. "Do it now! Shots imminent!"

Abe heard the warning in his earpiece and moved quickly. "Hey, everybody, I just heard the flight is leaving early, and we need to get going."

Ellie didn't hesitate. She was having the most fun of her life, and this was just more excitement. She jumped in the car, and Josh and Rosemaria did the same as Abe used his body to block Rosemaria since she would be the primary target.

He whispered in her ear as she was getting in. "Sniper."

The terror she felt set her veins throbbing in her throat. She plastered a smile on her face as she settled in next to Ellie. "Let's get the heck out of here," she said, with all the cheerfulness she could muster. "Ellie's got a plane to catch."

The third guard was yelling into his walkie talkie as he ran toward the front door of the house where he had been keeping his eyes on the hills above Macapa. "Sniper is at twelve o'clock straight up from Macapa and Mulholland. Use first street on the right to reach a two-story white stucco house. Sniper is set up about ten yards due east."

The SUV with Rosemaria and the others took off down Macapa, turned left, and sped down the hill. Meanwhile, the gardener came running from the back of the house next door and jumped into a black sedan that had been parked in front. The man who had been seated in the construction truck was waiting in the street to jump into the sedan as well. They raced down Macapa then up to Mulholland and turned right up a narrow street toward the house where the rifle had been sighted. They already knew from studying the area on maps that there was only one way in. Maybe they'd be lucky.

The third guard had been forced to almost crawl up the hillside in order to reach the sniper's nest. He grabbed onto tree roots and used outcropped rocks to find his footing. But it was slow going. He knew the killer would be long gone by the time he got to the top. And his colleagues wouldn't get up to the house in time. He stopped climbing long enough to tell the other two they needed to call for a police helicopter.

There must be a dirt road going through the hills that wasn't on the map, and even sending a helicopter might be too late. How the hell had someone managed to find a sniper spot after they'd cleared the area? There would be hell to pay.

As the SUV moved through traffic in the fast lane of the 405 toward the airport, Ellie turned to Rosemaria. "I'm sorry I'm having so much fun."

"Why would you say that?"

"Well, you being in danger and everything."

"Are you kidding? I was a cop for over ten years. If I didn't get shot at every couple of days, I figured it was a slow week."

Ellie winced. "Oh my dear, I hope that's not true."

"She's exaggerating, Mom," Josh said. "But if I were a criminal and she was after me, I'd just throw up my hands and let her arrest me. I wouldn't stand a chance."

Rosemaria looked down modestly. "Well, I'm not that good."

"Close."

"Well . . . yeah," Rosemaria admitted.

"See, Mom, you have nothing to worry about. You're going home to plan your wedding and look forward to your honeymoon."

"Oh poo. This is a lot more fun."

"I can't wait to meet your guy, Ellie," Rosemaria said. "He must be quite the catch for you to marry him."

"Oh gosh, he is." And for the rest of the ride, Ellie showed them pictures of herself and Elwin Targer and his beautiful house where they would live after their honeymoon in Florida. Her enthusiasm was infectious, and they listened to her ramble on all the way to the airport. Rosemaria almost forgot the attempt on her life as a flood of overwhelming affection for the woman who had brought Josh into the world filled her heart.

The SUV pulled up in front of United Airlines, and as Abe opened the door, Ellie turned to Josh and grabbed his hand. "I'm so happy, son. I've never been this happy in my whole life."

He hugged her. "You and Elwin are going to have a wonderful life together."

"You are the one who has made me truly happy."

"You call us any time you want," Rosemaria said. "If you're feeling worried and want to check up on us, don't hesitate. You hear me?"

"I will. But I'm going to be too busy working and making plans to bother you all that much."

"No bother, Ellie. But you behave yourself," Rosemaria admonished. "No more seducing men with your great haircuts. You found your guy; now you'll just have to stick with this one."

"You're funny." Ellie giggled.

McAdams opened up his door as Abe helped Ellie out of the car. Josh got out as Abe grabbed her suitcases from the back. He hugged her. "Bye, Mom. I'm sorry we couldn't do dinner as well. Love you."

Ellie bit her lip and blinked back tears. Abe took her arm and led her to the entrance of the terminal. She turned around and gave a little wave before reluctantly allowing Abe to usher her inside. McAdams stood on Rosemaria's side of the SUV, looking in every direction.

As Josh got in the SUV and settled beside Rosemaria, he let out a big breath of air. "Don't think I didn't know what was going on back there."

"I figured."

He pulled her close. "I know you're as good as I say you are, but still, this is getting awfully real."

"I know. And I'm sorry. But I promise you, it will be over soon."

"You can't promise me that."

"I know. You're right. But we're all going to do our best to find this person. It kills me to know you are in harm's way because of me. And I will do whatever it takes to make sure nothing happens to you."

He smiled. "Isn't that supposed to be the guy's line?"

"I know you'd do the same for me." She took her phone out of her purse, gave Josh a reassuring nod, clicked a button, and waited. "Vanessa, call me when you get this message. Let's set up the meeting with Sherilyn tomorrow or the next day. It can't wait." She clicked off. "See? I'm moving forward. And after Madelaine cuts the cast off my arm, I'll be unstoppable."

"I hope your plan to entice and pounce on your witness works."

"Don't worry. She'll be there. Vanessa will come up with an actor so handsome and famous even Sherilyn, who is scared out of her wits and has a boyfriend, won't be able to resist.

McAdams moved around to the driver's door and got in as they saw Abe approach the car. He got in as well. "She's off to Wisconsin," Abe said, "none the wiser."

"Good," Josh said. "Let's keep it that way. And that whole area was supposed to be cleared. What the hell happened?"

"We did clear it," Cameron said, "but somebody should have stayed up there and made sure nobody could get in from the top of the hill. Mr. Collins will have our backsides for this."

Rosemaria shook her head. "I'll make sure that doesn't happen. Whoever was up there didn't even get a shot off. Everybody did their jobs. I can't ask for more than that."

"Yes, you can. If we still have our jobs tomorrow, we'll do better."

CHAPTER TWENTY-EIGHT

The ice queen Mariah was luxuriating in her bubble bath the day after her botched attempt to blow the brains out of Baker. She scowled as she recalled scrambling down the hillside to her motorcycle and driving away on a narrow back road, intended to go to a house that was never built. She always had an escape plan and, like in business, was better prepared than the opposition. She knew from the get-go that her visibility on the target might be blocked, unlike the straight line she would have had from the Hollywood sign, which the cops had sealed off. But there was always a chance that between house and car, she might be able to get a shot off. Unfortunately, she realized her perfect hiding place had been blown when everybody started scrambling to get in the limo.

It had taken a little conniving to find out where the Sibley clan would be that day, and she had been lucky. She had been leaving an early breakfast meeting with some of her buyers at the Beverly Wilshire the day before and had seen Josh Sibley with an old woman who looked so much like him she had to be his mother. Then Sally Mankowitz said a realtor friend of hers had been asked by Vanessa to show the fifteen-million-dollar house on Macapa to some friends from out of town. Putting two and two together, Mariah figured maybe Sibley's mother was interested in moving to LA to be near her famous son. And she had been right, but she had blown a great chance to bump off the ex-cop, and she could have kicked herself. She had been prepared to wait to kill her until she had gotten rid of her old Hollywood roommates, but since the opportunity had presented herself, she figured she might as well take advantage of it. No harm, no foul. Next time, she'd have more time to prepare.

She wouldn't always be able to find the right people to get information regarding the whereabouts of Baker. She couldn't follow the target around all day carrying her rifle in the car. She had her own work to do, after all. She might have to kill the Baker woman up close and personal, which was fine with her. She didn't mind doing the killing herself as long as she wasn't unnecessarily exposed. She'd taken a risk today because she had looked forward to knocking off the Baker broad in front of her family and because fate had told her where they were, and that wasn't good. She needed to stay calm and remind herself why her father had called her *glacé* in the first place.

She drew a soapy sponge across her shoulders and lazily down her body. Her fiancé hated even an inch of fat on a woman, and Mariah worked hard in her home gym to make sure he was never disappointed. Every time she satisfied him in ways he had never dreamed of, her hold on him became stronger. She had discovered years ago that the most prominent and distinguished men in the country tended to be kinky as all hell. They constantly lusted after new and unusual sexual experiences. It took every bit of her imagination and ability to keep the men focused on her and her alone. That was how she had always gotten what she wanted from every single one of those self-involved, arrogant schmucks. Now she was with someone who was predictably normal when it came to sex, but even that type, who would have been satisfied with the missionary position for the rest of their lives, appreciated and came to crave the exotic pleasures she provided.

Marrying him and keeping him happy would provide her with everything she had ever wanted: social prominence, adulation, and more money. To accomplish that, she again contemplated who had to die. Sarah, with her two kids, sappy husband, and boring life, knew nothing, would probably never be a threat, and might be allowed to live. She hadn't made up her mind about Sherilyn, a dingbat with a dead-end job and an insipid boyfriend.

But the others had to go. Keith was long gone. Maisie was dead. That left Clyde, who was in deep hiding and might never show his face again north of the Rio Grande. She didn't want to leave him alive but might have no choice. Lorna had also completely disappeared. She didn't know that bubble head had it in her. It bugged the crap out of her that she'd been clever enough to escape. It also left Micco, who, even though he had managed to get rid of Sam and Stacey, was the obvious patsy who would take the fall for Ramin, David, and the rest. She could lead the cops all the way back in time to blame him for disengaging the alarm at the carpet store. She could arrange for him to be the one who had hired David's killer, and, in fact, he had been the one to hire the hit men. He had taught her everything she knew about the internet—hacking, searching, coding, and all the rest. She laughed out loud, remembering how much fun he'd had teaching her the very things that would come back and bite him in the ass. He might be contemplating going on the lam, but he wouldn't. He loved his art gallery too much. No matter how frightened he was of her, he loved his life and where he lived. She could take her time framing him. It would all come together after she killed the ex-cop.

* * * * *

The home of Jan-Michael Berenson where Rosemaria, Steven, and Jimmy sat and waited was in Cheviot Hills, not far from Twentieth Century Fox, now renamed Twentieth Century Studios. The house was a handsome split level suitable for a successful young actor working his way up the ladder to stardom. Besides his dark good looks, he had talent and a commitment to his craft. Rosemaria liked him right away. They were seated in his living room, which looked out onto the street.

"So, what exactly do you want me to say when she gets here?" he asked, looking at her and the two cops.

"Ask her to come into your office so you can talk about the script," Steven said. "We'll be waiting in there, and hopefully, she won't do a runner."

"I'll be in the room to the side of the front door," Rosemaria said. "If she heads in that direction, I'll step out and stop her."

"This is legal, right?" Jan-Michael asked. "It's not like kidnapping or anything?"

"She'll be coming here voluntarily, so no worries about that," Jimmy said. "Besides, Rosemaria will talk her into staying if she gets rambunctious."

"Stop scaring him, Jimmy," Rosemaria said. "He'll forget his lines."

"I hardly have any. I think I'll remember them." He looked out the window. "A car just pulled up."

"A red Honda hatchback?" Rosemaria asked.

"Yeah."

"That's her car."

"Places, everyone." Rosemaria said. "Break a leg." She looked at Jan-Michael. "My mom was an actress."

One ex-cop and one current cop scurried into the office while Rosemaria stood behind the front door, and Jan-Michael waited for Sherilyn to knock. She did, and he opened the door. Even working with agents every day and occasionally seeing big stars come through the door of the agency, Sherilyn still was awed at being asked by this incredibly handsome actor who was a household name to come to his house and talk about a script in person.

He ushered her in. "Hi, Sherilyn. Thank you for coming."

She handed him the script. "It was no bother. I'm flattered you read my coverage and liked what I wrote. I highly recommended it for someone exactly your type."

He headed down the hall, holding the script. "Let's go into my office where we can be more comfortable and discuss it."

She followed him and stopped short when she saw Steven standing on one side of the room and then Jimmy on the other. "What the heck—?"

Jan-Michael quickly backed out of the room.

"He didn't really like my coverage of the script, did he?" she asked, looking at Steven, deeply disappointed.

"Actually, he did like it," Rosemaria said from behind her. "There's a good chance his agent will try to package it for him."

Sherilyn whirled around. When she saw it was Rosemaria, she couldn't decide whether to be more upset than happy. "Really?"

"Absolutely. This could be great for your career."

Her initial excitement turned to dejection. "And all I have to do is agree to an inquisition by the three of you."

"Exactly. Have a seat."

Sherilyn sank down into the chair Rosemaria had indicated. "Go ahead. I might as well get this over with. I hope you feel a little sad for me when I end up murdered in my sleep."

"Mariah will never know you were here or that you talked to us," Steven said, pulling the desk chair around and sitting opposite her. "We had a great talk last time. Let's just see if there's more you remember that can help us."

"I already told you everything. I wasn't at the house all the time. I only went to spend time with Ramin. And when I was there, I avoided her."

"Lorna told us you were friendly with her," Steven said.

"When did she tell you that?"

"We interviewed her briefly over the phone when she was in Las Vegas," Steven said. "Then she disappeared again."

Sherilyn became alarmed. "See? That's what I said. That's what happens when one of us talks to you. She finds them and kills them."

Rosemaria knelt beside her. "Calm down, Sherilyn. Lorna's fine. She's somewhere safe."

"How do you know?"

"Trust me, okay?" Rosemaria sat on a footstool next to her father. "Were you friends with Lorna?"

"Kind of. She was nice, even though Clyde was cheating on her with Mariah."

"How do you know that?" Steven asked.

"One time, Lorna gave me the key to their room when she was going out because I needed to get some feminine products from her. So I was looking around the bathroom and Clyde came in and threw himself into a chair. He figured it was Lorna in the bathroom and kept saying 'Dammit, Lorna. Everything is screwed. We have to get out of here. Did you hear what I said? You should have seen her face when she suspected I knew her real name. She looked like she could have shot me then and there.' I walked out of the bathroom, and he just stared at me as I went out the door. He didn't say a word."

The three detectives, present and former, looked at each other. This was huge.

"Whoa," Jimmy said. "Clyde can tell us who she is."

"He never said what the name was?" Rosemaria asked.

"He sounded so shook up I just wanted to get out of there."

"And you just remembered this? You could have told me this before," Steven said.

"I'm sorry. It didn't seem that big of a deal."

"It was a big deal, Sherilyn," Rosemaria said. "And you knew it."

"I'm sorry."

"When Lorna went to Reno, Clyde left for parts unknown," Jimmy said. "Where do you think he might have gone?"

"He was dealing drugs and hanging out with losers. He's probably dead. I don't know where he could have gone, and that's the truth."

"What about Keith?" Steven asked. "He's disappeared as well."

"I had nothing to do with him. Nothing. He was older and creepy."

"Were Ramin and David friends with him?" Jimmy asked.

"Not really. But one time, they went to the bar Keith used to own, Los Desperados, some kind of biker bar." She laughed. "Really a great place for two rich spoiled brats. Ramin said Keith told him when he used to own it, he and Maisie lived upstairs. I went by with Ramin once. It was a real dump. It's gone now. I think it was a vacant lot for a long time."

This was getting better and better for the detectives.

"You could have avoided this by being more forthcoming in the first place, Sherilyn," Rosemaria said.

"Can I go now? I really do not remember anything else."

Steven stood up and helped her to her feet. "If you do, you need to call us. It's better for you if we find her. You know that."

She looked down at the script on the desk. "Do you really think his agent will package it?"

"There's a very good chance. And when Jan-Michael comes into the agency to discuss the deal, you can just pretend this never happened."

"Are you kidding? I'm erasing it from my mind as we speak."

She walked to the front door with the three detectives trailing behind. "Well, say goodbye to Jan-Michael for me. I wish we could have discussed the script."

"I'm sure that will happen later," Steven said. "Have faith."

"When it comes to show business, faith and hope are about all you have to cling to."

They said their goodbyes, and she walked out the door.

The detectives were all smiles. "So, what do you want to do first?" Rosemaria asked.

"Let's take a trip to Los Desperados and see what's there now. Sounds like the perfect place for Mariah and Keith to meet if the bar was abandoned, and he still had the key to a little love nest upstairs."

"Maybe that's where he met his tragic end," Jimmy said. "And I haven't had a chance to tell you, but forensics was able to augment and separate various bird and animal noises in the background during Clyde's call to Lorna. I passed the recordings on to Curtis, and he's going to run with it. He has friends with access to computer programs we don't have. "

"And once we find Clyde and get Mariah's real name out of him, you can take it from there."

"We'll toss a coin to see which team gets to visit Cajun country."

Jan-Michael came into the room. "I heard and saw nothing as instructed."

"Good man. I really appreciate you doing this for us," Rosemaria said.

"For Vanessa, anything."

"What did she do to earn such loyalty, if it's not too personal a question?" Rosemaria asked.

"We knew each other in acting class, and she believed in me. She got me hired on a show she had guest starred in, talked to the producer about casting me in a small part, and that led to a lead in a pilot for a new series. I owe her everything."

"She never told me that. That girl is so modest."

"Are you going out the back?" Jan-Michael asked.

"Yes," Rosemaria affirmed. "Ready, gentlemen? Through the neighbor's yard and to our car parked on the next block. You're sure they're not home?" she asked Jan-Michael.

"Positive."

"Then let's go and solve this mystery like the real-life detectives we are."

Jan-Michael watched them leave through the back door where Rosemaria's bodyguard Abe was standing on the porch waiting for her. He smiled and shook his head. This was better than anything his script writers could come up with.

Josh was on his cell phone at the dining table when Rosemaria came in the door. He waved, and she bent down and pecked his cheek, dropped her purse on the table, and sank down in a chair opposite him. Suzi left her perch by the window, flew over, and landed on Rosemaria's shoulder with a squawk, nuzzling close to her face. Josh clicked off his phone and smiled.

"You won't believe this, but we're still number one on the pop charts, and the movie is grossing several million over what they expected from a medium-budget romcom in Europe and Asia."

"What do you mean I won't believe it?" Rosemaria settled on a chair next to him. "I know a hit song and movie means more touring, but don't worry. I'm in good hands with Abe."

Josh laughed. "The singer of the hit song tours; the songwriter doesn't usually tag along."

"But you went to Europe with her."

"That's because we're friends, and she wanted to do me a huge favor."

"So, what's next for you then?"

"I'm signing with a PR agent that Miranda recommended, and I'll be going into the studio to start recording my first album."

"Awesome."

"I may sign with Joell's manager if he'll have me, and—this is the hard part—you know Joell wants me to open her shows in San Francisco next weekend and Seattle after that."

"Yes, of course you will. As I said, Abe will take good care of me if the crazed killer is still on the loose."

Josh frowned.

Rosemaria hurried to reassure him. "I just said that to be funny. I'm sure the killer isn't crazed."

Josh's look hardened.

"Gee whiz don't look like that. Just say yes, you'll go, and I'm sure we'll find this person who seems to be a little, you know, unbalanced. Curtis is going to help. I called him, and he agreed that as soon as we can give him a hint of where he may have gone, he's on it.

Josh shook his head and threw his hands in the air. "I don't know. You expect me to leave you alone again when this is going on?"

"You're not going to stop your life and career because I attract trouble. Remember, you promised me that. I try hard to avoid it, but it's going to happen. That does not mean you will not do your PR and record your album and tour and all the rest of it. If I in any way impede your progress, I will bury myself in this apartment and never set foot outside again." She grabbed his hand. "I mean it. I refuse to be the reason you don't succeed. Do you understand?"

Josh took both her hands in his. "Trouble? That's what you call this?"

"A minor irritant." She looked down at Suzi preening her feathers on the table. "At least no one can sneak in here as long as Suzi is on duty."

"Suzi?"

"Yes, exactly. I have a watch bird. She'll holler out some crazy thing as soon as anybody tries to come in. And don't forget Abe and all his video cameras."

He pulled her to her feet and took her shoulders in his hands. "Our bird is shedding feathers where people are supposed to eat."

"I know. I have no control over her. All our kids are spoiled."

"You'll have plenty of time to train Suzi to do better if you stick around here. Promise me you will stay home as much as possible and not run around attracting attention to yourself. Let your dad and the others find and arrest this woman, whoever she is."

Rosemaria swallowed and made a face, not wanting to lie. "Well—"

"Yes?"

"I will absolutely do my best to do as you ask."

"I guess I'll have to be satisfied with that. Meanwhile, since I'm still a big fat nobody, I have to go to Ken's studio and record a restaurant commercial. It shouldn't take that long unless the client is there and demands retakes."

"Take your time. I promise I'll try to teach Suzi some manners while you're gone."

He hugged her close and kissed her hard before studying her at arm's length and letting her go. He shook his head, smiled, and went out the door.

Rosemaria sighed and opened her laptop. "Suzi, you're totally unmanageable. That's probably why I love you so much."

She was staring intently at the screen when her phone rang. She saw who it was and eagerly clicked on. "Malcolm."

Curtis was in his den at his desktop computer, which had four screens surrounding the keyboard. Books, journals, and papers lay everywhere, and photographs of his years in combat zones and of himself with fellow marines covered the walls. "Rosemaria Baker, the woman who changed my life."

"I can only imagine what it's like being the father of two grown girls. Are they there? Can I talk to them?"

"They're both at work. I told them to enjoy their summer vacation before their senior year, but they insist on helping out. I told them I can handle all the school expenses, but they are very determined."

"Sounds like my girls."

"They'll call you later, and you can chat. Right now, I want to let you know what's going on with the case."

"I'm listening."

"Clyde was a lot more involved in drug dealing than his friends thought. He was in business with a lot of unsavory criminals from gangbangers to the Mexican mafia. His partner in crime was a guy called Blades who came into this country illegally from Nicaragua. His real name was actually Cesar Estaban. It seemed that Cesar had been arrested several years before bringing heroin across the border from Mexico and confined in a small-town Texas jail, but he escaped during transport to a court hearing in San Antonio. He was there or in LA for a few years before he was caught on video with gangbangers under surveillance but eluded authorities again. He was sent back by immigration authorities twice before he managed to stay off their radar.

"Apparently, he and Clyde had stayed out of trouble in LA by never cheating their drug sources and paying promptly. About the time that Lorna and Clyde lit out for Reno, Cesar was still hiding from immigration and trying to figure out how to stay in LA without getting caught again. Eric, who is my go-to guy when it involves computers and has the best contacts in government agencies, hacked into various cell phone servers, found Clyde's old phone, and saw calls between him in Reno and somebody on a throwaway in LA, probably Cesar. Lorna took off for Las Vegas, and Clyde disappeared. Immigration believes Cesar went back to Nicaragua.

"Cesar's mother, twenty-two-year-old sister, and eight-year-old brother live in San Carlos, Nicaragua, a small town near a rainforest reserve. If Clyde is there, we'll find him, and I had a talk with your friend Jimmy, who gave me some information that might come in handy as well."

"Will you be sending someone to Nicaragua? We will pay their expenses."

I'll be going down myself with someone I trust, and you won't pay for anything."

"You're sure?"

"You gave me my daughters. You know what that's worth to me?"

"All right, I won't argue. When do you leave?"

"I'll tell the girls tonight, find someone to say with them, and leave tomorrow."

"Whoa. You move fast."

"Kept me alive all those years in the desert."

"Good luck."

"You too." And he clicked off.

Suzi had gone back to her perch and was pecking at her seed bar. "Suzi, I know I told Josh I would stay put and hang around with you as much as possible, but while our prison was a lovely place and you got to spend quality time by the pool, we were still locked up. I totally empathize with you and your bird relatives who are forced to live in cages. Now that I'm physically fit again, I really don't see why I have to be hemmed in any longer. I must do something to move things forward." She picked up her phone and looked at Suzi. "You're the only person who could possibly understand me." She tapped in a number.

CHAPTER TWENTY-NINE

Los Desperados was no longer a biker bar. It and half the block were now a community garden where neighbors grew organic fruits and vegetables. Around a dozen people were hoeing, weeding, and plucking tomatoes off vines when Steven and Jimmy arrived.

"With all this digging and planting, you'd think they'd have run into Keith by now," Jimmy said. "If he was ever here."

"Mariah seems to know everything that happens before it happens. Maybe she knew it was going to be a community garden and dug deep."

They had dressed casually, but there was something about cops; they couldn't hide who they were, no matter how hard they tried to act like civilians. And that was okay with Steven. After all those years of retirement, he couldn't shake who he was, nor would he want to. The middle-aged Latinos easily recognized them as cops, gave them brief smiles, and went back to their work. Steven and Jimmy strolled down the sidewalk away from their car and surveyed the scene.

Jimmy said, "We're making a huge leap of faith that she killed him here, or somebody else killed him, and he's buried here. But GPR can find him if he's there."

"Does BHPD have it?"

"If we don't, we can get it." He took his cell phone out of his pocket.

Two hours later, the garden was cordoned off by yellow police tape, and an employee of Ground Sensory Detecting was maneuvering the ground-penetrating radar device carefully over and through the plants. Steven and Jimmy were leaning against their car when Larry drove up. He got out and glanced over at the GPR device being rolled through the garden and all the pissed-off neighbors looking on. "How long has he been at it?"

"About half an hour," Steven said. "He's got a long way to go, right, Jimmy?" He turned to his partner. "The guy with the GPR briefly explained how it works. It's not that complicated."

"But can take a while," Jimmy said. "Because of the digging and planting that's been going on here, it could be difficult to detect the right mass. If our murder suspect had time to dig—if, say, the bar was still here, and she was digging inside the cellar with no one watching—Keith could be six feet deep. In that case, if the screen sees an inverted *V* on the screen that deep, there's a good chance the GPR is looking at body. And because disturbed soil indicates something buried, they should find him if he's here."

"Too bad they can't actually see the body with that device," Larry said.

Steven chuckled. "Yeah, too bad it's not like in the movies. But it's more efficient than dogs, which is all we had in my day."

The three of them watched the device slowly moving down a row of plants for a few seconds, and Steven said, "He's going to mark everything he finds with a flag. What say we go get something to eat? We're not doing any good just standing here."

Five minutes, later they were at a diner on Hollywood Boulevard with mugs of coffee sitting in front of them.

"So, if the GPR discovers the body, what do you expect to find?" Larry asked.

"We'll see if there's any evidence on or around him," Steven said. "If he's been there for ten years, the medical examiner might figure out the cause of death, but as for clues to the killer, that's iffy."

Jimmy was more optimistic. "There could be shoes and belt buckles with the body. They don't disintegrate." He grinned. "Maybe a gun with Mariah's real name on it?"

Larry picked up a menu. "Let's order while I still have an appetite."

"Any progress on the Bel Air case?" Steven asked.

"We finally tracked down the teenage son and girlfriend in Georgia, where the family was from. The kid's a real piece a work—no ambition, drugs, sleazy girlfriend with a string of arrests. They're bringing them back to LA tomorrow."

"Sounds like you have your murderers," Steven said. "What kind of evidence do you have?"

"The murder weapon was a three-feet-long electrician's pipe cut from a longer one. After the bloody deed, the killer heaved it down the hill halfway to the house below, thinking it would stay well hidden in the brush. Unfortunately for the killer, the owner of the house had been told by the fire department to clear the brush or get a citation. Lo and behold, the owner found the pipe. He obviously knew about the murders, wasn't sure if there was blood on it, but called us anyway, and we picked it up. Turned out it did have the victims' blood on it and was the same kind of piping that was stored in the dead parents' shed by the electricians after they finished working in the house two months ago. The lock was not jimmied, so somebody had used a key, and according to the help, that key was stored in a kitchen catch-all drawer. Only somebody who worked or lived there would have known that."

"Classic killer couple," Jimmy said. "I've seen a lot of them on the Oxygen channel."

"Not to mention the Menendez brothers, which happened in our jurisdiction," Larry said.

"So, you're pretty sure these two kids are guilty?" Steven asked.

"Yeah, and we intend to get confessions from both. I'll interview the girl, and Osborne will grill the son. We'll do the usual: show pictures of the murder weapon, tell them we have fingerprints, tell one the other has flipped on them, and get something before they lawyer up."

"Very funny. His aunts or uncles will have lawyers on speed dial."

"Unfortunately, you're right. At least we have enough to keep them behind bars on remand. While they're in there cooling their heels, we'll get more evidence, and I'll bet the farm one of them cracks."

"Dream on, Kojak," Steven said. "You won't be allowed within a mile of those mutts."

"Who's Kojak?" Jimmy asked.

"A TV cop who made being bald sexy," Steve said. "Not that any of us have to worry about that."

Larry said, "Still, there might be something. Mariah's human, not supernatural; she's made mistakes."

"Clyde may be one of those mistakes," Steven added. "And if Clyde is hiding something, Curtis will squeeze it out of him."

Jimmy picked up his coffee cup and held it high. "That said, here's to Malcolm Curtis, a man not to be trifled with. I look forward to hearing how he sweet-talked Clyde into spilling his guts."

"First he has to find him," Larry reminded him.

Jimmy took a sip of his coffee and smiled. "With what I gave him, should be easy. As for me, I wouldn't mind a trip to Louisiana Cajun country. My second out-of-state investigation." He picked up his menu and studied it.

The other two picked up their menus as well to forget about murderers for a while and concentrate on their growling stomachs.

In short order, the waitress was back, placing their steaming hot plates of food on the table. Steven had just picked up his fork, and Larry was buttering his roll when all their cell phones beeped. They looked at their screens in unison. A body had been found.

* * * * *

Mack was alone in his cubicle cleaning up "paperwork" on his computer when he looked up and saw a man who was at least six feet tall, around fifty-six, trim and fit with an intent to murder on his face heading in his direction. Mack looked around in vain for anyone who could help him manhandle the maniac back to the lobby. Mack was tempted to pull his gun out of his drawer as the man started screaming.

"What the hell are you doing sitting here doing nothing while the person who framed and murdered my son is still running around free?"

"Mr. Marchand?" Mack ventured.

"After my people made it clear you're making no headway finding the person who ordered the hit on my son, I decided I better fly to San Diego myself and find out what the hell is going on."

Mack closed his eyes, struggling to hold on to his patience. "Mr. Marchand. Please sit down."

Marchand stood and glared at him for two seconds, then sat abruptly in the chair next to the desk. He leaned in close and whispered, "Tell me something I want to hear."

Mack backed away and coughed into his hand. "I can't talk to you while you look like you're ready to take a swing at me."

Marchand made a dismissive gesture with his hand. "Attack a cop? I'm angry, not stupid. I want to know what you're not telling the media."

Mack relaxed a bit. "I can tell you we are making progress. We've narrowed down the list of suspects to someone who lived in the house. I'm telling you this in confidence. I can't tell you who it is. Right now, the suspect is in the wind, but they can't hide from us forever. We're talking to people who may know where the person is, but it may take some time to track down those leads. I promise you, this case is high on our agenda. The cop who told your son she'd reinvestigate the case was shot. Only a miracle prevented her from being killed. I assure you, every cop in San Diego and LA has this case on the front burner."

The bluster had drained out of Marchand. He looked at Mack helplessly. "Do you have any idea how this has affected my wife? We bought another house out here so we could visit David in prison more often. When he was killed, I thought she'd go out of her mind. All she thinks about is clearing his name and finding his murderer. I never see her anymore. She's out here in California most of the time. She's lost all her friends; she's drowning her sorrow in food and has gained thirty pounds. She's consumed with this. And all I hear from everybody is 'We're working on it.'"

"We've spoken to the cops who investigated David's murder, and they've reached a dead end. No one in the prison has anything to say. But I do believe it's linked to the person we're after down here. I know it sounds trite to say we're working on it, but trust me: we have some of the best detectives in San Diego and LA on the case. I can guarantee you, without any reservation, they will not stop until this person is caught, convicted, and behind bars." Mack spoke with such certainty Marchand was taken aback.

"You really believe that?" he asked.

"I do. There is no doubt in my mind."

"Well, now I feel like an ass's hind end. Will you accept my apology for storming in here like this?"

"Understood and forgotten."

"Will you let me know what kind of progress you're making?"

Mack looked at him, an eyebrow lifted.

Marchand understood. "Never mind. I know you can't. But at least I can relax, even if my wife won't. Dealing with her is—" He stared out the window for several seconds. "Sorry, that's not your concern."

Both men stood up, and Marchand reached out his hand. "Thank you, Detective. If all goes as you say it will, the next time I see you will be under happier circumstances."

Mack nodded, and Marchand slowly made his way to the exit door.

Mack sympathized with Marchand and what he was going through and believed every word he had said to him. He and Loshi still had people to interview and were directing the search for Stacey and Sam, which most of them deemed a lost cause. But Coleman had filled him in on Malcolm Curtis and his search for Clyde. If he was as connected with private security companies and shadowy government agencies as Mack had been told, it could give them what they needed to find Clyde, who might very well lead them to the elusive Mariah.

CHAPTER THIRTY

Curtis had chosen as his compadre in tracking down Clyde another marine he had served with in Afghanistan. Robert Waknuk was born in Ukraine, immigrated to the US with his parents at the age of twelve, and became a citizen when they did. He had never considered any career option other than the marines, and only because of an injury to his right eye when his jeep hit a land mine near Bagdad had he agreed to leave his unit. He was in his mid-forties, a little older than Curtis, and while his eye prevented him from staying in the service, he was still six feet, four inches tall and more able bodied than men half his age. He could also shoot as well as anybody Curtis knew. Robert had grown weary of the security firm he worked for and the assignments that bordered on the illegal and immoral. Helping Curtis find a person of interest in a murder case who had possibly fled to Central America was right up his alley.

They had flown from Cleveland Hopkins International to Miami International and then to Managua, Nicaragua, where they had to change planes for the flight to San Carlos, then rented a jeep at the airport. The town had a population of about fifteen thousand and was located near Lake Nicaragua and the San Juan River. Curtis's friends had found the location of Cesar's house, and they drove through neighborhoods of pastel-colored shops and modest, clean homes. They spotted the house they were looking for, small and well cared for, and parked several feet past it. They walked back to the house, and Waknuk went around to the back while Curtis waited a minute before knocking on the front door, holding his Glock behind his back. A woman in her fifties, dark-haired and slim, opened the door a couple of inches. "*Que quieres?*"

"*Quiera hablar,*" Curtis answered. "*Sobre su hijo.*"

She tried to shut the door, but Waknuk appeared behind her, held her close with one hand, and muffled her scream with the other. "*Siéntese,*" he said, and she backed up to a chair with Waknuk still holding her and sat down. They heard a jeep pull up outside, and Waknuk stood behind the mother, an arm on her shoulder, his M9 Baretta pointed in the air. Curtis ducked behind the front door as it opened.

A girl in her late teens walked inside and stopped short when she saw the older woman sitting in a chair terrified and a tall, intimidating man standing behind her with a gun. A young boy came running in after her, laughing and yelling phrases Curtis didn't understand. He stopped then ran to his grandmother who held him in her arms. "*No nos agos daño!*" she cried.

Curtis closed the front door, his gun drawn, giving his best impression of a really bad dude, asked the girl, "*Habla usted Inglés?*"

The girl spun around and began backing away toward the woman and the boy. She kept her eyes on Curtis, terrified.

"Do you speak English?" Curtis repeated.

The girl seemed confused, not understanding.

Curtis glanced at Waknuk. "I guess we'll have to kill the kid. Maybe that will make them talk."

"No!" The girl ran to her brother and threw herself down in front of him. "Please. Whatever you want, you can have."

"I guess she speaks English." Waknuk smiled.

Curtis nodded at Waknuk, indicating that he should take the woman and the boy out of the room. Waknuk took the woman's arm and helped her stand up as the boy clung to her, his arms wrapped around her waist. The three of them walked toward the back of the house.

The girl stood up and looked at Curtis, fearful, her hands clenched in front of her. She spoke in a heavy accent. "Is this about my brother?"

"Over here." Curtis took her arm and set her down on the couch. He pulled up a chair where he faced her and the front door and window. "When did he come back?"

The girl swallowed hard, completely disoriented. She could barely get out the words as she whispered. "To Nicaragua?"

"Yes."

"He came back to this country but not to here. He stayed in Managua. That was maybe five years ago."

"What was he doing in Managua?"

She hesitated.

"I'm not with law enforcement, not DEA or CIA. Talk to me. I am not after your brother."

"He . . . he smuggled drugs through Mexico, like always." She spoke reluctantly, but the hard set of his face made her continue. "He sent money home. For a while he couldn't because he was hiding in LA, but he finally made it across the border to Mexico and then to Nicaragua."

"Was his friend Clyde with him?"

She almost gasped. "Is he . . . is he?

"Did Clyde come with him to Managua?"

She nodded. "Yes, they lived in Managua for a while but visited here a few times."

"Then what?"

"Then Clyde came down here by himself two years ago and said the drug trade was too risky, and he wanted to work in the indigenous area for the people who are raising cattle here."

"That's what he's been doing?"

"Yes, he found work. It's dangerous. They hurt people who won't give them the land, so they can burn the forest and graze cattle. People here are angry. The jungle and our reserves are our legacy."

"Where's your brother?"

"Maybe he went north again. I don't know."

"Where can I find Clyde?"

Her eyes darted around the room, searching for a way to avoid answering.

He nodded toward the back of the house. "Your family or Clyde. Choose carefully."

"He can't come here. He said there are people here who want to kill him and know this house."

"And?"

"I bring him supplies and take them to his cabin where he lives near the cattle."

Curtis stood up. "Robert!"

Waknuk came out of the back room with the woman and boy in front of him. The boy still clung to the woman. "What's up?" Waknuk smiled.

"We're taking a trip into the jungle."

The girl shook her head. "No! I can't take you there. He will hate me for bringing you."

Curtis looked her up and down. "So, you're worried about what he thinks? This gringo has a hold on you maybe?" He took the girl by her arm, led her toward the front door, and looked back at Waknuk. "Leave those two. We can always come back if—" He looked at the girl. "What is your name?"

"Marlena."

"Let's go find your boyfriend, Marlena. I think he's been expecting us for a while."

An hour later, they were in the jungle in the girl's jeep on a narrow dirt road with vegetation pressing in on both sides. Curtis was driving. Waknuk was in the back with Marlena. They passed areas of devastation caused by the cattle ranchers—ancient forests teeming with wildlife reduced to rotting trees lying inert on the ground along with decaying palm leaves scattered across the ground where grasses were beginning to sprout up. They saw a few heads of cattle looking at them curiously then continue to forage for food.

"How do you want to do this?" Curtis asked.

Waknuk looked at the girl. "How many guns does he have?"

"I . . . I'm not sure."

"If you want him to come out of this alive, you need to tell us, or he's dead. Do you understand?"

"He has two guns and a rifle. I don't know what they are. I don't know about guns."

"Where does he keep them?"

"He carries one pistol all the time. He has one in the car, and the rifle is in the bedroom in the closet."

"Will he be home now?"

"I don't think so. He'll be working."

"What do you think?" Waknuk asked Curtis. "You want me inside or outside?"

"I'll be inside with the girl. You can cover me."

"You got it."

The cabin was one of many illegal shacks in the area, provided by the cattle company for outside workers. As they approached, they could see there was no vehicle parked outside and drove up close to the front door. Waknuk stayed outside out of sight while Curtis and Marlena went inside. The interior was bare but clean with a couple of chairs next to a wooden table. The kitchen area had no running water, and there was no power. Kerosine lamps were scattered here and there on small tables, counters, and the floor. They sat in chairs and waited in silence: Curtis, patient, calm, while Marlena was filled with apprehension as she kept looking out the window, terrified of what might happen.

They had waited for almost an hour when Clyde's jeep pulled up beside Marlena's car. He hurried inside and saw her sitting at the table staring at him, wide eyed. "What are you doing here? Has something happened?"

Before she could answer, Curtis stepped behind him and grabbed Clyde's gun out of his waistband. He shoved him toward the table where Marlena was sitting, now in tears. Curtis slammed him into a chair next to her, and she clung to him.

"What the hell is this?" Clyde demanded.

"I ask the questions. You answer."

"Did Mariah send you?" His voice shook with fear.

"Pull yourself together, Clyde. It's embarrassing for your girlfriend to see you like this."

Clyde bent over and covered his face with his hands as if to stifle sobs. Then in one smooth action, he took a knife from his boot, grabbed Marlena around the waist, pulled her up, and put the knife to her throat.

"I'm leaving here right now, or I'll slit her throat."

Curtis kept his Glock trained at Clyde's head. He chuckled. "You're not going to kill her, Clyde, and you know it. And if you do, what's that to me? One way or another, you're going to answer my questions, and I really don't give a damn how."

Clyde held Marlena closer, then a look of despair crossed his face. He loosened his grip on her, and she took the opportunity to break free and gave him a resounding slap on the face that sent the knife flying across the room.

"*Bastardo!*" she yelled and slammed out the front door.

Curtis shook his head. "I don't think she's going to take you back after this, Clyde."

Clyde held out his hands in supplication, "I don't know what you want from me. I don't know anything. I swear."

Curtis smiled as Waknuk moved soundlessly behind Clyde and slammed the butt of his Baretta into the back of Clyde's head.

Marlena came back inside, furious, and opened her mouth to say something when Waknuk held up two sets of keys. "You might as well stay. It's a long walk home."

She slammed back out the door.

A few minutes later, Clyde found himself lying on his bed, his hands tied to the headboard. He tried to move but his arms didn't budge. Curtis and Waknuk were standing at the foot of the bed staring at him. There was no mercy in their eyes, and there was no use fighting anymore. He'd come to the end of the road.

"What are you going to do to me?" All the weariness of the last ten years of running permeated his whispered question.

"We know where you've been the last ten years; we know you've been hiding from the law and from Mariah. The question is, who scares you the most?"

"You already know."

"Yeah, we know she's the scariest female you ever ran into."

"You have no idea."

"Why don't you help us out, Clyde." Waknuk asked. "Tell us why she wants to kill you, why she's killed other people in the house."

"Why are you asking me those kinds of questions? Don't you work for her?"

"We work for the good guys, Clyde," Curtis said. "But that doesn't mean you can blow us off. Get that?"

"I get it." Suddenly a realization hit him. "Is Lorna all right? I can't reach her anymore."

"She's fine. Completely out of danger." Waknuk said.

"We don't have time to chitchat, Clyde. So let's get to it. What do you know about Mariah that is so important you think she wants you dead?"

"I knew she killed Ramin . . . or . . . I mean, I suspected her of having done it."

"Why did you?"

"I was the one who told her about the carpets being delivered by the Iranians and the fifty thousand Ramin was getting from the bank to pay them."

"How did you know?"

"A couple of guys I know heard about it. We hung out downtown where the Iranians had their warehouse."

"Gangbangers? Drug dealers?"

"Whatever. They thought about doing a heist but figured there were so many security cameras it wasn't worth it."

"Why not rob the Iranians and skip the middleman?"

"Are you serious?"

"Okay, so you told her, and somehow she managed to knock out the security cameras and the alarm. How did she get David to come there?"

"I don't know. Honestly, I don't know. I'm sorry. I didn't know she was going to kill Ramin. She promised to share the money with me."

"Did she share?"

"No."

"So you could blow the whistle on her any time."

"Yeah, and when David was killed in prison, I knew she had someone do it. And she had to know I would suspect her."

"For money and a little booty, you messed up your entire life and profitable business."

"There's something else. I found out her real name. The name she was born with, that she's been hiding all these years."

Curtis and Waknuk looked at each other and smiled. This was it.

"And what is her real name?" Curtis asked.

"Leonie Gautreau."

"And you found this out how?" Waknuk asked.

"By accident."

"We're listening," Curtis said.

"She had an old beater Keith had given her. She mostly took the bus, but she drove the car sometimes and wouldn't let anybody near it. She didn't have a license, but if she ever got stopped, she'd talk her way out of getting a ticket. She wanted to drive it to school one morning, but it was overheating, so she asked me to take it into the garage where I had a friend who was a mechanic. She took the bus to class while I drove the car to my friend's place and sat and waited for him to finish. He came to me holding an envelope and said he found it underneath the dashboard taped under the glove compartment with duct tape. It was pushed up against the wiring and messed it up. It was sealed, but I was curious and thought, *Why not?* We held it over hot steam coming out of a tap, and I pulled it open no problem. There was nothing in there but her birth certificate. Her name, Leonie Gautreau, was on there, where she was born, and her parents' names."

They all looked up as Marlena slammed open the door. "How much longer will you be talking to that"—her mouth curled into an angry sneer—"*cabrón?*"

Waknuk walked over to Marlena, took her arm, and, without a word, firmly escorted her outside, shut the door, and walked back to Clyde.

"Continue," Curtis said.

Clyde sighed hopelessly. "That's about it. I made sure the envelope was sealed perfectly as if it had never been opened. I was thinking we'd better tape the envelope back where it came from just as she came running into the shop out of breath. She saw me holding it, and she tried to pretend it was no big deal. I told her it was causing the problem with her wiring, and she said she had forgotten all about it. We sat and waited for my friend to finish with her car, and I tried to pretend I never opened the envelope, but I know she suspected." He shivered. "I didn't touch her after that, but sometimes I caught her staring at me like she knew. She had gone from hot to icy cold in one day. She scared the shit out of me."

"Do you remember her parents' names and the town she was born in?"

"No, but I took a picture of the certificate with my phone."

"Is it still on there?"

"That phone is long gone."

Curtis looked at Waknuk in frustration. "Damn!"

"But I printed out a copy the next day as a kind of insurance."

"You still have it?"

"In the dresser, top drawer in a wooden box."

Waknuk walked over to the dresser and retrieved the box from the drawer. He opened it, smiled, and handed the paper to Curtis. There in black and white was the key to possibly solving this whole puzzle.

"Tell me something, Clyde," Curtis asked, "Mariah, even then, was paranoid about anybody finding out who she was. Why would she hang on to a birth certificate that could expose her identity?"

"I thought about that, and I don't have a clue. It was the one stupid thing she did. But she couldn't hide it in her room. One of us might have found it, so she hid it in a car nobody would ever want to steal and nobody ever drove but her."

"We'll have to ask her when we find her."

"God, I hope you do."

Curtis stuffed the paper in his shirt pocket and began to untie Clyde. "Clyde you're going to be given a second chance at life. You lay low, and we'll find Mariah, or I should say, Leonie, and get her off your back." Walnut helped Clyde to his feet and tossed his car keys on the bed.

"What you're going to do is leave the area and go live somewhere else in Nicaragua, anywhere else. You're going to stay away from Marlena, leave your life of crime, and get a job doing anything that doesn't cause any more pain and suffering than you're already responsible for. We found you once, and we can find you again, and our employers have an endless reserve of money to pay us.

Curtis leaned in close. "You know how we knew for sure you were in Nicaragua?"

Clyde grimaced and shook his head.

"Birds."

Clyde looked confused.

"Forensics digital experts looked for ambient noise in your phone calls to Lorna, and there they were—parakeets, macaws, and more—two hundred species. Some of them that only live in the Indio Maíz jungle where you have been busy illegally destroying their homes." He smiled at Waknuk. "Karma, right?"

Curtis chuckled, drew the rope off Clyde's wrists, and threw it on the floor. "So you don't have to wonder anymore how we tracked you down. A little bird told me."

Clyde followed Curtis and Waknuk outside. Marlena was waiting for them, leaning against the hood of her car. Waknuk tossed her the keys, and she wasted no time getting in and starting it up, giving Clyde a final look at that should have vaporized the skin off his face.

Waknuk jumped in the back, Curtis rode shotgun, and they backed out to the road. Clyde watched them leave; a ton of misery and regrets for a life wasted swept over him. He wondered if there was anything left to live for. But he had managed to survive this long. He would keep on living, taking the high road. Curtis had made it clear—he had no choice.

Rosemaria was the first to get the news, straight from Curtis. "Don't disappoint me now," she said as soon as she answered her phone.

"We found him."

"And—?"

"He was very cooperative."

Rosemaria laughed. "I'll bet he was."

"I'm sending a written report to Larry, and he can share it with every-one else."

"What did he tell you?"

"Her name."

"Be still my heart."

"Leonie Gautreau. And he handed us a bonus: a copy of her birth certificate, which also tells us where she was born and the names of her parents."

"Holy moly. I wonder why she would save that. She was so careful in every other way to hide her identity."

"We wondered about that as well."

"What about Clyde? What did you do with him?"

"Left him to brood about his future. I'm sure he's repented of his sins and will walk the straight and narrow from now on. If not, I told him I could find him again just as easily as the first time."

"Have a safe trip home. Do you want to make a side trip here and receive all the 'atta boys' in person?"

"I'll skip that. Got to get home to my girls."

"Lucky you."

"See ya."

"Later." She clicked off.

CHAPTER THIRTY-ONE

The meeting of the godfathers-plus was in session in the conference room of the Beverly Hills Police Department. Judging by the empty water bottles on the table, the meeting had been going on for several minutes. In attendance were also Mack and Loshi and the raison d'être herself, Rosemaria Baker. Abe had decided his charge was safe in the hands of the BHPD and gone out for a snack.

"Forensics couldn't tell us anything about Keith except that he had a bullet hole in his forehead," Larry said. "Presumably put there by Leonie before she dug a grave four feet deep in the cellar of Los Desperados and rolled him in. We have no DNA to compare with his bone powder, but for some reason, Leonie left his belt on, which must have seemed too ordinary to bother with. She overlooked the inscription inside the buckle: 'From MT to KT' beside a heart symbol." He glanced across the table at Jimmy. "So you almost had it right."

"It's a gift," Jimmy said modestly.

"Or the Oxygen channel," Steven quipped.

Jimmy raised a water bottle. "Got that right." He took a long drink.

"I guess Leonie's attention to detail wasn't as acutely developed at age nineteen as it is now," Rosemaria said.

"I wonder what the heck Keith did to deserve her wrath."

Mack shook his head. "Poor Maisie, she didn't stand a chance against that barracuda."

"It wouldn't surprise me if Leonie provided the drugs to facilitate Masie's slide into oblivion," Rosemaria said. "Didn't have to murder her; just prey on her insecurities and let her destroy herself."

Her remarks threatened to engulf the room with gloom as they considered the tragic death of Maisie at age forty-two.

Loshi looked down at his iPad. "Curtis and Robert came through like gangbusters. Now that we have her name and where she was born, our digital forensic people tracked down her employers. She worked for two businesses in New Orleans: a chain restaurant and a car dealership. Which is amazing. She was young, didn't have much of an education at that age but still got decent jobs."

"She may be uneducated, but she's scary smart," Osborne said.

"Curtis and Robert would have loved to have met you all," Rosemaria said, "but flying from Managua to LA and then to Cleveland seemed like an unnecessary detour. Their report, as we all know. was incredibly detailed, but if we have any questions, Curtis says he will do a Zoom meeting."

Mack nodded in agreement. "We'll do that if we have to. Curtis and Waknuk did all the dirty work; now it's up to us to follow through.

"Our guys didn't find one picture of her," Loshi said. "She didn't have a driver license, passport, nothing."

"She was prescient." Rosemaria laughed. "She knew she was going to become a criminal and would have to hide from the law."

"I tracked her to the car dealership and then nothing." Jimmy turned to Loshi. "Did your people find any trace of her after that?"

"Nothing," Loshi answered.

"If her employers have records of her family, maybe they know what happened to her," Steven said. "Or maybe she stole the birth certificate and is somebody else altogether."

Rosemaria looked at him through narrowed eyes. "Okay, Dad, let's not throw cold water on our amazing breakthrough. My intuition tells me we're on the right track. She has a Cajun accent, uses Cajun expressions, is the right age, and can get jobs even though she's a kid. I'd bet anything it's her."

"So what happens to Clyde?" Jimmy threw out there.

Rosemaria grinned. "Curtis told him to straighten up and fly right, or he'll track him down again. From dealing drugs to destroying a rainforest. What a guy."

"He cared what happened to Lorna," Steven said. "That's one good thing you can say about him."

Mack shook his head. "Anybody in that deep with the Mexican mafia probably has a short life span. It's amazing he managed to hide from them this long. His partner Cesar is probably six feet under by now."

"Something else disturbing came up the past couple of days." Osborne said. "Walter Atkins bought himself a SIG Sauer P365 using the name of a con he put away a couple years ago. He drove up to a gun store in Sacramento to make the purchase. He's making weekly trips to an indoor target range." He looked at Rosemaria. "I'm sorry, but he's still a danger to you. We've had him followed."

Rosemaria was taken aback. "Darn, and here I thought he had forgotten all about me."

"Apparently not."

The room went silent as everyone mulled this over.

Finally, Steven spoke. "I'll talk to him."

"No, Dad, I'll do it. Don't worry. I know what to say."

"I'm not good with that," her father said. "Not at all."

"Abe will be my backup."

Steven was not reassured.

"Anything else to add before we adjourn this meeting?" Osborne asked.

"Our forensics team has been trying for weeks to identify the person whose blood was found in the parking lot at the health club," Loshi said. "Finally tracked him down through Interpol. He's a Chechen national, a thug for hire who was caught by the Russian military, fingerprinted and swabbed, and held briefly in Grozny. He escaped from Chechnya into Georgia where he disappeared. Whoever his friend, the sniper for hire, is, he knew how to locate him and get him into the US. Both are in the wind and will probably stay there."

Rosemaria shook her head in disbelief. "It's stunning that Leonie managed to find and hire them." She glanced around the room and spoke hesitantly. "But I have an idea on how to get her to show herself."

Larry had started to get out of his chair and sat back down. "This sounds interesting."

"What if we let it be known that, for a reason we can cook up later, Abe will not be with me at a certain time and place, and I will be completely alone?"

Steven frowned and shook his head. "Use you as bait?"

"Yeah. Why not? We could end this whole thing in a day or two. I've been thinking about it."

They all looked at her like she had lost her mind. Osborne's answer was definitive. "Absolutely not." He stood up.

"Why? I'll have protection she won't see. This kind of thing has been done before."

Steven smiled. "Over my dead body."

Rosemaria blew air out of one side of her mouth and slumped down in her chair. "Everybody was perfectly willing to have me go up dark alleys all by myself to catch lowlife mutts when I was a cop. I'm still that same person."

Osborne picked up his laptop and glanced around the room. "Anything else?"

"Yeah, now that that's settled, one more thing," Mack said. "Marchand came to see me. He was all fired up and pouring molten lava all over my desk, but I managed to calm him down a bit. I told him we had a lead on the real killer, and he seemed to accept that. His wife, on the other hand, has apparently gone off the deep end and has turned into a total fruitcake." He looked around the room and shrugged. "Just sayin', you never know what women like that will do."

"Good to know," Larry said. "And thank you guys for driving all the way up here to meet with us. They said it couldn't be done, but we're all working together like a well-oiled machine."

Loshi smiled. "Who's they?"

"That's one of those great mysteries even the best detectives in the Beverly Hills Police Department can't solve," Larry responded.

Mack held up his hand. "I just want to say I appreciate you guys having no hard feelings about us going to New Orleans."

"You caught the case in San Diego," Osborne said. "It's yours to follow through. I can't spare anybody to go with Jimmy, and Steven wants to stay near Rosemaria. It's a no-brainer."

"Then have a great trip, my friends," Larry said. "It's in your hands now. Keep us informed."

And the meeting of the godfathers was adjourned.

Rosemaria chose to walk with her dad down the stairs to the lobby where Abe was waiting, shooting the breeze with Sergeant Kowalski at the front desk. She couldn't leave without giving a hug to her old friend the sergeant, who had always ignored the politically correct regs that forbade such behavior. She held out her arms, and the great big bear of a man crushed the breath out of her lungs for a good thirty seconds, carefully avoiding her broken arm. "Come back to us. Courtrooms are dull. This is where all the fun is."

"That might be true, but I'd like to incarcerate a few more numbskulls first. I like that part of my new job."

With waves to Kowalski, the three of them went out the door and down the walkway. Steven's phone rang, and he stared at it at arm's length, puzzled. He pressed the button. "Steven Baker here." His face went white. "Stacey?"

Rosemaria and Jimmy reacted as Steven listened. They were rooted to the spot.

Abe couldn't allow them to stand on the sidewalk like statues leaving Rosemaria an open target, even outside the station, so he quickly ushered them inside the SUV. Abe jumped in the driver's seat, Jimmy into the passenger seat; Rosemaria sat with her dad in the back. Steven held the phone to his ear for several minutes. Finally, he said, "I agree. It's best you stay where you are for the time being. Do you remember the name of the boat?" He indicated with one hand he needed pen and paper. Rosemaria frantically fished around in her purse and came up with a pen and small pad. She gave them to her father.

"Hold on." He balanced the pad on his knee and wrote quickly and hard. "Where was it docked? . . . Anything else? . . . "Do you know the type of gun he used? . . . No, that's okay, but an automatic, not a pistol? Okay, that's helpful. . . . I assume you'll destroy this phone. . . . Sounds like you found a good friend. . . . We won't tell Micco, so don't worry; he won't be looking for you. Bye, Stacey. . . . Yeah, we're doing our best."

"Whew." Steven let out a huge breath. "Wow." He shook his head.

Rosemaria had started breathing again, and her lips were parted in anticipation. "Dad, don't keep me in suspense. Stacey's all right? What about Sam?"

"She's alive, but only by a miracle and a little help from a beach bum. Sam is dead."

"Oh no. Start at the beginning, and don't leave anything out," Rosemaria commanded.

"Yeah," Jimmy added.

Abe stayed cool and uninvolved; his eyes never stopped moving. "We can't stay parked here anymore. I'll drive around the neighborhood till you're finished talking, and then we'll drop Jimmy and Steven back to their cars in the garage." He pulled out and drove up to Santa Monica and into the residential area.

Steven began his recitation. "Micco came by their apartment and left a note that convinced Stacey and Sam to sneak out. He told them something about Mariah knowing where they were and that they weren't safe there."

"Micco?" Rosemaria was shocked. "He came all the way to San Diego to tell them that?"

"He drove them down to the marina, and they got on a boat he said was his. He took them on a jaunt out into the harbor. After they were out in the open water, he said he was taking them to Mexico and handed them a wad of cash. When they refused to go, he pulled a gun. Sam wrestled him for the gun and was shot. Sam yelled at Stacey to jump overboard, which she did. Micco threw Sam over the side while Stacey swam for her life. Micco shot at her blindly a few times while she was under water, managing to hit her once in the side, then gave up. She ended up on a deserted beach where a guy who lives in a tent patched up her gunshot wound and has been taking care of her ever since." Steven had remained impassive through the entire recitation but then shook his head in disbelief. "Yeah, really? Micco?"

Rosemaria was stunned as well. "Everything Mack and Loshi told us about him made me think he was the least likely of any of them to ever kill anybody."

"Do we bring him in or what?" Jimmy asked Steven.

"We don't even know if he went back home. He could have had his phone on forwarded when we called him."

"Criminy, Dad, you can't go up there. He has a gun. He killed Sam."

"If we arrest him, Leonie will find out, and she'll know that we know Stacey and Sam were shot, and Stacey is alive. She probably thinks both of them are dead."

Rosemaria smiled. "So, we don't tell him anything. Hopefully, he went back home, and we track him."

"It should only be that easy," Steven said.

Rosemaria relaxed. "Okay, Abe, we can swing by the station so Dad and Jimmy can get their cars, and I can get home to prepare for work on Monday."

Abe turned left and headed toward Santa Monica Boulevard.

"You're going back to work?" her father asked, not altogether pleased.

"Yep, they just told me this morning I can have my job back. Abe will drive me to the courthouse every morning, walk me to the entrance, and I'm good to go." She hugged her father and sighed. "I'm no longer a useless prisoner. Ain't it great?" She sat back and closed her eyes, contemplating the pile of cases waiting on her desk.

* * * * *

"Feel better?" Randy asked. Stacey was lounging in a hammock strung between two slender trees that were a part of the vegetation that shielded their campground from the road above and reinforced their privacy. Randy sat next to her in a simple aluminum camp chair.

"You were right. I needed to tell him. He said I should stay here."

"And so you shall."

"He won't tell Micco I'm alive."

"That makes sense. It keeps you safe."

"I'm not imposing on you by staying longer?"

"As long as you stay on your side of the divider, we'll be fine."

"I have so far, haven't I?"

"You've been very good about that."

"Can we have Chinese for dinner tonight?"

"After a couple more hours of reading and relaxing. Are you feeling any pain?"

"Just a twinge now and then. You know, it's kind of a crazy thing to say, but I don't think I've ever been happier in my whole life than I am right now."

"I feel the same."

* * * * *

Rosemaria was waiting for Atkins outside his office. He locked his door and saw that she was standing on the sidewalk a few feet away from him.

"Hello, Walter," she said quietly.

He stared at her with such contempt she could feel loathing emanating from his body. He made a move to get around her, but she immediately blocked his way.

"You need to listen to me, Walter, and I will never bother you again."

He lifted a hand as if to shove her aside, then noticed a very large, intimidating man move forward to stand behind her. Atkins backed up and glared. His words, despite his high-pitched voice, managed to come out in a growl.

"What do you want?" He stared at her through his tiny eyes and tried to look tough.

"Just this, Walter. I would like you to forget about me. I believe that's best for both of us. The police are tracking everything you do, everywhere you go, and are aware of every gun you purchase, legally or otherwise. They know when you pick your nose, scratch your ass, burp out of both ends, and have night sweats thinking about how you wrecked your career. That's on you, Walter. I was willing to make nice even though you acted like a jerk from the first time we met. But you chose to come after me. It drives you crazy to admit I outsmarted you, but you're not an idiot. There's no reason you can't make a go of your practice—nice location, by the way—and make a decent living. I urge you to move forward with your life. Join a twelve-step program, learn acceptance of the past. You can't change what happened, but you can give yourself a chance to have a decent future. I realize taking advice is hard for anyone, but I highly recommend you take this advice from me. Forget I exist. Because if you even think about hurting me, the hurt will come back on you a thousand times worse." She smiled. "Do we understand each other?"

Atkins shifted from one foot to the other, stared into the distance, and glanced at Rosemaria, then at Abe, who looked as if he wouldn't hesitate to kill him then and there. He nodded.

Rosemaria smiled. "Good decision. I wish you the best of luck."

She turned away and followed Abe back to the car; he opened the passenger door for her, and she got in. Abe shot one last look at Walter as he walked around the car, opened the door, then slid inside and drove off.

Walter watched the car pull away from the curb and accepted that his life just became devoid of meaning. Thoughts of revenge on Baker had started his mornings and filled his days. Now those thoughts had turned to dust and despair. No matter how torn up he felt about everything he had lost and the empty future he faced, he wouldn't let himself cry. He still had his pride. He quietly recited the lyrics to his favorite Springsteen song over and over again as he walked toward the parking lot and his car. But the tears came, and nothing he told himself could stop them.

CHAPTER THIRTY-TWO

The black SUV was on the 101 Freeway headed toward the 134 and the Burbank Airport. Abe was driving, and Josh was in the back with Rosemaria beside him. She was holding his hand as they both stared pensively out the window.

"When on Sunday will you be back?" Rosemaria asked.

"We're flying back around two. You don't have to pick me up. Joell will drop me off."

"Okay, but we wouldn't mind."

"Waste of gas."

"I'm used to you sleeping beside me again." She leaned on his shoulder. "It's not easy to let you go."

"It's only two and a half days this time."

"I know, but I seem to have become this horribly clingy fiancée who is bereft without you."

"You will never be bereft, and I'm sure you'll be up to no good the minute I'm gone."

"All I have is that meeting of the charity group at Chez Nous. How much trouble can I get into at the most upscale, snooty restaurant in Beverly Hills? They practically do a background check of everybody who makes a reservation."

"I'm sure that's an exaggeration."

"Only a little. They may not let me in."

"Vanessa's your best friend. She'll tell them to make allowances on your behalf."

"You need to get that album recorded and sell two million copies; then they wouldn't dare disrespect me."

"Yes, ma'am. Tuesday morning we'll be in the studio. Joell's musicians already have my charts and will be ready to make history."

"She's going all out for you—musicians, manager, PR person. You'll have your own posse before long. Where do I fit in?"

He pulled her close. "Don't worry. I'll find a place for you."

They were traveling up Hollywood Way but made a left turn before the airport entrance.

"Where are we going?" Rosemaria asked.

"It's a small airline up a few blocks. We're taking a plane that only flies between west coast and Nevada airports."

"Why doesn't she have her own plane like all the other rich celebrities?"

"She doesn't believe in it."

"Ah, she cares about the environment. I like her for that."

"And because she has such great taste in protégés."

"That goes without saying."

They pulled into a small driveway in front of a private hangar, and Abe glanced back at them. "I'll take your suitcase out of the back while you say your goodbyes."

Josh and Rosemaria unfastened their seatbelts, and he pulled her close. "Don't get into too much trouble while I'm gone," he whispered.

"Everything is being handled. My cops are on the case. I'll be sitting in front of the computer catching up on cases, especially the one I might be prosecuting. But more important than that, I wish I could go up and see Noor and Gilbert before they forget me. I'm worried they might not remember me when I finally see them again."

"They won't forget. Now wish me good luck and—"

A rap on the window stopped him short. Joell stood outside grinning.

He rolled down the window, and Joell bent down and smiled at Rosemaria. "It's so good to see you. Are you feeling better?"

"Thank you, Joell. I'm almost back to normal."

"Good to hear."

Josh opened the door and stepped out of the car, then leaned back in. "I'll call you tonight." He gave her a quick peck, and Joell took his arm as they walked toward the hangar.

"Have a safe flight," Rosemaria yelled after him as she watched Josh and Joell already deep in conversation. She felt a pang of jealousy but admonished herself for acting like an insecure idiot. He would become more and more famous, and she had better get used to women swarming all over him. Handsome, talented, and irresistible, who could blame them? Too bad for all those starry-eyed celebrity chasers—his heart belonged to her. She settled back contentedly and clicked her seatbelt back on as Abe steered the car back to Hollywood Way and home. She could hardly wait to dive into the caseload that awaited her on her laptop.

* * * * *

The smell of microwaved popcorn greeted Steven as he came in through the door via the garage. He saw a big bowl of popcorn on the kitchen table and a tall glass of Coke. By now, he knew his houseguest couldn't watch a movie without popcorn.

"Lorna?" he called out.

She came running down the hallway, dressed in a robe and hair in a towel. "Yes? Is everything all right?"

He held up his hands, smiled, and nodded. "Everything's fine. I saw the popcorn and wondered why you weren't sitting on the couch engrossed in a movie. I'm just being an overbearing, stressed-out old guy."

She took the towel off and shook her hair free. "I wanted to take a shower before watching a movie on TCM. Have you seen it? *The Postman Always Rings Twice* with Lana Turner and John Garfield. The original. I love that movie. She is so incredibly beautiful, almost unearthly; you know what I mean?"

"I do, and yes, I have seen the movie, and I'd love to see it again. But first I need to tell you something. So why don't you get dressed, and we'll have a talk."

She studied his face for a hint of clue but found none. "Is this good or bad? Will I be upset?"

"Change your clothes, and we'll talk"

She gave him a worried look before turning around and rushing down the hall to her room. Steven walked into his study, took off his jacket, and draped it over a chair. He wondered how she would take the news. At least he could tell her Clyde was still alive and in no present danger. That was something, but not much. He went back into the kitchen area, sat at the table, took a handful of popcorn, and crunched thoughtfully. He needed to find her another place to stay soon—something more permanent, maybe in another state.

Lorna came out of her room, her hair damp and stringy, hanging down over her denim shirt. She looked at him, her eyes pleading. "If it's something bad, something about Clyde, please just tell me."

"He's fine. No need to worry."

"Oh my God! You found him." She looked at him wide eyed, ready to jump out of her skin.

At that moment, she seemed incredibly young and vulnerable to Steven, more like eighteen than thirty one. "Calm down and just let me talk."

She bit her lip and swallowed. "I'm sorry. I'll be quiet."

"That's okay," he reassured her. "We found him in Nicaragua where he was—"

"Nicaragua?"

Steven gave her a look, and she settled down again.

"He was living and working near a small town that's situated next to a wildlife reserve. He moved there from Managua because, apparently, he and his partner, Blades, who I don't think you knew about, were up to their old tricks, working with drug smugglers up to the Mexican border and back. He must have known it was a matter of time before he got caught.

He didn't want to come back to the states because Mariah knew he had discovered something about her that put his life in extreme danger."

She let this sink in. "And she thinks I know what it is, so she's trying to kill me too."

"I'm afraid so. What he found out could lead us to her whereabouts, and she'll do whatever she has to in order to prevent that from happening."

"I guess you're not going to tell me what that something is."

"No. But I don't think Clyde will be calling you anymore now that he knows you're safe. His concern for you is about the only redeeming quality he has."

They both reacted as the doorbell rang.

"Go to your room," Steven whispered.

Her eyes fearfully flicked to the front of the house, but the drapes were drawn, and they couldn't see who was outside.

It's probably nothing, but let's be safe,"

She scurried down the hallway while he went to the front door. He looked through the peephole, relaxed, and opened the door.

"Senor Medina, come in, quickly."

Santiago didn't hesitate, and Steven closed and locked the door behind him.

"Have a seat," Steven said. "I'll call Lorna."

Santiago moved toward an overstuffed chair near the couch, but before he could sit down, Lorna rushed into the room and threw herself into his arms. "Santiago!" she said. "I've missed you."

"Why don't you two take the couch, and I'll sit in the chair?" Steven said. "What's going on, Santiago?"

"I've resigned from my job at the casino so I can provide a safe home for Lorna." He turned and looked at Lorna, who had a tight grip on his arm. "I didn't want to call you because I was afraid you'd say no. So I quit, drove all day, and here I am."

Lorna's eyes welled up. "I can't believe you did that for me. But what about your mom?"

"Mom is fine. When all this is over, you and I can go back to Vegas and get our jobs back. Till then, she's able to take care of herself."

"Where will we live?"

"We can stay in a motel for now and then figure something else out. I have a lot in savings, so don't worry about money."

Lorna scrunched up her face and chewed on a fingernail. "I want to be with you. I really do, and to be perfectly honest, until this very minute, I didn't know how much I wanted that."

"But?"

Lorna looked at Steven. "Would it be safe enough for me?"

"Not even close."

"I'm a security guard," Santiago protested. "I know how to handle weapons. I was trained by the Las Vegas Police Department."

"That all sounds good, but no. Checking into a motel, you need ID. Your car can be traced. If Mariah makes the slightest effort to find you, she will."

The two kids stared at him hopefully as he stood up and walked back and forth across the room. A thought had occurred to him. Maybe it was crazy but maybe not.

"What can we do, Mr. Baker?" Lorna asked. "We want to be together."

Steven sank back down into the overstuffed chair. "I think I have the solution, but it's predicated on my friend Sandy's reaction. She's a veterinarian, works out of her home, and has a guest house on her property. The last time I talked to her, no one was living there. I'll ask her if you can rent the guest house at a bargain-basement price. I can also ask her if she'll buy you a used car to drive temporarily and put it in her name—safer than any of us doing it. I'll give her cash for it. Don't worry about that now. You can pay me back later. Her place is not far from here. You'll have to park your car in my garage, Santiago. I'll ask if she'll come pick you two up."

Lorna was looking at him with eyes of wonder. "Wow. You and Sandy must really have an incredible thing going."

Steven shrugged. "You might say we're good friends."

She and Santiago turned and looked at each other, then back at Steven.

"Okay," Lorna said. "If you say so. But if we're going to be staying there, you know you can't hide the truth from us for long."

Steven smiled. "I'll go into my study and make the call."

CHAPTER THIRTY-THREE

Tourists had swarmed into town thanks to the perfect storm of three conventions and four bus tours arriving at the same time. His Stolen Sky gallery had started out with a fair number of customers in the morning, and apparently word of mouth had spread; by noon, the gallery was packed. And people had bought paintings; they hadn't just viewed. Micco could barely keep enough paintings on the wall and every half hour had to go back into the storeroom to unpack more. He and his assistant Janice had their hands full writing up delivery orders, which were now stacked high on his desk. He was gratified when three of his own paintings sold as well. He was in no way a snob about art, and when customers bought a painting because they loved the colors and wanted to decorate a room around them, he was supportive and encouraging. He never talked down to anyone, and he knew his attitude engendered repeat customers.

He sent Janice home at six and began to input the orders into the computer himself. She had grabbed sandwiches for the two of them around one, and he had managed a bite or two when he could sneak into his office for a quick break. Now he munched as he worked and sipped on coffee Janice had brought back for him. If business kept going as well as it had in the past two months, he might have to give her a raise. She had a boyfriend but still had bills to pay. He wanted to be fair.

Fair? What a joke. All day he had been too busy to think about Mariah and the fact that he was a double murderer. Sitting alone, contemplating his gradual slide into the dark slime that Mariah had pulled him into, he had to surrender the rules of normal behavior he used to live by. He could no longer afford a conscience and knew there would never be a comfort zone for him anymore. No matter how successful he became he would always have in the back of his mind that he had personally killed two of his friends and was responsible for the death of two more people. That's who he was now—a murderer. He could live with it or confess to the cops, pay the price, and ask for forgiveness. Redemption would come if he took that path and maybe even eventual peace of mind. But he couldn't do it. The thought of being locked up for years or the rest of his life was too horrific to consider. He'd have to tough it out and pretend it never happened.

Micco jumped to his feet and stood in the middle of the room, running his fingers through his hair, pulling at his face. He walked back and forth, staring at the walls covered with paintings seeing nothing. Who was he kidding? He was in agony. Mariah would never let him forget, would never leave him alone. She had called him five times, and he never answered. Hadn't he done enough? Clyde and Lorna had disappeared. Sarah and Sherilyn were innocent and could do nothing to hurt Mariah. Everyone else was dead. There was no one left to kill except Baker, and Mariah had said she wanted to do that herself. She hated Baker. Hated her profession, her authority, her successful friends, the people willing to give their lives for her, and most of all, she hated that Baker was loved— something Mariah strived for using her sexuality but never could achieve. Eventually, everyone saw through her grasping need for money and could no longer abide her pathological selfishness. Those who stayed too long at the party ended up regretting it and left for good. She must be doing a phenomenal acting role with her new fiancé to keep him around for almost two years. But it was just a matter of time. If she didn't marry him soon, it would be one more fake relationship to end in disaster.

He forced himself to relax and settled back down in his chair behind the desk. If he concentrated on work and contemplated his profits from just this one day of sales, he was somewhat comforted. Gradually, his imagination and his terrors lessened until his mind was filled with names, dates, addresses, figures, pick-up dates, and all the other minutiae of running an art gallery—his art gallery, that he had sacrificed everything for. After a few minutes he couldn't concentrate. He was too agitated.

He stood up abruptly, moved from behind his desk, threw himself down on the couch, and agonized for the hundredth time over the night that had changed his life. If only do-overs were possible—if only, if only, if only. Mariah had come to him that afternoon and said she knew how to make $50,000 in one night. He had reacted with scorn and skepticism, but she insisted they would merely be relieving a multi-millionaire of some cash he would barely miss. After a few drinks in her room, he agreed to drive her to an army-navy store in Hollywood, and she had him wait in the car. In a few minutes, she came out with a huge shopping bag and told him to drive to the spot in Griffith Park where she liked having sex in the woods near some picnic grounds. When he saw the black pants, jackets, and ski masks she pulled out of the bag, he almost lost it. But like the pathetically weak boy that he was, he allowed her to calm him down, murmuring sweetly as he grew harder and harder as she expertly used her hands on him. After he was drained of what strength and will he had left, she brought out a joint. A few tokes later, all of his misgivings had disappeared. Quietly reassuring, she convinced him to change his clothes and told him she would drive.

He was still woozy from the marijuana when they pulled up on a side street near Ramin's dad's carpet store. *Oh no*, he had thought. He couldn't do this to a friend. But he watched through a sleepy haze as she parked and then turned around and focused her eyes through the back window on the front door of the store. He had become warm and uncomfortable in the heavy clothes he had changed into. The warmth made him feel drowsy, and he nodded off. He awakened as Ramin walked out the front door and headed down the sidewalk. Mariah started the car, drove around the block to the back of the store, and parked up the alley from the back entrance. He had looked up at the cameras, and she assured him, "Don't worry. I knocked them out." He had taught her everything he knew about the internet, then she had easily leapfrogged over him and become more of a tech expert than he would ever be. He felt so logy he tried to remember if she could have drugged him earlier. She pulled him out of the car, took his black ski mask out of his pocket, drew it over his head, and told him to put his gloves on. She opened the back door of the store and reset the alarm, took a duffle bag out of the car, pulled her own mask on, and gave him his instructions.

They would wait for Ramin in the back room, Micco would grab him; she had an unloaded gun that she'd point at him, then they'd tie him up, take the money, and run. Easy. No one would speak a word; no one would get hurt. Micco had become wary and frightened. Gun? This was not what he had bargained for, but he was wallowing in the muck now. He had to play this to the end.

By then it was dark outside, and no lights were on in the store. He looked around the storage room as they waited on either side of the door. A large heavy safe stood on the floor in the far corner, rolls of carpets wrapped in plastic were leaning against the door of another storage room, and tall metal shelves holding wooden boxes stood against three walls. They waited silently for a few minutes then heard Ramin come in the back door and briefly reset the alarm. Ramin reached for the light switch as he came through the door, but Micco grabbed him and shoved him up against the opposite wall. The bank bag Ramin had been holding fell to the floor. Mariah had pulled out a gun and pointed it at him. "Just do as we say and you'll be fine," she'd said in a deep and what Micco hoped was an unrecognizable voice.

She pulled a cell phone out of her pocket and held it out to him. "Call David and tell him you need him at the store." Ramin hesitated briefly, then did as he was told. Mariah took the phone back. Micco had bent down to take a rope out of Mariah's duffle bag, and a shot rang out. He turned to see Ramin crumpled on the floor. Mariah was still crouched down from where she had taken aim. He watched in horror as he saw blood oozing from Ramin's chest and mouth. He was paralyzed with fear and horror.

She proceeded to push several boxes off one shelf, pulled two carpet rolls to the floor. "Pick up the bank bag and put the money in my bag," she ordered.

Trembling, Micco transferred the money. "Can we go now?" he had whispered.

"Now we wait," she said.

When David came through the back door, he called out Ramin's name. As soon as David saw Ramin lying on the floor he turned to flee. But Micco grabbed him, and Mariah slammed a narrow square steel pipe the length of a baseball bat into the back of his head, knocking him unconscious. Then she went about her tasks with methodical precision as he stood by inert and helpless. She pulled down a heavy shelf that landed close to where David had fallen. Boxes of tools spilled out all over the floor. She took out her gun and placed Ramin's fingers on the barrel and pressed hard. She walked to where David had fallen on the floor and wrapped his hand around the gun, pressed and let it fall. She picked up a bottle of floor wax from her bag; spilled it over David's chest, hand, and arm; and let it fall on top of him. She bent over David, grabbed his head, and slammed it into the edge of the steel shelf that had fallen near him. She had smiled up at Micco. "The pipe is the exact same size as the edge of the shelf. Can you believe the luck? I used this kind of pipe when I fixed up houses." *Fixed up houses? What the hell was she talking about?*

The rest of the night was a blur. He remembered Mariah picking up the pipe she had hit David with, wrapping it in plastic taken from her bag, leaving the back door wide open, being told to drop the empty bank bag in the parking lot, then walking quickly to the car and driving up the alley, through darkened streets, and back to the house.

From that night on, Micco felt removed from everything that went on around him. His life was pretense, an act. He had lost touch with whoever he used to be. Whatever Mariah told him to do, he did. She had no fear of the police, no fear of being found out and acted like nothing had happened, while his own morbid terror of being caught made him just as much of a patsy as David. She was certain that cops were stupid and would figure David and Ramin, being best friends, had conspired to steal the money for David's sake so he could escape the clutches of his overbearing father. They staged a fight to make it look like intruders interrupted them and stole the money, but something went wrong, and David accidently shot Ramin when David fell and hit his head on the fallen shelf. The empty back bag that had been dropped in the parking lot would prove someone else had been there later and had stolen the money. When the cops asked for tips, Mariah would call in anonymously and suggest just that.

If David were to be arrested and sent to jail, he had considered coming forward and telling the truth, but he knew if he did, he would end up as dead as Ramin. There was no way out. He was a loathsome coward and had gone into partnership with the devil.

His office had no windows, so he was unaware of the passage of time. When he finally picked himself off the couch, went over to his desk, and picked up his cell phone, he saw it was past eight and probably dark outside. It was time to quit. He logged out of his computer, took his sport coat off the rack, and slipped it on. Tomorrow he would enjoy another successful day, and thoughts of Mariah would be banned from his mind. As he turned off the overhead light and opened the office door, he saw the gallery was dark. He fumbled with the key to lock his office door and felt the muzzle of a gun at his neck.

"Walk to the reception desk and sit down," the coldest voice in the world ordered.

He walked slowly to the chair and sat, every nerve in his body convulsing, causing him to shake uncontrollably. He hadn't been in the same room with her for years. He had forgotten the evil that emanated from her icy tentacles when you were the object of her hate. He was afraid to look up.

"Have you missed me? I've missed you. I've missed you exactly five times as a matter of fact. So I thought I'd better come see you in person to make sure you're still alive." The voice grew even colder and more frightening. "Look at me, Micco."

He slowly lifted his eyes to see a figure in black, wearing a hoodie and a black Mardi Gras mask encrusted with rhinestones. An automatic pistol was pointed at his head.

"Do you like my new look? I stole the mask just for this occasion so you wouldn't see the new me in the society columns or on the news and say, 'I know her.'"

"I don't care what you look like now. I have no interest in anything you do."

"Why aren't you answering my calls?"

Micco's voice wavered, but somehow, he found the courage to speak the truth. What did he have to lose? "I don't want to do this anymore."

"I'm not sure I heard you correctly."

"Everybody's dead except Clyde, who's run off for good; Lorna, who managed to disappear; Sarah, who never had anything to do with you; and Sherilyn, who doesn't know anything about you then or now. What else do you want from me?" He hated the sound of his voice weak and pleading.

"Have you forgotten we've been partners since the day you hacked into the rug store security system and helped me steal fifty thousand dollars and kill Ramin?"

"You did that."

"So you say. You just murdered two of your friends all on your own. And let's not forget the young girl at the gym. You're a criminal, Micco. You could go to jail for murder."

"I know that. I want to forget what I've done and get on with my life in peace. You told me you have a boyfriend who inherited millions, and you're not exactly hurting yourself." He was so desperate he wanted to cry. "You've ruined my life. Why won't you just let me go?"

Mariah's voice was thick with cruelty. "You don't get to decide what I do and don't do. You will be my partner for as long as I say so. You will follow my orders, and you will answer the phone when I call. Avoiding me is not an option. I may need you to do something for me, or I may not, but that's up to me to decide."

He knew it was hopeless. He had sold out his life for a measly five thousand dollars. He could have started his art gallery without Mariah's money, with just the Indian money and a loan. But he was a weak and needy kid, and Mariah had played him for a fool. He felt tears well up in his eyes and fall down his face like a bullied schoolgirl. "And if I don't answer your calls?"

He sensed the smile on her face as she spoke inches away from his face. "I could leave you to the law, of course. But they might be too lenient. What will I do if you ignore me again? I'll leave that up to your imagination. Remember I told you years ago how I used to kill varmints when I was a kid? I shot at everything that moved. If they didn't die fast enough, I skinned them alive. You want to shed a tear for them, Micco? Go ahead. You've turned into such a sensitive guy. But if you try to avoid me again, it won't bother me one bit to do the same to you. Practice makes perfect. And I've had lots of it."

She backed away from him. "It's a long drive back to where I'm going and somewhat tiring. Don't make me have to do it again." She suddenly lunged at him, and he cowered and shrunk back in his chair. "Answer your damn phone!" He felt a heavy weight slam into the side of his head, and darkness overtook him as he slumped to the floor.

When he woke up, he was still sprawled on the floor, cold and shivering. His head was pounding where Mariah's gun had hit him, and there was blood on his shirt and his jacket. Some blood had smeared on the floor. There was only one chance for him to survive and escape Mariah's hold on him. Rosemaria Baker and her detective friends had to find her. Maybe he could make some sort of deal for himself once she was in custody. Until then, going to the cops was a death sentence. Nobody, including him, knew who she was.

CHAPTER THIRTY-FOUR

"Suzi, I'm going to leave this documentary about the birds of the Amazon on Netflix while I'm gone. Don't get depressed about your friends losing their homes. They're doing something about it. I promise. This documentary is all about that." Suzi was in the roomy cage that Loretta had bought for her, and she had a perfect view of the television.

Rosemaria fussed with her hair as she studied herself in the framed mirror in the living room. Madelaine had come over the day before and cut off her cast. Her arm looked a little shriveled, but Madelaine assured her that wouldn't last long. Vanessa had helped her pick out the black dress online and have it delivered in twenty four hours. It fit okay and showed off her figure but no cleavage. No men were going to be there so why bother wearing something revealing and showing off her assets, such as they were? Vanessa, being an actress and having been around glamor with a capital *G* for years, thought the dress a little plain. Plain was fine with Rosemaria. She didn't want to stand out. She wanted to observe without calling attention to herself. Leonie might be in attendance that night, and if there was any way humanly possible for that shrewd, diabolical woman to give herself away, Rosemaria wanted to be on top of it.

The possibility of that happening was such a long shot Rosemaria had to laugh at herself for even contemplating it. What could Leonie do to reveal her true identity? Make a public announcement? "Ha," she said out loud.

"Good job," Suzi said right back.

"Hey, You learned something new. Madelaine only said that to me about a hundred times. But I appreciate that you've finally expanded your vocabulary."

The doorbell rang, and Rosemaria swept her beaded handbag off the dining room table and went to the front door. "See you later, Suzi."

She opened the door and saw Kirsten, dressed in a blue cocktail dress and a matching blue jacket, roomy enough to hide her handgun in a holster on her hip. "Reporting for duty, ma'am."

Rosemaria closed and locked the door. "I hope nothing exciting happens the first time you sub for Abe."

They headed toward the elevator. "McAdams is driving and will be shadowing us in the restaurant. Have no fear, Ms. Baker. You're in good hands."

"Do you think she'll show?"

"I think that Mariah being one of these ladies is a remote possibility. But I could be wrong." She pressed the down button to the garage.

"I didn't tell my dad I was going to take you into my confidence about my suspicions that the killer is a young, rich charity fundraiser, but because you could be in the line of fire, I thought you deserved to know. On the DL, of course."

"Silent as a tomb."

McAdams was waiting right outside the elevator with the car doors open. They took their places inside the SUV, Rosemaria in back, Kirsten riding shotgun, and McAdams in the driver's seat.

Rosemaria leaned back and considered the possibilities the night could bring. Vanessa had taken to the new affluent world Larry and Loretta had opened up for her with ease. But she was never pretentious. She could play her role as wealthy matron and still be a close friend of somebody who shopped for furniture at garage sales. In the beginning, Vanessa had plunged into this new social set for the sake of Larry's career but now, Rosemaria could tell, she was actually enjoying herself and had made many friends. They had even elected her to head of the fundraising committee. Rosemaria hoped for Vanessa's sake that one of them wasn't a murderer. Her gut told her otherwise. As they neared Chez Nous on Rodeo Boulevard, she hoped it was merely indigestion.

The exterior of the restaurant looked like a French country house, white clapboard with large multipaned windows and outdoor seating protected by white railings and overhead awnings. The sign was small, next to the front entrance, where two round sculptured trees stood guard on either side. Kirsten got out of the SUV first then McAdams opened the door for Rosemaria. Kirsten walked a few steps behind. Inside, Rosemaria gave her name to the pleasantly officious maître d' who, speaking with a French accent indicated she was to go upstairs, away from the regular dining room that was packed with people at eight o'clock at night.

Vanessa was talking to someone near the top of the stairs and immediately broke off the conversation when she saw Rosemaria. She hugged her, a huge grin on her face. "You actually came. I thought maybe you'd chicken out."

"I wanted to, but I spent too much money on this dress to waste it."

Vanessa led her into a dining area that was decorated with cream wallpaper embossed with pastel flowered designs. Large impressionist paintings hung on the walls. The room was large and dimly lit, with recessed lighting and several dining area groupings. Rosemaria felt like it was set up more for a mass séance than a charity meeting. Several people were mingling while others had already seated themselves at the tables. Kirsten headed for the open bar but didn't order a drink.

"Just relax and enjoy yourself, okay?" Vanessa said. "I know it's not your kind of thing, but a lot of the ladies you met before will be here. There's a bar in the corner. So have a glass of wine." Vanessa spotted someone on the other side of the room and patted her arm. "Excuse me. I have to talk to Isolde for a minute.

Ah, to be an actress and be able to fit in any place you find yourself, Rosemaria thought. She felt comfortable in an interrogation room opposite hardened criminals and could grill them into spilling their guts no problem. But make small talk with women she had nothing in common with? She wanted to fade into the cream wallpaper. She spotted Drew at a table with Sophia and headed in that direction. Familiar faces were welcome at one of these things.

Drew smiled when she saw her and waved her over. "Have a seat, Rosemaria. You know Sophia from last time."

"Thank you. You rescued me from the world of mingling. I'm not good at that as you may have figured out already."

"How did Vanessa talk you into coming?" Sophia asked.

"She thinks now that I'm living in the 90210 zip code, I should meet people who haven't robbed banks or assaulted mini-mart owners."

"That's right. Vanessa told us you'd been a cop. But we haven't done either, I promise you," Drew said.

"How about you clue me in on who some of these women are, so I won't be completely in the dark?"

"So, who is the most interesting?" Drew wondered, glancing around the room.

"Anybody," Rosemaria reassured her.

"Okay, look at the tall brunette in the Stella McCartney near the bar," Sophia said.

"Translation?"

"The white, belted, no-back dress."

Rosemaria spotted the woman.

"Heather Perry. She is gorgeous and nice and always contributes a lot of time and money to whatever we're working on."

"Is she really that perfect?"

"Who knows what goes on behind closed doors, but she also has a sexy boyfriend who is loaded."

"My head is spinning already. Both of you are also nice and really loaded. My stereotype expectations are falling apart."

"You thought we'd be arrogant bitches clawing each other's eyes out?" Drew laughed.

"Exactly. Like in that old movie *The Women* with Norma Shearer?"

"I loved that movie," Sophia said. "The remake with what's-her-name—Warren Beatty's wife—was just god-awful bad."

"I actually saw the original with my mother at a theater in the Fairfax district that used to show old movies." Rosemaria said, "That was my view of wealthy women from an early age on."

"We didn't all inherit money or marry it." Drew said. "Some of us grew up in trailer parks with three siblings, like yours truly, and had a single mother who worked two jobs to support us."

"Damn straight," Sophia said. "I worked for a construction company for five years until we were hired to build an outdoor set for my future husband, the producer of the film. If he dumped me tomorrow and I lost everything, I could still find work as a bookkeeper in no time flat." She shivered. "Hopefully, that will never happen. I'd hate to lose my home gym and the masseuse who works miracles on my sore back."

Drew pointed. "Oh look, there's Alva Montez, the singer." She turned to Rosemaria. "She's single and has a slew of dancer boyfriends barely out of their teens. Every so often, she marries one, but she tires of them quickly." She laughed. "She's here for show mostly."

By now most of the women were seated, and the waiters were serving the salads.

"Where's the ladies room?" Rosemaria asked.

"It's two floors down. I think this restaurant was built in the dark ages," Drew said.

Rosemaria pushed her chair back. "I'll be back in a few minutes."

She walked toward the stairs and saw that Kirsten was following but not too close to be obvious. The first-floor dining room was still crowded as she headed down another flight. Going downstairs in high heels was a challenge, and Rosemaria hung on to the railing. "Don't you dare fall," Kirsten whispered behind her. "Abe would never forgive me if you broke more bones on my watch."

"Your concern is touching. I may look wobbly, but I have ankles of steel."

She finally got to the bottom floor and saw the women's room down the hall. "I drank too much water today, but I won't be long. And I have to make sure the paint isn't melting off my face."

Rosemaria pushed open the door. Kirsten checked the empty stalls, saw several women standing in front of the mirrors, and watched as Rosemaria went into a stall. She walked back outside and waited. Rosemaria was out in two minutes and was ready to go back upstairs.

"I need to go too." Kirsten said. "Will you come back inside and wait for me?"

"You're a big girl and can take of everything yourself. I'll just wait out here."

"You idiot. I meant for your own protection," Kirsten hissed.

Rosemaria sauntered toward the mirror at the end of the hall. "Please hurry. I'm missing all the fun."

Kirsten glared at her and went inside the ladies' room. Rosemaria sighed, gave herself the once-over in the mirror and before she could wipe a small glob of mascara off her face, a heavy-set woman came flying out of a hallway door and launched herself on top of Rosemaria. On her way down, Rosemaria hit her head hard on the edge of a table and was pinned to the floor by the obese woman. "Why are you wasting time here?" the woman growled. "Why aren't you out looking for my son's murderer?" The woman's hideous face was inches away from Rosemaria's. "What happened to my son is your fault, Baker! All of it is your fault!"

Rosemaria felt the woman's spittle hit her face. Before she was able to free her hand and punch the lady in the face the weight was lifted and the woman pulled off her. Kirsten and McAdams had grabbed her by the arms and quickly cuffed her behind her back. She struggled to free herself and swore a blue streak, but McAdams had her in a vise. He yanked her toward the stairs. By now a small audience had formed, and Kirsten said quietly to Rosemaria, "Follow us. We'll take you to the ER to check you out for a concussion."

Rosemaria shook her head. "I'm fine, just a little dizzy. I'll wait for you upstairs."

Kirsten knew by now it was futile to argue and followed McAdams as he forced Rosemaria's attacker up the stairs.

Rosemaria went back inside the ladies' room and washed her face, then walked back into the hallway. She had to steady herself as she made her way up one flight of stairs. She found a quiet alcove near the entrance and called her father. "Dad, I think I was just attacked by Helene Marchand. The woman has gone stark raving mad."

Her father was at his desk in his home study, and he bolted out of his chair. "What? Where was Kirsten?"

"It wasn't her fault. The woman got access to a room downstairs and must have been waiting for me. She's crazy like a fox, Dad. How many stalkers is a girl allowed to have?"

"Are you hurt?"

"Not at all. I wanted to let you know. Kirsten helped McAdams take her out to a squad car. I'm going back upstairs to join the party. I'll tell you all about it tomorrow, okay?"

"If you think you're okay, good hunting."

"You never let me down."

"Never."

And they disconnected.

Moving slowly, Rosemaria managed to find her way back to her table and her seatmates. Two other ladies were now at their table, and waiters were in the midst of serving them the main course.

"You look terrible," Drew said. "What happened?"

"Just a bit of an accident. I fell off my high heels going down the stairs."

One of the waiters set a plate of pasta in front of Rosemaria. "Vegan for you, ma'am, I believe."

Rosemaria smiled up at him. "Yes, that's for me." Vanessa was looking out for her as always. She looked at the other two ladies who had joined them at the table. "I think I met you both at Loretta's house at the meeting she had there."

One of them, a thirtyish redhead with freckles, nodded. She seemed a bit more formal than Drew and Sophia. "I'm Nancy Winfield. We talked briefly that evening."

The other lady smiled. "I'm Jackie Radcliff. We didn't have a chance to talk much before either. You seem to have gotten over your injuries."

"Yes, I had an accident. I tend to be a little clumsy at times."

Drew jumped in. "I'll say." She looked at the others. "Poor Rosemaria just tripped and fell while she was going down to the restroom."

"Luckily I was holding on to the banister, and not much damage was done."

"You must be close friends with the Collins," Jackie observed. Her smooth dark hair was cut to fall just above her shoulders.

"Not really. Their son is my ex-partner, and I needed a place to recuperate, so they volunteered their services."

"Loretta is such a nice lady," Jackie said, then looked taken aback. "Wait a minute. Loretta's son Larry is a cop. You were a cop, Rosemaria?"

"I taught him everything he knows." Rosemaria laughed. "But now I work at the Airport Courthouse as a prosecutor."

"That's incredible." Drew said. "Wow, I'm so impressed. All I did was fool around on the computer, and voila, surprise, surprise, I'm up to my eyeballs in money."

"Are you married?" Nancy asked.

"Engaged."

"Is he in law enforcement as well?" Sophia asked.

They were all looking at her as if her mundane life was worthy of inspection. "No, my fiancé is a singer-songwriter who mostly does commercials. But right now, one of his songs is number one on the charts, if I may brag a little."

"'New York Nights'?" Drew asked. "That's his?"

"Yeah, he wrote it for the movie."

The ladies seemed fascinated, even Nancy.

"Do you have a picture?" Drew asked.

Rosemaria took her phone out of her bag and scrolled through until she found the best one. She held it up for the others to see.

"He's very handsome," Jackie said.

"I'll say," Drew agreed. "Poor you."

"Why?"

"When he gets more famous, you'll be fighting off women with sticks. You better watch him every minute when that happens. Remember Angelina and Brad and poor Jennifer."

"I'll remember."

Vanessa, who was at the head table, stood up and turned on the mike she held in her hand. "If I could have your attention, ladies. I want to thank you all for coming and being a part of helping support the shelters. The heads of the various committees will now report on what they've done so far in planning the gala at the Beverly Wilshire. After they're through speaking, there will be a Q and A, and you can offer your own ideas on our silent auction and how to make sure we fill the ballroom to overflowing with generous attendees."

As the committee chairs got up one by one to speak, Rosemaria surreptitiously glanced at the women at her table as she pretended to listen: Sophia, who was possibly the wealthiest woman in the room but was nevertheless as unpretentious and down to earth as if she were still living in the humble surroundings of her youth; Drew, pretty and perky as a high school cheerleader who considered being a genius as normal as breathing; Jackie, with the easy smile, who didn't have as much money as the others but easily fit in with her wealthier friends and graciously accepted Rosemaria as a part of the group; and Nancy, the youngest regent of the UC university system, officious and focused on the task at hand, but she exploded in loud guffaws when Vanessa snuck a joke or two into her presentation.

Did any of these women at her table or the lady at the table next to her with the white dress and short platinum hair or Alva the boy-toy collector or the beautiful redhead in the backless Stella McCarthy have murder on their minds as they sat with their friends, planning how to raise money for the poor? Her usually reliable stomach was telling her nothing. Maybe the killer was not here. Or maybe her sixth sense was failing her because this event was so important to Vanessa, and Rosemaria did not want to ruin it for her.

She looked around the room at all the women who were paying rapt attention to what was being said. It was difficult to imagine any of them, including the women at her table, being a serial killer. What if she were completely wrong? What if she had everybody working on a wrong-headed theory that Leonie was in this inner circle of the rich and powerful? Maybe she was unconsciously resentful of the people she had been briefly allowed to interact with as Loretta's guest and Vanessa's friend. It was a lifestyle of seemingly no problems, no worries about having a secure home, bills paid, and able to wake up every day to unlimited possibilities. How could a serial killer reside in the midst of such a blessed existence? She felt Drew's eyes on her, questioning, seeing that her mind was wandering.

"It does get a little boring," Drew whispered. "You'll get used to it if you stick around long enough."

Rosemaria smiled and thought that this was not her world, and it never would be. But she could fake anything for as long as she had to.

CHAPTER THIRTY-FIVE

The detectives had rented a small SUV at the Louis Armstrong International Airport in New Orleans and headed straight to the Chevy dealership that was located a few blocks away on the way to their hotel. Gary Manzini, who now owned Manzini Motors since his father retired, was happy to talk to Mack and Loshi and told them his father had hired Leonie Gautreau when she was fifteen despite her having no office experience. The son still remembered the young girl who had worked as a file clerk part time. He had visited the dealership often as a child and learned the business from the ground up, doing menial chores for his dad, like washing cars and cleaning up the public kitchen area. He remembered Leonie being breathtakingly beautiful, blonde, outgoing, and friendly with the lightest blue eyes he had ever seen. He had a crush on her like all the other guys but was too much of a nerd to have approached her or done anything about it. At odds with her good looks was her Cajun accent, thick as sludgy swamp water, and she didn't seem to have had much of an education. She always took the bus, and even though one of the younger salesmen gave her driving lessons, she didn't apply for a driver's license even after she passed her sixteenth birthday.

At Mack's request, Gary looked up her records on his computer while Mack took notes—address, phone number, social security number, date of birth, and that was about it. Five years before, Gary's assistant had input records from fifteen-year-old paper files they then threw out. Could be the information was incomplete. Leonie had talked a few times about her father but didn't say where he was living other than somewhere up the Lafourche Bayou and had never mentioned her mother. She had refused to have her picture taken for her ID tag, and because his father was a softy he didn't push it. She pretty much had every one of the workers wrapped around her finger by the time she left after a year and a half. She didn't say where she was going, just that she needed to move on. The detectives left their card and asked him to call if he thought of anything to add. When the man asked why they were looking for her, Loshi answered that it was old business, nothing important.

Mack and Loshi were eager to learn more about the young Leonie, but they were bushed. Hotel reservations had been made for them at the Saint Charles Inn in the Garden District of New Orleans. It was located in a quiet, residential neighborhood. The lobby had an old-fashioned feel to it, and the rooms were elegantly simple. Even though the hotel was understated, they could tell it was expensive and suspected Larry had made the reservations himself—the perk of working with an ex-partner of the lady in peril who had unlimited funds at his disposal. After a good night's rest and a complimentary breakfast in the lounge, they would be ready for the drive to Neeva's Diner where Mariah had found her first job as a teenage waitress.

The next morning, they resisted the tempting spread laid out by the inn, figuring they might have to order a meal at the diner to ingratiate themselves. The drive to Neeva's in Metairie took only ten minutes. Mack and Loshi sat in the parking lot and contemplated what they knew about Leonie. Not much.

"We need to find out if her parents are still alive. What are the chances that someone who works here will remember her?" Loshi wondered aloud rhetorically.

"Fifteen years later? I wouldn't place any big bets on it."

"She seems to have been a quite memorable young girl."

"We're not going find out anything sitting here."

They got out of the car and went inside. It turned out the manager had only been working there for two months. He didn't know anything about a girl who had been a waitress there fifteen years before.

"How about records for that time?" Loshi asked the young man. "Would you still have those in the office?"

"We don't keep those here. The owner died a few years ago, and the heirs sold the franchise to a corporation headquartered in downtown New Orleans. Maybe they have records. But I doubt it."

"How about the names of other people who worked here at the time?" Loshi asked. "Somebody who might have known this girl."

The manager waved over a waitress who was standing by the kitchen opening about to grab a plate. She looked like she was at least fifty but had a sweet, lively expression on her face.

"Hey, Zelda, do you remember any of the waitresses from fifteen years ago? Were you here then? These here are two detectives from LA looking for somebody named Leonie."

Zelda's face perked up. "I never worked with her myself, but Sally May did and used to talk about her."

Mack and Loshi were all ears. "What did Sally May have to say about her?" Loshi asked.

"That Leonie was a real firecracker. Working here was her first job. She started out as a dishwasher and didn't mind the hard work at all. Then she got a job waiting tables and took to it like nobody's business. Made more money in tips than the rest of us put together. The customers loved her."

"Where can we find this Sally May so we can speak to her?" Mack asked.

"I think she moved in with her kids in Baton Rouge, or maybe it was Pensacola. I can't remember." She chewed on her thumbnail, wrinkled her brow, and scrunched up her face to think better. A light bulb went off in her head. "You know who would know is Carrie Sue. She was here at the same time as Sally May."

Mack blew out a load of air. This was like pulling teeth. "And how do we find Carrie Sue?"

Zelda held up a forefinger and whipped her phone out of her uniform pocket. "I'll call her right now. And Harry, you better bring that order to table five, or they're gonna start cussin' me out."

Harry hustled to pick up the order and deliver it to table five while Zelda dialed. "Hello? Carrie Sue? Zelda. . . . Yeah, everything's all right, but I have some detectives who need to talk to you here at the diner. Are you close? Can you come right over? . . .I'm sure they'll be happy to hear that. See you in a few."

Mack and Loshi were pleasantly surprised. "Thank you, Zelda. We'll wait in a booth, order breakfast, and give you a big tip. How's that?"

Zelda blushed. "Oh, I'm always happy to help out law enforcement. I know your job is not easy."

She led them to a table, and they ordered omelets and the melt-in-your-mouth pastries that seemed to be available everywhere in the area. She took their order with a smile.

"I love people who love their jobs," Loshi said.

"I've loved mine enough already. I'm ready to love not having to work."

"Won't you be bored? Won't you miss your old partner?"

"You can visit me in Baja."

"Don't think I won't."

Their food came about the time Carrie Sue came through the door. She was another lady who looked to be in her fifties or sixties with a friendly disposition. "So, what's this all about, detectives? How can I help?"

"We're looking for information about a girl who worked here fifteen years ago named Leonie Gautreau," Mack said. "Have a seat."

She slid into the booth next to Loshi. "What's she done?" Carrie Sue asked, all excited and nosy.

"Well, that's what we're trying to figure out."

"I only worked with her for two weeks, but Sally May knew her pretty well and told me all about her."

"Was there a lot to tell?" Mack asked between forkfuls of home fries.

"Oh yes, she was a very interesting young lady."

"Why don't you go over everything you remember, and we'll just sit here, have our breakfast, and listen," Mack suggested.

Carrie Sue licked her lips in anticipation, excited at having been given permission to share gossip—or, rather, information—about Leonie, and with cops, no less. They weren't about to brush her off as a silly old lady. They actually *wanted* to listen to her. She hardly knew where to start. She breathed deeply.

"When I met Leonie, she had been working here for a few months. It was her first job. She was a beautiful girl and had a lovely outgoing personality. At times, though, she could be a bit mercurial, especially during her breaks. She'd sit outside at the picnic table staring into space as if she'd rather be anywhere but here. If you said anything to her, she'd look right through you with those light blue eyes as if you weren't even there. A little scary, if you ask me. But then she'd snap out of it and be back to normal.

"After I'd been here for a week, she gave two days' notice and said she was going to work at a car dealership near the airport for more pay. She was saving to move away; she had confided in Sally May. According to Sally, the owner of the dealership had stopped in here for dinner, taken a liking to Leonie, and—this is all just gossip, mind you—but he took her out to his car, and she didn't come back for half an hour. The next day, she had a new job. Assume what you may from that."

Mack and Loshi just looked at each other as they chewed and said nothing.

"Anyway, after she'd gone, Sally May told me Leonie had told her a few things before she decided to be more tight lipped about her past. Apparently, she was from a small town on the bayou called Thibodaux where hardly anybody lives. Her mother had disappeared when she was a little girl, maybe run off to get away from her husband, and Leonie hadn't seen her since. Her father raised her but wasn't much of a prize, so she took off on her own as soon as she could save up a little money. She'd been working with her dad since she was eleven or so."

"She seemed to have talked a lot to Sally May."

"At first, she did. And then, like I said, a change came over her, and she never talked about her childhood again. At least that's what Sally May told me."

Mack was finishing up his home fries, which he had drizzled with ketchup. "Is there anything else you can tell us?"

"She was born in Thibodaux. I know that. She never said her father's first name, I don't think. Must be a doctor over there you can talk to. Somebody should know something. A town that small, everybody knows everybody else's business."

"Did she ever tell Sally May where she wanted to move to after leaving New Orleans?"

Carrie Sue scrunched up her face again to think. "Not specifically. But she talked about moving to a big city up north where she could get educated and make a lot of money. I forgot to tell you that. She talked a lot about becoming important and having a lot of money—to Sally, that is. This is secondhand information, you understand."

"What you've told us is invaluable." Loshi grinned. "You have been of more help than you know." He took out his card and handed it to her. "Call us if you think of anything else."

She took the card and handled it like it was a valuable jewel. "Oh yes, I will be sure to do that."

Mack took out a big wad of cash and laid it on the table for Zelda, who had helped uncover a fount of information. Now it was time to go back and have a chat with the elder Manzini.

It turned out that Earl Manzini lived with his wife in the Garden District not far from their hotel. Because it was within walking distance, they parked their SUV at the inn and strolled up a few blocks passed mansions that looked as if they were from another age. The Manzini mansion was in character with the rest of the neighborhood: white, flat roof, two stories with wraparound porches top and bottom with pillars every twelve feet. Black wrought-iron fencing surrounded the grounds with a gate that turned out to be unlocked. They walked up the flagstone walkway and climbed the stairs to the front door.

"Who knew selling cars paid so well?" Loshi observed.

"If we wanted to live in mansions, we wouldn't have become cops."

"Too late to cry about that now."

Mack pushed the buzzer, and they didn't have long to wait before the door opened. A middle-aged black woman with white hair wearing a light-blue maid's uniform opened the door.

Mack flashed his ID. "Detectives Mack and Loshi to see Mr. Manzini. We have an appointment.

"Please come in." She led them into a magnificent entryway, the focal point being a round antique mahogany table with a large vase filled with long-stemmed flowers. "Follow me."

The maid walked briskly down a long hallway with photographs of long dead men and women on the walls. The detectives felt like they were visiting a museum. She led them into a room lined with floor-to-ceiling bookshelves and more antiques. Earl Manzini himself stepped from behind a magnificent mahogany desk and greeted them with his arm outstretched. "Gentlemen, I'm Earl. Welcome to my home."

They shook hands all around, and Earl indicated for the detectives to make themselves comfortable in brown leather armchairs grouped around a glass coffee table. He sat in one as well.

"You said you have some questions about a girl, Leonie, who worked for me over fifteen years ago. Is she in some sort of trouble?"

"We appreciate your talking to us, Mr. Manzini," Mack said. "And yes, she may be in some trouble, but we're having a hard time locating her. We thought maybe you could give us some idea as to where she might have gone after she left your dealership."

"I barely knew her. She worked part time down in the repair and parts department."

"Is your wife at home, Mr. Manzini?" Mark asked.

"No. Why do you ask?"

"We know for a fact that you had a physical relationship with the girl."

Manzini's face turned red as a hot poker. "That is a damned lie. I don't know what you're trying to prove by coming here." He stood up. "I'll have the maid see you out."

"Sit down, Mr. Manzini," Loshi said. "We're not here because you had an illegal relationship with an underage girl. Not at all. And you don't need a lawyer. We just want to hear what you know about her. You must have had a lot of intimate conversations during your year and a half friendship. Enlighten us and we'll be on our way, and you'll never hear from us again."

Manzini shook his head in disgust and sank down in his chair. "I knew it would all come back to bite me. I was an idiot. She was like a drug. I'd heard about men getting involved with that kind of a woman before but never thought it would happen to me. I was addicted to her. I gave her money, hundreds of dollars every month. Then, when she decided to leave, she demanded ten thousand dollars from me or said she'd go to my wife. I was living a cliché. But I gave it to her, in cash, like she wanted. When I handed her the money, she looked at me like we'd never meant a thing to each other. She was like ice. She took the cash and walked away without saying goodbye, thank you, nothing. I might as well have been dead to her."

"I take it you cared for her?" Loshi asked.

"She was seventeen when she left me but miles ahead of her age. Not book smart—she never had an education—but worldly and wise like no other woman I had known. And so ambitious. She told me she was going to own her own business before she was twenty-five, and I believed her." He looked at the detectives. "Did she? Did she become that successful?"

"She did." Mack said. "Very."

Manzini chuckled. "I knew it. She was the most determined person I'd ever met. I wish my son had half of what she had."

"I doubt that, Mr. Manzini." Mack said.

"Why? What has she done?"

"Did she tell you where she was going when she left?" Loshi asked.

"Not then, but she had talked about going to Hollywood. But she didn't want to be an actress. She wanted to be around people who were successful. She figured if she learned how to design interiors or became a real estate agent, she could sell homes in Beverly Hills and meet them that way."

"Was there anything about her physically that you remember: a scar, tattoo, birthmark, any ticks or quirks?" Mack asked.

Manzini stared out the window as if remembering something pleasurable. "She was perfect." He reddened. "Yeah, I was that far gone. Pathetic actually. An old man and a young beauty. I felt lucky to have had her for only a short time." He stared out the window again, looking as if he were drifting back to their time together.

"No one's perfect, Mr. Manzini," Mack said.

"Of course, you're right. She was driven by greed. That was obvious. I tried not to think about that while I was with her, but I got the feeling she would do anything to get what she wanted. But I didn't care that she was using me. She made me feel like a teenager again. One day, we played hooky and went to a carnival that was traveling through a small town north of here. We went on rides and—I remember now, she took a spill when she was jumping across a creek to keep from getting her shoes wet. She landed on her hand, and her left wrist bent back funny. She didn't want to go to a doctor, so it always looked a little crooked and there was a scar there where a sharp rock had cut open her hand. No one would notice unless you were looking for it. She was still perfect."

The detectives looked at each other, and Mack leaned over and handed Manzini his card. "As I said, we won't be bothering you again, but you can call if you want to add anything to what you've told us."

The detectives stood and gave Manzini a pleasant smile, but he had a worried frown on his face as he walked to the library entrance with them. "You didn't tell me why you're looking for her."

Mack stopped and put a hand on Manzini's shoulder. "Be grateful you're still in one piece, Mr. Manzini. Some of Leonie's other conquests weren't that lucky."

The maid appeared and led the detectives back to the front of the house. Manzini gaped after them, wondering what on earth the detective could have meant by that remark.

Mack and Loshi walked leisurely toward the inn, taking in the beauty of their surroundings: classic Southern houses, immaculate landscaping, tree branches canopied over the street. It felt like a walk back in time as they imagined Southern belles in their giant hoop skirts tripping daintily down the sidewalk or traveling in horse-drawn carriages to their various social functions.

In a few minutes, they had reached their hotel. "What say we shower and change, walk around the French Quarter, and treat ourselves to some gumbo and hurricanes?" Mack asked. "We got a long drive to Thibodaux tomorrow. I want to let loose and pretend I'm a tourist."

Loshi held the door open for Mack. "You read my mind."

"You're going to miss me when I'm gone."

* * * * *

The car trip to Thibodaux was going to take at least an hour, and Mack didn't argue when Loshi volunteered to drive. The directions were complicated, so he figured Loshi could pay attention to the map on the screen while he enjoyed the scenery. He nodded off for a while, woke up, and found they were already in Lafourche Parish where Thibodaux was located. All along the highway were bakeries, their windows displaying a wealth of pastries enticing him, begging him to stop and partake. This state was a haven for pastry lovers like him. Maybe on the way back.

Thibodaux was not the tiny hamlet they had envisioned Leonie growing up in. It was a fairly large town with a population of almost 17,000 people—some rich, some poor. Very few of them had grown up in a shack on the bayou like Leonie. Or so said the sheriff they had called that morning and met with to request the whereabouts of a Mr. Gautreau who had a daughter Leonie. Sheriff Boudreaux, in his thirties, dark hair and complexion and speaking with a heavy accent they assumed was Cajun, told them everything he knew about the Gautreaus.

They learned that the sheriff's own daddy, who was sheriff for many years in Thibodaux before him, had told him the Gautreaus had indeed lived in a shack on the bayou, but Waylon had kept it in livable shape with his carpentry skills. He had shamefully ignored the needs of his wife and child and socked away most of his income for his old age. Everybody in town figured that the wife, downtrodden but still young and pretty, couldn't take it anymore and left with another man. The daughter, Leonie, who never owned a decent dress or pair of shoes when she was a little girl, ended up working for her father to earn her keep. The year before, Waylon had moved into assisted living because, after years of breathing paint and varnish vapors, he had developed stage four lung cancer. He'd gone the chemo and radiation route and didn't have much time left. Considering how he had treated his family, Boudreaux considered that more than fair.

Mack and Loshi left the sheriff's office and drove through a quaint area of downtown with several shops selling trinkets and souvenirs. Boudreaux had told them there was still the remains of a sugar plantation in town, including slave quarters and general store, a real tourist attraction, but it was not on Mack and Loshi's list of must-see sites. The assisted living place was not far from city central, and they parked in the lot and went inside. They identified themselves to the middle-aged dour receptionist, and she said someone would bring Waylon down to the lobby to see them. After fifteen minutes of waiting, they wondered if he had expired on the way down.

Waylon came in, a young nurse by his side, but upright and using a walker. Everyone introduced themselves, the detectives showed their badges, and Waylon spoke to them in a husky voice with an accent much like Boudreaux's. "The sheriff told me you was comin' to see me. All the way from California. You here to tell me something happened to Leonie?"

"She's disappeared, and we're hoping you can help us find her," Mack said.

Waylon was thin as a pencil and had only a few wisps of hair left on his head. His pants looked as if they were about to fall off. The nurse helped him sit on the loveseat across from the detectives. She smiled and excused herself. Waylon leaned forward, a sneer on his face. "What's that bloodless bitch done now?"

"That's what we're trying to find out," Loshi said, a little taken aback.

"You don't have to beat around the bush with me. Either she's dead or you think she killed somebody. Why else would two homicide detectives show up here? I may be old, but I'm not stupid."

Mack decided he had nothing to lose by being blunt. "We think she's responsible for the deaths of several people and may have killed one person herself. She hired someone to kill an ex-cop, but he missed and shot an innocent bystander instead. We don't think she's going to give up until the ex-cop is dead or we catch her."

Waylon leaned back against the love seat. His face broke into a wide smile, showing off a few empty spaces where teeth used to be, and he shook his head in amazement. "I can't say I'm surprised. She was a terror since she could crawl."

"Do you have any idea of where she could be?" Mack asked.

Waylon looked them dead in the eye. "If I knew, believe me, I'd tell you. She's not fit to be around normal people."

"We don't want to take up too much of your time, Mr. Gautreau," Loshi said, "but we'd appreciate anything you can tell us about her. It might help us find her."

"I got nothin' but time, officers. Visitors are as rare as a snowstorm in hell. I don't mind tellin' you what that girl was like. She was the devil personified. Ever since she first laid hands on one of my guns, she was out shootin' everything that moved—scared the wits out of my wife, I'll tell you. Murial took off for parts unknown, and I ain't seen her since. Leonie pointed the gun at her after Murial told her not to sass back, and when Muriel tried to take the gun from her, the crazy bitch pulled the trigger and almost shot Muriel's head off. What kind of creature does that to her own ma?"

"A deeply disturbed individual, I'd say," Mack answered.

"Deeply disturbed is damn right, and she was only ten, if you can believe that. She wanted to know all about fixin' up houses so she could earn herself some money. I let her practice on the shack we lived in on the bayou. It was small and not much to look at, but it was solid thanks to me. I was a carpenter and could fix just about anything and put in windows too, tight as a drum. My pa taught it to me, and I taught it to Leonie. She took to it like a pig to slop, easy as can be. I taught her about electricity and riggin' small explosives too for when I had to tear down houses and rebuild. Blowin' up parts of 'em was easier than takin' forever pullin' 'em apart."

"So did she work with you?" Loshi asked.

"Yeah, she did, and did a good job too. I never took no crap from her even though she scared me to death at times, and sometimes I figured she would send me to kingdom come in my sleep. But she saved enough money to get herself off to New Orleans by the time she was fifteen. Told me I'd never see her again, and I didn't. No loss, I can tell you that."

"After New Orleans, you have no idea where she ended up?"

"Well, I might have if you make me a promise beforehand."

"If we can, sure," Mack said.

Waylon hesitated and looked a little embarrassed. "Well, when you get back to California, I'd like you to send me an autographed picture of Clint Eastwood with him sayin' 'to my good friend, Waylon.' Can you do that? I'll take you at your word if you say it's really his signature. Always liked him."

Mack hemmed and hawed. "Ah well, we don't actually know anybody who knows Mr. Eastwood. That might not be all that easy."

Waylon glared at him.

Loshi nudged Mack in the side. "What about Rosemaria's friend Vanessa?"

Mack sat up ramrod straight, and his face broke out in a huge grin. "Good thinking, partner." Then, to Waylon: "I think we know somebody who can make that happen. You got yourself a deal."

Waylon proceeded to dig into his shirt pocket and came up with two newspaper articles folded many times over. "I gotta lotta time to read the papers in here."

Mack unfolded them and read the headline out loud. "'Balconies on Apartment Building in Miami Collapse.'" There was a picture of some of the residents being taken away in an ambulance. He looked at Waylon. "What's this?"

"Look at the other one."

He looked at the second sheet of paper. It was the front page of the *Miami Times* showing a girl on crutches walking out of the hospital. The article said she had been injured in the building collapse and, along with several other residents, was suing the building's owners.

"Under the picture it says she's Donna Saint-Saens, but that girl is Leonie. She never wanted her picture taken in her whole life, not at school, not for nothin', but I guess she got a little careless—reporter got her coming out of the hospital. And I'll tell you somethin' else. I'd be willing to bet my year's supply of chewin' tobacca that she caused the accident just so she could sue and make herself a lot a money. What do you think of that, officers?"

"Detectives," Mack said. "And yeah, we believe you."

"I hate to think that what I taught her about explosives got people hurt. She'd know how to do it with nobody knowing it was ever there and get herself some broken bones, just enough to sue the owners. She was that good."

Mack and Loshi stared at the picture of Leonie, clear as day, although a little crumpled.

"She would've had to give her social security number and show some ID when she was part of a lawsuit," Mack said.

"Probably stole somebody's name and number. Lotsa people do it."

Mack tucked the articles in his jacket pocket. "Waylon, if it's the last thing I do, I'm getting you that autographed picture of Clint Eastwood."

Waylon grimaced. "But you gotta catch her, officers. It makes me sick knowin' I'm responsible for unleashin' that monster on the world."

"Detectives," Loshi said. He took a swab tube out of his pocket and took the top off. "Do you mind if we get some DNA from you?" He stood up next to Waylon.

"Have at it." Waylon opened his mouth, and Loshi gave it a thorough wipe, then closed the swab.

"Thank you."

"Yeah, whatever. You don't have any chew on ya, do ya?"

"Sorry, fresh out," Loshi said, and Mack stood.

"It's okay," Waylon said. "And when you find Leonie, it's best you don't arrest her. Just shoot the bitch."

CHAPTER THIRTY-SIX

The "godfathers plus two" were having their second meeting in the conference room at the Beverly Hills Police Department, but by now, Mack and Loshi were no longer feeling like outsiders. Rosemaria's fate and their desire to nail Leonie were the overriding concerns for all of them by now. The frustration level in the room was high. They felt they were closing in on Leonie, but still, she remained far from their grasp. If, indeed, she was a part of the Beverly Hills social set that meant she was nearby and possibly aware of and mocking their every attempt to find her. They had barely touched the bagels and muffins the receptionist had thoughtfully provided for them early that morning. Everyone was speaking at once, and Osborne decided to take control.

"Hold it down, shall we? Let's go over everything we know to be true, what we merely suspect, and where we go from here. Agreed?"

Everyone sighed and nodded.

"Okay, here's what we know so far. Her real name is Leonie Gautreau, born in Thibodaux, Louisiana, parents Murial and Waylon. She moved to the New Orleans area, worked as a waitress, then at a car dealership, and entered into a relationship with the owner, for which we can assume she was generously paid. She told him she wanted to be rich and famous and study either design or real estate.

"We don't know where she went before she landed in Hollywood and changed her name to Mariah Venmore. She lived at the Hollywood house for free thanks to her relationship with Keith, studied design in school and real estate online, then was so impatient for money we suspect she robbed and killed Ramin, with, we think, Micco's help. She threatened the others in the house to keep their mouths shut and disappeared.

"After she left Hollywood, she moved to Miami, changed her name to Donna Saint-Saens and got herself a new social security number from someone of the same age who had died recently. She was in a terrible accident at an apartment complex, and although she probably strived to keep her face from being photographed, a news photographer took her picture as she came out of the hospital when she was released. She settled for an unknown amount in a lawsuit and disappeared. The lawyers have no idea where she moved after that or what her name is now.

"If what Rosemaria strongly feels is true, Leonie had David killed because he had asked Rosemaria to investigate his case, then she tried to kill Rosemaria to prevent her from going through with the investigation even though David was dead. She was also afraid that Rosemaria could identify her since she was the only cop who was up close and personal with her after Ramin's murder. Right now, she could be in Beverly Hills or a million miles away."

"We know Micco's been in touch with her," Larry said. "Why not arrest him, offer him a deal, and keep him in protective custody? He can tell us who she is."

"Maybe, maybe not," Loshi said. "He may only be dealing with her online and not know who she is anymore either. And if we put him in protective custody, she'll easily find out and possibly disappear."

"Agreed," Steven said. "We have a tail on him and a tracker on his car. We have to keep it that way as long as possible. She may contact him again, and we have taps on all his phones."

Jimmy shook his head in frustration. "I've reached a dead end after Miami. None of us are having any luck tracing her after that. Obviously, she changed her name again, but she had a lot of money after the Miami settlement and stealing the fifty thousand from Ramin. She may not have felt the need to get another job."

Steven disagreed. "No, being as ambitious as she was and if she's here now living as a successful businesswoman, she didn't waste any time sitting around doing nothing. She kept working, probably in something to do with design, architecture, something she was very much interested in. Jimmy, I'd check out Atlanta. That would be a ripe business atmosphere for her as a Southern girl to feel at home and get lost in. If we don't have any luck there we'll try New York."

"Lost is right," Mack said. "How do you find someone when you don't know her name or social security number? As for New York, fuhgeddaboudit. We'll never find her there."

"Facial recognition," Osborne said.

Jimmy laughed. "Only a few million women to check out on the streets of Atlanta, and hopefully, she hadn't had the plastic surgery yet."

"We need another lucky sighting by somebody who knew her," Loshi said.

"Let's face it," Larry said. "Unless she takes another shot at Rosemaria and we catch her at it, we're stuck." He glanced over at Steven. "Sorry."

"No offense taken," Steven reassured him. "Until we can narrow our focus, we won't be able to use her father's DNA to nail her. Unless we can get a warrant to secretly test every woman in her thirties who lives in southern California."

Larry grabbed a bagel and began to smear it with cream cheese. "I don't know about the rest of you, but getting absolutely nowhere has made me hungry." He took a big bite of his bagel, and the others followed suit.

"We still don't have a clue how Leonie found out about the Macapa Drive visit," Larry said. "We've been hammering the real estate woman for weeks, and she swears she told no one."

"I was so intrigued by watching her big lips move," Jimmy said, "I couldn't pay attention to what she was saying."

"I doubt if she's telling the truth. Leonie's not psychic," Osborne said.

"On another note," Larry said between bites, "too bad they're trying my murder case in Van Nuys. I was hoping Rosemaria would be prosecutor and question me on the stand. That would be a first."

"Admit nothing or she'll weasel the truth out of you," Jimmy said.

"Since we're on the same side, I should be safe."

"I remember the hung jury in the Menendez case," Steven said. It still gives me nightmares. I thought they might get away with it."

"I'd like to see Rosemaria go toe to toe with Tammy Berenson," Mack said. "Her besting that frizzy-haired, killer-loving defense lawyer would make my year." He almost snarled as he spoke.

Larry lifted his water bottle to toast. "I'll drink to that. And here's to Rosemaria. We'll keep her safe and find Leonie if it's the last thing we do."

They all drank deeply from their water bottles, and, feeling a lot better, they made short work of the bagels and muffins.

CHAPTER THIRTY-SEVEN

"I'm checking in with the boss. What's up down there?" Josh was sprawled on top of his bed at the Fairmont Hotel in San Francisco. Rosemaria was under the covers in bed. She'd managed to stay awake until one o'clock when he'd be finished with his concert and back at the hotel.

"Very witty for this early in the morning. Tell me how the shows went."

"Sold out the Bill Graham Auditorium, both nights. They love Joell in San Francisco."

"I'll bet they loved you too."

"Okay, so they showed some fond feelings for me as well. Joell and I sang a duet of "New York Nights," and then I rocked one of my R and B numbers with her band."

"How many encores?"

"Only one. I'm surprised she allowed me to have one both nights. She all but pushed me back onstage."

"She's in love with you, you know."

"She's a friend. That's all."

"On your part."

"That's the only part that matters."

"Go kill it again in Seattle. I'll be here waiting. Maybe Abe or Kirsten will take us out to dinner."

"Give yourself a hug from me."

"You too."

Rosemaria clicked off and looked at Suzi, who was sleeping in her cage. She suddenly felt lost and alone, which was ridiculous. Josh would be home tomorrow, and she had a protector across the hall twenty-four seven. But having to be constantly aware that someone was intent on ending her life was wearing her down. All she had ever wanted was to follow in her father's footsteps and uphold the law. Because of that, there had never been a shortage of bad actors who came after her, and she had dealt with them. But this time, she felt like she was in the crosshairs of someone so evil that she killed because of the pure pleasure she found in doing it. Rosemaria wanted her life back and had no idea of when that would happen.

Meanwhile, she had to ask Vanessa to get her Clint Eastwood's autograph. That might be the hardest favor she had ever asked of her friend. But Leonie's father had given them an incredible lead, and she would not disappoint him. After hearing about Leonie's impoverished childhood, it now made perfect sense that she would want to keep her birth certificate—a reminder of where she came from and how far she intended to go, no matter what it took. Leonie thought she had hidden it well, but she got careless, and the ancient wiring in her car proved to be her undoing. Rosemaria also needed to look at the Beverly Hills matrons for the little scar on Leonie's wrist the car dealer had mentioned without being too obvious. Leonie had probably had surgery to cover that up and the crooked wrist as well. But you never knew. She snuggled down underneath the covers and closed her eyes.

Her cell phone rang. "Jimmy, why are you calling me so late? Please don't tell me you're working."

Jimmy was seated at his desk in front of the computer in his bedroom. "I'm narrowing down companies that have to do with design, architecture, textiles, and that kind of thing in Atlanta. But I needed to ask you something. I'm checking company employment databases and looking at women her age who started working at around the same time. I'm also thinking that since she came into a lot of money from the settlement, she would be spending it in ways that wealthy women do. Any ideas?"

She sat up and put another pillow under her head. "Sounds like you've been doing a little bit of hacking, my friend, but I won't tell anybody. I'd be looking at spas, dermatologists, and possibly plastic surgeons. She might have begun the process of changing her face in Atlanta. If she had work done there, she'd want to keep her appearance up and might go to cosmetic spas. But not middle-class spas in shopping centers and not at the Four Seasons or other big hotels with cameras. Look at smaller, elite spas where privacy is everything. This is needle-in-a-haystack time."

"All right. I'll try that. And possibly, some traffic camera footage might stay in the computer for years before they clean it out. Maybe I'll get lucky, but it's a long shot."

Her voice softened. "I know you're working hard for me, Jimmy. Thank you."

"For you, Rosemaria, I'm trying to do the impossible. Sleep tight." He clicked off.

Two days later, Rosemaria's first day back in the Airport Courthouse prosecutor's office was exhilarating. As she made her way down the hall to her office, her friends and colleagues welcomed her back with hugs and well-wishes. Karen, her assistant, stood at the door of her office and handed her a decaf soy mocha from Starbucks and a bag full of scones. "Eat heartily, boss. We have a lot of work to do."

Rosemaria eagerly grabbed the bag and coffee and wasted no time scarfing down a scone before she sat down behind her desk. Since she had been too excited to eat at home, she was now starving. Josh had done his best to soothe her jittery nerves, but she felt like she was starting all over again and needed to prove herself. Before she'd gone out to meet Abe in the hallway of their building, Josh had taken her by the shoulders and looked her in the eye. "If they give you a minor case like the ones Karen sent you, it's only because they want to ease you back in. It's not because they don't have faith in you. Do your usual competent job and enjoy being back." He'd hugged her and handed her over to Abe, who was all business and stayed close behind her as they walked to the elevators.

Now, as she sipped her coffee in her familiar, cramped office, she was feeling energized and ready to proceed with the business at hand. She looked up at Karen. "What's it to be then? Am I prosecuting the graffiti artist who spray-painted the side of a gym with lewd but very artistically portrayed naked ladies, or is it the case of the instigator of a bar brawl in the Marina that sent five people to the hospital?"

Karen sat down in the chair in front of Rosemaria's desk. "Neither."

"Oh, which one is it then?"

"Late yesterday afternoon, the judge in the Rosa and Hector Oberman case decided the Van Nuys docket was too crowded and transferred the case to our courthouse. This morning, Lattimer announced that Reid would be first chair, and you would be second." She gave a half smile. "Welcome back to the trenches."

Rosemaria was stunned. "You're kidding."

"Reid has been here two years longer, so it stands to reason you're second."

"Of course, I know that, but still, I'm surprised Lattimer picked me."

"Everybody else is immersed in other cases, and this came down quickly. Lattimer had to make a decision fast so the two of you could hit the ground running."

"Did you set up a meeting with Reid?"

"At ten in his office. I put the hard copy in your inbox, and it's in your computer as well."

"I'd better study up on the case before I meet with him." She typed her password into the computer. "The most high-profile case in the city, and Lattimer assigns me."

"He has faith in you."

"But more in Reid, which stands to reason. Reid is fair and a good friend. We'll work well together." She smiled at Karen. "It's good to be back."

Reid Smith's office was somewhat bigger than Rosemaria's. It had room for a conference table, where they were sitting across from each other, laptops open. Reid was in his mid-thirties, with classic features and stylishly cut light-brown hair. When anyone met him for the first time, they immediately assumed from his speech and demeanor that he had class bred into him by a long line of impeccable family traditions. And they would be right. But Reid was not a snob, and even though he came from a wealthy family as Larry had, he was a hard worker and had achieved success as a prosecutor with brains, legal savvy, and dedication to his profession. Divorced with a four-year-old daughter, he spent most of his waking hours at the office and in the courtroom. He had successfully prosecuted the two armed robbers who had attempted to kidnap Rosemaria and was a good friend to her.

"The judge hasn't scheduled a hearing yet. Probably happen next week," Reid said.

"You have a bit of a head start on me and met the lawyers at the arraignment. Do you anticipate any surprises from either one?"

"So far, no motions for a change of venue and no motion from either side for severance. I imagine Lynette Strouse's lawyer might do so just before the trial starts, but that could be months from now."

"If she tries to sever, do you think Lynette will claim to be an innocent bystander?"

"Right now, she's madly in love with Liam and has a 'us against the world' attitude. As the trial proceeds, she and her lawyer, Helen Cooperman, may ask to sever, but I doubt Judge Levine will allow it. He's pretty strict when it comes to that. Lynette was there cheerleading the murder at the very least."

"What do you know about Cooperman? I've never dealt with her."

"Helen is competent and will do her best for Lynette. She wins her fair share of cases, but she is not in the same league as Tammy Berenson."

"I know Tammy's reputation. She's even more of a shark than the Menendez lawyer."

"I've never had the privilege of going up against her, but I've watched her win a few not-guilty verdicts when prosecutors thought they had a slam-dunk case."

"What do you think is in store for us?"

"Insanity, he heard voices, amnesia, 'some other dude did it,' attack the victims, attack the forensics, rush to judgement, he's just a child, last minute change of plea—you name it, she's done it. We can expect the worst."

"Parenticide is especially repugnant to jurors and the public. She'll have to come up with something spectacular to get past that. We have the physical evidence and consciousness of guilt for fleeing to another state."

"The 'abuse excuse' almost got the Menendezes off, and it's gotten murderers off in the past. Tammy may try it. And aunts and uncles on both sides might back him up. They'd rather accuse their own sister and brother of abuse than have their darling nephew convicted of murder."

"Yeah, I've seen that before. Grandparents throw murdered babies under the bus to keep their monster children out of prison. That's unfathomable to me."

"Expect to see Tammy be all over Liam, hugging him, patting his arm, ruffling his hair like he's an adolescent instead of a twenty-one-year-old adult."

"I've always found that especially sickening—lawyers treating murderers like they are their children." Rosemaria was building up a head of steam. "I can somewhat understand representing them but cuddling up to them like that? It makes my flesh crawl."

Reid chuckled. "Your sense of justice would never allow you to be a defense attorney, let alone cuddle up to felons."

Rosemaria acknowledged she was ranting and smiled. "I'm not a total hard-ass, you know. I've made deals with defendants before, but sometimes, I knew they were innocent and proved it. Sometimes they were victims of circumstances, but perpetrators who kill and devastate families, I want them locked up where they can't hurt anyone else."

"Before we manage to do that, we'll decide what evidence to show at the hearing. Our first exhibit will be the pipe with the parents' blood and the pipe from the shed that matched up to the murder weapon."

"Okay."

"She'll try to exclude it at the trial and maybe even raise a fuss at the hearing."

"That seems pointless. We're just showing what we have."

"She fights to the death from the opening bell. Expect that from her." Reid continued: "We have blood on shoes found in the trunk of the getaway car that matches the parents'. Testimony from the maid that only a person who lived in the house would know where to find the key to the shed."

"Do we include the will and the insurance policy leaving everything to Liam?"

"We can."

"How about the jewelry they stole and pawned on their way through Vegas?" Rosemaria shook her head. "They really were a couple of morons thinking they could get away with that."

CHAPTER THIRTY-EIGHT

The setting sun, the water, the clouds, and the mist all conspired to turn the horizon into a dazzling work of art. The beauty of the colors—gold, orange, and blue—took Stacey's breath away. She stood up from her supine position on the hammock and stretched. Finally, the pain in her side was gone. Yes, she was enjoying her time with Randy doing almost nothing, but if she could wish for just one thing at that very moment, it would be to sink into a bathtub filled with hot water and bubbles. She had roughed it for years in the mountains with Sam, but their cabin seemed like a five-star hotel compared to living in a tent and taking sponge baths. She saw Randy approaching from the steep path that led from the cliffs above them to the flat area below. He waved when he saw her, and she waved back.

He strode quickly toward her with a smile on his face, carrying bags from the Garden Wok Chinese restaurant. "I have a surprise for you."

"What is it?" She looked down at the bags he was holding.

"Not this." He held up the bags. "Although I know you love this restaurant. Have a seat." He gestured to two folding aluminum chairs next to a small table.

"Don't keep me in suspense."

"As soon as the sun has completely set, I'm taking you for a walk."

"Where? Is it far? Is it safe?"

"No, it's not far, and yes, it's totally safe. "We'll eat, watch the sunset, and then go on a little journey into the unknown."

"You're being very mysterious."

He took out the little containers of rice and savory dinner dishes and set them on the table. He handed her chopsticks. "Enjoy. The night is yours."

She looked at him askance but grinned and accepted the chopsticks. They ate mostly in silence for several minutes until the sun had disappeared, and the food was gone. Randy gathered up the remains and threw them into the covered trash can by the tent.

"We're waiting for complete darkness," he said.

Stacey nodded and refrained from asking any more questions, even though she was dying of curiosity.

When the sky had completely darkened, he reached out his hand and pulled her up.

"Don't let go. It's tricky, but I know the way."

They walked south for a few minutes along the side of the hill until they came to a very narrow path leading up past houses built on the side and on top of the hill. Dense foliage made the walk slow going. Suddenly, Randy stopped, and Stacey saw they were standing by a house built on a level patch of ground near the top. It was white stucco, had a wraparound balcony, and faced the ocean, but the shades on all of the windows were drawn.

Stacey became alarmed. "I don't know if we should be doing this."

He pulled her toward a sliding door beneath the balcony. "Come on." He slid open the door.

She hesitated, suddenly very frightened. "Why is there no alarm? Do you have permission to enter the house?"

She allowed herself to be pulled inside, into a room with only a couch and a couple of overstuffed chairs. "This isn't funny, Randy. Who owns this place, and why are we here?"

He sat on the couch in front of the window. "I own it, and we are here so you can live life a bit more normally from now on."

She looked at him as if he had gone mad. "You own it? Since when?"

"Escrow closed two days ago. I needed a couple of days to buy some furniture."

She realized her mouth was hanging open, and she abruptly closed it.

"I told you my parents left me money. It's just been sitting there earning interest—a lot of interest."

She sank down beside him on the couch. "But why now?"

"I think you know why."

"I don't. Tell me."

She faced him as he spoke in carefully measured words.

"All right. You already know a bit of my history and why I chose to live on the beach alone. But I've never told you that I was so broken I didn't want to live. I tried to get up the nerve to kill myself several times, but I just couldn't do it. So I settled for living an existence that was almost like death. I didn't want to see or be around anyone. Eventually, I had to venture up the hill to civilization to keep track of my money and get on the internet and such, but I was going through the motions of living until you came along."

Her face softened and she touched his arm. He took her hands in his.

"When I decided to buy this house, I swear I had no ulterior motives other than to make you happy. I'm way too old for you, I know that, and I will ask nothing of you except that you enjoy living as normal a life as you can, seeing that you can't go anywhere. But you can cook and take showers and sunbathe on the porch. It's totally protected from the view of neighbors." He stopped to take a breath, looking at her face anxiously, waiting for her reaction.

"I am so grateful to you, Randy. You saved my life, in more ways than one. And yes, we can be friends, and I will love living here with you."

Relief flooded through his body. Her words were a salve to his wounded soul.

"But there's one thing I don't agree with."

He felt a twinge of anxiety and waited, afraid to breathe.

She touched his face with her hand. "You're not too old for me, Randy. I'm thirty-two, and you're fifty-eight. That's nothing. You were so busy pushing me away you didn't notice that I've fallen in love with you. And I hope that until you feel the same way about me, you'll let me stay and try to make you change your mind."

He took her face in his hands, and they kissed, gently, with a tenderness he had never felt before. The happiness that had eluded him his entire life was sitting right next to him. He held her, and then her hands touched his neck and lightly stroked him.

He slowly pulled back and saw her eyes were filled with tears. "Are you sure?" he asked.

She wiped her face with her hand. "Of course, I'm sure, you silly man. Now, if I'm going to have a bath and you're going to take a shower so we can be totally clean when we celebrate this moment properly, you'll have to go back to the tent and get all our toilet articles."

He stood up and snapped to attention. "Yes, ma'am. I will walk back and carry them up to my car, and tomorrow night you can help me bring everything else back as well. I think we can retire the tent for good."

She stood up and put her arms around his waist. "Excellent. You did buy a bed, didn't you, and sheets and towels and such?"

"Of course." He hesitated. "I actually bought a king-size bed for one room and a queen-size for the other. I didn't know exactly—"

"You rat! You were prepared for me to throw myself at you."

"Well, I hoped."

She kissed him. "Like a piece of driftwood, I washed up on your beach, and now you're having your way with me."

"I haven't even begun." And he kissed her back.

*　*　*　*　*

Josh had broken off the recording session to attend an AA meeting in the basement of the Presbyterian church on Gower. He had become frustrated over an arrangement he couldn't figure out how to fix and had lashed out at the keyboard player, who had been offering a suggestion, and the producer, who was doing his best to read Josh's mind. Josh immediately apologized and knew he was pushing. He was too desperate to make every song perfect. He called an abrupt end to the session, said they would take the next day off, and walked out of the studio alone.

As he made his way up Hollywood Boulevard, crowded with tourists, residents, and a few homeless people, he realized he needed to stay grounded and not get carried away by the upward trajectory his career seemed to be on. He knew how obsessive he could be with his music—his unfinished Broadway musical that he never deemed good enough to show to anyone was a testament to that fact. He needed at least one day to look rationally at what they had recorded so far and assess what songs they needed to add or replace.

He also knew Rosemaria was right—Joell was in love with him. Everything she'd said and done when they were on tour made that obvious. She never made any blatant moves on him, but she treated him with kid gloves at rehearsals and had no problem deferring to him musically if he voiced an opinion. She went out of her way to share meals with him and hugged him too close when they said goodnight. She had provided him with the best studio musicians in town for his recording sessions and the best producer. He owed her everything. And it was stifling. Sooner or later, he would have to talk to her and face her anger or denial. That was part of his frustration. If he was going to be creative and productive, he needed to feel free.

Meanwhile, the church was nearby, and he felt better as soon as he walked down into the basement, smelled the coffee, and saw everyone gathered in a circle. Lenny was speaking, and he nodded a greeting at Josh. One day at a time. He would talk to Joell soon.

After the meeting he'd stopped by Martha's to make sure she was doing okay. Fortunately, her health seemed to be good, and her intake of Jack Daniels seemed to have miraculously lessened. He reassured her for the umpteenth time that she was doing him a big favor by subletting his apartment (even though he was paying the rent), and she could stay there indefinitely. As far as he was concerned, Martha would never be back on the streets again. After leaving her, he'd walked back to the recording studio parking lot and headed home.

Rosemaria was seated at the dining room table typing on her laptop when Josh came through the door. She looked up, surprised to see him and even more surprised when he walked straight over to her and pulled her to her feet. He ignored Suzi's happy squawking and circling and kissed Rosemaria before pulling back to look at her astounded face.

"I'm taking a day off," he said and looked down at her laptop. "Can that stuff wait?"

"Of course."

He led her into the bedroom, shutting Suzi out, and he began shedding his clothes. Rosemaria asked no questions and wasted no time tearing off her sweatpants and T-shirt. They came together standing naked in the middle of the room. Mouths melded together, their hands roamed each other's bodies, they fell on the bed. He pulled her on top of him and felt such a desperate need for her he was afraid he would come before he had a chance to bring her to orgasm. He touched her everywhere and kissed her breasts, and he heard her moan in pleasure. Then he was on top of her between her thighs and there was no holding back. They came at the same time and clung together, making the moment last as long as possible. They pulled apart and lay motionless for a few minutes, satiated, breathing heavily, perspiration glistening on their bodies. He went into the bathroom and came back with a large, dampened towel.

She looked up at him, wondering what had set him off. Was the recording going well? Not well? Was it something else? She wouldn't ruin this moment with prying questions. She would accept his sudden need for her and rejoice in it.

"I don't know what I did to deserve that," she said.

"Sorry I was so fast."

"Hey, in case you didn't notice, I had no trouble keeping up."

He grinned down at her as he carefully wiped the moisture off her stomach. "Yeah, I did notice that." He lay down next to her. "Did I interrupt something important?"

"More important than you? Never." She planted a kiss on his cheek.

"Suddenly, I'm very hungry."

"You deserve something really special." She noticed the look on his face. "No, no, I don't mean I'll make you something. Why don't you go get us a giant veggie burger and a mountain of fries at Vegan Victory down the street and two giant root beer floats?"

"No worries about calories?" He was already pulling his jeans on.

"None." She wrapped the towel around her and headed for the bathroom. "I'm enveloped in pleasure at the moment and will deny myself nothing." She waved and disappeared behind the door.

Half an hour later, they were seated at the dining room table, engrossed in eating their veggie burgers with a plate piled high with French fries covered with ketchup. Suzi sat on the back of one of the empty chairs grooming her feathers.

"So, are you ready for the hearing?" he asked.

"Well, since I'm just second chair, I'm mostly there to assist. Abe's having a fit because he doesn't like reporters swarming around us. He always meets me at the entrance when we leave and stays close to me when he escorts me to the car."

"The murder is a big story on the national stage, so reporters won't be going away anytime soon. Reid's a good guy. He'll give you a chance to make your presence known."

"He'll take charge of the hearing, but yeah, I'll probably fit into the actual trial in some way. I'm going over all the witness statements, and the cop in me is looking for more evidence."

They devoted themselves to their food for a few minutes, taking time to slurp their root beer floats.

"Any leads on the ever-elusive Leonie?"

"Jimmy and the other techs, here and in San Diego, are looking at any video they can get their hands on in Atlanta. Jimmy thinks that's where she went next, but it's been a few years. Who keeps surveillance video that long? If he finds anything using facial recognition that even resembles her Miami picture, he'll follow up on that. If I weren't involved in this trial, I would make myself useful somehow."

He used his napkin to wipe ketchup off her cheek.

"So, you're taking the day off tomorrow?" she asked.

"I thought I'd go up to the sanctuary."

"Good. Whatever is going on in the studio can wait." She chewed thoughtfully. "Do you really think they won't be angry with me when I see them again? Maybe they'll have forgotten me. That would just about kill me."

He finished off the burger and spoke with his mouth full. "You are their female human who they love. They will not have forgotten you."

"That will be the best part of finding that psychopath—seeing my kids again."

CHAPTER THIRTY-NINE

Rosemaria had just logged on to her office computer when Reid stuck his head in the door.

"We have a meeting in the judge's chambers in half an hour. Lynette Strauss wants to sever."

"Already? I guess her love for Liam wasn't as strong as her fear of twenty-five to life."

"The judge has a full schedule today and wants this decided this morning. Cooperman filed yesterday but failed to let me know."

"Let me check something on my computer, and I'll meet you there."

He gave a wave and was gone. She quickly looked up Judge Levin's record on severances and found out he didn't like them. In the words of the legal source she had looked up, his definition of "evidence presented against one of the defendants being antagonistic to the other, or creating juror confusion, which would lean in favor of the defendant" was very narrow. That was good for the prosecution, but you could never depend on what a judge might say. She turned off her computer and grabbed her purse and briefcase.

Reid was chatting with the judge's clerk when Rosemaria arrived at his chambers. Helen Cooperman arrived a minute later, all business, no smiles. She was a plain woman in her forties with short, light-brown hair, wearing a gray suit. Then they waited in silence for ten more minutes before Tammy Berenson finally came through the door. She and her frizzy blonde/gray hair were recognizable from her many media appearances, and she greeted them with casual disinterest. The clerk informed the judge everyone was present.

They took seats in front of the judge's desk as he read the motion papers in front of him. The lawyers glanced uneasily at each other, except Tammy, who seemed to be somewhat removed from the process. Judge Levine barely acknowledged their presence as he continued to read. Rosemaria had never been this close to him before and studied him carefully. He was thin, looked to be around fifty-five, had a full head of silver hair, and was wearing rimless reading glasses. She tried to read his expression, and it seemed to her he was trying to hide his annoyance, as if this were all a waste of time. Or, then again, she could be wrong.

The judge looked up, seeming a little grumpy. He addressed Cooperman. "According to this, you believe there is no evidence that your client was a part of any alleged crime and should not have the evidence against Mr. Oberman presented as evidence against her. You don't believe the jury will be able to discern that the evidence is solely against the other defendant and not against Ms. Strauss." He turned to Reid. "What say you, Mr. Smith?"

"Severance need not be granted solely because the defendant denies participation in the crime. And where evidence is admissible toward both defendants, severance need not be allowed. Furthermore, the record shows we have evidence and witness testimony against Ms. Strauss that is admissible as to her alone. The defenses are not antagonistic because they do not specifically contradict each other and therefore cannot be used to apply for severance."

"Ms. Cooperman?" The judge looked at her over his glasses.

"The evidence against Ms. Strauss is insufficient for a guilty verdict, and she will be judged according to admissible evidence against the other defendant."

The judge looked at Tammy, who appeared to treat this as nothing more than entertaining theater. "How about you, Counselor? You wish to weigh in on this?"

"I am happy to abide by your opinion, Your Honor."

"Very well." He pushed the motion to one side of his desk. "Whether or not the evidence against your client holds up is for a jury to decide. I find that there is no reason to sever the trials."

The lawyers stood and, almost in unison, said, "Thank you, Your Honor."

They filed out into the hallway and went their separate ways without speaking. When Reid and Rosemaria had walked a few steps, she said, "I think Lynette will turn on Liam as soon as the hearing is over. What do you think?" Rosemaria said.

He smiled. "I wouldn't be a bit surprised."

"My first meeting with the terrifying Tammy was a little anticlimactic."

"It's still early. She won't disappoint."

Karen was not at her desk when Rosemaria got back to her office. She was probably with Terrence, the other prosecutor she worked for. Rosemaria was eager to go over the witness statements and evidence against Lynette. There had to be something there they could use to get her to testify against Liam. Her cell rang, and she dug it out of her purse.

"Hi, Dad. What's up?"

Her father was driving north on the 405 in heavy traffic. He had his phone screen on. "You're not going to believe this."

"Uh-oh. Good or bad?"

"Mostly sad, I'd say. Last night your friend Drew had a huge party at her house celebrating her engagement to some famous designer."

"Yeah, Drew and Vanessa wanted me to be there, but I couldn't go."

"Well, Helene Marchand showed up uninvited—"

"No!"

"She demanded to see you and refused to accept that you weren't there. Drew's butler grabbed her, pulled her into a bedroom, and sat on her until he reached her husband."

"Did Marchand come and get her?"

"He did. Drew is not pressing charges, but both Marchands were warned not to make this a regular performance. You'd think getting hand-cuffed and made to sit in a patrol car for an hour last time would have discouraged her a bit."

"I feel her desperation, Dad. I really do. But at this point, I don't know what she wants from me or how I can help her."

"We'll find Leonie. You just concentrate on your job."

"Will do. It's good to be back."

"Love you."

"Love you too."

As soon as Rosemaria hung up, she dialed again. "Vanessa, hi. What are you up to?"

"Melissa and I are taking a walk down in the flats and going to visit a playground where she's made some friends."

"Sounds very democratic."

"Don't start," Vanessa warned.

"Sorry, just kidding. Listen, I heard about Helene's visit to Drew's house last night."

"Thank God most of the guests didn't even know she was there."

"How many people showed up?"

"Only two hundred of her closest friends. The usual crowd."

"I have a question for you. Could you ask Drew if she has video sur-veillance in her house and, if so, if she'd send it to me?"

"Why?"

"Just a hunch."

Vanessa stopped wheeling Melissa and sat down hard on a park bench, still holding her cell phone to her ear, "I have told you again and again, Rosemaria, you are not going find a murderer among my friends. And you are not going to ruin my first time planning a huge fundraiser at the Beverly Wilshire because of your obsessive belief that wealthy women are evil scum. Most of them are nice, hard-working women like Loretta. What do you expect to see on the video? A confession, a gun hanging out of someone's pocket? You're wrong this time, Rosemaria. And I'm asking you politely to leave my friends alone."

Rosemaria waited and said nothing. Vanessa finally couldn't take it anymore.

"Okay, I'm sorry. I know you always get your man and all that, but not here, okay? And not now."

Rosemaria didn't answer. Dead air was her friend.

"I'll ask Drew if she has videotape from the party. I think there was a videographer there as well." She sighed deeply. "You know I've always been happy to help you in the past. It's not that I don't want your killer found. Oh, hell, what's the use? I need the gala to be a success, it's true, but your life is more important."

"I promise your gala will be a big success. I will do nothing to ruin it for you. Honest."

Vanessa still sounded disgruntled. "Right."

"She can send the videos to my personal email address. And thanks for the autographed picture of Clint."

Vanessa stood up and began wheeling Melissa toward the playground. "I know his daughter. She's a great lady. Anyway, right now we're on our way to play with the poor unfortunates who live in the flats."

"Be kind to them."

"Later."

Rosemaria hung up. She didn't know what she was expecting from the video, but she hoped it was worth using her interrogating skills on her best friend.

Her phone rang. It was Jimmy. "I think I may have found something. A female, same age as Leonie, named Jillian Moss started working for a textile company that designs bedspreads, wallpaper, and draperies about a month after Donna Saint-Saens left Miami." He hesitated. "I hope you don't mind, but I asked Curtis for another favor."

"I don't mind if he doesn't."

"Well, since he has all these connections to security companies everywhere, I asked him if he could track down traffic cameras or businesses in the area that had cameras in the vicinity of the textile company during that time and might be inclined to save them in their computers."

"Who would save them for years?"

"He found some that still had the videos in their computer and had them sent to me. I've gone through all of them."

"That must have taken hours, No wonder you're up all night. Don't wreck your health because of me."

"Never mind that. I found a face that looks a lot like Leonie looked as Donna Saint-Saens in Miami. Not perfect facial recognition but close. She left the company after the president died unexpectedly of a heart attack. Could be Leonie."

"If it is, do you think she killed him?"

"Who knows? She disappeared after that."

"Maybe to New York? The ultimate destination for people who want to fulfill their hearts' desires?"

"Maybe."

"Good work, Jimmy. Send me a photo of the woman, okay?"

"Of course."

"Get some sleep."

"Later."

Rosemaria received the email of the party videos before noon. She stopped work on the Oberman case and two other felony cases she'd been handed, closed the door, told Karen no phone calls, and began to study the videos. The videographer had filmed and talked to dozens of party guests. Drew's cameras had caught everyone as they entered the foyer. Rosemaria watched all the interviews carefully more than once, trying to see if there was anything about any of them that she recognized, but there was not.

If Leonie had left well enough alone and never tried to kill her, she would be home free right now.

She checked her email and saw that Jimmy had emailed her the picture of Jillian Moss, the woman he believed was Leonie. Rosemaria printed it out and studied the hard copy carefully, trying to see if she bore any resemblance to the girl who called herself Mariah whom she had interviewed all those years ago or the photo in the Miami paper. Nothing in the woman's face looked familiar to her. She went through the party videos again to see if any of the guests looked remotely like the woman in Atlanta. Beautiful women who had had work done tended to have features that were alike, and there were many of those at the party, but none of them resembled the Leonie Jimmy might have found.

She replayed the footage of Helene arriving and being shoved into the bedroom and Victor showing up twenty minutes later. Rosemaria played his entrance again. Then again. As he came into the house and looked in on the crowd of people in the huge living room for an instant, she thought he showed a flicker of recognition. Then, just as quickly, it died. But who did he see—a mistress, a competitor, who? After a few tries, she managed to freeze-frame his face at the split second of the flicker. It might be her imagination but maybe—

A thought occurred to her. She grabbed her cell phone and hit speed dial. Jimmy didn't pick up, and she had to leave a message. "Jimmy, Rosemaria. Listen, Marchand's main office is in Atlanta. I want you to do a deep dive into the ownership of the textile company. See if it's owned by a bigger company that's owned by a conglomerate. I think we may be on to something."

Vanessa's big fundraiser was scheduled to happen in two weeks. She wanted to get this whole thing over with by then. Keeping her promise to Vanessa was important.

Rosemaria was having a difficult time concentrating on the vehicular homicide case that she might be handed if the Oberman hearing went as expected, and the trial was endlessly postponed by Tammy. The drunk driver was a state senator from Santa Monica who had been racing down a residential street at night. He had hit a woman walking home from her job at a convenience store and driven away from the scene. But the woman's husband had witnessed the hit and called the police with a description of the car. The senator had been caught, tested, and found to have a 0.108 alcohol level, meaning he was driving blind drunk. The case screamed for a guilty verdict, but Rosemaria imagined what the defense would be if he were represented by Tammy—it was the bartender's fault for serving him drinks after he reached the legal limit; he was suffering from PTSD after a bad divorce and couldn't judge how many drinks he had; he took a wrong turn and didn't know he was on a residential street; his brakes failed; his parents beat him as a child, and he was too busy having a flashback of being spanked to notice he had hit anybody. Tammy probably had a list a mile long that she pulled out for every case. Fortunately, Tammy was too busy to represent the senator.

She told Karen she was accepting calls and immersed herself in the hit-and-run case. But she could barely concentrate on her work wondering if what she suspected was true. What was taking Jimmy so long? She had just decided to go get herself a cup of coffee and chocolate cookie in the breakroom when her cell phone finally rang.

"Yes. What did you find?"

"You were right. Victor Marchand owns the conglomerate that owns the company that owns the textile firm."

"Holy smoke. I wonder if Leonie found out Ramin's father owned the company and targeted him on purpose? What do you want to bet she seduced him and squeezed money out of him? It must have appealed to her sick sense of irony to have an affair with the father of the boy she had framed for murder."

"We have to bring him in. I already told Larry and Mack and Loshi. They should be there when we question him."

"Did you get the video I sent?"

"Yeah, got it. We'll have him come in tomorrow. Your dad will probably report back to you immediately."

"Copy that, my friend. Later."

"Later."

Rosemaria knew she needed to focus on her work, but her mind was wandering in every direction. Would Marchand cooperate? Did he actually recognize the person he had had an affair with a few years before? Had she had more plastic surgery? Maybe he couldn't definitely say who it was. She had to calm down and concentrate. A few months ago, when Josh had asked her if she was going to be a cop or a prosecutor, she had jokingly said both. It was becoming very clear that, once again, she'd have to do just that.

CHAPTER FORTY

arry was standing next to Osborne near the receptionist's desk when two uniforms escorted Marchand back to an interrogation room. A lot depended on Marchand being willing to open up about his affair with Leonie, if indeed that were true, and being willing to identify the woman he saw at the party who had caused him to react for a split second. They had to make him realize how important the identity of the woman was but didn't dare tell him that she could be the person who'd murdered their son. If they bungled the interview, he might completely close down and leave. Marchand was a billionaire who ran a conglomerate. They were lucky he hadn't brought his lawyer with him.

Osborne went in first and sat opposite Marchand. Larry entered, smiled, and leaned against the wall, relaxed, a BHPD folder in his hands.

Osborne had brought his laptop and opened it to the freeze-frame of Marchand when he first entered Drew's living room. He decided to avoid the schmooze and get to the point. Maybe it would catch Marchand off guard. He turned the laptop around so Marchand could see the freeze-frame. "You saw someone you recognized," Osborne said. "Who was it?"

Marchand glanced casually at the screen. "I don't know who I saw. I saw a lot of people. I was worried about my wife. I just wanted to get her out of there and take her home before she made another scene."

"The woman we're looking for is a person of interest in several crimes. We don't know her identity or what she looks like. If you saw a woman you recognized, you could help us."

Marchand looked at them askance. "And why are you asking *me* who I recognized? Why single me out? You're not making any sense, and I'd like to know what you're not telling me."

Larry walked to the table and laid down his folder and took out several pictures of women who had been standing near the entrance when Marchand came in. He spread them out in front of Marchand. "The woman we're looking for used to work for your company, Fineman Textiles in Atlanta," Larry said. "She's probably changed her appearance since then. We just wanted to know if in one split second you might have recognized her."

Marchand studied the pictures one by one and shook his head. "I don't see anyone familiar here. Right now, I'm dealing with several business challenges, and my wife's behavior has taken a toll on me, gentlemen. You'll have to forgive me, but I'm having a hard time remembering that exact moment in time. If I briefly thought I saw someone I knew, it flashed through my head very quickly. Whoever it was, it wasn't as important as getting my wife out of there."

Larry opened a folder and showed Marchand a picture of Leonie as she looked in Miami. "When she worked for your company, she was using the name Jillian Moss, which we believe is false."

Marchand studied the picture and said she looked familiar, but he couldn't remember specifically having contact with her at work. "You have to remember, detectives, I rarely became involved with the individuals who worked for our various companies. If she was working for Fineman in any kind of low-level position, the chances of my even meeting her were very slim."

"Have another look, please," Larry said.

Marchand studied the photos again. "These ladies look nothing like the one you just showed me. Is one of these women the one you're looking for?"

"We don't know," Osborne said, "and we certainly don't want to accuse an innocent person of a crime she didn't commit."

"I wish I could help you, but I can't." He slid out his chair and stood up. "If there's nothing else, I need to get back to my wife."

The detectives stood as well. "Thank you for coming in," Osborne said.

After Marchand left, Larry had a thoughtful look on his face. "I think I know how we can draw her out, but we'd need Marchand's help."

"I wouldn't count on that."

"He needs to be carefully manipulated into telling us the truth. We need someone who is not in the least bit intimidated by money or power to talk to him, someone who can stand up to him and appeal to him as a father. And tell him the person he may have slept with could very well be his son's murderer without having him go off the deep end, track down the woman he thought he recognized, and kill her."

"And the person we assign this chore is . . .?"

"Think she'll do it?"

"In a heartbeat."

*　*　*　*　*

Victor followed a uniformed cop out of the interrogation room to the exit door and down the stairs. He told the police officer his car and driver were out front. After his driver opened the door and Victor had sunk into the soft comfort of the leather seats, he was silently apoplectic. Recognize her? Of course, he had recognized that bitch from the Miami picture. He was never so happy to get someone out of his life as when Jillian Moss or whatever the hell her name was hit the road out of Atlanta. But as far as which one of the women in the pictures was her, he was not sure. They all looked alike to him—dark hair, dark eyes, attractive, thin. None of them looked like the blonde, green-eyed Jillian he had known. He didn't even remember the moment caught in the camera's freeze frame when he must have seen someone who looked like Jillian—hell, he didn't even remember the camera. He was so caught up in his wife's drama and so eager to get her home, the moment, if he had it, had been quickly forgotten.

To this day, he suspected Jillian had something to do with Maury Fineman's death. She had probably assumed her affair with Victor would lead to her taking over as president of Fineman Textiles—her, a young girl with zero experience. Her chutzpah was off the charts. He hadn't touched his wife for years. Her obesity repelled him. She had wasted no time putting on the pounds after a shotgun wedding that resulted in the birth of his boy, David, the only good thing that came out of the marriage. Sex with Jillian was phenomenal, like nothing he had ever experienced. But business was business, and she was not qualified.

When Victor said no, he had suspected that Jillian somehow engineered Maury's fatal heart attack. She became enraged when Victor still refused to hand over the presidency to her. She screamed obscenities at him and began throwing valuable art objects against the mirrored walls of his office until he pressed the button for security, and they came running. It took two guards to hold her down and get her the hell out of his office and out of the building. She left messages on his cell phone threatening him with videos of them having sex, which would have caused his wife to file for divorce and cost him a good portion of his assets. Jillian insisted on meeting him at a sleazy bar in Adair Park where his driver and limo would stand out like a sore thumb. It wasn't enough for her to get the million in cash out of him. She got her rocks off making him feel like the lowlife, stupid sucker he was.

He stared out the window, contemplating how his wealth had not protected him against the oldest con game known to man. He had a business luncheon at the Peninsula Hotel in half an hour, unavoidable meetings the next two days with the president of a wine label he was considering dumping, and one with the president of a computer chip company his conglomerate had recently taken over, then all he wanted was to fly back to Atlanta with his nutcase of a wife and forget his sordid history with Jillian.

* * * * *

Rosemaria was on board with Larry and Osborne's plan for Victor, but she didn't have a whole lot of time to think about it. She had to focus on her job first. The Oberman hearing was next week, and she wanted to concentrate on the strategy Reid had drawn up for them. First, they would present the court with crime scene photos and testimony from the medical examiner. Then they would show photos of the murder weapon and offer the testimony of the neighbor who found it. Rosemaria would question the maid, who would make it clear that no one knew where the key to the shed was except members of the family. They'd show Walmart footage of Lynette buying the masks. They would introduce a video from a camera attached to a house several blocks from the murder site showing those identical masks being worn by the murderers as they exited their parked car and walked toward the Oberman house. That same video would show that Liam and Lynette, wearing those masks, parked and exited the car at 2:45 and came back to the car and drove away at 3:10, which was the estimated time of the murders. This was the same car Liam and Lynette had been driving in Houston when they were apprehended. Reid expected this would be enough evidence to bind the case over for trial. They would save other testimony for the trial.

After the hearing, it was just a question of how long Tammy would seek to delay the trial and what possible reasons she would come up with for doing so. When you have an obviously guilty client, the usual strategies are to attack the victims, the detectives, the forensic scientists, and the witnesses and to find other suspects who could have committed the murders. Tammy was arguably the scrappiest defense lawyer in the country. They could expect she would throw every kind of defense lawyer BS at the courtroom wall and see what stuck and, if none of it did, would throw some more BS at the wall.

Rosemaria was not in the least bit intimidated by Tammy. She had zero respect for the woman and was looking forward to beating her in court. But with Tammy's reputation for asking for endless delays, Rosemaria figured she would deal with many other cases before the Oberman trial was finally on the docket. Considering the kind of lawyer Tammy was, after delaying the trial for months, and possibly years, she'd probably argue at some point that it was unfair to her client that he had not received the speedy trial he was legally entitled to. Rosemaria smiled. She'd bet any-thing that was exactly what would happen.

She looked at her watch. It was time to call Larry and find out where the best place to corner Victor Marchand was where he would not be able to avoid her.

* * * * *

Victor had let Merritt Eiland talk him out of selling Melova Wines for now. Eiland had practically gotten down on his knees and begged for a chance to prove he could boost profits in the next six months. Victor was embarrassed for him and agreed. If he was this motivated, maybe he could actually accomplish what he promised. They were just finishing up their business when Eiland's desk phone rang. He listened for a few seconds and hung up. "My receptionist just showed your wife into the conference room. She said it's an emergency."

Victor almost knocked his chair over getting to his feet. "I know where it is." He walked down the hall and around the corner and opened the door to the conference room. He saw an attractive woman standing by the shiny hardwood table. "Where's my wife?"

Rosemaria walked toward him, and he backed away. She closed the door and locked it.

"What the hell?"

He tried to move around her to open the door, but Rosemaria stood her ground. "You need to listen to what I have to say."

"There are cameras in this room. You're not going to get away with any entrapment bullshit."

"You've had enough of that Victor, wouldn't you say?"

"Who are you?"

"I was the cop who interviewed everyone in the house after Ramin was murdered. But I didn't do my job, and your son, an innocent man, went to prison. He was murdered by the same woman who killed Ramin, and now she's after me."

"I know who you are. My son was killed because you went to see him. I have nothing to say to you. Don't make me have to use force to get you out of my way."

"You wouldn't be able to do that, Victor, so I suggest you sit down and give me five minutes of your time. I know all about you and Jillian Moss, and I don't think that's something you want all over the news." Rosemaria was doing a little guesswork here but knew she'd hit the nail on the head when Victor's face went white.

"I have no idea of what you're talking about."

"You don't need to play the almighty chairman of the board with me, Victor. You fell for her, and she took you for some big bucks, and now you're just as big a schmuck as the guy who works at the corner carwash. No better, no worse. The chickens have come home to roost, and now we're going to have to ruffle some feathers."

"You have a lot of nerve for a cop, talking to me like that. If you're accusing me of something, I have a right not to say anything."

"I'm not a cop anymore, just another victim of Jillian Moss."

Victor sank into a chair. "You have five minutes."

Rosemaria sat down opposite him. "Did you recognize someone when you walked into the party?"

"I may have, but I honestly don't remember who it was. They all looked alike in the pictures the real cops showed me."

"If Jillian is living the high life in Los Angeles, you're going to help me spring a trap and catch her."

"All right, so I had sex with this person, and she blackmailed me and took me for a lot of money, but I am not getting involved in any plan to trap her. Why the hell should I?"

"This woman we're talking about purposefully tracked you down, seduced you, and forced you to pay her money. She toyed with you like you were an aging Ken doll. And do you know why?"

Victor's shoulders sagged, and he sighed heavily. "No, why?"

"Because she found immense satisfaction in having sex with the father of the boy she framed for murder."

Victor bolted upright. "That's not possible."

"As God is my witness."

"How do you know?"

"We've had the best detectives in San Diego and LA investigating the case. We're sure."

"I don't believe it."

"And I'm next on her list unless we can identify her and arrest her before she gets another crack at me."

Suddenly Victor's face turned white, and he looked as if he were about to pass out or have a heart attack. Rosemaria panicked. Good lord, she couldn't let that happen. The rest of the team would kill her. She opened the door and yelled down the hall for someone to bring a bottle of water. In two seconds, the receptionist came running. Rosemaria grabbed the bottle of water, opened it, and handed it to Victor. "Drink."

He brought the bottle up to his mouth and tried to swallow some of the water. Half of it dribbled down his chin. "What do you need me to do?"

* * * *

Josh was still asleep when Rosemaria began to prepare breakfast at the dining room table. She wanted to have a good view of the big TV. Breakfast preparation consisted of her pouring granola into a bowl and pouring rice milk over it. The automatic brewer had made the coffee without any effort by her. She had a place setting and coffee cup for Josh as well should he choose to get up early after a long night in the recording studio.

Victor Marchand was scheduled to be on a national morning news show, and she hoped she wouldn't have to wade through too much irrelevant chitchat and lame jokes before they finally got to him. She munched on her granola, and when Suzi hopped on the table, she shared a few kernels with her. Josh didn't need to know, and besides, it was sugar-free. How bad could it be for Suzi?

During a commercial for yet another drug for yet another disease she'd never heard of that frightened the TV audience into believing they had whatever ailment it was meant to cure, she sipped her coffee and hoped

Larry's plan would work. She sat up straight, put down her coffee cup, and concentrated on the TV screen. Victor was being introduced.

Tasha Jones, the zaftig black woman who hosted the show, was effusive in her praise of Victor's accomplishments. She sounded almost reverential as she spoke.

"Mr. Marchand, it's an honor to have you on our show. We know you prefer to avoid publicity even when you help raise money for charities like Miles of Smiles that change the lives of children all over the world or Desert Water, a nonprofit that digs wells to help small communities in several African nations, so there must be a special reason you agreed to talk to us today."

Rosemaria thought Victor looked smashing in his dark blue suit, light-blue shirt, and pin-striped tie. She had to admit he was a handsome man for someone his age. He looked so much better than the last time she'd seen him. He projected an effortless aura of authority and charisma and awarded Tasha with a dazzling smile. "Actually, I came to talk about one of those charities, but you're right. I do have a business proposition for the right person. It's something I've been contemplating for a while."

"Does it have anything to do with a pastime you enjoy but rarely have time for?" Tasha teased, already knowing the answer. "I've read about how, as a young man, you loved spending time on the water, sailing on your uncle's sloop. Which is what, by the way?"

Victor's eyes lit up as he spoke. "A sloop is a one-masted sailboat that is faster than a ketch and great for racing. The sails are heavier, but with only one sail, it's more difficult to handle in a strong gale. When I was in my teens, I loved cutting through the water at lightning speed, feeling as though my uncle and I were alone at sea, using our skills to bend nature to our will. I'm sure it wasn't as dangerous and dramatic as that, but that's how it felt and how I remember those times."

"I can see how much you loved it."

"Well, as I get older, I've been thinking of not only getting back out on the water while I'm still strong and relatively fit but also building sailboats and using everything I've learned to custom-make them according to my specifications."

"And, as I understand it, you're looking for a partner."

"As you know, I have several large business enterprises already, but still, I'd like to explore the possibilities of shipbuilding, not only sailboats but large cabin cruisers as well. Because the actual building is far out of my comfort zone, I'm looking for a small business partner who preferably already has the infrastructure to build boats and knows the business a lot better than I do. I don't want to just buy another big successful business. I want to build my own from the ground up with the right partner. I can do the research and hire experts and all that, so even if the right candidate doesn't have any experience in building sailboats, I'd like to team up with someone I can trust who has the ability to hit the ground running, and we can learn together. I don't have a lot of time to waste at this point in life, and I'd like to be involved with a business I love. It will give me an excuse to test run our products out on the water. I can't think of anything more fun."

"Are you actively searching for businesses who have that infrastructure?"

"I've interviewed a couple of people and am considering them, but I'm open to meeting more and making a decision soon."

Tasha turned to the camera. "So, if anyone out there has the knowledge about building boats and the qualifications Mr. Marchand is looking for, or even if you don't, I sense this could be a huge business opportunity for you." She glanced at Victor, then back at the camera. "This man has the golden touch, and I predict that whoever Victor chooses will end up profiting mightily." She looked at him. "Can you stick around after the break and talk about Miles of Smiles?"

"That's why I'm here."

"We'll be right back with the incredible Victor Marchand."

Rosemaria turned off the TV just as Josh came out of the bedroom in his bathrobe, his hair wet from the shower.

"He just made the pitch. It sounded good."

"Think Leonie will bite?"

"I'm wondering if Tasha hit the money part hard enough. These interviews he's doing are supposed to appeal to Leonie's greed. Plus, we figure she'd love nothing better than to fool Victor again. It would appeal to her sadistic nature to finally go into business with the man who had rejected her and whose son she had killed."

"Hopefully, she'll be watching. How many more shows is he doing?"

"He's doing two of those daytime talk shows where women sit around and gossip about celebrities and talk about their pet peeves and then another morning news show tomorrow. They love having famous people come on and promote their charities."

"How's his wife doing?"

"I think he sent her back to Atlanta on their private plane."

"Strange couple."

She picked up the box of granola and held it over the bowl at his place setting. "Should I make you breakfast?"

"Please."

She poured in the granola and then the rice milk. "It's delicious if I do say so myself. I'll get the coffee."

He grabbed her arm as she went by. "Woman, you are amazing."

She bent over and gave him a peck on the cheek. "Don't I always aim to please?" She came back with the coffee, poured some into his cup, and set the pot down on a trivet.

He crunched his granola. "That you do. And as a reward, I will agree to marry you when you're out of danger."

"I already trapped you, and we're engaged. And yes, as soon as we put Leonie away, you're mine."

"That's the price I pay for living with a gourmet cook."

"Don't get smart with me, or I won't heat up your frozen dinners in the microwave."

"If I write you a song, will it get me off the hook?"

She grabbed his hand before he could reach for his coffee cup and looked deep into his beautiful blue eyes. "You've said that before, and I'm still waiting."

"Patience is a virtue."

"Aha. Here's another platitude for you: 'The road to you-know-where is paved with good intentions.'"

"You may change your tune when my CD comes out."

"Really?"

"Really."

He shrugged. She grinned. They sat that way for several seconds before resuming their excellent breakfast.

* * * *

Larry and Vanessa had been watching Victor on the morning show as well. Melissa was in her highchair eating toast and jam, and most of it was on her face. Her parents were thoughtfully sipping their coffee.

"You seriously believe one of my friends could be this psychopath?" Vanessa asked, fire springing into her eyes.

"Calm down. If one of them is, indeed, Leonie, this is a way we might be able to get her to come forward. We have no idea what she looks like now. We know she worked for Victor in Atlanta, but he says he barely remembers her. And this Leonie character has been driven by greed her entire short life. If she knows Victor and figures she can convince him to take her on as partner, she'll be richer than she's ever dreamed of. Leonie has always used men as ATMs, and here is another perfect opportunity to prove how irresistible she is. It's never failed her in the past. Why should it fail her now?"

"Your case has a lot of assumptions and suppositions. The killer could be someone else entirely. And hopefully, she watches talk shows."

"I haven't told you everything about this case. Believe me, we are on the right track. The next move is Leonie's. Victor is bound to recognize her when he meets with her up close and personal."

"Maybe he won't."

"If he does, we've instructed him not to let her know."

Vanessa sighed deeply. "I'm not mad."

Larry smiled. "It could be someone you barely know."

"I have to continue with my plans for the gala at the Beverly Wilshire. I could be talking to this person every day." She proceeded to wipe toast and milk off Melissa's face. "Please find her soon. For Rosemaria's sake and the sake of my gala."

Larry looked over at Melissa. "Your daughter has that funny look on her face she gets after breakfast."

Vanessa laughed and picked the baby up out of her highchair. "Don't worry, Daddy. I'll take care of it."

He took his briefcase off the hallway table. "How long until they're potty trained?"

"*They* could take years, so don't hold your breath." Then she added, "Love you, have a good day" and disappeared down the hall.

He went out the front door thinking he loved his daughter to the moon but would never have made it as Mr. Mom.

CHAPTER FORTY-ONE

Leonie was in her home office enjoying the view of the downtown skyline. The promos the day before announcing Victor Marchand would be on various morning shows were hard to miss. She had watched one and felt her life was about to change. As always, when things threatened to go badly, her luck always brought her back from the brink. There was no doubt she would partner up with Victor. He had looked straight at her and not recognized her at Drew's party. Her fiancé would provide the building infrastructure Victor was looking for. Her fiancé, who had his eye on running for public office, had pretty much been ignoring the crumbling, all-but-forgotten furniture building business he had inherited, along with three other, more successful businesses, from his parents.

If Victor showed any hesitation whatsoever, she was certain her persuasive powers would overcome his reluctance. The factory was there, dilapidated as it was, but it was perfect for what Victor said he was looking for. It was situated near the port of San Pedro and could be transformed into a boat-building site with very little effort. Together, she and Victor would transform the company with an infusion of cash, and with his talent for making money, profits would soar. Maybe she wouldn't even need her fiancé anymore if she could talk him into signing the business over to her. It wasn't like it was making him much money. She doubted if he even gave it much thought. His intention of running for office had been a threat to her from the beginning and was part of the reason she felt she had to eliminate people from her past life. They might have been able to recognize her when she had to play the candidate's wife, not something she had been looking forward to.

She knew now that Micco was the only person who might be able to figure out who she was. He knew her voice but not her face, and his computer skills put her at risk. She had stolen his .45 automatic when she had visited him at his art gallery and briefly considered using it to kill Rosemaria, then dismissed the thought. Micco had already shot Sam and Stacey with it and, like the amateur he was, had locked the gun in his safe—easy enough to break into. She had video of him taking the boat out with Sam and Stacey that fateful night, and that was all she needed to force him into a corner. She had decided he would have the honor of eliminating Rosemaria himself and would be given a choice of doing that or going to prison for the rest of his life. Either way, she intended to get rid of him. There was no time to waste. She picked up her cell phone.

Micco was at work at the gallery when his phone rang. He walked into his office and clicked it on. "What do you want?"

"Is that any way to talk to your partner?"

"I'm not doing anymore dirty work for you."

"Well, I think you are. The Baker woman is your next target. Do you want to me to do it myself with your gun?"

"I figured it was you who had stolen it."

"You also have a rifle in your gun safe in your office. Use it or whatever gun you have. I don't care. Just do it."

"With a bodyguard sticking to her like glue every morning, noon, and night? How am I supposed to do that?"

"I found out she likes to spend time alone after work on the roof of their condo building. She sits out there by herself and makes her bodyguard stand outside the door so she has some semblance of freedom for a few minutes a day. There are lawn chairs and a table and potted plants for shade. You can sneak up there during the day using the service stairs, pretend to be an air conditioner repairman, and wait for her. After you shoot her, just walk back down the stairs, and you'll have plenty of time before the guard figures out she's been there too long."

"The bodyguard will never let anyone in there, and I can't sneak in the night before because he will thoroughly check the place out before letting her out on the roof."

"So shoot her while she's in the hallway, and he's checking out the roof. Or follow her and find another time when she's alone. You figure it out."

"I'm not doing it."

"I don't see how you can refuse."

"Well, Mariah, there's something you don't know. Stacey is still alive."

Leonie was stunned. "What?"

"She jumped off the boat while I was shooting at Sam. She disappeared under the water, and I thought she had drowned. After I threw Sam overboard, I kept shooting toward shore where she would have been heading, but I couldn't be sure I hit her."

"So what's the problem?"

"I drove down and looked for her in the area where she could have swum to shore. I never told you where that was. And I found her. I know where she lives."

Leonie was at a loss for words.

"I told her and Sam everything before I shot him. If she talks, we are both cooked."

"You have to tell me where she is," Leonie hissed.

"Have my .45 delivered to me by special delivery, and I will tell you where you can find Stacey. After you deliver my gun along with two hundred thousand dollars, I will disappear. We'll owe each other nothing. You can do as you please. Rid yourself of the ex-cop or let her live. I don't care. But I will be out of your life forever. Here's the address where you can send my .45 and the money." He gave it to her.

Micco clicked off the phone and made a call.

Leonie was devastated. Her world was crashing down around her. She had been excited about getting a meeting with Victor and convincing him to take her on as partner. With Baker gone, the path would be clear. She had everything set up to blackmail Micco into killing her, then framing him for the murder. Now he'd managed to throw a monkey wrench into her plan. Should she even bother to meet Victor? Should she just disappear again after being so close? Maybe New York? But she loved her life in Beverly Hills. It was everything she had dreamed of her entire life as she planned and schemed. She wasn't used to losing. It had never happened to her.

Two hours later, Leonie was still sitting alone in her home office. She walked to her wall safe and took out a few stacks of cash. Using a fake name, she called a messenger service on a burner phone to come pick up a package containing Micco's gun and two hundred thousand dollars in cash from a restaurant where she was waiting in a wig and sunglasses. She paid the messenger in cash and gave the man the address in New Mexico where Micco had told her to send it. Then she had called Victor's home office number, given her credentials, using a different identity than the one she was currently using and been granted an interview. After she was certain Victor's offer was not some elaborate trap cooked up by the cops to trap Baker's would-be killer, and after she was certain Victor did not recognize her, she would give some plausible explanation for the small deception. Extreme caution had always served her well. She told him yes, she was in Beverly HIlls but could fly to New York if necessary. No worries. He would call her with a time and place himself.

But was it all for nothing? With Stacey alive it would only be a matter of time before she felt safe enough to call the cops and tell them what she knew. Maybe she already had, but according to what Micco had said, she was still hiding out. Leonie would know where she was as soon as Micco had the money. There was no guarantee he wouldn't just take the money and run but she hoped he wasn't that stupid. He knew better than anyone what she was capable of. After her meeting with Victor, she would take care of Stacey herself. As for Baker, that would have to look like an accident. She needed to work on that. She couldn't afford another investigation right now. She could make killing Stacey look like a break-in. No problem there. But as for Baker, killing her and making it look like an accident would be a challenge.

* * * * *

Victor's meeting with his next potential partner was to take place on the outdoor patio of the Polo Lounge. She had insisted. In the past few days, he had met with five women and seven men who had the qualifications to be an asset to his company, but that, after all, was not the purpose of this charade. He wished he'd never agreed to it, but refusing would have shown an egregious lack of interest in catching his son's killer. He left his car with the valet and made his way to the lounge. He told the maître d' he was waiting for someone but passed up the offer of a glass of wine by the waiter. He needed to keep his wits about him. His irritation was growing when the woman finally showed up fifteen minutes late. He watched her glance around the patio, notice him, and make her way toward his table.

He was immediately panic stricken. Her hair was cut short and dyed a reddish brown, and dark sunglasses covered half her face, but he could tell by the way she moved and carried herself that this was indeed Jillian or Leonie or whatever the hell her name was. He could barely keep a smile on his face as she approached. Her friendly demeanor showed she had no idea he had recognized her. And up close, she looked so different from Jillian he could hardly believe it was her. He stood; they shook hands and took their seats. She ordered a glass of white wine from the waiter and looked at Victor expectantly.

"I have to confess I am nervous meeting the famous Victor Marchand in person." Her voice had matured and was an octave lower than he had remembered.

"Nothing to be nervous about," Victor said easily.

"But there is. You're famous but very private and elusive. You're one of the richest men in the world, but you don't flaunt your wealth. That's very intimidating."

"Well, I'm actually not intimidating at all. I'm extremely friendly and open to hearing you tell me why you want to be partners with me."

She looked up as the waiter came by with her wine. "I can order now if you don't mind. I'll just have the avocado salad."

Victor hadn't bothered to look at the menu. "I'll have the same."

She lowered her sunglass briefly and fastened her big brown eyes, formerly an emerald green, on his face. "I think I'm a perfect fit for you."

If only you knew, Victor thought. "How so?"

She pushed the sunglasses back on her nose. "You've looked at my résumé, I presume?"

"I have. You are involved in a little bit of everything—import-export, construction, real estate, design, publishing. The construction part of your business seems to be the largest and most profitable."

"Exactly. I was lucky, came in with a lot of lowest bids, received some government contract work and a large high-rise downtown."

"But nothing in your résumé about boats."

"That's true, but my fiancé does have a small furniture building company that has been ignored for the past several years. The infrastructure is still there, it's right near the water, and I think it will be an easy switch. And small and personal, as you were looking for."

"So I'm confused. Will I be dealing with him or you?"

"Me, of course. Believe me, I will have no problem having him sign over the company to me even before we're married. He has zero interest in that company and prefers to spend his time on yachts rather than building them."

"I see."

"Exactly. He is the complete opposite of you and will be no problem, but the company is there waiting for you and me to make it incredibly successful."

"I'm liking the sound of this."

"Really?" She seemed as excited as a little girl.

Victor had been through this before and remembered well her playing the innocent while spinning her web.

The waiter came with their salads, and they barely looked at them.

"Why don't you email me information on this business of your fiancé's, and we will talk again."

Her face lit up with a tremendous smile. She had even changed the shape of her teeth. "You won't say yes to anyone else before we meet again, will you?"

He picked up his fork. "Absolutely not. I promise you."

"Wonderful." She was even better at it than before. Indigestion hit him like a rock in his stomach. But he kept eating and pretending. It wasn't easy.

An hour later, Victor was on his way home to Bel Air, a house he loved for its seclusion and incredible view and a house he probably would not see again for quite a while. He was supposed to have called Detective Coleman by now, but he had no intention of doing so. He'd also forgotten to take the woman's wine glass with him so they could get a sample of her DNA. Too bad. He must have been insane to think he could identify her and then walk away and have nothing to do with the investigation and trial. As soon as she knew he was involved, she would blackmail him and threaten him. His life as he knew it would be over. She had murdered his son and several others. If he helped put her in jail, he was a dead man. He would pack as soon as he got home and hire a private jet to fly him to one of the islands in the Caribbean. He would check out for a month or so and do business online. His wife would have to fend for herself. Let somebody else deal with her hysteria for a while. Coleman wouldn't find him, and even if he did, they couldn't force him to do a damn thing. He didn't have the best lawyers in the country on retainer for nothing.

Abe was driving Rosemaria home when her phone rang. Larry. Maybe Victor had ID'd Leonie. "Larry, give me some good news."

"Victor vamoosed."

"Damn. I did not see that coming."

"It had crossed my mind, so I should have had someone there. Like an idiot, I trusted him. She murdered his son, for crying out loud."

"Fear is a strong motivator."

"He had three meetings today: one at breakfast, another one at his office, and the other at the Polo Lounge. So far, he's met with six women but kept the names a secret. He claimed he didn't want to single out an innocent woman unnecessarily, but I think he had another agenda."

"What?"

"I think maybe he knew something about the murder of Maury Fineman, and covering his ass and not exposing his affair are more important than finding his son's murderer."

"I think he was scared out of his mind of Leonie."

"That too."

"Do you think one of the women he met is Leonie, and he recognized her?"

"We'll be going to the Polo Lounge and the other places he met the women and show pictures."

"How do you know what pictures to show? There are hundreds of women involved in Vanessa's charity, and there's a good chance she's not one of them."

"We'll give it a try."

Her phone announced another call.

"I've gotta go, Larry. Let me know if anything breaks. We're getting ready for the hearing tomorrow. We're sure it'll be bound over, but if you want to dig up more evidence for us before the trial, we wouldn't be averse to that."

"We're doing our best."

She clicked her phone. "Vanessa, I was just talking to your husband."

"Is he making any progress?"

"We just had a little setback, but he's dealing with it. What's up?"

"You've probably been really busy, but my birthday's coming up, and a friend is having a little get-together for me."

"Oh no. I'm sorry. I did forget."

"No biggie, but I'd like you to be there if you can."

"Of course, I'll be there. When is it, and where is it?"

"It's my friend Meredith's top-floor apartment in the historic art deco building in West Hollywood just down from Sunset. Maybe you've seen it. They've been making renovations and just reopened it. It's gorgeous. Built in the golden age of Hollywood. So far, she is the first and only tenant. She's inviting six of my best friends I've known forever. I'm so overloaded with committee meetings and having to deal with a lot of people I barely know, I thought just a few of us relaxing and talking about nothing important would be just the ticket."

"So email me the address and date and time, okay?"

"Will do."

"What would you like for your birthday?"

"As if."

"See you then, valley girl."

CHAPTER FORTY-TWO

eonie's mind was racing. She knew exactly what she needed to do but didn't have much time to implement her plan. One of her friends on the committee called to tell her an actress friend of Vanessa's was having an intimate birthday party for her. Vanessa would be staying over after the party so she and her friend could go shopping together the next day. Neither Leonie nor the committee member who called her was invited because it was a very exclusive group of those closest to Vanessa, but she suggested they organize their own get-together for Vanessa and include Loretta. It would be an excuse to score points with one of the richest, most influential women in town. They needed to organize it soon before anybody else thought of it. Leonie had said it was a great idea and would call her back.

If her research yielded the kind of information Leonie hoped for, and the art deco building was as old as she knew it must be, this would be the perfect chance to rid herself of the Baker woman for good. It would be counted as a tragic accident. There would be no reason for a murder investigation. Afterward, she would drive down to San Diego, find the house where Micco had told her Stacey was hiding, deactivate the alarm system, break in, and shoot Stacey and her boyfriend as they slept. She would pull out drawers and yank clothes out of the closet to make it look like a robbery. Child's play. All the way back to LA, she would be celebrating the demise of the ex-cop and Stacey the blabbermouth, and, in a week, she'd meet with Victor again and seal the deal on their partnership.

Meanwhile, Micco would be the person of interest in the murder of Stacey and her boyfriend if the attempted robbery didn't play out. The videos the police would find would show Micco taking Stacey and Sam out in the boat before he shot Sam and Stacey swam away. Nobody, not even Micco, could prove she had anything to do with any murders. He didn't even know her current identity. Besides, Micco was undoubtedly in another country by now.

Suddenly, life was looking fabulous. How could she ever have doubted that everything would work out for her? Hadn't it always? Maybe not the bungled attempts to kill Baker, but this time, Baker was as good as dead. The next night, she would check out the apartment building and make preparations for a perfect murder.

* * * * *

The Oberman hearing went as Reid had predicted. Tammy did not show her hand and did not object to any of the evidence the prosecution introduced. It was not everything they had by a long shot but enough for the judge to bind the case over for trial. Tammy barely looked at them during the hearing as if even taking a moment to cast contemptuous glances at the prosecutors was a waste of time. She conferred with Helen Cooperman as necessary but pretty much gave her the same derisory treatment. Apparently, Tammy couldn't care less that she was creating hard feelings in the lawyer representing a client who could turn state's evidence and testify against Liam. Rosemaria didn't think she had ever witnessed such a display of hubris in the courtroom.

After they left the courtroom, Rosemaria and Reid speculated that Tammy's lack of concern over the evidence and incurring Cooperman's wrath might be because she intended to have Liam admit he killed his parents but had some brilliant excuse lined up, and so whatever Lynette testified to was irrelevant. They anticipated that the trial that was for now scheduled to proceed in four months would be a roller-coaster ride neither she nor Reid had ever experienced before. Rosemaria couldn't wait.

In her office, Rosemaria took a call from the security company that Abe worked for. The plans for tonight were verified, and Abe and Kirsten were waiting at the entrance. She looked at her watch and saw she had time to make some last-minute notes on the Oberman case before they slipped her mind. And just an hour before, Karen had put a case on her desk that demanded her attention. A gang shooting in Venice that had resulted in the death of a five-year-old black girl, T'neesha Wright, who had been playing in her front yard when a bullet slammed into her chest, had aroused the ire of the entire community—black, Latino, and white. This time, there was no hesitation about giving the cops as much information as they could about what they had witnessed. The shooter, sixteen-year-old Sancho Arroyo, had been identified and found hiding downtown in a homeless squat on Sixth Avenue. He had been arraigned that morning and was cooling his heels in the city jail. The little girl was known on her block as a ray of sunshine with the brightest smile anybody ever saw. Everybody wanted blood. The real target of Sancho Arroyo's rage, fifteen-year-old Jose Marcos, who had escaped without a scratch, was still on the run. He had no family in LA and no funds. The cops expected him to turn up soon.

Sanford Blair was Arroyo's lawyer, a tough but reasonable man Rosemaria had dealt with before. He wanted to set up a meeting to talk about a possible deal. The community was hungry for a trial and justice for little T'neesha. Looking at the photos of the girl as she was before she was killed and at the crime scene broke Rosemaria's heart. No way was Arroyo getting out of this with a manslaughter plea. This was second-degree murder, and unless T'neesha's parents pushed Rosemaria to cut a deal for fear he might get off in a jury trial, she would dedicate herself to putting Sancho in prison for as long as the law and the judge would allow. She had no time for sob stories about his age. Fifteen or fifty, a murderer belonged behind bars where he wouldn't be able to kill again.

* * * * *

Leonie had settled inside the electrical room in the basement of the twenty-story building where Vanessa's party would take place on the top floor. Vanessa's friend was the first and only tenant to move into the building so far. Leonie had dressed head to toe in her black spandex outfit, but now her ski mask lay on the chair beside her. The day before, in preparation for her reconnaissance mission, Leonie had found the schematics for the ancient art deco building on her computer and was relieved and delighted that there was only one elevator. There was no guard, and she had easily disabled the security cameras when she entered and enabled them when she left. There had only been a doorman behind the counter in the lobby, and he had left after the realtor for the building had shown his last client the available apartments.

Entering through the service entrance in the back of the building the previous evening had been no problem. She had taken the elevator up to the penthouse floor where the party would be held and placed a tiny camera by the light fixture that faced the elevator so she could monitor who was entering the elevator on her iPad. Although the apartments had all been updated, Vanessa's friend lived in a building that was so old the elevator was still only outfitted with one brake. The owners and contractors were eager for new buyers and had not prioritized elevator brakes. It was an accident waiting to happen. She had already studied the elevator cables and knew exactly where to place the induction heating device that she had perfected herself and could adjust and time perfectly the melting of the main elevator cable. She would have to carefully gauge when Rosemaria and her bodyguard would be entering the elevator. She would begin the melting process a little early and then the weight of the two of them would cause the cable to snap. The one irritating and unforeseen snafu was that the ancient air conditioning system sometimes, but for only a few seconds, knocked out her camera setup. She was certain she could work around that. The melting of the cable would be undetectable by anyone investigating the aftermath. Everyone would assume it had been a faulty cable that had caused the elevator to be sent plummeting down fifteen stories to the fifth-floor brake. Lawsuits would ensue, and the owners of the building would go bankrupt. Not her worry.

Leonie waited patiently as the realtor and potential residents arrived and departed. They went up and down the elevator, oblivious to the fact that she held their lives in her hands. She wondered if Baker's female bodyguard Kirsten or the big guy Abe would be going down the elevator the same time as Baker. It was no big deal to Leonie who it was. She fully expected that everything would go off without a hitch, and no clues would be left behind. She would retrieve the camera at a later date. It was so cleverly hidden behind the light socket that even the accident investigators would fail to find it. Leonie could hardly contain her excitement. She would have preferred a prolonged death for the ex-cop because of all the aggravation and inconvenience she had caused, but dead was better than alive.

After two hours of waiting, sitting on a hard metal chair behind a nook near the equipment panel, she saw on her iPad that Vanessa was the first to arrive. Then more friends of Vanessa whom Leonie had never met. Undoubtedly out-of-work actresses who wouldn't fit in with the snotty Beverly Hills crowd. Every now and then, the camera would get fuzzy for a few seconds because of the damned air conditioning system. That was annoying but nothing that would derail her plan. She had a long wait ahead of her as she observed the Baker woman and her bodyguard Kirsten, the last two people to arrive, get into the elevator at the same time as two of the potential tenants.

She watched as the realtor and his last client went out the door, then for three hours, she sat still and waited, her mind wandering over the last decade of her life, and feeling immense satisfaction over everything she had accomplished. She didn't dare lose focus and risk getting distracted by surfing on her iPad for fear of missing the moment when the Baker woman pressed the lobby button inside the elevator.

Leonie began the heating process, ready to accelerate it at the first sign of Baker coming out the door. Two of Vanessa's friends were the first to leave, then another and another. Two more guests left, leaving only Baker and her bodyguard still in the unit. Several more minutes passed as the cable heated up and was nearly ready to melt. The heat was intense and she sat as far away from the cable as possible. Finally, Leonie's anticipation came to an end—Baker and the bodyguard appeared. She immediately speeded up the heating process. Saying goodbye at the door took several more exasperating minutes. But all that unnecessary hugging and cheek kissing these women indulged in was enabling the cable to arrive at the perfect breaking point. She wanted to get this over with and head down the 405 to San Diego. After several excruciating minutes, Baker and the bodyguard were walking toward the elevator. The bodyguard pressed the down button. Leonie held her breath.

As the two women stepped into the elevator, the air conditioning again made the iPad screen fuzzy for four seconds, but the down button inside the elevator had been pressed. The elevator began its descent, and Leonie heard the scraping sound as it fell, then a loud bang as it hit the only safety brake on the fifth floor. She removed the bits of coil that had broken apart with her heat protective gloves and placed them in a small black canvas bag. She rolled up the tarp she had laid over the opening to the cable machinery below, which had caught falling debris from the coil apparatus. She knew after her successful experience in Miami, this would be treated as another tragic accident, and forensics, even Baker's faithful and thorough friends, would find no remnant of the coil. The Baker woman was out of her life. Leonie made her way out of the building via the service entrance and walked to her car, her head down, covered by her hoodie.

She drove down Santa Monica Boulevard doing the speed limit and heard sirens in the distance racing toward the accident. She would pull off at an exit on the 405 and throw the tarp and vacuum in a gas station dumpster. In two hours, she would be in San Diego and then, in another half hour, south of the city, where Stacey had found shelter with her new boyfriend. In case she had spilled her guts to this guy, he had to go as well. She had Google Earthed the area of the shore near their house and figured out it would be best to park her car half a mile away, then make her way along the bottom of the hill, walk up the path to their house, turn off the alarm if there was one, and give them each a double tap in the head and body as they slept. They would be sound asleep and never know a moment's panic before dying. Then she would quickly rummage through their belongings and take anything of value. It would be considered by the cops to be a fatal break-in. As she stared ahead at the highway, she had never been so focused in her life; every nerve in her body was tingling with anticipation. The drive was over two hours long. She had anticipated doing the home invasion at two in the morning. Her timing would be perfect.

She found the area she had been looking for without a hitch. The GPS guided her to a residential street where she could park. She sat for a few moments and carefully studied every house where insomniacs might spot her and her car. She could find no outside cameras on any of them. Noiselessly, she exited her car and walked down a path to the bottom of the hill half a mile from the beach. She found the path that led to the house where Stacey was staying and walked carefully and slowly up the hill. The houses were far apart. No one had their lights on. Everyone was asleep. From several yards away, she could see the security lights in the eaves of the house. If she came anywhere near the door, the lights would come on and possibly an alarm.

She made her way up the side of the house and saw a locked panel on the outside wall where all the power for the house was located. She used her automatic lock pick to open the panel door and studied the wiring. She quickly disarmed the alarm, disabled all the power in the house, and closed the panel door. She walked to the front door and unlocked it with her lock pick. She opened the door and listened for any hint of a sound. Finding none, she crept inside and closed the door.

She had studied the house plan and knew the master bedroom was down the hall to the right. She reached into her jacket pocket and took out her Beretta, then grabbed her suppressor out of the other pocket and screwed it on. She saw the door was not closed, which made for a quiet entrance. All she had to do was open the door and shoot. She pushed it open slowly and was pleased there was no squeak.

The heavy drapes let almost no light in from outside, but she could make out two bodies, the tops of their heads showing, one small and another a little bigger, lying close together under a thick quilt, so close it was almost as if they were one person. Ah, true love, isn't it grand? Too bad all that great sex had to come to an end. She stood at the foot of the bed and sent four taps into each of the lumps on the bed. Then four more for good measure. Not a sound.

She looked around and saw a large dresser against one wall. She moved quickly—no reason to stay one second longer than necessary. She placed the Beretta on top of the dresser, pulled out drawers, and rummaged through the contents. There was a small desk under the window, and she opened a metal box that contained a wallet with cash and some credit cards. She took all the cash but left the credit cards. It was imperative that she move as swiftly as possible, but she had to rifle through drawers in the living room as well to make the robbery look real.

But first, she picked up her Beretta and walked over to the bed. She noticed there was no blood staining the quilt from either body. She felt a terrible premonition wash over her as she pulled down the quilt. The bodies were dummies. She turned to run out of the room, but when she reached the doorway, Baker's face was inches from hers.

"Looking for me?" Leonie only had a split second of shock before she felt Rosemaria's fist land a punch in the center of her face. The pain was excruciating. She wobbled, the Beretta dropped from her hand, and she was about to fall when two patrolmen grabbed her. One of them ripped Leonie's mask off as blood gushed from her nose. She passed out and hung between the two patrolmen limp as a rag doll.

Rosemaria looked into the face of Jackie Radcliff who had been so unassuming and friendly, never having shown a hint of the loathing she had felt for Rosemaria. Rosemaria grabbed Leonie's right wrist and pulled up her sleeve. There it was—just the hint of a scar. Easy to miss.

A few minutes later when Leonie felt herself regaining consciousness, she saw she was handcuffed to a gurney about to be lifted into an ambulance. Her nose and mouth had been bandaged, and she stared with impotent rage at the people staring at her. Baker was standing behind the ambulance along with several men she assumed were detectives. She tried to move her hands but couldn't. She wanted to scream with frustration as Baker looked down on her with an amused expression on her face. How could this have happened? She had planned everything so perfectly.

"Jackie," Rosemaria said. "I can't believe this. You always seemed like such a nice lady."

Leonie grunted her response and her eyes narrowed into slits.

"Something you failed to realize, Leonie," Rosemaria said, "and should have known after your debacle on Macapa is that the security firm the Collins hired to protect me was ordered to treat me like the pope or the president of the United States. Whenever I was planning to go anywhere, they checked the place out a day ahead of time and made sure it was secure. Imagine their amazement when you showed up with your little camera and scoped out the control room in the basement. They figured you were up to no good then and there and decided to follow you home. I guess you didn't notice."

Leonie tried to lift her head off the gurney, and gurgling noises came out of her mouth.

"Oh, we'll explain to you how we thwarted your attempt on my life and how we knew you were coming here later."

Leonie pounded the back of her head into the gurney, and her face went rigid as stabs of intense pain shot up and down her nose and sinuses.

"Try to rest for now, Leonie. You have some busy days ahead of you. Oh, and don't worry about the damage to the elevator; they were planning on reconstructing it anyway." Rosemaria nodded to the EMTs, who shoved Leonie all the way into the back of the ambulance.

Mack and Loshi, who had been standing next to Rosemaria, patted her on the back, then jumped into the back of the ambulance. As it headed for the hospital, two sheriff's cars followed, running lights and sirens.

The whole gang watched as the ambulance drove up the street headed for the freeway entrance: Larry, Darryl, Steven, Jimmy, and Rosemaria. Then they meandered up the street to where their cars were parked. "I'm glad we played it out to the end," Jimmy said. "Four attempted murders are better than two."

"We have her for Sam's murder," Rosemaria said. "And we can build cases on the others."

Rosemaria walked away from the group and took out her phone and clicked a number. "Josh."

Josh was standing at the living room window with Suzi sitting on his shoulder. He was relieved to hear her voice. "Did it go off as planned?"

"Both places. Everybody was fantastic. Vanessa said it was like being in a disaster movie."

"Are you on your way home?"

"I am. I'd like a few hours' sleep tonight, but tomorrow, can we please drive up to the sanctuary in the morning so I can see Noor and Gilbert?"

"We can do that."

"After we visit our kids, I'll be in the mood to go to the station and watch Larry and Darryl question Leonie. Hopefully, she'll be out of the hospital in a couple of days."

"Do I dare ask why she's in the hospital?"

"Oh, didn't I tell you? She resisted arrest and sustained some injuries to her face."

"I won't ask whose fist she walked into to. Drive safe. I'll probably be asleep when you get here, but you can wake me if you want."

"I just may do that. I'll be home before you know it."

She clicked off her phone and looked at Larry. "There's still one thing that pisses me off."

"What's that?"

"That miserable coward Marchand. We could have avoided all this if he hadn't run off with his tail between his legs."

"I'm sure you'll have a chance to tell him that when you haul him in for Leonie's hearing."

"If he wanted to keep his sordid past a secret by hiding on an island in the Caribbean, he has a rude shock coming."

Larry smiled. "That's my girl."

* * * *

It was drizzling the next day as Josh and Rosemaria drove up the coast toward Santa Barbara in Rosemaria's car, a better choice in the rain than Josh's ancient Mustang convertible. Instead of looking at the scenery as they usually did, they held hands and stole glances at each other, just happy to be free of restraints, with no worries about assassins.

"I guess our kids will be sleeping in their dens tonight. No room for us in there."

"It would be a little wet sleeping on the ground in our usual place in our sleeping bags."

"That's okay. I'm just holding my breath until I see them. Cats don't like wet weather. What if they don't come to our meeting place?"

"For somebody who just helped catch a mass murderer, you sure do a lot of worrying."

"I'm a mother. I can't help it."

Forty-five minutes later, they drove through the entrance of the sanctuary. By then, the drizzle had turned to heavy rain. They took rain jackets with hoods out of the back seat and put them on. Justin, the manager of the sanctuary, came out of the office to greet them, holding a huge black umbrella over his head.

"When I saw the weather report, I put up a big tarp where you guys usually meet so you won't get quite so wet. All the other cats are inside."

Rosemaria's face was getting splattered by rain, but she barely noticed. "Will they come out to meet us?"

"Why don't you go find out? You have the key."

He closed his umbrella and hopped in a covered golf cart. Josh and Rosemaria climbed in the back. He drove them to the outer gate of the cat enclosure, and his passengers got out; he gave a wave and drove back down to the office. Josh opened the outer gate with his key, then the inner gate, and they walked toward their meeting place by the huge rock where Noor loved to lie in wait. They stood near the rock, rain pounding on the tarp, faces wet, and waited.

"Should we call out to them?" Rosemaria asked.

"They know."

When Rosemaria saw Noor and Gilbert, their fur soaked and glistening from the rain, walking down the path toward them, she was filled with an overwhelming longing for them. She knelt and reached out to them. "Babies!"

They didn't hesitate for a second and leaped to her side. She wrapped her arms around them as they licked her face and pushed against her, vying for her affection. Even though their tongues felt like sandpaper, she welcomed every lick. She petted and hugged, and the tears wouldn't stop flowing. "I didn't forget you guys," she murmured. "Not ever. Not for a minute."

She was so overwhelmed with happiness the rain and mud didn't faze her. She threw herself down on her knees and gloried in the attention they were giving her. They were Josh's gift to her. She saw Josh looking down at her as the cats bounded back and forth and rolled in the mud. On a sudden impulse, she unzipped her jacket and pulled it off. She stood up and began walking toward the lake. She knew Noor and Gilbert were the only cats who had been allowed outside while she and Josh visited and had no worries she might disturb the others.

She ran toward the lake. She wanted to celebrate and cleanse the past two months from her psyche. She stripped off her muddy clothes and took a flying leap into the water. The chill was a shock, but it reminded her that her senses were charging on all cylinders. She saw Josh standing by the water's edge and Noor and Gilbert dipping their paws in the water, trying to decide if they should jump in too. Rosemaria sunk down underneath the water, stayed under for several seconds, then exploded to the surface. She flipped her hair off her face, then slicked it back. She would always remember this glorious day. The objects of her love were waiting for her on land, and nothing was better than that. She slowly waded toward them.

CHAPTER FORTY-THREE

eonie was seated at the table in an interrogation room in the women's jail in San Diego when Mack and Loshi walked in. Seated next to her was her attorney, the formidable Price Harrington, a handsome, silver-haired man in his fifties who commanded respect from law enforcement and the accused alike. With the millions of dollars at Leonie's disposal, it was no surprise she could afford someone of his stature. But there had been no fiancé anywhere in sight since the arrest. He must have remembered he had urgent business in another country.

Mack and Loshi introduced themselves, then sat opposite Leonie and her lawyer. Behind the two-way glass, Rosemaria, Steven, Larry, Jimmy, and Darryl watched the human wreckage that used to be the beautiful Leonie. She was dressed in her prison blues, her nose and mouth covered in bandages, but enough of her face was visible to show she was still simmering with rage. Her brown contacts were gone, and her icy blue eyes glittered with loathing for the two detectives.

"As I made clear on the phone, gentlemen," Harrington said, "Ms. Gautreau has nothing to say, but we will be bringing charges against prosecutor Baker for assault on my client."

"Charge away, Mr. Pennington," Mack said. "There were several witnesses, myself included, who will swear that Baker acted in self-defense against an armed intruder who had attempted to murder two people while they slept."

"That will be for the courts to decide, Detective. Meanwhile, why are we here? I will be representing my client at the hearing in a few days, and until then, she will say nothing to you."

Loshi smiled. "We're here because we wanted to give your client an opportunity to come clean and avoid the death penalty."

"There is no death penalty in California."

"You know as well as I do, Counselor, that it still exists. It was merely suspended by a worthless, gangster-loving governor who has never had a gun pointed at his face. We can get her on death row. We'll just have to wait a few years for her to get her ultimate reward. If she confesses, the prosecutor will withdraw the murder one, murder-for-hire charge regarding Sam Oliver."

"You have nothing but supposition for that charge, and it will easily be disposed of at the hearing."

"The hearing will include charges of the attempted murders of Rosemaria Baker, Kirsten Lowell, Stacey Fields, Lorna Selverino, and Randy Meisner." Mack said. "And as for the murder one charge, Jill Sussman, the prosecutor, should be here with our witness shortly." He looked down as his phone lit up, and he read the text message. "Ah, I believe our prosecutor is in the building."

"Really, Detective," Harrington asked, "are these kinds of dramatics necessary?"

"I assure you, Counselor," Mack said, "we won't take up much more of your time. We just want to be fair to your client."

At that, Leonie snorted, causing her to wince in pain.

There was a knock at the door. It opened, and a plump, diminutive woman who looked to be in her fifties, with gray hair cut short and simple and dressed in a conservative blue suit, came in. "I'm sorry to be late, but I had to wait until my witness was released into my custody." She turned around and waved at someone in the hallway, and Micco, his hands cuffed behind his back, came into the room, accompanied by a sheriff's deputy. Leonie's eyes widened when she saw him, and she took a huge intake of breath, causing her to choke and gasp for air. Harrington was livid as he patted his client on the back.

"This is outrageous. I demand that you call an ambulance. Once again, you have given us cause to bring charges against you for purposely causing harm to my client."

But Leonie was shaking her head and staring at Micco. "You?" she managed to get out.

Sussman stood next to Micco, who was looking at Leonie with a derisive smile. "My witness was your client's partner in crime and will testify against her. He recorded their phone conversations and your client's instructions to him. He is throwing himself on the mercy of the court and will take whatever punishment is coming to him for the pleasure of putting your client behind bars and never having to communicate with her again. I've listened to the conversations, Counselor; they are quite revealing. Add to that the undisputed charges of attempted murder of five people, and I'd say your client has boxed herself in beautifully."

Leonie slumped in her chair, started to put her head down, then pulled back as soon as the tip of her banged-up nose touched the table. Sussman nodded at the deputy, and he escorted Micco out of the room. "It's time to talk, Leonie," she said. "You're done. David Marchand, Ramin Hassan, Amy Rothman, Sam Oliver, and Keith Tomlin are crying out for justice. There may be other victims too. We will track them all down, and you will be convicted. Your only hope to save yourself from the death penalty is to tell us everything and hold nothing back."

Harrington put his elbow on the table and leaned his forehead on his hand. He had a losing hand, and he knew it. He sat up. "Let me talk to my client."

Mack nodded, then looked at Leonie, who had shrunk into herself physically and emotionally. "As Rosemaria told you, Leonie, she was treated like the most important person in the world by the security company Collins hired. You could never have conceived that a human being could be treated with such an inordinate amount of love and respect, so you failed to take that into consideration when you made your plans. The security team found your camera, watched your every move, was aware of your electrical skills, figured out what you had in mind, made sure no one was on the elevator, even caused the air conditioning and your camera to misfunction at the same time, giving Kirsten time to reach in and press the down button and for the two of them to scoot around the corner where your camera couldn't see them.

"As soon as you left the apartment building after scouting out the premises, contractors came and constructed a temporary emergency brake on the nineteenth floor should you decide it wasn't just Rosemaria you planned to kill. Security followed you down the 405 and found the evidence you threw in the dumpster. Micco told Sussman you wanted to rid yourself of Stacey once you discovered she was alive. We took a helicopter to San Diego, prepared the house, and sent Stacey and Randy on a prewedding honeymoon to Hawaii, which is where they are now. Stacey will also be a witness against you.

"You never loved anyone or had anyone love you back, Leonie. Your fiancé has disowned you. That's why you could never understand what Rosemaria had and you didn't. You're all alone with only your lawyer on your side. And things will only get worse. The best you can do is escape death. That's it. Take the deal or leave it because personally, I don't give a damn."

Rosemaria was staring through the glass at the scene in the other room. Listening to Mack, she almost felt sorry for the pitiful figure in the blue jumpsuit who used to have the world at her fingertips. Rosemaria did have friends; she did have people who loved her and had taken care that she was safe and protected. That was worth a whole lot more than a huge bank account. Leonie started out with nothing and was willing to sacrifice everything for money. Now she was back to where she began, and never again would she have a chance for anything more. Love and friendship were everything. Everything else was dust in the wind.

EPILOGUE

The top was down, and the warm breezes from the Pacific Ocean were ruffling their hair as Josh drove his beloved classic silver-blue Mustang up the Pacific Coast Highway. Rosemaria looked bewildered. "We're not going to the sanctuary. We're not going on a picnic at the beach. Exactly where are we going?"

"Just enjoy your Saturday, and don't ask any more questions."

"I'm a lawyer and former cop. It's what I do."

"And I'm standing on my Miranda rights and not talking."

"You've obviously hung around me too much."

They drove in silence for a while.

"If you'd brought the CD of your album, we could be listening to that," Rosemaria said.

"It won't be ready for release for another three weeks."

"How long before it shoots to number one, and I hear the song you wrote for me?"

"With the publicity campaign my PR people have already initiated, the CD might show up somewhere near the middle of the charts. Joell will be pushing it as well, so maybe a little higher."

"Did you have that talk with her?"

"I'm thinking after everything that's happened, it won't be necessary."

"You know best."

They were passing Pepperdine University and the ocean overlook point where they liked to picnic and look through the binoculars for whales who might be visiting.

"Any idea which song will turn out to be the breakout single?"

"You never know what the public will like. Your song is pretty damn good, but I'm a little old fashioned, and I'm in an industry where kids rule the market. I can only hope my retro style appeals to them."

"You won't change how you write and sing just to sell CDs, will you?"

"Nope. I'll be me, and if I fail, I'll just keep writing jingles to make money."

"And you have the musical. Don't forget the musical. Broadway beckons as well."

"So far nobody in New York is beckoning me regarding that."

"You have to let producers hear it first. I have some ideas about how to—"

"I promise I'll listen to your advice on our next trip up the coast."

"Fat chance."

They passed Zuma Beach, and Josh slowed to look at road signs where the turnoffs from the highway looked a lot alike. He made a right turn onto a narrow road, drove up the hill, and turned left into an overgrown lot. He kept going up a dirt driveway and parked the car.

"This is it." He opened the door and got out of the car while Rosemaria sat and waited.

"This is what?"

Josh came around, and the passenger side door, and helped her out.

"How do you like the view?"

She looked out over the broad expanse of blue water and surrounding hills. "It's beautiful."

"How would you like to look at it every morning?"

She looked at him in wonderment. "Did you buy this lot?"

He came to her and took her hands in his. "I wouldn't do that without asking you first. But one of the musicians I met on the European tour is about to put it on the market and told me he'd give me a great deal on it before he does. We can't afford more than the lot right now, but I'm expecting we can build in about a year or two." He looked at her, and she still seemed to be recovering from his revelation. "What do you think?"

Rosemaria was dumbstruck. "I'm—I'm overwhelmed."

"In a good way?"

"In a very good way." She looked into his eyes and saw the anticipation on his face. "Yes. Let's do it!"

He wrapped his arms around her and held her close. "There's something else I have to ask you."

"Yes?"

He held her at arm's length. "Now that you're free to live a normal life again, I want us to get married. Nothing big, no party, just a small ceremony with close friends and family, maybe in two weeks?"

She smiled and touched his face with her hand. "I agree. And let's invite your mom and her fiancé. And maybe Curtis, Melissa, and Tiffany?"

"Uh-oh, it's getting bigger."

"Larry and Vanessa have a big house, and she'll organize everything. . . . Speaking of houses, I wonder if Tammy will still be asking for delays in the Oberman trial by the time we start building ours?"

"From what you've told me, that's a possibility. We'll make sure your home office faces the ocean, so you'll have a great view while you figure out how to foil her unexpected moves."

"I have so much work to do before then."

"I'd appreciate it if you confine your work to your offices and the courtroom and stay out of harm's way."

"I'm dealing with criminals. Staying out of trouble is kind of impossible."

"Especially for you."

She grabbed his arm, and they stood looking out over the view that would soon be theirs. Rosemaria thought about what Vanessa had said to her one day at the Collins house when Rosemaria had been feeling especially depressed about her lack of freedom and ability to work and be with Josh. "Life is a series of yin and yang," she had said. "As bad as it gets, that's how good it will be." Vanessa was right. Things had been very bad for a long time. Now the good was here to enjoy for much longer. And Ellie had been right as well—God didn't let her be killed when life was so incredibly perfect.

Two weeks later, in Vanessa's living room, with the groom wearing a black suit, white shirt, and blue tie and the bride resplendent in a white cocktail dress, which had been picked out by Vanessa, that clung to her curves, Rosemaria and Josh exchanged their vows. Bearing witness to the joyful occasion were father of the bride, Steven Baker; mother of the groom, Ellen Sibley; and her fiancé, Elwin Torger. Also in attendance were best man Larry Coleman, matron of honor Vanessa Coleman, and Loretta and Andrew Collins. Flower girl Melissa tottered toward the bride and groom, holding a little straw basket, randomly dropping rose petals on the pink walkway ribbon, and occasionally falling on her plump bottom and uttering hysterical peals of laughter.

Melissa and Tiffany had flown in from Cleveland with Malcomb Curtis and were ecstatic to see Rosemaria again after over a year of being apart. Karen, her faithful secretary, was there, glowing with pride and happiness. Jimmy and Darryl were dressed so spiffy Rosemaria barely recognized them. Mack and Loshi had driven up from San Diego and still looked like cops in their off-the-rack suits, but Rosemaria thought they looked perfect. Madelaine, who had given her such loving care, came alone. Kirsten, Abe, Cameron, and Raul, who had put their lives on the line for Rosemaria, had also been invited, and Rosemaria was grateful they'd chosen to come. Terrance, who had picked up the slack in the office, and Reid, her new partner in the courtroom, were there solo. Surprisingly, Joell had broken off in the middle of a tour to be there. She stood by herself and watched the ceremony with a bittersweet smile as she forced herself to witness the end of a dream she'd known all along was hopeless. And Ken Jordan, who had kept Josh afloat during the drinking years and given him the break of his life when he hired him to write the theme song for *New York Nights*, was there with his wife, Marla, and son Kevin. Jenny, Ken's secretary, who had been the inventor of countless alibis when Josh had failed to show up to auditions, was there with a date. If not for her, he wouldn't be here.

The many tears shed during the ceremony were balanced by the laughter, the flow of sparkling grape juice, and a number of toasts made to the happy couple. But the most important toast of all, which threatened to degrade the makeup that Vanessa had so flawlessly applied to Rosemaria's face, was the toast by the groom to the bride.

Josh lifted his glass toward Rosemaria and said, "To my wife, the woman who chased away my demons, who has always believed in me, always challenged me to do better, and is out to save the world even if it means risking her own neck. I will always have your back, dearest, and love you more than you know."

As everyone lifted their glasses and sipped their sparkling juice, Rosemaria choked back tears, determined not to let mascara run down her cheeks and ruin Vanessa's perfectly applied makeup job. She lost that battle.

THE END